AUTHOR		CLASS	F
RAMSEY E			
TITLE Kummersdorf connection		No. 67982530	

D0418210

The Kummersdorf Connection

Other Futura Spectaculars:

Eric Ramsey

The Kummersdorf
Connection

Futura Publications Limited
A Futura Book

A Futura Book

00688608

First published in Great Britain by
Futura Publications Limited in 1978

Copyright © 1978 by Book Creations, Inc.

ISBN 0 7088 1471 9

Printed in Great Britain by
Hazell Watson & Viney Ltd
Aylesbury, Bucks

Futura Publications Limited
110 Warner Road
Camberwell, London SE5

Richard Gore, in the *National Geographic* magazine, asked at the tail end of an article on the cell, genes, and genetic engineering if man should attempt to control his own destiny. If so, he asked, who is to decide what man will become?

This novel attempts to deal with those questions, although the characters and events are purely figments of the author's imagination.

ERIC RAMSEY
Cambridge, Wisconsin

PROLOGUE: April 1945

Gustav Predel stepped out of the one-story administration building and lit a cigarette with shaky hands while waiting in the cold mist for the messengers from Berlin. Early morning began with a cold rain. By late afternoon, the overcast had deepened and turned into fog and a thin drizzle, chilling him to the bone.

He had not slept in forty-eight hours, ever since the Russian artillery shelling began in the east. The night before, under clear skies, the bright flashes appeared on the horizon, followed a minute or so later by the dull rumbles of explosions, like thunder in the distance.

That day the sounds of the shells grew much louder, evidence that the end was at hand, although they could no longer see the flashes.

A plain black Mercedes sedan, a portion of its top blown away, pulled through the main gates of the compound and came to a halt in the central courtyard a few feet away from Predel. Two men in Gestapo uniforms got out.

"Heil Hitler," Predel said, raising his right arm.

"Dr. Predel?" one of the men asked, neither of them returning the salute.

Predel nodded.

"We have orders from the Führer." Both men mounted the stairs and entered the building, brushing past Predel.

Predel hesitated a moment, then turned and followed them into his office. He had been expecting some kind of word from the Reichs Chancellory Bunker ever since he learned the Russians could not be stopped.

At the afternoon staff meeting the day before, they had debated the wisdom of destroying the station and its test animals on their own and then escaping to the West and the Americans or the British. All seventy-three of the project scientists and technicians sat in the lecture hall when Predel entered from the back of the room and walked to the podium.

"I trust you have all read the contingency plans I distributed this morning," he began without preamble.

Everyone nodded, but no one said anything. Predel took a deep breath and continued.

"The Russians are twenty-seven miles away, and I am told we have nothing with which to stop them. It is now only a matter of hours or perhaps a few days at the most before they overrun us."

"Have we gotten word from Berlin?" one of the project scientists asked.

Predel turned toward the man and shook his head slowly. "No, and I doubt if there will be any help from them. We are on our own."

The man who had spoken got to his feet, the contingency plan in his hand. "We cannot do this, Gustav," he said with feeling. "I for one have worked all of my life on this project. And we as a coordinated research group have worked since the early thirties. Now we are close, so close. We cannot give it up, we cannot simply destroy everything and then walk away as if it meant nothing."

"Exactly the point, my dear Stromberg. We must destroy this facility and everything it contains. Especially the test animals. The world is not ready for our research. If the Russians or the Americans caught us with this, we would all be dead men."

Stromberg, an older man with thick white hair that

flowed down around the collar of his white lab coat, threw the plan to the floor.

"Perhaps, Gustav, but our work would endure."

"Don't be a fool," Predel said, angry now. "Do you think that anyone else will continue with this project? Do you think for one moment that the Russians have the finesse or the Americans the courage?"

"Without direct word from Hitler himself, I will not allow this to happen," Stromberg said, and he sat down.

Predel looked at the others. All of them were silent. He realized that for the first time since he had begun work here as the head scientist and project administrator he didn't know what they were thinking, either collectively or individually.

Nor, he thought as he entered his office behind the two Gestapo men, was he sure of his own feelings. Although he had written the contingency plan to destroy the facility, he, like Stromberg, wanted to hang on, to continue the work.

But now that decision was being taken out of his hands.

The Gestapo men were seated across the desk from him, and he waited for them to speak.

"We have just come from the Reichs Chancellory Bunker," one said.

Predel nodded.

"At fifteen-thirty hours today our Führer died. One of his last orders was that this facility and everything in it be destroyed."

Predel stared at him for several seconds, not believing what he had just heard. It was impossible. Hitler—dead? How?

The second man broke the strained silence, his tone conciliatory. "There is nothing we can do to soften the blow, *Herr Doktor*. The war is lost."

Predel began to speak, but the first man cut him off. "It is up to us now, Dr. Predel, to make certain there will be a Germany in the future. If this facility should become known to the world, it not only would guarantee the end of the German nation, but it also would sign the death warrant of the German people."

"The National Redoubt?" Predel asked softly, his voice hoarse with emotion.

"No," the Gestapo officer said and stood up. "This facility must be destroyed within eighteen hours. After that the Soviet army will overrun you. That cannot be allowed to happen."

Predel looked up, dazed, as both men turned toward the door. "And if I cannot?" he heard himself saying.

One of the men went out the door, but the other turned back a moment. "The fate of the German people rests squarely on your shoulders, *Herr Doktor*. Do with it what you must. We will help."

"How?"

"We are going to attempt to slow the Russians."

"You have troops?"

"A hundred of them, mostly old men and children. It is the end," the Gestapo man said, and he turned and went out the door. A few moments later Predel could hear their car start, then drive away.

The research facility was enclosed in a compound two hundred meters on each side. It was surrounded by a high, electrified, barbed-wire fence with a main gate facing east and a smaller service gate on the west side. The center of the compound was dominated by the main administration and laboratory building that housed offices, laboratories, lecture halls, and three complete operating theaters. Along the east fence, more buildings housed workshops and laboratories. On the north was personnel housing, on the south Jewish inmate barracks, and along the west fence were the buildings that housed the test animals.

Leutnant Abel Brenner hurried from the administration building and crossed the compound to his quarters. Like the others, he had not slept in forty-eight hours, and he was dead tired, although his mind was alive with speculation and fear.

For the last two days they had all hoped that somehow the Russians would be stopped but assumed that the Führer would be sending trucks and men to move the camp to the mountains near Salzburg. If there was to be a National Redoubt, now was the time to begin it. Colonel Predel's contingency plan was nothing more than a piece of paper—a thing written for the files so that when a final board of inquiry met to see how the situation had been handled, they would look good.

"We had no way of knowing if we would be rescued, so we had to write the plan," Predel would tell the board. And after that everything would be all right.

Only now, Brenner thought bitterly as he entered his building, everything was finished. The Russians were close, the Führer dead, and the mighty *Wehrmacht* only a name. It was over. Over. The word kept running through his mind.

Upstairs on the second floor, Brenner entered his small room, grabbed the standard issue officer's Luger from his desk, and snapped the clip into the butt of the handgrip. He slipped two extra clips of ammunition into his pocket, then looked around the tiny cubicle in which he had lived for the past three years.

In addition to the small cot and the wooden desk beside it, the room was bare. Brenner had never spent much time here; most of his hours had been devoted to his laboratory in the Test Animal Section. Even when at the university his quarters had been similar, and there, too, he had spent most of his time in the library or laboratories.

He was a young scientist with much to learn, but a scientist nevertheless. Which meant he was detached from political concerns. It did not matter if the Germans or the Russians or the Americans were in charge. It did not matter who was footing the research bills as long as the research continued.

Until this evening Brenner had respected Dr. Predel. Only now did he realize that his loyalty was misplaced. Predel, like so many other scientists who became administrators, had developed into a political animal. Science now came second.

Predel's plan called for the immediate and complete destruction of everything within the compound—the laboratory equipment, the files, the Jewish inmates, and the test animals.

"And there is no other way but by fire," Predel told them at the briefing minutes ago. "Everything must be burned. Everything."

"The test animals, too?" Brenner asked incredulously.

"I'm afraid so," Predel said, turning to him. "There is no time for anything else."

"We cannot," Brenner shouted.

"The Führer ordered it."

Brenner started to protest, but Predel cut him off and dismissed the meeting, asking only department heads to remain. The compound and everything in it was to be soaked with gasoline, kerosene, and alcohol, and set on fire. Then they would make their way to the west in civilian clothes and give themselves up to the Americans. What happened after that no one knew.

There was nothing he could do to stop it, Brenner told himself as he left the room and hurried down the back stairs. But Predel's plan called for the destruction of the test animals by fire. They would be burned alive.

"It has to be this way," Predel explained. "The Americans will arrive soon after the Russians are finished. We must make it look like the compound was burned accidentally. If we shoot the Jews or test animals, we will be hunted as mass murderers."

That was Predel's worry, Brenner told himself as he slipped out the back door and hurried over to the west side of the camp. He was not going to allow the animals to die like that.

The rain had stopped, but the sky was still overcast

and the camp lights were turned off. Already the pervasive odor of gasoline filled the air. Brenner quickened his step. He didn't want to be caught in the middle of an inferno before his work was finished.

The building in which he worked was the eighth in a row of sixteen identical buildings. Already men were working on the fourth, splashing gasoline and diesel fuel inside and out.

He slipped in the front door and hurried through the small lab into the section where the animals were caged. The smell of alcohol, mixed with the odor of urine and defecation, was strong, but it was a smell he was used to.

He stood in the middle of the room, which was lined on either side with large cages. He held his breath as he listened to the sounds and waited for his eyes to adjust to the dim light.

The animals were restless. He could hear them moving in their cages. For a moment he almost believed nothing was wrong. He was here only to check on his animals. In a moment, when he had them quieted down, he would return to his room to get some sleep and be back in the morning. But then he heard voices shouting and the sounds of several trucks grinding to a halt near the center of the compound.

It would not be long now before the camp would be set on fire.

One of the test animals whimpered and Brenner moved toward it.

"Was ist los?" he asked softly. The animal got to its feet from where it was curled on its straw mattress and moved toward the front of the cage.

They were so close, Brenner thought as he looked into the almost human eyes that stared at him. Another month, another year, two at the most, and they would have it.

The animal watched as Brenner reached into his pocket and withdrew the Luger. He slipped the safety off, pulled the ejector back and released it, snapping a round into the chamber.

He reached into the cage and petted the animal; then he withdrew his hand and raised the Luger, the barrel only a few inches away from the animal's right eye. Brenner's hand was shaking and his stomach churning.

It was a waste, such a criminal waste. The animal stared impassively at him, its large brown eyes glinting liquidly in the darkness.

"I'm sorry . . ." Brenner started to say, when he heard the sharp staccato burst of a machine gun.

He snapped around as the animals jumped and began screaming and snorting, rattling the bars of their cages. A second and then a third and fourth machine gun began firing; he could hear men screaming and shouting as the firing became more and more intense.

It was the Russians, it had to be, Brenner thought as he raced through the lab to the front door. They had broken through faster than expected.

Everything was lost. They were dead men.

He cautiously opened the door in time to see a truck coming down the road in front of the buildings. A machine gun mounted on the tailgate was firing into the group of men who had been pouring gasoline on the buildings.

At first it was too dark for Brenner to see who was in the truck, but suddenly the camp lights came on and he froze. The trucks bore the insignia of the *Waffen SS*. The soldiers firing the machine guns were Germans.

Brenner slammed the door and hurried inside, his mind racing.

The Gestapo had brought orders from the Führer to destroy the camp and everything in it. Now the *Waffen SS* was here killing everyone. Why? What the hell was going on?

The gunfire was getting closer, and the animals were howling and screaming. Everything was lost. Everything they had worked for was gone. It would all be destroyed. Not only the test animals, the equipment, and research notes, but the brains, the scientists, and technicians; everything would be lost.

Brenner looked around. It could not be allowed to happen. Could not.

He rushed to the rear entrance, unlocked the door, and opened it a crack. A couple of meters away, the fence was bathed in light. Beyond it the clearing sloped sharply upwards into the forest that rose nearly three hundred meters above the camp.

The backs of all the lab buildings were deserted; the gunfire and noise were concentrated at the center of the camp.

The lights were on, however, which meant the generator was working and the fence still electrified. There would be no way to escape through the main gate; and the rear access gate, which he could see from here, was locked. He would have to go over the fence.

Brenner hesitated a moment longer, his eyes resting on the red sign attached to the fence: V.ORSICHT!—HOCHSPANNUNG. Then he hurried to the animal he almost shot. The docile one.

Outside he could hear someone shouting orders, someone else screaming for mercy, then more gunfire.

Brenner pulled a key ring from his pocket, unlocked the cage, and swung open the heavy metal-barred door. The animal cowered at the back of the cage. Brenner pulled it to its feet by its collar.

"Kommst du," he said gently, and he led it out of the cage and down the narrow aisle.

This was the only way, he told himself, his stomach churning again. At all costs someone would have to survive to carry on the work. At all costs.

Brenner went to the back door, opened it a crack, and peered outside. The lights were still on, but now the gunfire had moved on toward the administration building. It would take several more minutes before order was restored and a building-by-building search begun. In the meantime, Brenner would be over the fence and gone. Beyond that point he did not know what he would do, except stay away from the Russians—and his own countrymen, as well.

He pushed the animal outside, ahead of him, and nudged it toward the fence.

The animal stumbled forward and then turned and looked back at Brenner, its myopic eyes seemed almost questioning. In its three years of life it had never been out of its cage. Not once. Now it did not know what was expected of it.

Brenner's knees were going weak, threatening to collapse at any moment, as he prodded the animal toward the fence.

There would be other animals, other laboratories, other chances to work. There would have to be.

"Geh!" Brenner said sharply, and he pushed the animal forward.

The creature turned after a moment, studied the clearing and the forest beyond, and then sprang toward the fence, contacting the metal with all fours. For an instant the beast went rigid as the five-thousand-volt charge slammed into its body. Then a low, terrible howl emerged from its throat as it began convulsing, its fingers and toes clamped rigidly around the wires, holding it firmly in place. Sparks shot out in all directions and smoke began to curl from its body as the flesh started to cook.

A few seconds later, the circuit breakers broke contact and the animal slumped to the ground. Brenner leaped to the fence and scrambled over as vomit rose out of his stomach and spewed down his jacket.

He was over and on the other side seconds later. In a dead run he made his way up the clearing and into the thick underbrush at the edge of the woods.

Behind him he could hear a truck racing toward the lab buildings. In a few moments they would discover the dead animal by the fence. With any luck they would assume it had merely gotten loose, tried to climb over the fence and been electrocuted.

It was nearly dawn. The eastern sky was beginning to turn gray and the lights in the compound below were pale now. The gunfire had stopped more than an hour ago. From where Brenner was watching, he could see the test animals being herded toward the main gate, where the *Waffen SS* trucks were positioned like a gigantic funnel. The gates were open and other trucks, their engines running in the chill morning air, lined the narrow dirt road that led east. The animals would have to go out the gate, and the trucks would have to jockey around so the creatures could move down the road.

He was cold and hungry, and at first he was unable to figure out what was happening. As far as he could tell, every project scientist and technician, as well as the one hundred and fifty Jews, had been murdered. The only ones left were the SS troops and the test animals.

Once the funnel was formed, he made the connection. The Russians were advancing from the east, and the animals were being herded directly into their path. It was one insane, last-ditch stand.

But why? Why waste nearly fifteen years of work on one last desperate gamble that was doomed to fail?

Brenner shivered and hunched his coat high around his neck. Within a half hour everyone would be gone. The camp would be deserted. The diversion the animals caused would give him a couple of extra hours —plenty of time for him to descend to the camp, change into civilian clothes, destroy his ID cards, and take one of the civilian cars.

With a little luck, he would get so far away that he would not be connected with this facility or Berlin. He would pose as a medical doctor in the town he happened to be closest to when he was captured.

It was a weak story, but he was counting on confusion to make it stick.

After that . . . the thought trailed off. Someday there would be another laboratory, other animals. The work done here would continue.

PART ONE
Fall 1977

CHAPTER 1

It was early morning when the young man emerged from the plain brown brick building at 4 Fremdenstrasse and walked slowly toward the center of town. He was a solidly built man, standing two meters tall and weighing nearly one hundred kilograms. He carried himself erect with a military bearing. His short-cropped hair, square, regular features, and steel-blue eyes made him seem unfriendly though he neither smiled nor frowned.

The shopkeepers sweeping their sidewalks did nothing to acknowledge his presence as he passed by. His routine had been going on for several years now. Every morning as they rolled up the gates in front of their shops and began sweeping their sidewalks, the young man was heading downtown.

This morning, like every morning, he entered the small post office and handed across the message handwritten on a plain white piece of paper. He waited until the clerk telegraphed it to the address in East Berlin before he paid.

The message was no different from what it had been on any other morning. "AUNTY IS WELL. NO CHANGES TO REPORT." It was signed simply "NEPHEW."

He was dreaming about fishing with his son. It was early morning, and from the small rowboat where they sat, the lake looked like a flat piece of glass stretching toward the tree-lined shore. Smoke rose lazily from the chimney of their cabin, and he knew that in a few minutes his wife would be calling them in to breakfast.

A telephone rang, its jangling a long ways off, and he looked up, curious that it would ring out here on the lake. Then he realized he was dreaming and fought to stay asleep. The telephone rang again, then his wife mumbled something.

Nathaniel Gleason was fully awake when Pat rolled over in bed and nudged him.

"The office," she mumbled and handed the phone across to him.

He took it from her without sitting up or opening his eyes. "Yes?"

"Mr. Gleason, this is Carlson. I hate to bother you so early, but you're needed."

"What time is it?"

"A couple of minutes past four, sir."

"This a Red Light?" Gleason asked.

"Ah . . . no, sir, Amber," his administrative assistant said hesitatingly. Such codes were not normally used on open lines.

Gleason sighed heavily. "Who's running this one?"

"Sylvan Bindrich, sir."

"Be right there," Gleason said, then sat up and reached over his wife, hanging up the telephone. For a moment he looked down at her face turned sideways toward him. She was asleep. She would not remember anything when she got up, but he kissed her. "Love," he said and then threw back the covers and got out of bed.

Sylvan Bindrich, head of Missions and Programs, was not an excitable man. And although he ran his department efficiently, he never seemed to be in a hurry.

"The pacing is entirely up to us," he told Gleason once. "If we move fast, so will they. It's nothing but a game. Besides, who needs ulcers?"

There was a note of urgency in Carlson's voice, Gleason thought, as he showered, shaved, and quickly dressed. Whatever the Amber Light was, it was important. Important enough to get Bindrich out of bed and to put in a call to the head of Gleason's department— Operational Services.

Most departments worked autonomously. Little joint divisional work was done. Each department sent its reports and summaries around to the others, but multi-divisional meetings or briefings were rare.

The bombing of the Utah radio towers, the Bay of Pigs, the Cuban missile crisis, and, more recently, the defection of the MIG-25 pilot to Japan had caused multidivisional stirs that lasted in some instances as long as a month.

Gleason only hoped that this morning's Amber Light would not turn out to be such a project. He was scheduled to take his wife and son on vacation in three days; whatever was happening this morning he wanted over with by then.

The trip from Chevy Chase to Langley was made simpler by the deserted early-morning highways; within an hour he was showing his security badge to the marine guard at the front gate. Carlson was waiting for him at the elevator, and they rode up together.

"What have you got for me?" Gleason asked the younger man, who always appeared clean-shaven no matter what time of the day it was.

Carlson shook his head slowly as he watched the floor indicator. "Not a thing. Bindrich is keeping the lid on this one."

"Not even a hint?" Gleason asked, irritated.

"Afraid not, sir," Carlson said, looking at him. "He declared the Amber Light and put out the call for you and a few others."

"Who?"

"A couple of recording technicians and Marty Romberg."

"Soviet Research?"

"Yes, sir," Carlson said as the elevator slid to a stop and the doors opened.

They emerged onto the fifth-floor corridor, showed their badges again, and continued down the hall toward the briefing auditorium next to Bindrich's office.

"Anyone else?" Gleason asked.

"Not that I know of."

When Gleason had joined the CIA nearly twenty years before, directly out of the University of Wisconsin Law School, it was with the understanding he would have nothing to do with cloak-and-dagger work. And he had learned, to his pleasure, that very little of it was done anywhere, despite the spy novels' portrayals. Most of the work done by intelligence services was the kind Gleason especially enjoyed, what he called chess play.

The job of the CIA was not only to gather intelligence on foreign powers, friendly or otherwise, but also to make connections and correlations of that data for whichever administration was in power, correlations that could be used to make foreign-policy decisions. And those correlations struck Gleason as nothing more than a vast chess game. The appointment of one cabinet member here, the construction of a new hydroelectric plant there, the assassination of a political figure in another place—all added up to delicate maneuvers on a gigantic board. Figuring out what the next move would be, and when and where it would happen, was Gleason's job. And he loved it.

Bindrich was exactly the opposite.

Carlson held the door for Gleason, who entered the briefing room. About a dozen men and a few women were seated in the front rows of seats in the darkened, theaterlike room. This room, which had a seating capacity of more than a hundred, is typical of CIA expenditures, Gleason thought, as he and Carlson moved down the side aisle and took seats in the third row. Everything is overdone. He was sure a hundred people had never gathered in one room in the complex for any reason.

By definition, interdepartmental autonomy and the secret nature of their work prohibited large gatherings.

Sylvan Bindrich, a stoop-shouldered man of at least sixty, stood at a podium. Behind him was a large screen onto which was projected the image of a man, obviously Russian, who appeared to be in his late forties or early fifties.

When Gleason and Carlson sat down, Bindrich began.

"Sorry to get you out of bed so early, but it couldn't be helped," Bindrich said in a harsh, grating voice.

"What have you got?" Gleason spoke up. "And who are the others here?"

"This is coded Triple Sixes. I'll have the need-to-know personnel list to you directly after the briefing. Most of the others here are from Romberg's section, plus a couple of Vietnam experts and two recording technicians."

"Who's the Russian?" Gleason said, and Bindrich glanced over his shoulder at the image projected on the screen.

"He's the Triple Sixes," Bindrich said. He looked down at a file on the podium in front of him, cleared his throat, and began. "Last night at eleven o'clock Paris time, this man, Viktor Vasilievich Kozhevnikov—pronounced Ko-*shev*-na-kof—contacted one of our low-profile men. He knew of his existence as well as the proper blind number and sequence." Bindrich looked out at his audience for a moment before he went on.

"Kozhevnikov has been assigned to the KGB's First Chief Directorate, Division of Disinformation, since that division was formed in the NKVD shortly after World War Two. Most recently he was assigned to Hanoi, and in the last year, Saigon. Last night he popped up in Paris with his wife. Presumably his assignment in Saigon is completed, he is being rewarded with a Western European vacation; and then he will return to Moscow for permanent assignment there."

"A defection?" Gleason asked.

Bindrich nodded slowly. "Possibly, but this one could be a bit tight."

Alarm bells began jangling along Gleason's nerves as he suddenly remembered where he had heard the Russian's name. He could see his vacation sliding away in the distance. "Wasn't this the man behind the Polaris scheme in the Med?"

"The same one," Bindrich said. "He asked our man to arrange an open-ended meeting in Munich in four days."

"Specific location?"

"A small tobacconist's shop downtown."

"Is it clean?"

"We're checking it out now," Bindrich said, and he looked away from Gleason toward the others. "We'll have to make our first go or no-go recommendation for the director within twenty-four hours. That will give us slightly less than seventy-two hours to set up. That means you have twenty-four hours to come up with everything there is to know about our friend Kozhevnikov. I want it from before day one. Parents, grandparents, schooling, girlfriends, wife, children, promotions, and especially his projects. I also want to know specifically what he is doing in Paris, how long he's been there, who he's seen and why, and what is likely to happen to him when he returns home."

No one said anything. After a moment, Bindrich grunted. "All right, get on it, and keep me posted every two hours."

The others rose to leave, and Bindrich turned again to Gleason. "I'd like you and Romberg to stick around."

Gleason nodded, then turned to Carlson. "Dig out what you can on this character, Howard. I know we've got something on him from the Polaris incident in the Mediterranean. I think it was in the early sixties."

"Nineteen sixty-four," Carlson said. "It was before my time, but I heard about it. How about the others? Should I call them in?"

Gleason shook his head. "Let's leave this as routine for now. I don't want to make any waves. We might as well keep the personnel list as small as possible for as long as possible."

"Yes, sir," Carlson said. He got up and left with the others. Bindrich motioned for Gleason and Romberg to join him in his office.

CHAPTER 2

It was after two in the morning when the taxi pulled up, and Viktor Kozhevnikov got out. As the cab pulled away, Kozhevnikov lurched drunkenly across the narrow sidewalk, up the one step, and into the lobby of his hotel. At the desk, the concierge sniffed disapprovingly as he handed over the key, then went back to the paperback he was reading. As Kozhevnikov stumbled toward the elevator, he noticed the two husky men seated at opposite sides of the lobby. Both were pretending to read newspapers, but he knew they had seen him and were relieved. He had been missing for nearly four hours now.

The ancient elevator doors opened and Kozhevnikov lurched inside and pressed the button for the fourth floor. After the doors closed and the cage started up, he straightened his tie and brushed back his hair, emitting a long, tired sigh.

The first step was accomplished. He had gotten past his guards without incident. The second battle, the biggest one, was about to begin.

Kozhevnikov was sure Nadya would still be awake and that, like so many evenings in the past, they would not get to bed for several hours. It would take that long for her tirade to run its course.

He was not looking forward to it, but then, he mused wryly, he never looked forward to it. But tonight especially, he hoped she would give up her vigil and go to bed. Mornings dulled the edge of her anger, and her rantings were less strident.

The elevator clanked to a stop and the doors slid noisily open. Kozhevnikov stepped into the dimly lit corridor. A light was shining from beneath their door. His heart sank. Nadya was waiting.

He unlocked the door and entered the suite, which consisted of a small sitting room and an even smaller bedroom. Nadya was seated on the sofa. When he closed the door and turned to her, she looked at the travel clock on the coffee table beside her.

"Good evening, Vitya," she said, using his pet name sarcastically.

"Sorry I'm late, my dear," Kozhevnikov said softly. "I didn't realize the time."

"Yes you did," she said, the direct rejoinder stopping him momentarily. "As you did the last time, and as you will the next. Nothing has changed."

He had no answer to her challenge, but this evening he wished he could make her understand what he could not even understand himself.

He went across the room and bent to kiss her cheek, but she pulled away. When he straightened, she glared at him.

"You've been drinking."

"Yes," he said, turning away from her and loosening his tie. He slipped off his jacket, laid it over an easy chair, and then sat down and began undoing his shoelaces.

She watched him in silence. When she spoke, he noticed the anger in her voice just below the surface, ready to boil up and explode at any second.

"Where have you been all this time? Bolotin was concerned."

"I was out walking. That's all. Paris is a beautiful city."

"It's a dirty city. I want to know where you were until two in the morning."

"Walking, nothing more," he said, looking directly into her eyes. She was still a beautiful woman, even by Western standards. Although she openly despised anything Western, she used French body lotions and American cosmetics that she bought at the large exchange store in Moscow. Only foreign currency could be used there, and where she got the cash he could only guess; but it was an easy guess, one he didn't want to think about tonight.

At fifty-two her hair had not grayed, nor had her face or breasts sagged badly. During the day, when she was dressed and made up, she looked like a woman of thirty-five, and even now she looked young and vibrant, much like the girl he had married nearly thirty-five years ago. The only ugliness about her was the deep-set scowl lines on her face.

"And where were you walking that you had to take the trouble to elude your bodyguards? Can you tell me that?" she continued.

"It's a little game, that's all," he lied, knowing she could sense his fabrication. "I wanted to be alone. Without anyone watching. Do you understand?"

She shook her head. "I only understand, Viktor, that you are a high-ranking member of the Komitet. That you have done fine work. And that in the very near future you will be a division chief. Very soon."

Kozhevnikov started to protest, but she cut him off.

"No, Vitya, hear me out. Going from a peasant boy to a soldier in the war and now to a division chief is a long way to rise. And it is even a longer distance to fall."

Kozhevnikov laughed bitterly. "Such a long way, really, Nadyenka?" he said, using her informal name. "And would it be such a terrible blow to you? Do you forget so easily how it was? The boats on the lake? The sleighs in the winter? The picnics? The walks in the forest? The lovemaking in the summer fields?"

She slapped the arm of the sofa impatiently. "It is you who does not remember the cold winters in unheated rooms. The endless cabbage and potatoes and black bread. The boredom, the peasants, the filth."

"We were happy——" he began, but she interrupted him again.

"Happy because we knew we were leaving all of that. We were heading toward Moscow. We were going to have a nice apartment, nice clothes—even an automobile. And we have all of that now. Don't lose it for us, Vitya, with your insanity."

She suddenly fell silent. Kozhevnikov, weary, lay back in his chair and closed his eyes. He could see the mountains, the air clear and clean in the spring, the rivers swiftly moving and cold with the melting snow. It had been a time of expectations, a time of dreaming; yet they had been happy and content with what they were doing. Each day was a pleasurable new experience.

Then in Moscow, after their daughter drowned, the city seemed to close in on them; the smog, the dirty river, the grimy buildings, the stupid and ambitious people pressed in on them from every direction.

The war had been terrible, but he did not realize how bad it really was until he returned to find one of every three men missing, never to return. To find meat impossible to get, fuel oil nonexistent, fresh produce scarce, housing impossible, and the demands upon his loyalty stringent beyond belief.

He continued his work for the NKVD, took more night courses at the university when it reopened, and threw himself into the rebuilding of his country, Nadya at his side. As terrible as it was, they felt in their hearts that they were the ones who were going to make it a better place for their only child.

But the city became oppressive after her death, work became demanding, and Nadya began to grow distant.

At which moment, he asked himself now, had their fate begun to hang in the balance? Had a fulcrum shifted somehow, causing them to teeter slowly to the wrong side? Were these ideas only imaginary? Or was this merely life?

He opened his eyes. Nadya was staring at him. A tinge of fear was mixed with her expression of satisfaction that she had gotten through to him and was making him see the error of his ways.

"What is troubling you?" she asked.

Kozhevnikov was surprised by the question. "I'm tired."

"It's two in the morning."

"No. I'm tired from work. The Vietnamese are not our people. The Chinese will have them soon, and everything we did there will be wasted."

"The Americans lost," she said. He laughed.

"The battle, perhaps; but they will win the economic war sooner or later."

"What's happening to you?" Nadya asked, her voice again harsh and demanding. Kozhevnikov's gut tightened. "Is your brain addled? Is everything we've worked for going to be lost by your stupid comments?"

Everything is already lost, he wanted to say to her but held his tongue. She continued, "Say something like that to the wrong person and you will get your wish— we both will be back to Umsk and cabbage, or worse, Butyrki."

Kozhevnikov got up slowly and went into the bedroom, leaving the door open. Nadya remained on the sofa, fear written on her face.

He wondered what would become of Nadya if he lost his position. Would her lover, whoever he was, allow her to fall, as well? Most likely he would, Kozhevnikov told himself, and it gave him no comfort from his guilt.

He stood by the dressing table studying his image in the mirror. His eyes were red-rimmed and his complexion sallow from the strain he had been under the past three months, ever since he had made his decision. He was not a stupid man, nor did he wear blinders like his co-workers. Once a man had seen beyond the mountains, he would never be content to remain in the valley. And that was unfortunate, because the valley was often nicer. Wherever he went he would wear the label of a traitor.

And those left in the valley? Would the sun still shine for them? Would he lead a terrible, dark army back to destroy everything he had loved and held dear?

Nadyenka. What would become of her? What had become of her? For the past five years, during his assignment in Hanoi and then last year in Saigon, she had returned to Moscow at least three times a year, each time staying longer and longer. And, shortly after each trip, Kozhevnikov was promoted one rung higher. With each move came a newer and larger apartment, more food, more liquor, more money, more power.

Was it worth it? If she had not set out on this course, would he ever have seen beyond the mountains? Or would he still be content in his ignorance?

Nothing made sense any longer, especially what he had set in motion this evening. Did the Americans value life any more than his own countrymen, or were their blinders just a different brand?

He turned away from the mirror, suddenly conscious that Nadya was behind him. She stood in the doorway watching him. The anger and fear were now gone from her face, replaced by a weariness that matched his own.

"Where have you gone, Vitya?" she asked softly.

He shook his head. "I don't know."

"Can you return?"

"I don't know that, either."

Tears formed in her eyes and slid down her cheeks, but she made no sound. He wanted to go to her, to hold her in his arms, but he couldn't. He had lied to her. It was too late for him now. He could never return.

CHAPTER 3

"You know Marty Romberg, our Soviet Research chief?" Sylvan Bindrich asked, as he indicated chairs and a leather-covered sofa for them to sit upon.

Gleason nodded at the small man who peered back at him through thick glasses. "We've met," he said.

"I asked him to join us because I·think we'll be leaning quite heavily on him and his department before we're finished."

"Why are you involving me?" Gleason asked. But Bindrich did not answer until they were seated. Gleason sat down in an easy chair and the other two faced him on the sofa.

"Your name came up specifically," Bindrich said.

Gleason's brows knitted. "Kozhevnikov mentioned my name?"

Bindrich nodded. "Mine as well, and both of our exact positions within the company."

"It wouldn't strain credulity too far to assume they have our entire organizational chart," Romberg said precisely. "We have theirs."

"Does that include our deep-cover people, Marty?" Bindrich asked.

"Certainly," Romberg said without hesitation. "But to what level is anyone's guess. He did have Douville's name and correct number."

"Yes," Bindrich replied dryly. "Which might indi-

35

cate nothing more than sloppiness on Douville's part and not a high level of expertise on Kozhevnikov's. I just want to make sure he's not playing games with us."

Gleason watched the exchange with growing impatience, which Bindrich noticed.

"Sorry, Gleason. I didn't call you in to talk around you."

Gleason nodded but said nothing, waiting.

"But before I lay it all out, I want to know what connection you have with Kozhevnikov."

"None," Gleason said. "As I indicated in the briefing, I've only heard his name in connection with the Polaris incident of '64. Carlson is digging out what we have on him now."

"No other contact with him?"

"None."

"Not during the war? Army intelligence?"

"What are you getting at?" Gleason asked, his impatience rising.

Bindrich smiled. "He wants you and me, as well as one of our operatives in Copenhagen to be present at the Munich meeting in four days. I can figure the Dane, and I can even figure myself since I run Missions and Programs. But your name comes up a complete blank."

"I can't help, unless it's a defection, in which case he'll need me to verify data."

"Perhaps," Bindrich said thoughtfully; he fell silent.

Gleason lit a cigarette, inhaled deeply, and sat back in his chair. Bindrich took a tape cassette from his coat pocket, plugged it into a small machine on the coffee table in front of him, and punched the rewind button.

"Before I play this, I'd better give you a little background," Bindrich said.

Gleason resigned himself to what would probably be another long mission. It had been five years since he had taken a vacation, and it looked now as if this year's plans would also have to be canceled. Pat would be disgusted, Kevin would be unhappy, and it would open up a whole new round of pressure on him to quit the CIA and get a job in the private sector.

"Dennis Douville is one of our deep-cover people in Paris. We put him there shortly before the Paris peace talks began. After that mess was over with, we kept him there to keep tabs on everything."

The cassette clicked to a stop, and Bindrich looked up. "Douville has been cooling his heels for the last eighteen months or so, with little or no traffic from us or anyone, until last night. At eleven o'clock Paris time, Kozhevnikov telephoned Douville on his blind number. He instructed him to meet him in twenty minutes at a downtown discotheque. Alone."

Gleason's eyebrows rose, but he said nothing.

"By the time Douville contacted me and I gave him the go-ahead, there was nothing he could do to set up anything from his end. He managed to strap on a T-111, which Kozhevnikov apparently did not detect, and after the meeting, transmitted the tape via the embassy's crypto channel directly here."

"How do we know the man is Kozhevnikov?" Gleason asked.

Romberg answered. "We won't, until we meet him in Munich."

"I see," Gleason said.

"For now, we're going to assume he's who he claims to be," Bindrich said, "at least until the go or no-go decision tomorrow morning."

"And the tape itself?"

"Too much was lost in the transatlantic transmission and re-recording for any positive voiceprint ID; but Romberg doesn't rule out the possibility that the voice is indeed Kozhevnikov's."

"We have voiceprints on him from Saigon last year," Romberg explained. "But this tape is inconclusive."

"So Douville showed up at the discotheque," Gleason prompted.

"Right," Bindrich said. "The meeting was short; it

lasted only three or four minutes. And Douville evidently had some trouble with his tape unit—the first portion of the meeting was not recorded."

Bindrich punched the play button and turned up the volume. Gleason sat forward as the voices came through the heavy background noise.

One of the men was obviously French; the other man spoke English with a heavy Russian accent.

". . . be gone from here and I don't want to be followed. Do you understand that?"

"Oui."

"This is what must be done. Exactly," the Russian continued. "In four days, at four o'clock in the afternoon, local time, I will meet with a representative of your company at the Wansee Tobacconist Shop in Munich. The address is Nineteen Georgenstrasse. At that meeting I will give more instructions."

There was a burst of static, and then the tape cleared.

"In the meantime, a safe house must be set up no more than an hour's drive from the city. A double who will be prepared to assume my identity for possibly thirty-six hours must be provided. At the safe house Sylvan Bindrich, your chief of Missions and Programs, Nathaniel Gleason, head of Operational Services, and Svend Erik Rafn, your deep-cover man in Copenhagen must be present. Do you understand all of that?"

"Oui."

"Good. You must also understand one other thing. This operation must be kept extremely low-key. Your need-to-know personnel list must be kept to a minimum. There must be no leaks. None. This is too important."

"Is there anything else?" Douville asked after a pause.

"No," the Russian said, and then the tape went blank.

"That's it?" Gleason asked, looking up.

"That's it," Bindrich replied, nodding.

"And Douville had nothing to add?"

"Nothing except that Kozhevnikov—or the man claiming to be him—was alone."

"Unusual."

"Very. If the man is Kozhevnikov, he would have had to elude his bodyguards to make the meeting. And he'll have to do it again in Munich."

"Risky."

"Yes, it will be, unless we're being set up for some reason."

"Like what?" Gleason asked.

"Like getting us out of the woodwork and then disposing of us."

Gleason smiled. "Isn't that being a little melodramatic?"

"It's happened before," Bindrich said without humor. "And it is a valid consideration which will have to be dealt with before any decision is made."

Gleason nodded. "What about Kozhevnikov? What have we got on him? As I said, my knowledge of him is limited to the Polaris thing."

"We know quite a bit about him because of it," Romberg said, sitting forward.

"Go ahead, then," Bindrich said, and Romberg smiled.

"First off, Kozhevnikov has been assigned to the Department of Disinformation ever since the war.

"The department is one of the more active arms of the KGB, and, of course, makes use of political assassinations, kidnappings, strikes, riots, and leaks to the international press to misinform the general public in the Western world, as well as enemy country secret services. They do a good job of it."

"Save us the political history lesson, Marty, and get on with it," Bindrich said harshly. Romberg ignored him.

"When I say 'misinform,' I mean they attempt to

make their enemies believe one thing, while in actuality another thing is true. Handled properly, the Department of Disinformation is the Soviet government's strongest weapon."

"And Kozhevnikov himself?" Gleason asked. "Where does he fit in?"

"Very high up," Romberg said. "He began as a cipher clerk, then became a field man, and finally was admitted to the department's Committee of Planners about the same time he was allowed to join the Communist Party.

"Five years ago he was assigned to Hanoi, along with a number of other Russian advisors. We learned that the Russians were there early in the game but kept it under wraps. The Chinese were a part of the fray, and that was out in the open; but we saw no reason to help the Soviets by acknowledging their presence."

"I should think the opposite would have been true," Gleason said.

"Not so," Romberg countered. "The Soviets were there exclusively to work disinformation plots on us, as well as on the government of South Vietnam. It would have helped them if we had acknowledged their presence. In our dealings with Moscow, we would have had to tread carefully so as not to step on any toes in public. As it was, we were playing games with them below the surface."

"Well, it didn't work. They won," Gleason said.

"Yes, they did," Romberg said academically. "The Western world began to believe that the government of South Vietnam, the government we were trying to defend, was corrupt. It was one of Kozhevnikov's schemes. The Western world, the Americans especially, began to believe the war was totally unjust and immoral. After all, we had Calley, we had the napalming of innocent citizens, we had——"

"Get on with it," Bindrich snapped.

Romberg turned to him. "Am I to brief this man, or not?"

"Brief him, but make it short."

Romberg nodded primly and then turned back to Gleason. "Suffice it to say then that Kozhevnikov's work in Hanoi was brilliant and successful. When our people pulled out of Saigon, Kozhevnikov and his staff moved in. But by then the job was finished, and it was only a matter of time before he was rotated."

"How did we know all of this, and why didn't we do anything about it?" Gleason asked. "I've got to confess I know next to nothing about that situation. I've had my nose buried in Western European operations for too long."

"We didn't act," Romberg responded, "because we would have had to acknowledge the Soviet presence in Vietnam, which was impossible at the time. But we began to get an idea of what was happening there because of Kozhevnikov, whom we first got to know in the Mediterranean in 1964."

"Polaris," Gleason said.

"Exactly. That was one of the few Kozhevnikov schemes that, fortunately for us, did not work. It was his plan to leak radioactive wastes in the harbor waters around every port where American Polaris nuclear submarines docked. Then, by passing that information on to the local newspapers, worldwide sentiment would rise up against the American navy. It would have severely hampered our nuclear-submarine operations."

"Ingenious."

"Yes, like most of Kozhevnikov's work."

"What stopped the plan?"

"Sloppy field men. A pair of them got caught in Marseilles with a truckload of lead-shielded barrels, each containing fifty-five gallons of seawater loaded with plutonium waste, strontium 90, and a number of other exotic by-products of a leaking submarine reactor. Under pressure both men talked, and both came up with Kozhevnikov's name. We have been watching him from that moment on."

"So now he's in Paris?" Gleason asked.

"Possibly," Romberg said. "As of two weeks ago he was in Saigon and due for rotation back to Moscow. He'll probably be promoted to Chief of the Disinformation Department. Meanwhile, he's been rewarded with a Western European vacation. His wife is with him most likely."

"Children?"

"None that we know of."

"I see," Gleason said, sitting back again in his chair. All thoughts of his vacation gone, he tried to build a mental picture of the man they would be dealing with. So far nothing indicated why Kozhevnikov should suddenly want to defect. Just the opposite seemed to be true. If the man who contacted Douville was indeed Kozhevnikov, he was probably working another sophisticated disinformation plot.

He voiced that opinion to Bindrich. "And if that's the case, he's playing a dangerous game for himself."

"Yes," Bindrich agreed. "He's an important man with the KGB. And for someone as important as he is to place himself on the front line makes no sense. Which is the only reason I'm inclined to suspect he is defecting."

"But why?"

Bindrich shrugged. "We'll have to find that out. You and I and Rafn, in four days."

CHAPTER 4

It was just after six o'clock in the morning in Copenhagen. For two days it had rained on and off. A stiff wind had come in from the northwest and now lashed the rain against the windows of Svend Erik Rafn's second-floor apartment.

He emerged from the bathroom, pushed back the heavy black drape that covered the door and placed the last batch of 16mm photographs he had just developed next to the others drying on the newspaper-covered dining room table.

A cigarette dangled from the side of his mouth and the front of his shirt and tie were speckled with burn holes from which the hot ashes fell unnoticed.

He went to the living room window, pushed back the drapes, and looked down at the deserted street.

He had covered his trail from Berlin last night quite well, he thought; first to Munich by plane, then Luxembourg by car, Paris by train, and finally Copenhagen by plane. And at each point, he made sure he was not being followed.

He smiled, his teeth stained yellow from the three packs of Camels he smoked a day, and turned away from the window. He had been right after all. It would give him perverse satisfaction to gloat over his triumph —gloat and then collect the bonus he was going to demand. He didn't need the extra money. He was com-

43

fortable in his bachelorhood; his needs and wants were relatively few. But the only thing the Americans understood was money. The importance of any project was measured in terms of how expensive it was. This project had been important from the beginning, and now the Americans would pay dearly.

He stubbed out the butt of his cigarette in an overflowing ashtray on the cluttered lamp table by the sofa, lit another, and went back to the dining room.

His East German contact had taken one hundred and fifty photographs of the area around Szczecin on the Polish border. Individually, each photo showed very little. An earth-moving truck traveling along a highway; a small convoy of buses carrying construction workers; three men in Soviet uniforms; an area of forest cleared away with deep, well-like pits being lined with cement. But collectively the photographs told a story that he would write up as an offensive missile site on the East German–Polish border, manned entirely by Soviet technicians.

Rafn smiled to himself as he peered through his thick, wire-rimmed glasses at the drying photos.

The CIA director and the American president, as well as his Council of Forty, were going to lose sleep over this one. But there would be very little they could do, except to inform the Soviet government that they knew what was going on. The Soviets would thus lose the edge of surprise. And although the missile site would remain operational, it would become less of a threat than if it had remained a secret.

It was only a game, Rafn told himself, an expensive game.

Later this morning, after the photos dried, he would take the package to the American embassy for delivery via diplomatic pouch to Washington, D.C. Afterward he would take a vacation. Spain would be nice this time of year.

In the efficiency kitchen, he opened a bottle of bock

beer, then went back into his living room where he sat down at his desk. He wound some paper into his typewriter and began his report.

When he was finished, he would include the ribbon and carbon paper in the package, a precaution he had learned during the war.

The telephone on the desk next to his typewriter burred softly, the bell muted by the cotton wadding he had stuffed around the clapper. He let it ring twice before he picked it up.

"Yes?" he said flatly.

"Herr Rafn?" a deep voice answered in German.

"This is he," Rafn said, also in German.

"I'm happy I caught you at home," the man said, hesitating a moment. "But your machine parts have arrived."

"Yes? Where?" Rafn said, sitting forward.

"They are the French parts and are now at the Meissinger Warehouse in Munich. You know the place?"

"Yes, I'll be there."

"The parts must be moved immediately, Herr Rafn," the man continued. "They cannot be left long. They must be shipped out very soon."

"I understand," Rafn said, somewhat impatiently. "I will be there."

"Auf wiedersehen," the man said and hung up.

Rafn slowly replaced the telephone on its cradle and sat back, lighting another cigarette. The code sequence had never been used before with Rafn and was only supposed to be used in case of emergency. He had to go immediately to the safe house the CIA maintained in Munich.

Whatever they wanted would have to wait, he told himself as he went back to his report. It could not be more important than what he was working on now.

Although he had worked for the Americans since World War Two, he had never liked them. They were too excitable, and too predictable. Both attributes were the opposite of what Rafn found interesting.

The Russians, on the other hand, had depth. When they were dishonest in their dealings, they did it with finesse. The Americans wore their lies on their sleeves, plain for everyone to see.

Rafn smiled to himself. The biggest game of all was the one he was playing with himself. He was born a Dane, fifty-five years ago in Jutland, but he remained a Dane in name only. Any country in the world would jump at the chance to use his services. But he had chosen the Americans. Why?

It was a question he had asked himself from the beginning, when he had worked for the American military intelligence unit that first contacted his Danish underground group.

"You Americans have only one thing going for you," he told the CIA director once. "And that is your cigarettes. Nowhere else in the world are the cigarettes any better."

"That's a pretty poor excuse, Rafn," the director chided.

"Don't search for a better reason," Rafn said softly. "You might be surprised, and just a little disturbed."

That conversation had taken place before the cold war between the Americans and the Russians had gone too far. Since that time his loyalty had never been questioned.

He was a Danish citizen, he worked for the CIA, he accepted the assignments and money and that was enough. His methods, his continued employment, and his contacts were never discussed.

"I'm loyal only to myself," he told the director. "And as long as working for you causes no problems, I'll continue. But pressure me, get too close to me, or try to play games with me, and I'll leave. And no one will find me."

He got up and went back into the kitchen for another beer. For the first time in thirty years, he was being pressured. He felt it in the man's voice on the telephone, and he didn't like it.

But he smiled. They would wait. They would have to wait.

CHAPTER 5

It was raining in Vienna when Sigmund Schiller emerged at noon from the building at 7 Rudolph Square. Traffic was heavy and it took him nearly an hour to make it across the city to his hotel by cab. In his room he began packing his suitcase and stuffing papers into his attaché case. The flight to Berlin would be delayed by the weather, but he wanted to wait at the airport in case the weather suddenly lifted and the flight was cleared for takeoff.

Schiller was a large man, but when he moved it was as if he were part cat, making no sound, his feet gliding across the floor. It had come from long training in the Israeli Secret Service. His father was still part of the service, as was his younger sister. They were a family of what his mother called "secret keepers and gatherers of justice," titles all of them were proud of.

He had spent most of the morning with Simon Wiesenthal, the famed Nazi hunter who was gathering information on former SS and concentration camp personnel since the war. Wiesenthal, himself a Polish Jew from Galicia, had spent four years in concentration camps and the experience turned him into a dedicated man. It was Wiesenthal who uncovered the information that led to the capture of Adolf Eichmann in Buenos Aires. And Wiesenthal continued to provide

48

the Israeli Secret Service with information on other former Nazis.

But this time around, Schiller thought as he closed his suitcase and locked it, Wiesenthal had been able to provide little information on the man the Israelis now sought.

Schiller picked up the telephone and had the operator place a call to the airport for him. When the connection was made, he looked at his watch.

"This is Walter Goldmann. I have a reserved seat on Lufthansa flight five-seventeen. Has it been cleared for departure?"

"I am sorry," a feminine voice cooed. "The weather is not expected to lift for at least two hours. If you would rather not wait at the airport, we would be happy to call you in plenty of time for——"

Schiller cut in. "That's not necessary, thanks," he said and hung up, cursing under his breath.

Even the weather was fighting him.

He sat down on the bed and pulled the attaché case to him. On the top of the files was a faded black-and-white photograph of a man wearing a long white laboratory coat. He was tall and thin, with a hawklike nose and sharp, angular features. In one hand he held a bundle of papers, in the other a cigarette.

Two weeks ago Schiller had seen the photograph for the first time. He was called to the military intelligence section of the Israeli Secret Service housed at the air base just outside of Tel Aviv. Ushered into the small briefing room, he was introduced to three other men, all military intelligence, plus Ezra Wasserman, his immediate superior in the secret service.

"Gustav Predel," Wasserman said, handing the photograph across the table to Schiller after he was seated.

Schiller took the photo and studied it a moment before he looked up. "You want me to find this man?"

Wasserman and the others nodded. "Predel is, or was, a medical doctor who worked at the Deutsches

Bundeskrankenhaus in Berlin before the war. Around 1940 he disappeared."

"That's a long trail," Schiller said carefully. "Why do we want him?"

David Sherman, one of the military representatives, snapped forward and was about to speak, but Wasserman motioned him back. "We must move dispassionately, lest we muddy the trail, David."

Sherman settled back in his seat after a moment, but Schiller could feel the tension that suddenly pervaded the room. He held his silence until Wasserman turned back to him.

"This will not be an easy assignment, Sigmund," Wasserman said, choosing his words. "But we think it is important."

Eichmann, Schiller could understand. But this man, Predel, he had never heard of. What had he done that demanded this kind of attention?

Wasserman continued.

"We have very little information on Predel, aside from a few eyewitness accounts. But what we do have requires that he be found."

"If he is still alive," Schiller said.

"He is alive," Sherman said. "He must be."

Schiller glanced at him and then turned back to his chief. "Am I going to have some help on this?"

"I'm afraid not. You're on your own."

"Why?" Schiller said directly. Something was wrong, he could feel it, and in the short embarrassed silence that followed he tried to come up with the reasoning. On every other Nazi hunt all the stops had been pulled out. Budgets and manpower were virtually unlimited. The information piled up. But this was totally different.

Wasserman sighed and sat forward, folding his hands in front of him on the table. "There are some very compelling reasons why you must work alone on this, Sigmund. Alone and in complete secrecy. Only those of us here know what we are going to do, besides

Begin himself. And it must be kept that way. Do you understand that?"

Schiller nodded slowly.

"All right then, I'll explain everything to you. But first you must agree that if you do not want to take this assignment, which is your right, you will never speak of it to anyone. Never. Do you also understand that?"

"Yes," Schiller said; he could feel his heart pounding against his ribs.

"The only knowledge we have of Gustav Predel's life is between 1932 and 1940. We do not know where he was born, what schools he attended or whether he had a medical practice. We only know that he showed up at the Bundeskrankenhaus in 1932. And after that period, after 1940, our information is blank. He was at the hospital one day and gone the next. He was never included on any killed or missing-in-action lists, nor were any directives or correspondence ever issued regarding him."

"We know eight years of his life," Schiller prompted after a moment.

"Yes, and we know very little of that period. Most of our information comes from a few eyewitness accounts."

"May I question the eyewitnesses?"

"No!" Sherman shouted, slapping his open palm on the table.

Schiller turned toward him, surprised at the violence of his outburst.

"It's impossible," Wasserman said. "Of the seven witnesses, three have committed suicide, two are in a mental institution, and one is a hopeless cripple."

"And the seventh?" Schiller asked quietly.

Wasserman looked at Sherman, whose complexion had turned gray.

"The seventh woman is my wife," the old man said. "And I will not allow her to be questioned."

Schiller had always believed that situations were

based in causality. The more complex the situation, the more the causes behind it. Like a good detective, Schiller patiently waited for causes to become apparent before he tried to understand the situation. With the older man's outburst, one of the causes behind this unusual situation now dropped into place.

Schiller nodded and waited for Wasserman to continue.

"The testimony of these women was taped. The transcripts of those tapes are here," Wasserman said, pushing a bundle of seven file folders across. "In each case the name of the woman has been changed to protect her. The circumstances, however, are true."

A second cause fell into place and Schiller, too, sat forward. "You want me to find Predel and kill him," he said simply, staring directly at Wasserman.

"Yes," the man said softly.

Schiller held his stare. "You aren't offering me any backup. If I am caught, you're going to deny any knowledge of me or my mission."

"Yes."

"But it must be done by someone. If not by me, someone else."

"Yes."

Schiller continued relentlessly. "Before I agree to this, you must tell me the entire story."

"It's in the files," Wasserman said, his gaze wavering.

"I want to hear it from you," Schiller said. "And then I want you to give me the direct order."

Wasserman blinked, slowly got up from his chair, and moved so that he stood behind the older military man whose wife was one of the seven. "You don't have to stay, David," he said to him.

"No, I will stay, and I will brief this man," he said and turned to look down the table at Schiller. "My wife was a very fortunate woman, Captain Schiller," he began, using Schiller's rank for the first time.

Wasserman remained standing and the others stared

across the room at the wall, but the man's gaze remained locked with Schiller's.

"In 1931 I was twenty-two and my wife twenty. That year we were married at Schwäbisch Hall. One year later she became pregnant, and complications began. She was admitted to the hospital there, but was transferred to the Bundeskrankenhaus in Berlin where she remained for two months, finally losing the baby."

"Predel was her doctor?" Schiller asked.

The man nodded, then continued. "She underwent several operations, the nature of which was never specifically explained to us. After that she could not get pregnant. We wanted children, Captain, and we tried, but it was to no avail.

"Both of us were arrested for supposed subversive actions against the Third Reich in 1937. I was shipped to Sachsenhausen near Berlin, and I heard my wife was sent to Ravensbrück, which was the women's camp in Mecklenburg.

"I survived somehow, although I now have a metal plate in my skull, and both my legs are wooden. But even more miraculously, my wife and I were reunited about six months after the war ended."

His gaze had not wavered, but now Schiller could see tears forming in his eyes.

"You must understand, Captain Schiller, that when my wife and I were separated, we were young. But when we were reunited, we had both aged fifty years. It did not diminish my love for her, but we have had an unspoken agreement since we came to Israel that I would never ask what was done to her during those years. Never once have I asked her what hells she had to endure. It was easy enough for me to guess. We just picked up our lives the best we could."

"But she has talked finally," Schiller said gently.

"Yes, she has talked. And so have six others," he said. The tears were now streaming down his cheeks.

"My wife has cancer. She will only live a few more months. And now she wants to purge her soul."

Schiller held his breath, knowing what was coming.

"Before Predel left the Bundeskrankenhaus he murdered as many as five thousand Jewish women. My wife was among the few survivors. At first the women were forced to mate with Jewish men, then later with SS and Gestapo enlisted men. The women who could not become pregnant were subjected to a series of operations and radiation treatment. For what purpose we do not know. One woman who became pregnant had her belly slit and sewed open so that the development of the fetus could be watched each day. She died before coming to term.

"Another woman had most of her stomach and intestines removed, and her womb was enlarged to fill the cavity. She was artificially inseminated so that she was carrying twelve developing embryos. She, too, mercifully died."

"And your wife?" Schiller heard himself ask as if from a long distance.

"My wife has no breasts, no ovaries, no uterus, no fallopian tubes, not even a vagina. Everything was removed." The old man's voice had gotten softer and softer and finally it had cracked. He stared straight at Schiller.

"Gustav Predel," Schiller said.

Sherman nodded. "Find him, Captain Schiller. Find him and kill him."

Schiller returned the photo to his attaché case, snapped the cover down, and locked it. For two weeks he had scoured his sources in Israel for more information on Gustav Predel before moving his search here to Vienna and Simon Wiesenthal.

So far he had drawn a complete blank, except that he learned from Wiesenthal that Predel received his medical degree from the University of Heidelberg in

1930, was admitted to general practice in Berlin, then joined the Bundeskrankenhaus staff two years later.

His next step would be to go to the attorney general's office in West Berlin and then the Bundeskrankenhaus itself.

Somehow he would find Predel. Find him and kill him. Slowly. Cause him as much pain as possible. Although he knew he would probably need help from the Americans in West Germany, he would keep his real intentions an absolute secret.

After he had killed the man, he would return to Israel, where his identity would be changed. And even if he were arrested and brought to trial for murder, he would not talk. He could not, for the sake of the many hundreds of women still alive in Israel and other parts of the world who had been submitted to the inhuman indignities of Predel.

CHAPTER 6

The rain which had blanketed Europe from the north-west for two days finally subsided, leaving the skies overcast. In Munich it was dark and a chilly ten degrees Celsius; but traffic was heavy along the Maximilianstrasse with late afternoon shoppers and workers hurrying home to dinner.

The two electronics technicians who would operate the monitoring and recording equipment arrived late last night. Dennis Douville flew in from Paris in the morning, a few hours before Gleason and Bindrich arrived with Martin Romberg. Hans Villmeier, the CIA operative attached to the army's logistics office in Munich, arrived after dinner.

Bindrich, standing at the window of the third-floor apartment, watched a bus lumber by and stop at the corner a half block away. A woman and an old man with a cane got off and went around the corner.

Across the street another man and woman sat in the window of a bar, deep in conversation. Bindrich knew they were watching the front door of the apartment building.

The rear entrance was locked from the inside and the door was wired so that the lights in the apartment would flash if it were forced The telephone was cleared, and the walls, floor, and ceiling were swept before they arrived. The day before, people in the apartments above, below, and to either side of them were checked, and for the first time since he arrived in Germany, Bindrich felt somewhat comfortable, although Rafn still had not shown up.

Bindrich turned away from the window to face the others.

"Nothing yet?" asked Gleason, who sat slouched on the sofa.

Bindrich shook his head. "I think the perverse bastard is doing this on purpose."

Gleason's eyebrows rose. "Frankenheim said he called and told them he'd be delayed——" Gleason began, but Bindrich cut in.

"That's Rafn's style. Make us think he's playing the game when he's really taking his own sweet time," Bindrich said with outward calm, but he could feel his blood pressure rising.

Everything in this operation depended upon strict timing. They were well into the second day, and in less than forty-eight hours everything would have to be set up and ready for the meeting at the tobacconist's shop. They needed every hour of that time.

And yet, Bindrich mused, as he stood by the window, he was not going to allow any operative to get his goat, even if the man were the best, and even if the green light depended upon what information he might supply them.

"Gleason has had no prior connection with Kozhevnikov? You're sure of that?" the director asked early yesterday morning.

"Positive," Bindrich replied.

"That leaves Rafn, who may have had contact with him during the war."

"I have been operating under that assumption, sir," Bindrich said. "We have nothing in our files on such a connection, but Rafn worked for U.S. military intelligence before and during the fall of Berlin. His unit had some contact with the Soviet military intelligence unit operating in that area. But we have nothing conclusive."

The CIA director, a new man who had been recently appointed by the president, chewed at his lip thoughtfully.

For an old hand such as Bindrich, the decision was simple. But Bindrich knew, from long experience under a half-dozen different directors, to keep silent unless he was asked.

The director looked up after a moment. "What do you think, Mr. Bindrich?"

Bindrich sighed inwardly. "I think we should set up for the meet in Munich and then base our decision on Rafn's information."

The director's face lit up. "Good thinking. But I'll want you to contact me with the final decision. I'm taking this to the president."

"Sir?" Bindrich said, sitting forward.

"Sorry," the director said, "but the president told me specifically that in any dealings with the Russians he is to be consulted first before any action is taken. The arms-limitation talks are scheduled to go into full swing next month and he doesn't want anything to interfere."

"The timing might be critical."

"I'll keep myself available. And the president has already been informed of this situation. He's agreed to act fast as well. We just can't step on any toes."

A solid brick wall had been thrown up before them. Now Rafn's tardiness was shoving them up against it; Bindrich didn't like it. Not one bit.

The apartment was large. Off the living room to the left was a huge kitchen, and to the right, down a short corridor, were three bedrooms and a spacious bathroom. The place had been used since its construction in 1957 as transient quarters for American military officers and their families on temporary duty with the army logistics office. It had also been used as a CIA safe house, so that none of the neighbors found anything unusual in the arrival of new faces from time to time.

Romberg was asleep in an easy chair across the room. Douville and Villmeier were reviewing the files on Kozhevnikov, and the two technicians were in the kitchen eating when the telephone rang. Gleason sat forward and picked it up.

"Yes?" he asked quietly.

Bindrich moved away from the window.

"Thanks," Gleason said a moment later and hung up. "An old man with a cane just entered the front door."

Douville and Villmeier looked up and drew their guns as Bindrich moved across the room to flip off the light switch by the door. A moment later the light in the kitchen went off and the technicians appeared in the doorway. Bindrich motioned them to keep silent.

Their movement to this apartment could have been monitored; anyone watching the apartment would have seen all but the technicians arrive.

Bindrich did not like it at all.

The two operatives took up positions on either side of the door, and Bindrich was ready to open it and jump to one side.

A few minutes later they heard footsteps in the hall outside. And then someone knocked on the door.

Bindrich moved to one side. "Yes?" he said.

"Herr Bindrich, this is the *Hausmeister*. There is a package for you."

Bindrich held his breath for a moment. He recognized the man's voice from talking with him earlier. "Just a moment, please," he said, nodding for Douville to turn on the lights and step away from the door.

Once the lights were on, Bindrich carefully opened the door and looked out into the hall. The red-faced *Hausmeister* stood a few inches away. He was holding a large manila envelope; when he saw Bindrich, he smiled.

"This was just delivered for you, Herr Bindrich."

Bindrich opened the door all the way and took the envelope from the man as he surveyed the hallway. There was no one else there. "Thanks," he said, and the *Hausmeister* nodded and then turned and lumbered back the way he came.

Bindrich closed the door and tossed the envelope to Villmeier, who was heading for the kitchen where one of the technicians was filling the sink with water.

Within fifteen seconds the envelope was soaked and the technician was carefully opening it. Inside was the German edition of a Gideon Bible.

"What the hell . . ." Douville started to say when someone knocked at the door again.

"Herr Bindrich, it is the *Hausmeister* again, please."

Bindrich was across the room and had opened the door as Douville shouted for him to stop; but it was too late.

An old man, the stubble of three days' gray whiskers on his chin, stood in the corridor pointing his cane directly at Bindrich.

"Bang, you are dead, Herr Bindrich," said the old man, and then smiled, showing his yellow teeth.

CHAPTER 7

"Do you always operate this way, Mr. Rafn?" Martin Romberg said, sniffing disapprovingly after they were introduced.

Rafn ignored him, directing himself to Bindrich, who had recovered his poise. The others were gathered around him in the living room.

"This is a sloppy setup, Bindrich," Rafn said harshly. "You can tell from a hundred meters that the back door has been wired; and your people in the *Gasthaus* across the street stick out like sore thumbs."

"How long have you been in Munich?" Bindrich asked, holding his temper in check.

"I arrived this morning, a half hour before Douville," Rafn said, smiling. "As a matter of fact, I had dinner at the table next to your people across the street."

"Congratulations," Bindrich said dryly.

"At least the opposition isn't watching. You're safe."

"Why didn't you come up earlier? We've been waiting all afternoon," Bindrich said, his frustration rising again.

Rafn smiled. "I was waiting for Villmeier to show up."

"And if he hadn't?"

"Then I would have supposed you were pulling some kind of operation here in West Germany, against the Germans, in which case I would have cleared out."

Bindrich took a step forward. "Look here, Rafn——"

"Don't pressure me, Bindrich. I'm not working for you. I never have and never will."

Bindrich stared down at the man, but Rafn's slight smile never wavered. Gleason broke the strained silence.

"We didn't call you here for this, Mr. Rafn," he said. "Your name was mentioned to us by a Russian."

Rafn's gaze snapped to Gleason, and for the first time there was genuine surprise in his expression.

Bindrich was seething inside, but he knew that Gleason was right. They couldn't pressure this man. Besides the fact that he was a damned good operative, he was also a Danish citizen, not a U.S. citizen. And if he skipped, there would be nothing they could do about it. Any pressure they brought to bear on him would ultimately result in embarrassment to the United States. Rafn was truly independent.

Bindrich decided he was just tired, suffering from jet lag. And he was concerned about this mission. If Kozhevnikov was playing games with them, and they fell for it, the ax would come down on his head. He was due for a promotion, and he did not want anything to interfere with that possibility.

"Does the name Viktor Vasilievich Kozhevnikov mean anything to you?" Bindrich asked softly.

Rafn turned back to him. "Indeed. I saved his life in 1945."

"While you were with our military intelligence in Berlin?"

Rafn nodded. "Where is he now?"

"In Paris right now, but we're expecting him here in Munich probably tonight or tomorrow."

"And my name?"

"Kozhevnikov mentioned it to our man in Paris whom he contacted two days ago."

Rafn fell silent for a moment, and when he looked up his eyes narrowed. "A defection?"

"That's what we're hoping you can tell us," Bindrich said. He motioned for Rafn to sit down; when they were all settled, Bindrich explained everything they had so far. When Bindrich was finished, Rafn lit his third cigarette since entering the apartment.

"He, as well as his wife, are being monitored in Paris?" Rafn asked.

Bindrich nodded. "He's being loosely tailed by four of his own people working in pairs. But so far they haven't gotten very close to him. He has managed to elude his bodyguards for up to three or four hours a day. But yesterday our people managed to keep up with him."

"What did he do?"

"Nothing much," Bindrich shrugged. "Had dinner alone, went to a couple of art museums, and then returned to his hotel."

"He's establishing a pattern so that when the switch is made here, his people won't become suspicious."

"We figured the same thing," Gleason said.

"What about his wife?" Rafn asked.

"She sticks pretty close to their hotel," Bindrich said.

"And what have you done here in Munich?"

"We've checked out the Wansee Tobacconist Shop. It's clean. As far as we can determine it's never been used before."

Rafn nodded. "And the safe house he asked for?" he said, and he looked around the apartment. "Surely you're not going to use this place."

Bindrich shook his head. "We've got a place south of here on the Starnberger See, near Seeshaupt. It's off-season and too cold for tourists."

"And the double?"

"We found an actor who'll do the job. He won't be here until tomorrow afternoon."

"That's cutting it a bit close. How about his briefing?"

Romberg spoke up. "There's very little we can do until we've established a pattern on Kozhevnikov's actions. And we're assuming that whenever he sets up the switch he'll give himself a couple of hours to brief his double."

"We're also assuming he'll be sending his wife home ahead of him," Bindrich added. "The switch would be impossible otherwise."

Again Rafn fell silent as he finished one cigarette, stubbed it out in the ashtray, and lit another. When he looked up his expression was thoughtful.

"There's not much I can tell you about Comrade Kozhevnikov. I knew him for about three months during the war, but he is not the typical Komitet man. He thinks too much."

"Typical or not, he's up for promotion. Probably to Department Chief," Bindrich said dryly.

Rafn smiled. "I have a feeling that his rise within the KGB isn't entirely his own doing. Perhaps his wife. . . ." he let the sentence trail off.

"You mentioned something about saving his life," Romberg said after a moment.

Rafn turned toward him and nodded. "It wasn't much. The military intelligence unit I was assigned to worked with the Soviet Intelligence Service before Berlin fell. I ended up with Kozhevnikov. Shortly after we were assigned together, we were cornered in Berlin by a couple of SS commandos on the run. I managed to take them both out before they could get Kozhevnikov. That's all."

"After that?" Bindrich asked.

"We worked together for a couple of months, and then I went my way and he went his."

"How close did you get to him?" Bindrich asked.

"The usual stuff," Rafn said casually. "Late-night talks over ideologies, the Nazis, and the women we had known. He was married then, and all he could talk about was his wife. He didn't think much of the war or the military. He just wanted the war to end so he could go home."

Bindrich got up from his chair, went to the window,

and pushed the curtains back. The traffic had thinned out, and it had begun to rain again. The couple still sat in the window across the street. Bindrich laughed to himself—they stood out like sore thumbs.

When he turned around Rafn was watching him, a sour look on his face.

"You know, Bindrich, every time you do that it's like sending up a flare."

Bindrich ignored the comment. "What do you think, Rafn? Is he defecting, or is he playing games with us?"

"Defecting," Rafn said without hesitation. "Otherwise why bring me in on this? And why tip his hand that he knew of Douville's existence, the blind number, and the code sequences? And why call for yours and Gleason's presence?"

Bindrich came back to his chair and sat down. He was not impressed with Rafn, and now he was beginning to actively dislike him. "Why do you suppose he called for your presence here?"

Rafn's eyes narrowed again, and he stubbed out his cigarette. "Bindrich, don't pressure me. If you want to fuck up this operation, then count me out. But if you want me in on it, I'll run it from now on."

"Like hell you will," Bindrich stammered.

Rafn laughed and got to his feet. "Good luck," he said, and he headed for the door.

Bindrich jumped up. "This won't work without you," he said.

Rafn stopped and turned back toward him. "You're goddamned right it won't work without me, but it won't work with you running the operation. You're desk-bound, Bindrich. You're not a field man." He nodded toward Douville and Villmeier, who had remained silent through all of this. "Ask your own people. Every thing has been sloppy so far. Every goddamned one of us may be compromised already."

Bindrich was seething inside, but he forced himself to calm down. Apparently Rafn was the one man Kozhevnikov could trust. And without Rafn, Kozhevnikov would go sour on the entire setup.

"What do you want?" Bindrich sighed finally.

"We'll finish the briefing here tonight; then we'll leave at two-hour intervals. I want everyone out of the city, even out of the country. And then I want you to return individually to the Starnberger safe house."

"What about the tobacconist's shop?" Bindrich asked.

"I'll take one of the technicians with me, and we'll stay in town. As soon as we're set up we'll come to you. By then the double should be here. I want to talk to him before the switch."

"What about monitoring the operation?" Bindrich asked. "I figured we'd do it from here."

Rafn shook his head. "Too close. We'll have to do it from Starnberger. Douville and Villmeier are going to be your legmen?"

Bindrich nodded. "Yes, I want to keep the personnel list as small as possible."

"Good," Rafn said. "They'll have to work alone, in random shifts. If Kozhevnikov's people get wind of the fact they're being watched, it'll blow the entire thing."

"What about the switch itself. . . ?" Gleason started to ask, but Rafn interrupted.

"Kozhevnikov apparently knows what he's doing, and there's nothing we can do until after the meet. He's evidently got this entire thing worked out from his end. It's up to us to keep the hell out of his way."

CHAPTER 8

Any one of a hundred things could go wrong during the next forty-eight hours, Kozhevnikov told himself. Maybe it would be for the best. Maybe Nadya was right in believing that they should leave for Moscow and forget the whole thing.

But he couldn't, he told himself for the thousandth time. He could not. He shook his head, and Nadya caught him.

"What is it now, Vitya?" she asked, concerned.

Kozhevnikov looked up at his wife, who stood in the bathroom alcove of their tiny first-class train compartment, ready for bed. She was studying his face, and for an instant he felt a sharp pang of guilt. Could she guess what he was doing?

"Nothing," he said. "I'm just tired. It's been a long day."

"Let's go home in the morning," she said seriously. "We can finish our holiday in Moscow, with our friends."

"Your friends," he corrected, and the instant the words left his mouth he regretted them. It was one old wound among many.

"Don't start that again," she snapped, ducking back into the bathroom to finish washing her face. "It's a wonder you've become department chief with talk like that. But if it continues, you certainly won't go any further."

I don't want to, Kozhevnikov wanted to shout at her, but he held his peace. It was no use. The damage had been done.

"Seriously," she said, "let's go home."

Kozhevnikov sighed. "We have two weeks left and I intend to spend at least five days in Bavaria."

She looked around the corner again, her face wet and soapy. "Why?" she snapped.

Again the pang of guilt stabbed at his insides. "After five years of Vietnam, I want the mountains."

"And the Urals are not mountains?"

"We've been over this a hundred times, Nadya. Let's not do it again."

"I simply want to know what fascination Germany has for you," she said. "It's a postage-stamp-size country of stupid former Nazis who overeat, overdrink, and overdo everything else. Their music is terrible, their food inedible, and their manners boorish."

Kozhevnikov laughed out loud, something he had not done for years. "Careful," he chided, "you're sounding decidedly Western European."

The remark hit home, and she was speechless for a moment. She was still a beautiful woman, he told himself. Perhaps too ambitious, but that was a fault many people had.

No, she had not changed over the last five years. It was he who had changed. And there was no way he could backtrack. What terrible price was he going to have to pay for what he knew now? Was it worth it?

"As much as I want to go home," she began, a sudden calmness coming to her voice, "and as much as you want to be left alone, I will not do it."

Kozhevnikov held his breath, his chest suddenly constricting. How much did she know? How much of this conversation was being monitored by the watchdogs in the next compartment?

Nadya finished in the bathroom, and when she came

back into the compartment there was a slight smile on her lips.

"Perhaps I have been too hard on you, Vitya," she said sweetly, brushing his cheek with the palm of her hand. She took off her robe and climbed into the narrow bed beside him.

He reached over, turned off the light and settled back.

"Perhaps there is a girl in Munich?" she asked lightly. "Perhaps you would like to see her? It is of no consequence to me. I'll wait for you to indulge yourself, and then we'll return home together."

Nadya had stopped talking, and Kozhevnikov listened to her breathing until it deepened and became regular. She was asleep. If everything went well at the tobacconist's shop, he would have to engineer her return to Moscow.

But that, he told himself as he turned over on his side, would be relatively simple. He had not used his ultimate weapon against her yet, nor would he unless it became absolutely necessary.

He turned the thought over in his mind. Did he love her or not? For the first time he did not know the answer.

He still felt tenderly toward her. After all, they had been married for more than thirty years; since they were children really. But did he love her?

He tried to imagine what she was like in bed with another man. Did they make love in the nude with the lights on? Or did they make love in the dark, her dress merely pulled up around her hips?

The thought did not make him jealous. He could not envision Nadya in that situation, although he knew it had happened and would continue to happen.

He finally drifted off to sleep, his mind locked on the image of her in another man's bed. It certainly was more palatable than the other thing—the thing that had driven him to call Douville. He did not want to think about it. He knew he could not handle it well. But it was there, lurking at the back of his mind like a gigantic black monster ready to devour him.

Rafn was there, too. He could feel the man's presence.

CHAPTER 9

The plaque on the heavy oak door on the third floor of the Government Center Building in West Berlin read GENERALSTAATS FÜR KREIS BRANDENBURG. EINTRITT.

Inside, Schiller found himself in a small, wood-paneled office. An older woman sat behind a desk overflowing with papers. She looked up and smiled.

"May I help you, *mein Herr*?" she asked.

"Yes," Schiller said. "I'd like to speak with the attorney general, if he is in."

"I'm sorry, he will not be in this week. Can anyone else help you?"

Schiller pulled out his identification card and handed it across to her. "Walter Goldmann, Israeli News Service. I'd like to speak to someone concerning World War Two records."

The woman glanced at his identification and then looked up at him, her expression darkening. "May I ask what this is in reference to, sir?"

"The Bundeskrankenhaus," Schiller said.

"War crimes?" the woman asked simply, and Schiller nodded. "One moment, please," she said, and she picked up the phone and dialed two numbers.

"There is a gentleman here from the Israeli News Service who wants information on the DBK and its operations during the war. Will you speak to him?"

A moment later the woman hung up the phone, re-

71

turned to Schiller his ID card, and nodded toward the narrow corridor which led to the back of the building.

"Miss Vogel, the assistant attorney general, will see you. Third office on the left."

Schiller nodded his thanks and went down the corridor. He knocked at Vogel's door and entered. A youngish, attractive woman got up from her desk and held out her hand.

"I'm Gertrude Vogel," she said.

Schiller took her hand and smiled. "Walter Goldmann, Israeli News Service."

"Pleased to meet you," she said and indicated for him to sit down. When they were both settled, she looked at him with a touch of curiosity. "You're interested in the DBK?"

Schiller nodded.

"Whatever for?" she asked.

"I'm looking specifically for one man, a Dr. Gustav Predel. We're doing a story——"

The woman smiled. "May I see your identification, Mr., ah, Goldmann?"

Schiller pulled out his identification and handed it to her. She studied it a moment and then handed it back.

"I don't think you want me to call the INS, so why don't you level with me?" she said with a straight face.

"I don't understand——" Schiller began to say, but again she cut him short.

"You are no more an INS correspondent than I am Eva Braun," she said directly. "And your name is probably not Goldmann. My guess is that you work for the Israeli Secret Service, and you're supposed to track down this Predel. Correct?"

Schiller said nothing. He supposed his cover was flimsy but it would only be apparent to someone accustomed to looking for subterfuge. Only he did not know how far he could go with this woman. The Germans had never been highly cooperative with the Israelis in their search for war criminals. And although each state's attorney general's office was supposed to actively search for Nazi war criminals and bring them to trial, they did not do their job with any enthusiasm, preferring to forget that period of history. What little help the Israelis received from Germany was normally through the few Jews who had remained in the country after the war and a very few Gentiles who were genuinely concerned about what had happened during Hitler's regime. He hoped merely to see any document that would show what had become of Predel after 1940. Now, it did not look too promising.

The woman smiled again. "I thought as much," she said, and she sat back in her chair, crossed her legs, and waited for him to regain his composure.

"You remind me of my sister," he said, wondering why he should say such a thing.

The woman laughed. "Is she in the business as well?"

He nodded.

"Well, if you don't mind talking with someone who reminds you of your sister, what can I really do for you, Mr.——"

"Let's leave it at Goldmann, all right?"

She nodded. "If it makes you comfortable—but I will check on your credentials."

"You won't find anything," he said straight-facedly.

Her expression darkened slightly. "Is it that important?" she asked; when he did not respond, she continued. "You said Gustav Predel. Was he a medical doctor?"

"Yes," Schiller said. "The best information we have is that he was stationed here at the Deutsches Bundeskrankenhaus from 1932 until 1940."

"And after that?"

"He simply disappeared. We have found nothing on him after that time."

"And you . . . your people want him badly?"

"Yes," Schiller said simply. "Can you help me?"

"I doubt it," she said, reaching forward and picking up the phone. "Hilde," she said after a moment. "Check through our DBK files and see if we have anything on a Predel, Gustav. A medical doctor. He was assigned there from 1932 until 1940. We're especially interested in his reassignment."

When she hung up she again sat back in her chair. "What did Dr. Predel do that interests you?"

"Medical experimentation," he said.

"You can't talk about it?" she asked.

Schiller shook his head.

"And what if you find him?"

"I would merely like some information about him, Fräulein Vogel. After that, you can forget I was here."

She smiled. "Impossible, Mr. Goldmann. It is up to the German courts to decide just who was and wasn't a war criminal. If you interfere you will be prosecuted. Beyond that . . ." she said and spread her hands.

"But will you give me the information?" he asked.

"Yes, however I am required to tell you that you are not allowed to search for this man within West Germany. Any information you may gather must be forwarded to this office for dispensation."

"I understand," Schiller said.

"If anything should come of this, you must also understand that I will testify to the fact that I informed you of the law."

Schiller nodded, and someone knocked at the door. The woman looked up.

"Yes, come in," she said, raising her voice.

The older woman from the front desk entered the office and laid a thin file on the desk. Then she left without a word, closing the door softly behind her.

Gertrude Vogel opened the file folder and scanned the three pages it contained. A few minutes later she closed the file and looked up at Schiller, an odd expression on her face.

"What is it?" he asked, sitting forward.

"I don't know," she said distantly. "But I don't think you're going to have much luck in your search."

"Why?"

"I've only heard of things like this," she said mysteriously. "I've never run into them before."

"What is it?" Schiller asked impatiently.

She focused on him again. "We don't have much more on Dr. Predel than you apparently do," she said, and she handed the file across to him.

He quickly scanned the three pages. The first sheet was Gustav Predel's birth certificate from Baden-Baden, the second his graduation records from the University of Heidelberg in 1930, and the third, orders assigning him to the Bundeskrankenhaus, Division of Research, in 1932.

The orders were stamped with the letters W.O., below which was a swastika, the signature of Dr. Paul Joseph Goebbels and the date *12.7.40*. July 12, 1940.

Schiller looked up. "This stamp at the bottom with Goebbels's signature. What is it?"

"That's what I was talking about. There were a number of top-secret projects going on before and during the war. Many of them were under the direct authority of Goebbels's Propaganda Ministry. Of those projects a select few were considered so important that they were under the direct authority of Goebbels himself, answerable only to Hitler. Those projects were never subject to written orders. Everything was done verbally, which is the W.O. notation. It stands for *wörtliche Ordnungen*—verbal orders. So to whatever your Dr. Predel was reassigned in 1940, it was important, it was top secret. Nothing will be written about it in any of the records that have been found."

She spread her hands again. "I'm sorry, Herr Goldmann, but I can be of no help to you, whatsoever. I do not believe you will ever find your man."

Schiller's mind was racing. He would not simply give up at this point. He could not. Even if it meant working on it for the rest of his life, he was determined to stick with it. But there had to be a clue somewhere.

"In 1940, he was reassigned to work directly for Goebbels . . ." Schiller began, and the woman nodded.

"After that, as you can see, our records are blank," she said.

"Yes," Schiller said. "But what projects did the Nazis have going in 1940?"

"I don't understand what you're getting at," she said.

"Besides Peenemünde, what other research projects were the Nazis working on? What important projects?"

"Besides rocket research? God, there were literally hundreds. Nuclear research, germ warfare, medical experiments——"

"Medical experiments," Schiller interrupted. "Where were they done?"

She shrugged. "Throughout the country. Mostly in places like the DBK and in concentration camps."

"There was no central location?" Schiller asked.

The woman shook her head. "I'm afraid not, Herr Goldmann. I'm afraid you're hitting a dead end. It's been too long. And without written records. . . ."

Schiller stood up abruptly and held out his hand. "Thank you for your help," he said.

She stood and shook his hand. "I'm sorry I could not give you more. But while you are in Germany, be careful. I would hate to have to prosecute you."

"That won't happen," he said and left her office. If the hospital did not have anything on Predel, he would be at a dead end.

CHAPTER 10

The rain had finally stopped, and the weather was chilly with a low, overcast sky. A cold, northwesterly wind ruffled Rafn's white hair as he stood on the balcony overlooking the Starnberger See.

The gloomy weather matched his mood. This entire operation was sour and had been from the beginning. In the last twenty-four hours Rafn had listened to Douville's tape at least two dozen times. Every time it ended he felt uneasy.

Something was wrong, drastically wrong. Rafn did not believe that people's basic natures ever changed. If a boy grew up to be a lighthearted man, he would always be a lighthearted man, even though his life might be terrible.

During the war Kozhevnikov had struck Rafn as a good man, a man of high principles and morals, and a man for whom decisions came easily.

But now, the man on Douville's tape was a totally different animal. Rafn could sense it.

Gleason came out on the balcony, but Rafn did not turn around. In the last hour the lake had become choppy with whitecaps and the motion of the waves seemed to draw him forward.

"Bindrich just came in," Gleason said, breaking the silence. "He wants to talk to you."

Rafn said nothing as he studied the lake. People

were like the lake. At first glance their lives and actions seemed purposeless; but if one studied them long enough a pattern emerged. Rafn could see now that the waves were moving ahead of the wind in long, uneven rows, their pattern scattering as they broke on an outcropping of rocks a half mile away.

"You don't particularly care for him, do you?" Gleason said, and Rafn turned around.

"What makes you say that?"

"I don't know," Gleason said, shrugging. "You don't seem to like Americans in general."

Rafn smiled at the naiveté. "That's not quite true, although your Mr. Bindrich is a fair example of an American."

Gleason returned the wan smile, but shook his head. "I think I'm a little more typical. Wife, kids, home, a couple of cars, a color TV, vacations whenever possible."

Rafn turned away to look out across the lake again. "You've just described Comrade Kozhevnikov," he said softly.

Gleason joined him at the low wooden railing and offered him a cigarette. Rafn declined and lit one of his own instead.

"I prefer Camels to your filter tips," he said without turning.

After a few moments of silence, Gleason asked, "Did you get to know Kozhevnikov very well during the war?"

"Well enough."

"So well that something besides Bindrich is now bothering you," Gleason said it as a statement rather than a question.

Rafn did not answer. Instead he was remembering two men in black uniforms dead at his feet in the ruins of a bombed-out building. It was night, but the sky was lit up with a sharp yellow-red glow from fires throughout the city. The sounds of gunfire and shells exploding were very close. Next to him stood Kozhevnikov, visibly shaking.

"You know your life belongs to me now," Rafn said in German, their only common language.

Kozhevnikov's brows knitted. *"Bitte?"*

"It is an old custom. I've just saved your life, and it belongs to me now. For the rest of your life, I will be responsible for you."

Kozhevnikov smiled in understanding. "Treat me well then, my friend," he said.

Rafn turned to Gleason, who was studying his profile. "You know, people who work for the KGB are not the bogeymen you've been led to believe they are."

Gleason smiled. "Nor are we the bogeymen Soviet children believe we are."

"No," Rafn granted, "and Comrade Kozhevnikov is very much like you. His material values are slightly different, but his wife, his job, and his country are his world. He loves his life at much as you love yours."

"I understand that," Gleason said. "But what's bothering you about this operation? Besides Bindrich, I mean."

"Bindrich doesn't really bother me," Rafn said. "He's a deskman like you, but he, unlike you, is trying to play the field operative. And he doesn't have the fortitude for it."

"And Kozhevnikov?" Gleason asked.

Rafn again looked out across the lake. "Consider yourself, Gleason. You love your family, your things, your orderly little existence. Consider yourself defecting. Consider yourself contacting a KGB deep-cover man, setting up a meeting, knowing that soon you will be leaving the United States for the Soviet Union. Consider that within six months you will have told the Soviets every single thing you know about the CIA, about your military, about your governmental structure. Consider it, Gleason, and then tell me your feelings."

"I couldn't do it," Gleason said without hesitation.

"No, and neither could Kozhevnikov. You two are cut from the same material. You could be brothers except for the geography."

"And yet he is doing it."

Rafn nodded. "Yes," he said. "But why?" He turned again to Gleason. "What would it take for you to do the same thing?"

Gleason could not answer so fast. When he did he shook his head. "I don't know. I can't imagine."

"But Kozhevnikov has," Rafn said softly. "So why is he coming to your side? There is no reason for him to defect. Just the opposite, he has every reason to stay where he is."

"That's what's bothering you?" Gleason asked.

"Yes. I can hear it in the tape. Kozhevnikov is a frightened man. So frightened he's willing to give up his country." Rafn blinked. "What's troubling him?"

"I'll tell you what's troubling him," Bindrich said, coming out on the balcony.

Rafn and Gleason looked up.

"He's tired of the party line. He wants out, that's all."

"Perhaps," Rafn said noncommittally.

Bindrich glanced at Gleason then turned to Rafn. "What about the tobacconist's shop? Is it ready for the meet?"

"The place is clean," Rafn said. "Gleason can show up early and browse through the pipes until Kozhevnikov arrives. They can talk, then we'll take it from there."

"I don't like it," Bindrich said.

"Why?"

"What if they grab Gleason?"

Rafn shook his head. "If this is a plot to grab someone, they'll wait until they can get all of us."

"But you don't believe that."

"No. And I'm suggesting Gleason because it will

show Kozhevnikov we're not playing games. That we are laying it on the line for him."

Bindrich turned to Gleason. "How do you feel about it?"

"It's all right with me," he said. "I tend to agree with Rafn's assessment. He's the only one who's had personal contact with Kozhevnikov."

Bindrich again turned back to Rafn. "And afterward?"

"That depends upon Kozhevnikov. I'm sure he will have specific instructions. If we smell a rat we can back out."

Bindrich thought a moment and then nodded. "All right. He and his wife showed up in Munich this morning. We've got our people on him. As soon as he's established a pattern we can brief the double."

"Has the man arrived yet?"

"He'll be here this evening."

"Is he prepared for trouble?" Rafn asked.

"What do you mean?"

"Kozhevnikov wants the double to switch places with him so he can talk with us. If he decides not to defect, he can switch back. But if he does, we'll have to pull the double out of the firing line without making it look like we're kidnapping Kozhevnikov. There could be trouble."

Bindrich thought about it for a moment. "We'll brief him," he said.

CHAPTER 11

"The Deutsches Museum is located here in the middle of the Isar River between the Ludwigs and Cornelius bridges," droned the tour guide monotonously.

It was a dangerous game he was playing, and now that the meeting with the Americans was less than an hour away Kozhevnikov was becoming nervous.

"Actual construction of the museum was begun in 1906, but the complex was not formally opened until May 7 of 1925."

Kozhevnikov looked at his watch. It was shortly after three. And then he looked up at the tour guide, pretending interest. To the left and slightly behind him, one of his bodyguards feigned interest in what the short, squat German guide was telling the group of tourists.

They stood near the back of the huge assembly hall, which fronted directly on the Ludwigs Bridge.

"This museum contains the world's largest collection of natural science and technology masterpieces. It was founded to demonstrate the development of all technological fields in chronological order. And as such, it is the pride of Germany."

Kozhevnikov was certain that his wife had already spoken to Bolotin, the man in charge of his bodyguard detail, because it was becoming increasingly difficult for him to break free. Yesterday morning while he was shopping downtown his attempt to evade them had failed—they anticipated his moves and kept up with him. Last night, too, it was difficult to leave the hotel. Bolotin had stationed a man in the front and another at the rear exit and gave a twenty-mark bribe to the bellboy to allow him to use the service entrance off the kitchen.

"Beyond this assembly hall is a courtyard that leads into our library. It contains more than three hundred and fifty thousand volumes in German and in many foreign languages. Beyond it are the main exhibition halls."

Last night, after he returned to the room, Nadya wanted to argue again, but he went to bed and pretended to sleep in order to escape her tirade. He didn't sleep all night; instead he lay awake thinking about the meeting and the days ahead.

"We will move now to the library itself. The remainder of our time will be spent looking at the exhibits themselves." There was a smattering of applause, and the group began to move through the assembly hall and out the door into the courtyard.

Six months ago in Vietnam he had made his decision. He would engineer his vacation to Europe. Done. He would contact Douville. Done. He would ask for a meeting with Gleason, Bindrich, and most importantly, Rafn, here in Munich. Done.

What then? he asked himself as he moved along with the tour group. If he was going to make the meeting on time he would have to break loose from his guards within the next fifteen minutes. And if Gleason, Bindrich, and Rafn was actually there, if they had set up an acceptable safe house, if they had found a double—what then? As the group crossed the courtyard and entered the library building, Kozhevnikov edged toward the middle of the group and the bodyguards fell behind. By this time tomorrow he might well be on his way to the U.S.

He sighed anxiously. He was giving up his country.

His job. His wife. Everything he loved. For what? Did his reasons, his half-formed suspicions, justify such traitorous action?

The tour guide was leading them at a brisk pace through the lower stacks of the library, and when they turned the corner, Kozhevnikov quickly ducked around one of the long shelves and headed down several aisles in the opposite direction, toward the entrance.

Rushing past the main desk and out the front door, he crossed the courtyard and reentered the assembly hall. Arriving at the opposite entrance, he hesitated at the doors leading to the parking lot. His bodyguards were not in pursuit. They would be searching for him in the library and would be occupied long enough for him to get a cab and hurry to his meeting.

And what would Nadya say this time? They would have another argument. And he was certain that he would have to start one if she didn't.

If the Americans had set up everything, he would send Nadya home to Moscow. Considering what she told him on the train, it would not be a pleasant task. Nevertheless, he would have to do it in order to switch with his double.

And even if the Americans did not believe him, even if he were going to have to return home to Moscow himself, wouldn't it be over between him and Nadya? Wouldn't what he was going to have to say to her end their marriage?

One thing was certain, he told himself as he hurried across the parking lot. He was a confused man. At this point he didn't really know what he was doing or why. Everything seemed out of focus. He supposed he would have to get used to the feeling; it was something that would stay with him for the rest of his life.

But the reason he would do it loomed up in his mind. He shuddered and quickened his step. The Americans would have to believe him. No matter what, they would have to.

CHAPTER 12

The Wansee Tobacconist Shop was the closest thing to a supermarket for pipe smokers that Gleason had ever seen. Although he did not smoke a pipe, he appreciated the hobbylike intensity with which pipe smokers pursue their vice. Pipes of all sizes and shapes, humidors, pipe racks, specially designed ashtrays, and other gadgets filled the endless displays down several long aisles.

It was a self-service shop, with cash registers near the front door. At a counter along one wall clerks helped customers select a particular blend of tobacco.

The place was busy and no one noticed Gleason as he browsed through the pipes.

He had viewed this part of the operation with some trepidation. Even though he was a deskman, as Rafn put it, he was enjoying his role now that he was actually here.

"Nathaniel Gleason, isn't it?" asked a man who spoke English with a heavy Russian accent.

Startled, Gleason spun around and looked into Viktor Vasilievich Kozhevnikov's face. The man had aged somewhat from the photographs Gleason had seen, but he looked typically Russian—high forehead, deep-set eyes, heavy eyebrows, a flat nose, square features, and an uneven haircut. He was wearing a poorly cut gray suit and his tie was knotted crookedly.

"Don't stare," the Russian said, amused, and Gleason turned back to inspect a pipe he had just picked up off a shelf.

"Kozhevnikov?" he asked under his breath.

The Russian moved beside Gleason, picked up a pipe, and began to examine it. "Did you come here alone? Are others outside?"

"I'm alone," Gleason said.

"Good." Kozhevnikov nodded. "I want you to continue moving around the store, looking at the pipes. Stay away from everyone else."

Gleason nodded, put down the pipe and moved a few feet down the aisle. A few moments later Kozhevnikov moved close to him.

"Is a safe house ready?" he asked.

"Yes, we've got a house on the Starnberger See, outside of Seeshaupt."

"Good. Sylvan Bindrich and Svend Rafn—are they there?"

Gleason moved a few feet farther down the aisle, and when Kozhevnikov again moved alongside of him, he nodded. "They're waiting with your double. When does the switch come?"

A man carrying pipes came down the aisle, and they fell silent until he passed.

"Listen carefully," Kozhevnikov said.

Gleason detected a note of urgency in his voice. He suddenly realized that this was not a game.

"I'll arrange for my wife to leave for Moscow on the morning flight to Helsinki. Then I'll lose my guards and drive immediately out to Dachau, the concentration camp museum. I rented a small black Audi. The license is Z104. Can you remember that?"

"Yes," Gleason said, his heart pounding. "What time?"

"I'll be there at noon. Have my double there, along with Rafn. No one else."

Gleason moved to the end of the aisle, turned the

corner, and stopped by a display of lighters. Kozhevnikov moved past him and stopped a few feet away.

"My bodyguards won't be close enough to recognize a switch. We'll switch clothes in the car. Perhaps you'd better send a van instead."

Gleason turned to look at him. Kozhevnikov was studying a lighter with pop-out pipe scrapers, reamers, and tampers.

"We'll send a van," Gleason said, turning away.

After a short interval Kozhevnikov followed him to a large display of humidors and pipe racks. Two men stood talking about fifteen feet away, and Gleason lowered his voice.

"Are you sure you weren't followed today and that you won't be followed tomorrow?"

"Absolutely. But if I can't elude my guards immediately, wait at the museum. I'll be there sometime during the day."

"And then what?" Gleason asked. He could feel Kozhevnikov watching him.

"Then we talk, Gleason. You, Bindrich, Rafn, and I."

"And when we are done, what then?" Gleason asked.

"Don't play games with me," Kozhevnikov said quietly.

Gleason could sense his anger and cursed his own stupidity silently. He would never be able to explain it if Kozhevnikov suddenly balked.

"Sorry," Gleason said.

"This is of vast importance, Gleason. I must be absolutely certain everything is properly arranged. What I want to discuss is of the extremest importance."

"Are you bringing something with you?" Gleason asked, but Kozhevnikov moved down the aisle.

For a moment Gleason was sure Kozhevnikov was leaving the store, but the man stopped at a display, bent down, untied, and retied one shoe.

Gleason moved and stood behind him. "How do we know you aren't pulling some kind of operation on us?"

"Don't be a fool," Kozhevnikov said, standing up and facing Gleason. "We don't put our top agents on the front line." He turned and strode out the door, nodding at the clerk by the cash register.

Gleason stood watching the door; then suddenly feeling conspicuous, he left the shop.

If Kozhevnikov did not show up at Dachau tomorrow, it would be no one's fault but his own.

As he headed away from the tobacconist's shop, one thing Kozhevnikov said kept pounding through his mind. "This is of extreme importance. . . ."

Gleason suddenly felt cold; he pulled his coat up around his neck and hurried to a taxi stand a block away.

They would know what he meant soon enough. In less than twenty-four hours.

CHAPTER 13

"Fräulein Vogel from the attorney general's office sent me here to Xerox some records from World War Two," Sigmund Schiller said to the records clerk at the Bundeskrankenhaus.

The room was located in the basement beneath the main building of the huge hospital complex. Unlike the modern structure above, this part of the hospital was old. Apparently it had not been heavily damaged during the war.

"Fräulein Vogel?" asked the clerk, an older man, looking up at Schiller.

"Yes," Schiller said. "Specifically she wants records on personnel who were in the research facility and transferred out before the end of the war."

The clerk shook his head. "The attorney general's office has all those records," he said.

"Their records are incomplete."

"This is highly irregular," the clerk said. Schiller casually reached inside his coat for the flat Beretta in its shoulder holster.

"I don't know anything about that. All I know is that Fräulein Vogel sent me here to look at those records."

"One moment, please, sir," the clerk said. He picked up the phone on the counter and dialed a number.

Schiller's fingers curled around the weapon. At this

range the man would die instantly. But how much time would he have to search the records? Probably not enough.

The man was talking on the phone. "This is Gunther Braunschweig at the Deutsches Bundeskrankenhaus records division. Is a Fraülein Vogel there, please?"

Schiller tensed. He had nothing against the man, but he had to see the hospital's records. Without them he would almost certainly fail.

"No, that is not necessary," the clerk was saying. "I can telephone her later this afternoon, or tomorrow. *Danke schön.*" He hung up the phone and looked up. "I'm sorry, but I wanted to confirm that Fräulein Vogel sent you here. We have so many crackpots."

"She wasn't in?" Schiller said, relaxing slightly.

The clerk shook his head. "No, but I suppose I can let you see what records we do have," he said, sighing. "Follow me, please."

Schiller withdrew his hand from inside his coat and followed him around the counter and into a huge, vaultlike room with row upon row of filing cabinets and shelves crammed with files, books, and cardboard cartons.

A section near the back had been screened in by a tall fence with a wire door. Braunschweig produced a key, opened the door, and entered the area. Like the rest of the huge room, it was crammed with files and steel shelves.

"World War Two records," he said. "What information are you looking for specifically?"

"Transfers of personnel from the hospital's research division in 1940."

"That will be easy," Braunschweig said. "The administrator's office keeps a log of everything that goes on in the hospital. Every day the staff summarizes the previous day's happenings, which includes personnel changes, operations, acquisitions of new equipment, and the like—everything but daily admissions and discharges." He smiled primly.

"These logs are the hospital's complete records?" Schiller asked.

"Heavens, no," the clerk said, amused. "They are only a summary—what you might call an index. And for each entry there is a file. I assume you would prefer to look at the daily log for the year 1940. If you find what you are looking for, we can locate the specific file."

He moved to the back of the room, where a group of metal shelves held large, leather-bound volumes, each stamped with a swastika and date.

He pulled down the book for 1940 and then turned and shuffled back to the front of the room, where a small table and chair were located by the door.

"This book cannot leave this office. If you find something you need, call it to my attention and I will take the request through channels. By tomorrow we can have the appropriate documents photocopied for you."

He laid the book on the table and then looked up at Schiller with a pinched expression on his face. "The attorney general's office has all these records, so I don't know why you were sent."

"Our office doesn't have copies of the logs, however," Schiller said, guessing.

"True," Braunschweig said, "but as I told you already, they merely summarize what is contained in the files themselves."

"I understand," Schiller said. "Thank you for your help. I shouldn't take too long."

"I hope not," Braunschweig said and shuffled back to the outer office.

Schiller immediately sat down and opened the book to the first page, dated *1 Januar 1940*. The first entry was *0003 Uhr*—three minutes after midnight. Lötte Hildebrandt had been successfully operated on for gallstones by Dr. Dieter Schwalbach in operating theater 4 East.

Schiller quickly scanned the entries. On the fifth page, still under the first of January entries, was the notation *Forschungen,* research. Beneath the heading Gustav Predel's name leaped off the page at him. He could feel the hairs raising at the nape of his neck.

At four-thirty in the morning, Dr. Predel personally supervised the arrival of twenty-five Jewish women from the Ravensbrück concentration camp in Mecklenburg. Below that was the notation *tot,* dead, followed by the names of fourteen women.

Schiller stared at the entry, holding back the lump in his throat and controlling his shaking hands as best he could. It was true: Predel was a mass murderer. Although he believed the women's story, seeing it now in a book of hospital records made it more real for him.

He thumbed further into the book. The twenty-five women's names appeared sooner or later under the heading *tot.*

But then, near the middle of the book, under the date *16 Juli 1940,* was a brief notation that the Special Jewish Research Section of the DBK was being dismantled. A list of personnel followed, some with transfer orders to other hospitals and some to concentration camps.

One list of names—Gustav Predel and fifteen doctors—was set aside from the others. Next to it was the notation W.O., with the swastika and Goebbels's rubber-stamped signature.

Only this time someone had added a notation beneath Goebbels's name. The ink had faded, and Schiller had to pick up the book and hold it directly under the sole light bulb that dangled from the high ceiling. It was a single word: *Tiefensee.*

Apparently it was the name of the town to which Predel and the fourteen others had been sent.

"Tiefensee," Schiller said half under his breath as he laid the book back on the table and left.

There were still thirty-seven years of Predel's life to fill in. But this was a start. He was not at a dead end.

In the outer office, the clerk rose from his desk. "Did you find what you were looking for, sir?"

Schiller shook his head. "I am afraid you were correct. There is nothing in those records the attorney general's office does not already have."

The clerk was smugly pleased. "I didn't think so," he said.

"But thank you for your cooperation, Herr Braunschweig. Your assistance will not go unrewarded," Schiller said, smiling. Braunschweig stood mouth open, wondering just what reward would be coming his way.

Leaving the hospital, Schiller drove his rented Volkswagen to an Esso station for a road map. Back in his hotel room, he spread it out on his bed and began methodically searching the names of all the towns, after he checked the map's index with no luck.

Working in ever-widening circles from Berlin, he finally found what he was looking for and his heart sank.

Tiefensee was a small town thirty kilometers northeast of East Berlin. It was now in the East Zone.

He got up from the bed and went into the bathroom to splash cold water on his face. Although he was a large man, his facial features were diminutive and unmarked. His baby face had been a curse to him all his life, but now that he was getting older, it was becoming an asset. He often passed for a much younger man.

The Americans were the only ones operating with any effectiveness in East Germany. Schiller supposed that he was going to have to contact them for help now.

Predel's trail led in that direction, and Schiller was going to have to follow it with caution. Wasserman had told him he would receive no backup. The Americans might cooperate with him, but once they contacted the Israeli Secret Service about the operation and were told Schiller was on vacation, they would back off. Schiller was completely on his own.

He would have to work fast, he told himself. If he could get to Tiefensee, he would find someone who remembered Predel.

He had the hotel operator dial the American embassy, and when the embassy operator came on the line, he gave only the code sequence.

"Seven-one-seven, please."

"One moment," the operator said and clicked off.

A few moments later a man came on the line. "Yes?" he asked brightly.

"This is Muskrat. Have Nathaniel Gleason contact Walter Goldmann at the Alsterhof."

"Yes," the man said and hung up.

Schiller put the phone back on its cradle, pushed the map from the bed, kicked off his shoes and lay down. The message would not get to Langley for at least thirty-six hours, and it would take another day or so to get a response.

Schiller only hoped that Gleason was busy and would not contact the Israeli Secret Service first for confirmation. If that happened, someone else would come to see him. He would have to wait, now—and watch.

CHAPTER 14

Andrei Andreevich Bolotin stood at the open door, an apology on his lips. It was nearly ten o'clock at night and Kozhevnikov had just returned to the hotel. Bolotin and another bodyguard had been waiting for him in the lobby. When he arrived, Bolotin followed him upstairs.

"I'm sorry to bother you like this, Comrade Kozhevnikov," Bolotin said with much deference in his voice, "but we were concerned about your well-being."

"So?" Kozhevnikov asked, raising his left eyebrow.

"We lost you at the museum. Your wife was quite upset."

"What do you want, Bolotin?" Kozhevnikov asked harshly.

"Comrade, I have been charged with your safety. But it is becoming increasingly difficult——"

Kozhevnikov cut him off. "I am on holiday, Andrei Andreevich and I will not be bothered like this again. Do I make myself clear?"

Bolotin blinked and nodded, but said nothing.

"In the future, I want you to maintain a low profile. I don't want to see you, and I don't want you to speak to me or my wife again unless spoken to first. Is that also clear?"

"Yes, Comrade Kozhevnikov, but my responsibility is——"

"Good evening," Kozhevnikov said and shut the door, his heart pounding. It was getting close, very close. Tomorrow's meeting at Dachau was going to be difficult. It was going to be hard to evade the bodyguards long enough to make the switch. And then, if everything worked out, his double's escape was going to be even harder.

He turned away from the door. Nadya was standing in the doorway to their bedroom, ready for bed. There was a stern expression on her face.

"He will report this, of course," she said.

Kozhevnikov ignored her, crossed the room to a low *Schrank,* and poured himself a cognac in a small snifter. When he turned back and took a drink, Nadya was still staring at him.

"Is she that good, Vitya?" she asked harshly. "Is she so good that you must toy with your bodyguards like this?"

"There is no woman here, Nadya," he said tonelessly.

"Then what?" she asked, her voice rising.

"I merely want some freedom a few hours each day," he said.

"What?" she asked incredulously.

"I need some freedom from this rigid holiday, from Bolotin—and from the Komitet and Vietnam."

"And that includes me?" Nadya asked.

"Yes, Nadya, that includes you. Especially you," Kozhevnikov said, taking a deep drink. He would remember this moment for the rest of his life. But it was the only way.

Nadya, hurt, stepped forward, then stopped. "What is happening?" she asked, but Kozhevnikov casually waved her off.

"No theatrics, Nadya. I'm too tired, and it has been going on too long. Even before Hanoi."

"What are you saying, Vitya?" she asked, with disbelief in her voice.

"You know quite well what I'm talking about. And don't call me Vitya. Not tonight."

Her mouth was moving, but no words were coming out.

"Shall I spell it out for you?" he asked, leaning back against the *Schrank*. He tried to be nonchalant, but it was difficult. Despite what she had been doing ever since he had joined the Soviet Intelligence Service, he still loved and respected her. If he could only erase what had driven him to contact the Americans, he would be trying to bring her back to him, not destroying their marriage by forcing her to run home.

She said nothing, but he could see the tears forming in her eyes. He forced himself to continue.

"Shall we discuss Comrade Bushkin? He was the first, I believe. The chief cipher clerk, wasn't he? That was in the KI days. Then there was Zalonzy, the division clerk in the Third Directorate. Ten years ago it was Boris Marakov, who lived not too far from us. And then in Hanoi it was——"

"Stop it," she screamed. "Stop it, Vitya, stop it now!"

Kozhevnikov wanted to rush over to her, but he stayed where he was, a slight smile on his lips. "Don't you want me to continue, Nadya? Perhaps we could discuss your present lover. The man to whom you want to return this very moment."

"I did it for you," she said through her tears.

Kozhevnikov laughed out loud. "Come, Nadya, that's worse than the American movies you hate so much." He took another drink and then set his glass on the cabinet. "You're an ambitious woman. Too ambitious."

"I didn't love any of those men," she said, taking another step toward him.

"But you gave your body to them," he said coldly.

"Yes," she shouted. "Yes, and every minute I was thinking about you."

"No, my dear," he said, his tone softening. "You

were thinking only of yourself. You were thinking about the new apartments, the new furniture, the new clothing. You were thinking about the car and the prestige of being married to a high-ranking Komitet man. Nadyenka Ivanovna Kozhevnikov: Why, she is the wife of that department chief! A lucky woman."

"That's not true, my Vitya, that's simply not true."

"Then why, Nadya?" he asked softly.

She pushed a loose strand of hair away from her eyes, pulled her bathrobe tightly around her, then crossed the room to sit on the arm of the sofa. Minutes later, when she looked up at him, the tears were gone, replaced by a sad, tired expression. For the first time since he had made his decision he was not so sure it was the correct one.

"Twenty years ago, after we lost Sasha, when I was ill, we were given a permit to hire a housekeeper. She was a young Jewish girl. She stayed under our roof for nearly six months. Remember her, Vitya?"

Kozhevnikov was suddenly cold. He remembered the girl clearly.

Nadya continued. "I was ill. You were young, and she was fresh and pretty, and you took her to bed. Do you remember that, Vitya? Do you recall it clearly?"

"So it's revenge," he said, still cold. It was true, he had taken her to bed, mainly out of frustration. It was a difficult time for him as well as for Nadya. After their daughter died, Nadya reacted by becoming ill, while Kozhevnikov needed comforting. He needed the warmth of a lover, something Nadya was unable to supply. So he took the girl to bed. She was so completely intimidated by him that she submitted.

One evening he returned home and the girl was gone. He tried to trace her but with no results. The girl had simply disappeared. After a time Nadya recovered, and he forgot the incident.

"No, it's not revenge. There's no revenge in my spirit."

"But you were hurt," he said, his voice a long distance away.

"A little," she said, smiling sadly. "But later I understood why you needed her. We both had our own needs during that time, and I was willing to forget. I loved you, Vitya, and I still do."

Kozhevnikov was about to protest, but she waved him off. He fell silent.

"She was Jewish. And you were a member of the NKVD. You had been selected for advancement, and they were watching you very carefully. I didn't find that out until much later, but at the time I suspected something was wrong. The promotion cycle came along and you were overlooked. At first I didn't become too suspicious, but when you were turned down the second time, I knew what I would have to do."

"Which was to go to bed with my superior," Kozhevnikov said, a harsh edge to his voice.

"Yes," she said simply. "Otherwise you would still be a minor division clerk."

"And would that have been so bad?"

"Tell me you haven't enjoyed your position and your power," Nadya snapped.

He was weakening. If she hadn't said that, he knew he would have blurted out what he had done in Paris. But now his resolve strengthened again. If he had never risen in the ranks of the organization, he would never have learned what he had learned nine months ago.

If there were parallel universes, was there one in which Nadya had not done this? Was there a Nadya and a Viktor somewhere who were still very much in love and happy? It was nice to think about, but it was a fantasy. What was done was done, and they could never go back.

"I want you to leave for Moscow in the morning," he said flatly. "Alone. I will stay here for a few days."

Nadya rose and shook her head. "No."

"Yes," he ordered. "And when I return I will have made my decision."

Disbelief crossed her face and then her features hardened. "I have worked too hard and too long for us to let you throw it away like this."

"You have worked hard, I grant you that, my dear. But not for us—for you. Don't you think I know about the American money you spend at the exchange store? Don't you think I know about the favors you have received from your current lover? Let's not play games any longer."

"I'll ruin you, Viktor Vasilievich," she said imperiously.

"Perhaps you will, but it will be your ruination as well. You are too old to continue this intrigue much longer. Kept women are usually much younger."

The comment hurt her deeply, he could see it; but he relentlessly pursued his argument. "I will become a department chief because of my work, not because of your machinations, Nadya. Granted, at first my success was because of you. But that is no longer true. What will become of you in the next few years? You will need a husband to comfort and support you in your old age. Who will it be? One of your lovers? Will one of them give up his wife and position for you?"

"Vitya . . ." she said, coming forward, but he waved her off.

"In the morning you are returning to Moscow. I have already made your reservation. When I return I will have made my decision."

CHAPTER 15

After the war the concentration camp at Dachau, just north of Munich, was made into a permanent museum so that the world would never forget what was done to the Jews. Rafn sat in the driver's seat of the Volkswagen van parked outside the main gates. Through the wire-mesh fence he could see the statue that had been erected in the central receiving area. Beyond that the crematory building's tall brick chimney rose obscenely into the sky.

Rafn and the actor had been parked here since ten-thirty. Gleason, Bindrich, and the others were at the safe house near Seeshaupt, and they were ready for the switch.

Rafn turned in his seat to look back at the actor, Raymond Johnson. He sat in his underwear, a thin terry-cloth robe thrown over his shoulders.

"Nervous?"

Johnson looked up. "A little, I guess."

"You do bear a striking resemblance to him," Rafn said, and it was true. With a wig and some makeup, the man looked amazingly like Kozhevnikov.

Johnson smiled slightly. "My one big role, and I won't have an audience."

"The pay isn't so bad though."

Johnson turned away and said nothing. He was frightened, Rafn guessed, but he hoped the man was not so frightened he would blow it. There was no way they could prepare for every contingency, so Johnson would have to think fast. One slip, one uncharacteristic move, one telephone call from Kozhevnikov's wife, and the operation would fall apart at their feet. Rafn was not particularly concerned, but he knew Johnson was.

He turned back in his seat, lit another cigarette and continued staring out the windshield at the museum.

It was a weekday, and off-season, so there were only a few cars in the huge parking lot. Three people emerged from the crematorium a hundred meters away and slowly made their way back to the killing trench, a concrete-lined trough cut into the ground. Jews had bled to death there, their blood running out the drain into fifty-five-gallon barrels. Human blood made excellent fertilizer.

Rafn had no feelings about the Jews. They were merely unfortunate people who had borne the brunt of Hitler's megalomania. Now they were fighting back, and Rafn admired it; but he felt no sorrow or pity for them.

His mind returned to the problem of Kozhevnikov. Gleason had confirmed his impression that Kozhevnikov was troubled. He had seemed intense, harried, and somewhat frightened at the tobacconist's shop. And his cryptic comment that this was of vast importance was also bothersome.

Rafn wondered if there was any significance to Kozhevnikov's choice of this place as a meeting point. Why Dachau? Was he trying to tell them something?

He inhaled deeply on his cigarette, then rolled down the window and flipped the butt outside.

They would find out soon enough. He hoped that Kozhevnikov had not gone the way of so many other operatives he had known: men who worked on the front line so long they became shell-shocked, lost their nerve and were on the run. They were not running toward something but away from themselves and the things they had done.

General MacArthur once told Congress, "Old soldiers never die, they just fade away." Maybe old operatives never died, either. At least not natural deaths. They just ran away. Frightened. Alone. Confused. Uncertain.

Was this Kozhevnikov now? Was he such a man? Rafn hoped not.

Kozhevnikov was tired. He had not slept much in the last four nights, and now this morning at the airport there were bags under his red-rimmed eyes and his mouth felt foul.

The guards had been informed that Nadya would be flying to Moscow alone. Bolotin had assigned one man to return with her, leaving only three to look after Kozhevnikov. Now, he could feel, they were watching him say good-bye to his wife.

They took a cab to the airport and did not say a word to each other during the drive; nor did they speak while her baggage was being checked and her ticket prepared. They waited at the boarding gate while the other passengers boarded the Finnair jumbo jet. Nadya looked up at him.

"You don't look well, Vitya," she said softly, a note of concern in her voice.

"I'm tired," he said. "I did not sleep well last night."

"Neither did I . . ." she said, and she looked toward the door that led to the boarding ramp. Nearly all the passengers had boarded the plane. She turned back to him. "I'll have to leave in a moment. Are you sure this is what you want?"

He nodded. "Yes."

"Will you get some rest?" she asked.

"I'll try."

"And will you return home to me, husband?" she asked, her voice now barely a whisper.

He took her in his arms and held her close. "I love you, my Nadya," he said.

"I have always loved you, Vitya," she answered, and they parted. She looked deeply into his eyes. "Return to me. Return home and we will spend the rest of our lives together."

He was about to reply, but she brushed his cheek with a kiss and then turned and hurried through the door to the boarding ramp, leaving him standing alone in the empty passenger lounge.

He moved to the windows, trying to find her. He could not see her, and after a few minutes he turned and left the lounge.

Return to me, Vitya, she said. Return to me. The sentence ran over and over in his mind. He would never see her again unless something went wrong. But if it did and he returned home, it would never be the same between them.

It was nearly ten-thirty by the time he returned to the hotel. Bolotin would have his men posted at the front and rear entrances, and the third would be standing just outside his door. They were not taking the chance that he would go off by himself. But they were foolishly inept men who really didn't know their jobs at all.

Had they bothered to check the other rooms on this floor they would have discovered that a woman identifying herself as Victoria Perez had rented adjoining suites two days ago. No one in the hotel had seen the woman. She reserved the rooms by telephone and sent a messenger to register, paying in advance.

Had Bolotin known about this, he might have become suspicious if he discovered that one of the rooms opened on the same corridor as Kozhevnikov's room, while the adjoining suite opened around the corner, just across the corridor from the stairwell.

Kozhevnikov loosened his tie and turned down his

coat collar, then donned a long, heavy robe, pulling it tightly around him. From his suitcase he extracted the bottle of champagne and, selecting a few flowers from the vase on the bureau, opened the door and stepped out into the corridor, feigning surprise that Bolotin was there.

"Andrei Andreevich, I did not know you would be here," he said.

"Comrade?" Bolotin said, eyeing the champagne and flowers.

"I am seeing a friend," Kozhevnikov said. He marched down the corridor, knocked once on the last door on the left, produced a key, unlocked the door, and entered the suite.

It would take Bolotin several minutes to find out who was registered in this room. When he did, he would find that the woman had rented the adjoining suite but had not been seen entering the hotel yet.

By then it would be too late.

Kozhevnikov quickly threw the champagne and flowers down on the bed, took off the robe, straightened his coat and tie, and entered the adjoining suite. He listened at the door, holding his breath, but could hear nothing. He opened it a crack and looked out. The corridor was deserted.

Quickly he stepped out, shutting the door behind him, and in a few steps was at the stairwell door, which he had previously made sure was kept unlocked.

He guessed that the front door would be watched as well as the doors leading from the kitchen, since he had gone out that way the last time.

In the lobby, he hurried into the coffee shop, and without stopping, went out the street entrance. As he expected, none of the guards were in sight. He quickly crossed the street, turned the corner, and hurried away.

Two blocks down, he hailed a cab, which he directed to a parking garage across town. Twenty minutes later he paid the driver, entered the garage, and retrieved the small black Audi 50 he had rented two days ago.

Rafn was about to light another cigarette when he noticed the Audi coming down the road in the rear-view mirror. It turned into the parking lot, and as it came closer, Rafn picked out one man driving. No one else was in the car.

"It's him," Rafn said quietly, and Johnson moved forward.

"Kozhevnikov?"

"It looks like him, but stay where you are," Rafn snapped.

The Audi swung in front of the van and parked a few meters away. The license number was Z104.

Rafn waited, glancing in the rearview mirror from time to time, but no one had followed the Audi.

A few minutes later Kozhevnikov got out of the car and slowly walked toward the van. Rafn stepped out and closed the door behind him.

Kozhevnikov stopped a few meters away and stared at him impassively. "It's been a long time, my friend," he said in German.

"Have you been keeping yourself fit?" Rafn said.

Kozhevnikov smiled and said, "I'm as well as can be expected."

"And your wife?"

"She left for Moscow about two hours ago."

"Your guards?"

"Confused, but they won't give us any trouble," Kozhevnikov said, and he looked beyond Rafn toward the van. "Is my double here?"

"He's in the van waiting for your instructions."

"How is he?" Kozhevnikov asked, looking again at Rafn.

"Frightened."

"So am I."

"Don't tell that to the Americans," Rafn said.

Kozhevnikov did not smile. "If they have any sense they will be frightened, too."

Rafn was about to reply, but Kozhevnikov broke in. "It will not do for me to be gone too long this time."

Rafn nodded. They went back to the van and climbed in through the side door. When the door was closed Rafn nodded toward Johnson, whose eyes were nearly bulging.

"What do you think?"

"He is passable as long as he is not seen too close for too long," Kozhevnikov said. He turned to Johnson. "How is your Russian?" he asked in Russian.

"I'm fluent in it," Johnson stammered.

"How so?" Kozhevnikov asked, his brows knitting.

"Though my father was Swedish," Johnson said, regaining some of his composure, "my mother was Russian. I learned it from her. And I learned it at school."

Kozhevnikov turned to Rafn. "He's passable. But he won't be able to speak. His voice isn't the same."

Rafn nodded, and Kozhevnikov turned back to Johnson.

"Listen closely, my man. If you make a mistake and are discovered, it will be very bad for all of us."

"I understand," Johnson said. "They—I was briefed earlier."

"All right. Switch clothes with me now and then return my car to the parking garage near the *Bahnhof*. Take a taxi to my hotel and enter it through the coffee shop. Go immediately to the dining room and have lunch. Stay for at least an hour."

"Yes?" Johnson prompted.

"Take a bus tour of the city after that. I'll give you the ticket. It ends at five o'clock. The bus will leave you off at the hotel. Go to your room, call room service, and have them bring you dinner. Tell them you're not feeling well, that you are going to stay in your room this evening and perhaps tomorrow. Tell them you're not to be disturbed. Bolotin, the chief of my bodyguard detail, will check the desk and find your message. He won't disturb you."

"What if he does? What if he wants to speak to me?" Johnson asked. He was clearly becoming more and more worried.

"If that happens, go right to bed. When you do not answer the door, Bolotin may enter. When he sees you asleep, he'll leave you alone."

"What about tomorrow?"

"Tomorrow I want you to sneak out of the hotel at three in the afternoon. Call ahead and have the desk rent you a car. Drive out here and park where I parked the Audi. If the van is here, we'll be ready to take you back. If it isn't, take a brief tour of the museum, then return to the hotel and stay in your room. The next day at the same time, come back here. By then, at the latest, the van will be here for you."

"And if the van is here, how will you get me out?"

"Don't worry. We'll get you away from here without any trouble."

Johnson started to say something, but thought better of it. He sighed deeply. "Wish me luck," he said, and he took off his robe to switch clothes.

CHAPTER 16

Sylvan Bindrich stood up and stretched. "Coffee, anyone?" he asked.

Kozhevnikov looked up at the man—his true adversary, the only major adversary in this room—and shook his head. "I don't like coffee. I'd prefer some cognac."

"I'll get it," Villmeier said, and he got up and left the study.

Bindrich took a cigarette from Gleason, who was seated at the long table across from Rafn and Douville. When he had it lit, he put one foot on the chair. "We were talking about Hanoi. And your office there."

Kozhevnikov nodded.

"Why did you dismantle your Hanoi operation and move it to Saigon?"

Kozhevnikov allowed himself a slight smile. "We felt that if there were going to be any further disinformation operations, they would be centered around Saigon. Your military had just departed, but we knew a number of your people were left. Mostly journalists."

Marty Romberg spoke. "It's my understanding that your office was set up in the old American embassy. Why?"

"No particular reason," Kozhevnikov shrugged. "Let's say the victors were claiming the spoils."

"When was that?" Bindrich asked.

"Thirty days after the last of your people were evacuated by helicopter from the embassy grounds."

"And now your people are moving out," Bindrich said.

Kozhevnikov nodded. "We're done there. The dismantling of my office was actually begun ninety days ago, with the first transfers."

"And you?"

"I was the last to go. Only a few technicians are left."

"Any operatives?" Bindrich asked, leaning forward.

Kozhevnikov shook his head. "Not from my department—at least not in Saigon. Most of our people are now in Bangkok and other places in Thailand."

"We'll want specific names, locations, and assignments," Bindrich said.

"Agreed," Kozhevnikov replied. At first he was concerned about the Americans. But now that concern had changed to wariness. These men were no different from anyone in the KGB. They were professionals. The country they worked for was the only difference. At least that was true for everyone but Rafn who had said nothing for the past three hours.

Villmeier returned with the cognac and handed it to Kozhevnikov who looked up and nodded his thanks.

On the drive here from Dachau, he and Rafn had not spoken more than a few words. And when they arrived at this house, isolated from its nearest neighbors by four and a half square decameters of dense woods, Rafn merely introduced Kozhevnikov to the others, and then sat at the long conference table in silence.

Villmeier also brought in a pot of coffee. When everyone had poured themselves a cup, Bindrich continued his questioning.

"You are being transferred to Moscow? To KGB headquarters itself?"

"Yes. To the First Chief Directorate. Department of Disinformation."

"We understand you are being promoted to chief of that department. Is that correct?" Romberg asked.

Kozhevnikov turned to him. "That is the rumor. However, nothing official has been said to me."

"Why the trip to Europe?" Bindrich asked.

"I requested the holiday. It was granted on the basis of my work in Vietnam."

"But it wasn't meant to be a holiday."

"No," Kozhevnikov said. "I engineered the trip to contact your people."

"Which you did," Bindrich said dryly.

It was coming now, Kozhevnikov could feel it. He nodded.

"Why?" Bindrich said softly. "Are you defecting?"

"Possibly," Kozhevnikov said.

Bindrich slammed his open palm on the table. "What the hell kind of answer is that? Are you defecting or are you playing games? What the hell do you want, Kozhevnikov?"

Kozhevnikov looked at the men seated around the table. To his left was Gleason who, like Rafn, had said little during the past three hours.

At the end of the table, flanking Bindrich, were two technicians. One of them was operating the tape recorder and the other was watching the meters of an electronic instrument that continually swept the room.

Seated next to Rafn was Douville, and standing at the window was Villmeier.

As Kozhevnikov understood it, the house belonged to Villmeier's mother-in-law, who had not been here in the last fifteen years. It was maintained weekly by a caretaker from nearby Seeshaupt. The old man came to clean and make repairs on weekends. He wasn't due for another three days.

At Kozhevnikov's words Rafn sat forward in his chair, his eyes bright. Of all the people in this room,

Rafn was the key. If Kozhevnikov could convince him, everyone else would fall into place.

Kozhevnikov stood up. "I want to take a walk."

Bindrich started to protest, but Rafn stood up and cut him off. "All right. Who do you want to come with you?"

Kozhevnikov studied his old friend's face for a moment. "You, Bindrich, and Gleason. No one else."

"All right," Rafn said and came around the table.

Bindrich hesitated a moment, then sighed deeply. "The rest of you take a break. Get something to eat." He got up, and along with Gleason, followed Rafn and Kozhevnikov out the door. In the living room they put on their coats, went through the house and tromped out the side door.

They followed the path to the lake and began to walk along it as Kozhevnikov tried to figure out the best way to tell them what had been eating away at him.

The sky was darkening already, and the wind had picked up. A new bank of clouds scudded in low from the northwest. It would probably rain again, but Kozhevnikov was not thinking about the weather.

"Is my life still yours?" he asked Rafn.

Rafn smiled. "That is the custom. But it seems as if you have done well without me."

They were walking slowly up the deserted beach, Rafn beside Kozhevnikov, and Bindrich and Gleason slightly to the left and behind them. In the distance, around the curve of the shore, they could see a resort hotel, but it looked closed and empty like most of the other places around the lake.

"I need your help now," Kozhevnikov said. "I need you to understand what I am going to say."

Rafn said nothing, and Kozhevnikov stopped to look out across the choppy lake. Then he began talking to the three men. "Three years ago I had to return to Moscow for a directorate committee meeting. I remained there for five days to do some work in my office. Mostly personnel lists and operational data. Things that were more easily done there than in Hanoi," he began.

"Since I was on a semipermanent assignment away from Moscow, my office was being used by another department—the T Directorate. It concerns itself with the espionage of scientific and technical data."

"Wasn't it unusual for another department to take over your office space?" Gleason asked.

Kozhevnikov glanced back at him and shook his head. "Not really. Space is at a premium even in our new headquarters. Our organization is actually quite a bit larger than yours, but we were not so lavish in the financing of a new building. Since my staff and I were gone for five years, it was not unusual for office space to be reassigned. At least temporarily."

Kozhevnikov again turned to stare across the lake. "While I was there I happened upon a file with a red flag, which meant it was of extreme importance. I did not look at the material it contained, but I remember the notation on the jacket was 'The Kummersdorf Papers.' When I asked about it, I was told to steer clear. That it was none of my business, that the need-to-know list included personnel only from the T Directorate."

"Was that unusual?" Bindrich asked.

"Not in itself," Kozhevnikov said without turning. "If such a sensitive file were not lying unguarded on a desk, I might not have begun to wonder. But something else struck me as odd. This was the jacket itself. In our directorate, we have file jackets that are coded to departments. Blue files for T Directorate, green files for Disinformation, yellow for Clandestine Operations, et cetera. Although this file was clearly marked a T Directorate operation, it was in a jacket that belonged to the division that handles Jewish Affairs."

Kozhevnikov turned to Rafn and looked deeply into

his eyes. "For three years I have been troubled by this, my old friend. It is what has driven me to contact you. What I am about to tell you is the truth. I am not working a disinformation plot on you, as Bindrich suspects. You must understand that."

"Go on," Rafn prompted gently after a long pause.

It was cold, and Kozhevnikov shivered. "That file bothered me, and when I returned to Hanoi, I began a quiet investigation of my own. Very low key, very careful so as not to create any suspicions. But an assistant director of a division does carry some weight, so I was able to carry out this little operation."

"And what did you find?" Rafn asked.

"Nine months ago I learned that one hundred thousand Jews, mostly women, have been quietly and carefully taken from cities like Moscow and Leningrad and transferred to someplace in Siberia. It has something to do with the Kummersdorf Papers file, but exactly what I don't know. I only know there is a connection."

"What is happening to those Jews?" Rafn asked softly.

"Supposedly they are being given farms. It's part of the Agrarian Reform Project to develop Siberia. But I have learned that in fact no such farms exist."

"What are you saying?" Bindrich broke in.

Kozhevnikov turned to him. "A hundred thousand Jews have been taken to Siberia. They have not been given farms. The file outlining all of this was in a Jewish Affairs folder but marked for the Scientific Espionage Directorate. Everyone is very quiet about this, which means it's a highly secret operation."

"A pogrom?" Gleason asked softly.

Kozhevnikov jerked around toward him. "I think so," he said.

CHAPTER 17

Bindrich looked at his watch. It was six in the morning, exactly eighteen hours since Kozhevnikov switched with his double in the parking lot. Marty Romberg and Nathaniel Gleason had provided instant confirmations of all the data Kozhevnikov was throwing at them. All, that is, but the data behind his reason for defecting.

One hundred thousand Jews, he had told them. Bindrich was becoming more and more certain that Kozhevnikov was indeed working a disinformation plot on them. The theory was simple, but he had to admire the man's execution of it.

First: Set up a possible defection to the West by a high-ranking Komitet man. Someone the Americans would like to have.

Second: Meet with the Americans and sell them a bill of goods so unbelievable it is fantastic. This second stage was bothersome. In order to pull it off, the Russians would have had to send an outstanding actor, a man who could be very convincing. Kozhevnikov was such a man. Outwardly very sincere. But inwardly?

Extra frosting on the second point was the introduction of Rafn to the scheme. Kozhevnikov had been selected for this operation not only because of his acting ability, but because of his connection with Rafn.

Evidently they knew exactly who and what Rafn was. It was a disturbing fact, but one they would have to live with. At least it proved that Rafn was not the hotshot operative everyone thought he was.

Third: Once the Americans had bought the bill of goods and acted upon it, the Russians would be able to prove that the Americans were accusing them of pure hogwash.

"A pogrom, Mr. President? Don't be silly. What is this—more of your human rights silliness?"

The headlines would be embarrassing. Exactly the kind of scheme Kozhevnikov was famous for.

Bindrich slumped back in his chair as he thought it out. Kozhevnikov and Rafn were talking quietly with Gleason. Douville and Villmeier had gone to bed, and Marty Romberg was listening again to the tapes that the recording technician had made.

There was one disturbing element in all of this. What was Kozhevnikov going to do once the Americans were convinced? Was he going to come to the U.S., assume his new identity, and eventually make his escape back to the Soviet Union? If that was their plan it was a very dangerous game for them. Surely they understood that once he was on American soil, his debriefing would be accomplished with drugs.

Maybe they had worked that out as well. Maybe Kozhevnikov truly believed what he was telling them. Maybe he was unwittingly involved in a disinformation plot against the U.S. Maybe they had planned it this way all along.

A plus point on the side of this theory, at least in Bindrich's mind, was the fact that Kozhevnikov had told them nothing they didn't already know. Except for the fact that Kozhevnikov knew about Rafn and Douville, he had told them nothing of real importance.

Bindrich sat forward. "Kozhevnikov. What do you want out of this?" he asked.

Kozhevnikov and Rafn both looked at him. "Two

things," Kozhevnikov said after a moment.

"First, I want a new identity in your country. Papers, a job, a little money, some plastic surgery perhaps. I want a new life."

"And secondly?" Bindrich prompted.

"Secondly, but more importantly, I want the assurance that something will be done to help the Jews. Perhaps some political pressure can be brought to bear on my government by yours. The Nazis were the scourge of the earth. I don't want my country to end up the same way, even if it means going outside for help."

Bindrich smiled. It fit. It all fit. But they were not going to fall for it. "You're lying," he said simply. "This is all bullshit, and you know it."

Kozhevnikov seemed unperturbed. "I thought you might have that attitude——" he began and Bindrich cut him off.

"It would have been a nice scheme, Kozhevnikov, but I've been around too long to tumble for it. It would have been a feather in your cap."

"Six months ago I knew I would be talking with you," Kozhevnikov said. "And I also knew you would doubt my sincerity. So I began looking around for some means of convincing you."

Bindrich was suddenly less sure of himself, but he said nothing. Kozhevnikov continued, slowly and deliberately.

"Several months ago I came across a man by the name of Jan DeHeus. He is stationed in Bangkok, Thailand, where he is working with some of the personnel from my office. DeHeus is supposedly the liaison man between us and the Thai supporters of North Vietnam." Kozhevnikov smiled.

"His cover was quite good, I'll grant you that. I never would have discovered him if I hadn't been specifically looking for someone to prove my point here." He turned to Rafn. "You remember DeHeus, don't you? He worked in the same underground unit that you did during the war. He was young then, but he was quite good I am told."

Rafn said nothing, nor did his facial expression reveal even a hint of what he was thinking, but Bindrich was holding his breath.

"DeHeus, of course, is in reality nothing more than a CIA deep-cover operative. As a matter of fact, Mr. Bindrich, he works directly for you. Much like my friend Svend Rafn here works directly for the director." Kozhevnikov fell silent momentarily, an amused expression on his face. "Shall I continue?"

"Yes," Bindrich managed to squeak.

"DeHeus is paid from your nonbudgeted fund. Line one-seventy-two. A very sophisticated setup." Kozhevnikov sat forward. "I didn't blow his cover. I wrote no memos, I told no one. If this works out here, DeHeus will continue his work, which is quite good."

Bindrich's lips were moving but no sound was coming out. Gleason and Romberg were staring at Kozhevnikov. Rafn was smiling.

"What I am saying to you, Bindrich, is that I am not working a plot on your organization. I am defecting. And now I have laid all my cards on the table, as you say. What will you do?"

Bindrich rose slowly, turned without a word, and stiffly went out the door. For forty years he had worked in the intelligence community. For a time he had even been an operative. But never had he received a shattering blow like this.

If they knew about Rafn and about DeHeus, two of the best deep-cover men in the CIA, wasn't it reasonable to assume that they also knew about everything else? About Cuba, about Los Angeles, about Hyannis Port, and all the rest?

Bindrich went to the telephone in the front hall, asked for the overseas operator, and gave her a number in Washington, D.C.

One thing was certain, Bindrich told himself. They

were not going to let Kozhevnikov slip by them. Like the man said, this was just too damned important, Jews or no Jews.

After a few minutes the connection was made and on the fourth ring the telephone was answered.

"Yes?" It was the director. He sounded sleepy.

"Bindrich."

"What have you got?" the director asked, the sleepiness instantly leaving his voice.

"This is for real," Bindrich said guardedly. Although it was highly unlikely the phone lines were being monitored, he was careful with what he was saying out of long habit.

"Can you talk?"

"No, sir, but this is some pretty heady stuff. I'll get a telex off to you later this morning. But for now I think we should have a green light."

"The president said——" the director began, but Bindrich interrupted.

"Listen to me, sir, he knows about line one-seventy-two as well as lines sixteen and four-fifty-eight. Do you understand what I am saying?"

There was a long pause on the line, and when the director came back he spoke with less authority, a hesitant, uncertain note in his voice. "Nonbudget lines?"

"Yes, sir," Bindrich said, suddenly tired.

There was another long hesitation, and Bindrich was about to speak when the director was back.

"I think we should discuss this with the president."

"There is no time."

"What do you suggest?"

What did he suggest? What was the answer? Yesterday he had been sure he had the answers to everything, that this was going to be a fairly easy, albeit important, operation. But now?

"He's telling us something that could be potentially embarrassing to us if we acted on it without confirmation, but disastrous if we don't. It all depends upon the proof."

"And he's not providing it?"

"No, sir," Bindrich said, glad at least that the director was picking up smoothly on what he was saying.

"So what are you telling me?"

"Let's send him back to gather data. He made it out once, he'll have to make it out again."

The director hesitated again. "What do you think the chances of success will be?"

"We'll keep surveillance on him as best we can. But I'd still say less than fifty-fifty."

"That's not very good, is it?"

"No, sir, but as it stands he's no good to us now."

"And there is no time to think this out?"

"No, sir," Bindrich said.

The director hesitated again. "What do you recommend?"

"I'm not going to recommend anything this time, sir. The decision is yours." Bindrich had already stuck his neck out far enough, and he would be damned if he was going out on the limb any further. Let the director earn his salary.

"Then go ahead," the man said with surprising firmness in his voice. "I'll explain the situation to the president. He'll understand. Meanwhile, when will you be returning?"

"Tomorrow, if all goes well here."

"Be careful, Bindrich. Be very careful. It will be disastrous if something goes wrong and we end up with egg on our faces."

"I understand, sir. Good night," Bindrich said, and he hung up the phone and returned to the study.

No one had moved from the time he had left until now. It was as if an artist had painted the tableau.

He sat down heavily in his chair, poured a stiff shot of cognac into his coffee cup, and drank it straight down. The liquor burned in his throat. Within a half hour his ulcer would flare up, but it didn't matter at this point.

The others in the room looked at him, waiting for him to speak.

"You're going to be returning home," he said finally to Kozhevnikov.

Kozhevnikov looked stunned. Gleason and Romberg sat forward in their seats, but the expression on Rafn's face did not change.

"What are you saying?" Kozhevnikov asked after a tense moment. "I'm going home?"

"We need more information. If we are going to act on what you told us, we'll need proof."

"Impossible."

"Then there is no way for us to make a deal. We'll take you back to Munich and drop you off wherever you want after we pick up our double."

"You bastard," Kozhevnikov said, rising from his seat.

Bindrich slammed his fist on the table. "Don't bastard me, you fucking parrot. You came to us, remember? You wanted to play the game; you play it our way now. Otherwise you can go back to your cozy little office and rot in fucking hell."

Kozhevnikov leaned toward Bindrich, both hands on the table. "I'll blow your entire organization wide open. There won't be a hole deep enough for you to hide in."

Bindrich smiled, then nodded at the tape recorder. "Wouldn't it be disastrous for your career if those tapes fell into the wrong hands?"

Kozhevnikov glanced toward the machine. The anger seemed to melt off his face. "I can't return," he said softly.

"You'll have to. We'll put a contact in Moscow for you. If you get in over your head, he can get you out."

"It's not that," Kozhevnikov said, sitting down. "It's my wife. She suspects."

Bindrich's eyes narrowed. "What?"

"She knows nothing about what I have told you, but she suspects me. She knows something is going on. And she is a loyal party member."

The expression on Bindrich's face turned to disgust, and once again Kozhevnikov's voice rose up in anger.

"Don't give me that look, Bindrich. Being a party member in the Soviet Union is no different than being a Democrat or Republican in your country. You have two parties, we have one."

"There's no way around it. You bring us proof."

"I cannot."

"Look, Kozhevnikov," Bindrich said, "you can't expect my government to approach your government with something like this, purely on speculation. Christ, even you admit you're not sure of your facts. If I had defected and you were sitting on this side of the table, would you expect your people to act?"

Kozhevnikov looked deeply into Bindrich's eyes, then turned toward Rafn, who had sat impassively through all of this. "What do you say, Svend? Do you believe me?"

Rafn nodded his head slightly. "Yes, I do, but for once Bindrich is correct. We need more information, Viktor. We can't act without it."

Kozhevnikov turned again toward Bindrich, but his eyes were not focusing on anyone. "My God," he said, the words coming out of him softly.

Bindrich started to sneer, but Rafn glared at him.

"I'll return," Kozhevnikov said in a barely audible voice.

Bindrich could feel a great pressure lifting. "We know it won't be easy, but——" he began, but Kozhevnikov waved him off.

"Don't give me that, Bindrich. If I'm going to return, I'll go of my own free will, not because of those tapes. I'll go because I believe a hundred thousand Jews are on their way to their deaths. I want it stopped. The fact that it's happening in my country makes me a traitor. Do you understand? A traitor."

Kozhevnikov again turned to Rafn. "Listen to me, Svend," he said, his control returning. "Don't let them compromise me. I'm sure that my inquiries about the Kummersdorf Papers and the Siberian operation have been noted. And because I have frequently evaded my bodyguards, I will be under some suspicion for a time. Any sudden inquiries from this side would be bad for me. Do you understand what I'm saying?"

"Yes, I do, Viktor."

Kozhevnikov turned to Bindrich. "I don't know how long this will take, but under no circumstances do I want you to contact me."

"Agreed. But what about DeHeus?"

Kozhevnikov smiled bitterly. "He's of little consequence. But don't worry, I won't blow his cover. I'm the traitor, remember?"

CHAPTER 18

Villmeier returned to Dachau with Kozhevnikov to effect the switch with the double. The plan was for Kozhevnikov to wait in the Volkswagen van until the double showed up and went through the museum. On the way out, Villmeier would create a disturbance that would delay his guards. The double would walk to the van, where he would quickly switch clothes with Kozhevnikov, who would get in the rented car and wait for the bodyguards to catch up.

Villmeier figured he would be able to delay the guards less than a minute. It would be close, but it could be done.

At the safe house, it was nearly three o'clock in the afternoon. Gleason was on the telephone to his office, and Bindrich, Martin Romberg, and Rafn were in the study.

"Kozhevnikov mentioned that Kummersdorf may be connected with the Nazis," Romberg was saying.

"In what way?" Rafn asked. He was tired of this entire operation now. It was completely out of his hands, and he wanted to start on his own vacation.

"Station Kummersdorf West was the German's original rocket research station in the thirties. In 1936 it was moved to Peenemünde on the north coast. It was there that Von Braun developed the buzz bombs and V-2 rockets."

Rafn shook his head. "What does that have to do with the hundred thousand Jews being sent to Siberia?"

"Maybe nothing," Bindrich interjected, "but we're going to check it out."

Rafn turned to him. "Kozhevnikov will be in a touchy position."

"It doesn't matter. I'm returning to Langley with Romberg to dig up whatever we can. We'll send the information to you by diplomatic pouch. You'll have to drive up to Bonn to pick it up in the next day or so."

"What are you getting at, Bindrich?"

"While Kozhevnikov is in Moscow, we're going to dig up what we can find here in Germany. Kummersdorf West and Peenemünde are both in the East Zone, so you'll have to use your contacts there. But there still may be answers here."

"What the hell are you talking about?" Rafn exploded. "Didn't you hear what he told us? His life is on the line."

Bindrich glared coldly at Rafn. "You are working for us, Rafn, not Kozhevnikov."

"I won't have anything to do with this. I'm working for the director, not you."

"The director expected you might say that. If you would like to talk to him, feel free to do so. I am merely relaying his orders."

"And if I don't go along with this insanity?"

"Your employment with us will be terminated," Bindrich said. Rafn started to rise, but Bindrich waved him down. "Consider one other thing, Rafn," he said. "If you're not going to work this operation, we'll have to get someone else. Maybe someone less adept. Maybe someone who will knock over the milk can for Kozhevnikov."

It was Rafn's turn to glare at Bindrich. "You sonofabitch," he said.

"Then you'll take the assignment?" Bindrich asked lightly.

Rafn nodded. He was being forced into the dirty business. It was his own fault, he told himself. He should have expected something like this. But there would come a time when he would get his chance at Bindrich, and when it happened it would be sweet.

Gleason came back into the room, a perplexed look on his face. "I've got to fly up to Berlin," he said to Bindrich.

"What's up?"

"Sigmund Schiller, an Israeli operative we've done business with before, is in town and wants to talk with me. He used the seven-one-seven code."

"Goddamn it," Bindrich said angrily. "The code book is more public than the Manhattan telephone directory."

Gleason shrugged.

"Do you want me to come along?"

"I don't think it's necessary. I'll fly up there and find out what's bothering him, and then return home."

"Don't make it too long," Bindrich said. "We're going to need you in on this operation. We'll have to crank up a network in Moscow to watch Kozhevnikov and get ready to grab him if he needs us."

PART TWO

CHAPTER 1

The *National Weekly* newspaper parking lot was nearly full when Laurie Andrews pulled into her stall and got out of her red Corvette convertible. Phil would be mad at her for coming in late, but it didn't really matter. He would fuss and fume for a few minutes and then forget all about it.

Besides, she told herself as she entered the modernistic building in the heart of downtown New Orleans, after this weekend, a little of Phil's bitching would be a welcome relief. At least he was one man who was sure of himself.

Upstairs, she entered the noisy newsroom, and by the time she arrived at her desk near the front, a half-dozen people told her the old man wanted her in his office.

She laid her purse down, checked for messages, and then slowly walked over to the managing editor's office.

Phil Shapiro was on the telephone when she walked in, and he waved her to a seat. Stanley Karsten, the librarian, was also seated in the office, a stack of files on his lap. When Laurie sat down across from him, he nodded.

"Goddamn it, Melissa, if you can't handle it, we'll get someone who can," Shapiro was shouting into the phone. He listened a moment and then, somewhat calmer, nodded his head. "That's better, sweetheart. I'll expect to hear from you this afternoon. Bye."

He hung up the telephone and looked across his cluttered desk at Laurie. "Where the hell were you all weekend—shacking up with some stud?" he growled.

"Don't knock it if you haven't tried it," she said sweetly.

"Goddamn it, I tried to get you all weekend. Where the hell were you?"

"On the ocean—out of sight and out of hearing."

"Leave a number after this."

Laurie shook her head. "My weekends are my own, remember?" she asked. Shapiro was about to shout at her, but she cut him off. "I'm here now. What's the flap?"

He looked at her for a moment, then sighed and sat back in his chair. "What do you know about the Nobel Prize?" he asked.

The question caught Laurie completely off guard. "I don't know," she said, trying to decide exactly what he wanted. Shapiro was famous for putting his reporters on the spot. He would spring a question on them, check for their reaction, and then assign a story based on how the reporter fared.

"Not a hell of a lot. Alfred Nobel, a Swede, invented dynamite. When he died he left his estate to be given as prizes for literature, science, medicine."

"Not quite correct, but close," said Karsten, a bald, older man, looking up from his files. "Alfred Bernhard Nobel set up a perpetual endowment fund for the prizes. Each year's dividends are divided among the winners. A board of directors manages the fund, while separate boards for each prize work year-round deciding who should be honored."

"There are five prizes," Shapiro said, picking up from where Karsten left off. "Peace, chemistry, physics, physiology and medicine, and literature."

"And sometimes more than five people share those prizes," Laurie added.

"Entirely correct," Karsten said, as he withdrew a large sheet of paper from a file and handed it to her. "Here is a list of all the Nobel Prize winners to date, including the 1976 winners. The 1977 selections are coming in now."

Laurie looked at the list, then looked up at Shapiro. "What's the assignment?"

Shapiro smiled, got up from his chair, and began pacing the room, something he always did whenever he was thinking out an assignment that he particularly liked.

"A few years back Irving Wallace did a novel about the Nobel Prize winners. He showed them as real people. People who did something interesting enough to attract the attention of the Nobel Prize Committee."

"I read it," Laurie said.

"Don't interrupt," Shapiro snapped, and he continued his pacing. "There was a minor character in that novel, a gal, I forget her name. At any rate, she was a newspaper woman doing stories on each of the candidates. But I mean real stories. Stories about their little foibles, their troubles, the skeletons in their closets."

"She wasn't very well liked, as I remember," Laurie said dryly.

Shapiro turned on her. "That was fiction, sweetheart. This is the real thing."

"What the hell am I supposed to become," Laurie said, sitting forward, "a lady mudslinger? Bullshit!"

"Listen to me, darling," Shapiro said, coming around his desk to her. "This is a natural. I don't want anything like that broad in the novel. I want the real thing. These people who win the prize, they're looked upon damn near as gods. They all live on Mount Olympus, and once a year a few of them are brought down out of their ivory towers for the world to get a look at them. But no one really sees them. Not really."

Laurie looked up at him skeptically but said nothing.

"I want you to take a good hard look at this year's winners and do a series of pieces on them. I want to know about the work that led to their receiving the prize. I want to know about them as human beings. I want to know about their background, about their future, now that they've won the prize. I want to know everything about them. I want the stories to come across so that both the little old lady in Duluth and the college prof in Boston can understand what makes these people tick, and what it takes to win a Nobel Prize."

"And I'm supposed to earn these winners' confidence and write the pieces. Christ, what the hell were you doing this weekend?"

Shapiro went back around his desk, sat down, and lit a cigar. "I've had my fill of crap this morning. Melissa just called me from New York and told me she's not going to be turning in anything on Jackie this week. She says the lady is tired of reporters bugging her. I told Melissa that if she wished to continue her employment with us, at fifty big ones a year plus expenses, she would damn well send us the best goddamned story that had ever been done."

"You're telling me the same thing, right?" Laurie said, wondering if her weekend had really been all that bad. The scuba diving off Grand Isle in the Gulf was fun, but the man she was with was like all the others she had ever known. He talked a good line, but once he came under fire he folded up. After watching him in action underwater, she could not be overly enthused about his bedroom prowess.

"That's the bottom line, sweetheart," Shapiro was saying. "We let you screw around in the Canary Islands after those 747s crashed, and you came up with a good story. Since then, you haven't done shit. It's time for you to earn your pay again."

Laurie sighed. There was no way she was going to give up forty thousand a year. But one thing was certain. After this assignment was over, she was going to complain to Shapiro about Melissa's earning fifty thousand. That was going to change.

"How much time do I have?" she said with a straight face.

Shapiro lit up. "That's my girl," he said, and he turned to Karsten. "We've got about six weeks, right?"

Karsten nodded ponderously. "Correct, Mr. Shapiro. The recipients will be in Stockholm to receive their prizes exactly six weeks from today."

"How about expenses?" she asked. During her three months in the Canary Islands, she had lived like a miser. This time it would be different, and she was going to fight for it.

"Unlimited," he said expansively, and Laurie sucked in her breath. "I don't give a damn where you go, what you have to do, or who you have to pay, but I want the stories. One on each winner. And I want them good. Solid. Hard-hitting. Meaty pieces. Real circulation builders."

"How about the award presentations?" Laurie asked.

"You'll be there, sweetheart. And I'll even spring for a formal gown."

Laurie relaxed. This was turning out to be better than anything she had ever worked on. In fact, she told herself, it could be fun. "Where do I start?" she asked.

Karsten handed her a copy of a telegram. "The first prize was just announced this morning. This is a copy of the telegram sent to Dr. Hans Meitner, in Wisconsin. We got it from our people in New York."

Shapiro was on his feet again, puffing furiously on his cigar. "Meitner won this year's prize in physiology and medicine for his work with genes."

Laurie focused on the telegram: ". . . FOR YOUR WORK IN GENETIC ENGINEERING WHICH HAS LED TO

THE DEEPER UNDERSTANDING OF LIFE ITSELF AND THE HUMAN CONDITION . . ."

She looked up again and Shapiro was excited. "Meitner is the first to be formally announced. And you'll be starting out with a good one."

"What do you mean, a good one?" Laurie asked.

Shapiro nodded toward Karsten. "Stan has already dug up some material on him. Listen to this. Meitner is the classic recluse scientist. He's working now at the University of Wisconsin in Madison. He's a bachelor. Always has been. No one up there knows him. There's never been anything done on him, other than a short piece about his work now and then. And no one seems to know anything else about him, except that he came to the States from Germany after the war."

"He is a little odd," Karsten said, handing her a thin file.

"And coming from Stanley, that's a hell of a pronouncement," Shapiro said happily. "Who knows, maybe this Meitner is a faggot. That'd make a hell of a story. Faggot Flees Fatherland."

Laurie groaned. "I'll get started right away," she said, standing.

"Give it a week," Shapiro said more seriously. "If you take that long for each candidate, you'll have plenty of time to get ready for Stockholm."

"How about the others?"

"Check back with Stanley in the next day or two. The other candidates should be formally announced by then. We'll ship you the files."

"All right," Laurie said, and she turned and went out the door.

"Christ," Shapiro said after her, "wouldn't it be great if he were a faggot?"

CHAPTER 2

It was a few minutes after nine o'clock in the morning when Hans Meitner, an older, stoop-shouldered man with a mass of white hair reminiscent of Einstein, mounted the steps of the Genetic Research building and entered the swinging glass doors. Two hours ago, deep in thought, he had left his home on the west side of Madison and walked the six miles to his laboratory.

The first step was now completed, he told himself for the thousandth time. One individual DNA molecule that made up a single gene in a human cell had been isolated and decoded. By itself, it was a monumental achievement. But there was more, so much more to be done.

In each human cell there were as many as a hundred thousand individual genes, each with its own coded DNA, each with its own set of instructions for the manufacture of some aspect of a human being.

The gene Meitner had isolated four months ago was one that ordered its group of cells to manufacture the protein that made up hair, specifically blond hair.

The next step would be to change the coding so that the altered gene would produce brown hair.

Meitner shuffled past the elevator and headed up the stairs to his third-floor office and laboratory, unaware of the people staring at him in the narrow lobby.

With the ability to locate a specific gene and change its code, only one step would remain, that of cataloging every gene within a cell.

At the Lawrence Livermore Laboratories in California six months before, Meitner had seen a machine called CYDAC, which used a microscope to scan chromosomes, each of which was made up of hundreds of genes. A computer hooked up to the microscope was able to sort the chromosomes at the rate of a hundred thousand a minute. Somehow a similar system, by which each gene type could be identified and separated, would have to be worked out.

Suddenly he stopped on the stairs between the second and third floors. He could visualize a machine adapted to this purpose. The first DNA molecule was a crystalline structure which showed up under X-ray bombardment. Perhaps the physicists would have the answer for his problem. Perhaps the bombardment of the cell by the smallest and quickest of particles in a particle accelerator would display the individual DNA molecules. Each separate gene could then be tagged with a specific type of radioactivity that was so short-lived it would cause no biological damage to the DNA. The computer, working faster than any human could imagine, would sort the individual genes.

Sort the individual genes. That was the key. It had to be.

Meitner rushed up the stairs two at a time and burst into the third-floor corridor. Several people stood in the doorway to his laboratory, but he was not really conscious of them as he pushed past.

A young woman, one of his graduate assistants, spun him around and kissed him on the cheek.

"Dr. Meitner, you've done it. You've done it. You've won. Oh . . . it's so wonderful, you've won."

For a long moment he stared at the girl. "Kathy . . ." he started to say, but then someone else took his hand and pumped it vigorously. He looked up into the eyes of Robert Stewart, the dean of the College of Letters and Sciences.

"Congratulations, Hans, we all knew it was going to happen," the man said, smiling.

"I don't understand," Meitner mumbled. At once he became aware of thirty-odd people crammed into the lab. Some of them were drinking champagne, others were smoking, flicking the ashes on the spotlessly clean floor. All of them had been talking at once, but now their smiling faces turned his way.

His mind raced, trying to figure out what they were celebrating. Was it a holiday? Or someone's birthday? Dr. Stewart offered his congratulations.

"He doesn't know yet," someone shouted, and Dr. Stewart leaned closer to him.

"Haven't you heard the news yet, Hans?"

"What news?" Meitner asked, shaking his head. "I've just arrived."

"This," Stewart said, withdrawing a telegram from his pocket and holding it out. "It came for you this morning."

Meitner took the telegram and fumbled in his coat pocket for his glasses. When he had them on he looked around at the others in the room. They were waiting expectantly for him to read the message. He looked down, and as he read, his hands began to shake.

THE SWEDISH FOREIGN OFFICE ON BEHALF OF THE NOBEL FOUNDATION OF STOCKHOLM IS PLEASED TO INFORM YOU THAT YOU HAVE BEEN SELECTED AS THE 1977 RECIPIENT OF THE NOBEL PRIZE FOR PHYSIOLOGY AND MEDICINE STOP THE SELECTION WAS MADE FOR YOUR WORK IN GENETIC ENGINEERING WHICH HAS LED TO THE DEEPER UNDERSTANDING OF LIFE ITSELF AND THE HUMAN CONDITION STOP MORE SPECIFICALLY RECOGNITION IS GIVEN TO YOUR SIGNIFICANT WORK IN THE ISOLATION AND IDENTIFICATION OF A HUMAN GENE STOP

THE AWARD CEREMONY WILL TAKE PLACE IN
STOCKHOLM DECEMBER NINTH STOP DETAILS TO
FOLLOW STOP
OUR SINCEREST CONGRATULATIONS STOP

He looked up. Someone offered him a glass of
champagne, but he waved it aside and turned to Dr.
Stewart.

"I want to offer you my congratulations again,
Hans," Stewart said.

Meitner numbly shook his head. "I can't accept this,"
he mumbled, and Stewart laughed.

"Don't be modest, Hans. Of course you can accept
this. It's rightfully yours. You have won the Nobel
Prize. The highest accolade man can bestow on his
fellow man."

Meitner's eyes narrowed. There was no way he
could accept this prize. It was not possible.

With acceptance of the prize would come publicity.
With publicity would come recognition. And with that
sooner or later someone would step up and shout, "I
know you, Dr. Hans Meitner. I know you well. And
I will expose you."

It could not be allowed to happen. He was so close
to the solution. So close. There was no time for this
foolishness. There was precious little time.

This morning, like every morning for the past month
and a half, Meitner had been spitting blood. And
deep within his chest he could feel a dull rattle. He
had not seen a doctor, because he knew he would be
ordered to stop work.

He had no intention of stopping work—not for the
malignant growth he was certain existed in his lungs,
and certainly not for the silliness of some prize.

It had taken him thirty-five years to get to this
point, to the point where he could see some progress,
where he was no longer wandering through the middle of a gigantic, puzzling universe. He would not be
cheated of his victory. He could not be.

The telegram slipped from his hands and fluttered to the floor as tears began to well up in his eyes.

His carefully constructed world was crumbling down around his head. If it continued he would never finish his work. He would not be allowed to.

He turned and shuffled out of the lab, unaware that everyone was watching him silently with a mixture of pride, awe, and pity in their expressions.

As he made his way slowly down the stairs and then back outside, headed for home, he let his mind wander back, farther back in his memory than he had ever let himself go since he had come to America. And he was a little boy again on the Rhine. A little boy and happy.

CHAPTER 3

Gleason parked the rented Opel Rekord in the driveway and made his way up the stairs and into the house. Another storm front had settled in over Southern Germany directly on the heels of the previous one that had dumped two and a half inches of rain on them. These clouds threatened to bring more of the same cold, blustery, rainy weather.

Rafn was seated by the fireplace. A number of books were spread out around him, and an overflowing ashtray was at his side. When Gleason entered the room he looked up and took off his glasses.

"I didn't expect you back," he said.

Gleason studied his face for a moment, wondering how he was going to take this. "I have to talk to you. Something has come up."

"Yes?" Rafn asked, laying a book aside and giving Gleason his full attention.

Gleason came across the room and perched on the edge of the sofa. "I've been in Berlin with Sigmund Schiller."

"And?" Rafn asked.

Gleason nodded. "His assignment may tie in with ours."

Rafn stubbed out his cigarette and sat forward, interest on his face. "Have you spoken with Bindrich yet?"

Gleason's eyes narrowed at the unexpected question. "No, but . . ."

"Perhaps we should not be having this discussion, then. Perhaps you should give him a call."

"No," Gleason snapped impatiently.

Rafn seemed amused. "Am I in the midst of a power struggle?"

The comment released the tension that had suddenly gripped Gleason and he laughed. "Not unless you intend to create one yourself."

"I don't like this operation," Rafn said flatly. "I didn't from the beginning, and I am liking it less the further I get into it. Now, unfortunately, you are going to add another variable. Sigmund Schiller."

"Perhaps fortunately," Gleason said, once again his patience strained.

Rafn sighed. "Continue."

Gleason stared at him. Perhaps Bindrich was correct. Rafn was an obnoxious sonofabitch. But he was the best. "Sigmund Schiller is tracking down a Nazi war criminal by the name of Gustav Predel. Doctor Predel. Does that name mean anything to you?"

Rafn thought a moment, then shook his head. "No. What were his crimes?"

"He was a medical doctor stationed at the German Federal Hospital in Berlin before the war. He headed a medical experimentation team for the Third Reich."

"A lot of that went on during the war," Rafn said disinterestedly. "What does that have to do with us?"

"Perhaps a lot," Gleason said, warming to his subject. "Predel was reassigned from the hospital in 1940 to work on some project directly under Goebbels's Propaganda Ministry."

"Not unusual."

"Granted. But whatever project Predel was working on was so supersecret that no written orders were ever issued. Everything was done by word of mouth, evidently directly through the chain of command from Hitler to Goebbels to Predel. No in-betweens."

"I still don't see . . ." Rafn began, but Gleason continued.

"Hear me out. Schiller managed to dig up a record on Predel from the hospital's archives. And in this record was a single word notation, Tiefensee, which is the name of a small town just northeast of East Berlin."

"No doubt Dr. Predel experimented with Jewish women," Rafn said offhandedly.

Gleason nodded.

"The Siberian operation Kozhevnikov speaks of involves Jewish women."

Again Gleason nodded.

"And the Kummersdorf Papers that Kozhevnikov spoke of may have some relation to the Nazi research station, Kummersdorf West, which was located somewhere near Berlin. Also correct? Am I following your line of reasoning so far?"

Gleason started to nod his head vigorously, but then he realized Rafn's voice contained a tinge of sarcasm.

"Really, Gleason, that is stretching things a bit even for you, isn't it?"

"Why not the connection?" Gleason snapped, indignant now.

"Number one: The Kummersdorf Romberg mentioned was a research station headed by Von Braun and a bunch of other engineers who played with rockets. What does that have to do with Jewish women?"

"I agree that the connection is tenuous. And at this moment I don't know the answer to that question. That is your job."

"Number two," Rafn continued relentlessly. "You tell me that this Dr. Predel was reassigned to Tiefensee—which I take to mean you are assuming is the site of the Kummersdorf rocket station—in 1940. Yet the station, according to Romberg, was moved to Peenemünde on the north coast in the mid-thirties."

"I hadn't thought of that," Gleason said, deflated. "But can it be a coincidence? The name Kummersdorf, I mean."

"Probably," Rafn said. "Kummersdorf means sorrowful village in English. It could be the name of a dozen places."

"But this wasn't the name of a place, as such," Gleason persisted. "It was the name invented for a research station."

Rafn chuckled. "The Germans have always been that way. Sorrowful village has a nice sound."

"For a rocket research station?"

Rafn shrugged. "What's your point?"

"Predel was assigned to a research project near Berlin. The Kummersdorf that Kozhevnikov speaks of may have been a research station near Berlin. Predel experimented with Jewish women. A hundred thousand Jews, mostly women, have been transferred to Siberia. Predel's project was so supersecret there were never any written orders. Kozhevnikov's project is so supersecret that only a few select people within the KGB know anything about it. Predel's work was scientific. That is, Predel was more than a medical doctor, he was a scientist. The file containing the Kummersdorf Papers was in a KGB Jewish Affairs folder, but it was marked for the Scientific Espionage Directorate. Coincidence? Perhaps. But I believe there are enough similarities for us to follow up with Schiller."

"You want me to work with Schiller?" Rafn said tiredly.

Gleason nodded. "Yes. I think you should follow it up."

"I don't."

The directness of the statement stopped Gleason momentarily.

While he recovered, Rafn lit a cigarette and said,

"Then I'll work alone on it. Alone and very fast. Once the KGB finds out inquiries are being made, Kozhevnikov is finished."

"Goddamn it, man, are you so sure of yourself?" Gleason said, jumping up. He was frustrated and mad now.

Rafn stared up at him impassively. "More sure than I am of you and your bunch."

"What the hell do you want? Why don't you go over and work for the opposition? Maybe Bindrich is right, maybe you're nothing more than a self-serving, conceited old man. A pure sonofabitch."

Rafn was grinning. "He's right, you know. I am nothing more than a self-serving, conceited old man. I do things my way."

Nothing was working. Rafn was right, this operation had started badly and was getting worse by the minute. And right now Gleason felt like an amateur trying to play games with a pro. He was sorry he had ever been pulled into this mess. Maybe Bindrich knew the secret buttons to push to get Rafn to work, but he certainly didn't.

"All I am asking, Rafn," Gleason said after he took a deep breath and forced himself to calm down, "is that you go up to Berlin and talk with Schiller. I am convinced there may be a connection between Predel and the Kummersdorf Project in Siberia."

Rafn started to speak, but Gleason held him off.

"Let me finish. Let's leave Schiller out of this for a moment. If you're going to poke around for information on Kummersdorf, you'll have to use your East German network. Correct?"

Rafn nodded, but said nothing.

"Every time you use a network in an enemy country, you risk being discovered. Granted?"

Again Rafn nodded.

"If you are discovered and they dig up what you are working on, it will blow the whistle on Kozhevnikov. Also correct?"

"Correct," Rafn said. "Which is why I am against making any inquiries from this end. At least until we get Kozhevnikov out."

"That's neither here nor there. You are going to make the inquiries. Unless you turn tail and run out on this."

For the first time Gleason was having an effect on Rafn, who seemed a little uncomfortable.

"I told Bindrich I would do what I could, but that does not include babysitting an Israeli fanatic," Rafn snapped.

Gleason ignored the comment. "Now suppose, just suppose, you do work with Schiller. His search for Predel will lead you into the East Zone. At least as far as Tiefensee. The Soviets hate Nazi war criminals more than we do. So if you are discovered. . . ."

"Schiller and his search will be a decoy," Rafn said, finishing the statement for him.

"Exactly," Gleason said. He could see a crack in Rafn's armor. "Use Schiller's search for Predel as a cover operation. We don't give a damn about Predel. He could not have been that important, otherwise we would have heard of him."

Rafn smiled. "Now you are thinking like a true intelligence officer—using people to your best advantage."

"It stinks."

"The whole business stinks, Gleason. I suggest you get out before it ruins you."

The statement stopped Gleason momentarily. Rafn was right. If he got out, it would make Pat and Kevin happy at least. But not until this was finished.

"You'll do it?"

"Yes," Rafn laughed. "You've convinced me. I'll use Schiller until he drops; then I'll dump him."

"You bastard," Gleason said.

The rain had begun, but the tall, solidly built young man with short-cropped hair, square features, and steel-blue eyes did not seem to notice it as he left his apartment and headed down the street toward the post office.

Unaware of the shopkeepers who stared out their windows at him, he walked ramrod straight with a military bearing.

At the post office, he sent his routine message: "AUNTY IS WELL. NO CHANGES. NEPHEW." Then he paid for it and left.

The clerk wondered why this man sent messages to East Berlin daily. On many mornings he wondered about the address and the significance of the messages, but as usual did nothing. Better to leave things like this alone.

CHAPTER 4

The light from the heavily overcast sky shone flatly on the highly polished wood floor in the large room. Kozhevnikov stood at rigid attention with his wife, his immediate superior, Sergei Borisovich Antipov, and the chairman of the KGB while the premier spoke. No one else was in the room.

"Yours, my dear Comrade Kozhevnikov, will be an unsung welcome. Unlike Gagarin, your name will not be known, you must realize."

Kozhevnikov said nothing. He was thinking of Rafn and how like Nadya he was.

The premier, a bull-like man with thick, black hair, stood up and came from behind his desk, carrying a leather-covered box. A gold star was stamped on the cover.

"You have done good work for us, Viktor Vasilievich," he said, stopping directly in front of Kozhevnikov. His eyes penetrated him. Panicked, Kozhevnikov wondered if he could see inside his soul. But it was impossible for any man to do that, he told himself. Not even the premier of the Union of Soviet Socialist Republics had that ability.

Party lines, party lines, how suddenly sick of party lines he had become.

The premier opened the box and from its velvet recess withdrew a heavy medal attached to a thick red ribbon. It was the Order of Lenin, the highest medal of honor in the Soviet Union.

The premier handed the box to Nadya and leaned forward to slip the medal over Kozhevnikov's head. His fingers were thick and pudgy, and for a moment he had difficulty unfolding the ribbon; but then it was done. The bright red contrasted sharply with Kozhevnikov's black suit. The premier grabbed Kozhevnikov by the shoulders, pulled him forward, and kissed him firmly on the lips. When he stepped back he was smiling.

"Your people owe you a great debt of gratitude, Viktor Vasilievich. You will be remembered by us as a true hero."

"Thank you, Comrade Premier." Kozhevnikov said the required words thickly.

The premier nodded and turned to the KGB chief. The smile left his face. "Stay," he said. Then he turned and went back to his desk.

Kozhevnikov, Antipov, and Nadya turned stiffly and went out of the room through the tall, double oak doors which led to an outer office. No one was there except the premier's personal secretary, a middle-aged man who did not look up as they passed into the corridor.

Antipov, thin and ferretlike, turned and stiffly drew Kozhevnikov to him, kissing him on the lips. When he stepped back he managed a slight smile.

"May I also offer my congratulations on a job well done, Comrade Kozhevnikov."

"Thank you, Sergei Borisovich," Kozhevnikov said formally.

Antipov turned toward Nadya and smiled warmly. "I must apologize, my dear, but I have a car waiting to take you home. We must talk business with your husband. I will make sure he returns early. I promise."

"Thank you," Nadya said, and turning to her husband, brushed his cheek with a kiss and hurried down the corridor.

When she was gone, Antipov turned to Kozhevnikov, the expression on his face now cold and impersonal.

"There are men of former high station in Lubyanka Prison who also wear the Order of Lenin," Antipov said sharply. "Do not take this as a sign of weakness on our part. It would be a dangerous assumption."

Kozhevnikov said nothing. His heart was pounding and a warm flush was creeping up his neck.

Antipov studied his face for a moment. "Come," he snapped, and he turned and headed briskly down the corridor opposite from the way Nadya had gone.

They took the elevator from the third floor down to the basement garage where a black Zotz sedan was waiting for them. Kozhevnikov and Antipov got into the back seat, and without a word the driver took them out of the building and through the gates of the Kremlin Palace. They quickly sped away toward KGB headquarters, located just off the peripheral highway circling Moscow.

It was cold in the unheated car, and it had begun to snow in the deepening gloom of afternoon. At one time Kozhevnikov had been excited by this city. Things were happening here. The people were bright and alive. At times he could even forget about his wife and her lovers, about the poor housing, about the pollution. But now he looked out upon a dead, lifeless scene: There was little traffic on the roads, very few people in the streets, and none of the bright lights of Paris or Munich.

Was this what happened to all traitors once they had made the decision to leave their country? Did their home suddenly become a cold and lifeless place? Would the United States seem brighter and more alive?

He had seen photographs of New York, Detroit, and Los Angeles. They had not seemed any better than this. What was he trading for?

Antipov stared straight ahead, and Kozhevnikov wondered what the man was thinking about. He had never been a very pleasant person, and this afternoon he seemed particularly harsh. How much did he know? How effective had Bolotin's surveillance really been in Paris and Munich? Had they played games with him just to see how far he would go? Had they followed him to his meetings?

The double had said nothing when he entered the van in the parking lot at Dachau. He had been out of breath and frightened. Kozhevnikov wondered now if Bolotin had discovered his true identity and was letting him continue with the charade.

Perhaps, Kozhevnikov thought, they were on their way to a First Directorate Tribunal, which was the way the Komitet's internal matters were handled.

Once a man appeared before a tribunal, he usually disappeared a month to six weeks later—usually it was called reassignment to a foreign post.

The foreign post was a thinly disguised euphemism for a plot of land less than a meter wide, two meters long, and two meters deep—a grave. An assignment from which there was no return.

In twenty minutes they were on the Moscow Circumferential Highway. In the distance Kozhevnikov could see the thick stand of trees in which the new KGB headquarters building was nestled. They would be there in just a few minutes.

"Put that away," Antipov said, breaking the silence.

Kozhevnikov looked his way. "Comrade?" he asked.

"The medal. Put it away. We are not conducting a state function for you. The medal is unnecessary."

Kozhevnikov fingered the heavy medallion for a moment. Technically once the medal was awarded, no one, including the premier himself, could order any man to remove it. The medal could be worn daily, although most people wore it only for state or official functions.

But Kozhevnikov complied, slipping it into his side pocket. If he were going to end up at Lubyanka, it would do him no good, as Antipov had clearly pointed out. But if he were going to be dressed down, then promoted to department chief, the medal would only make things worse. Soviets did not like their heroes tarnished.

They pulled off at an unmarked exit, and within a few minutes were winding their way through the trees. Within a couple of miles they came into a clearing crisscrossed with power lines, across which a nine-story glass, steel, and cement building stood.

The road turned left sharply, and they stopped at the sentry post by the main gate to show their badges. The guards scrutinized them closely and motioned for them to move on.

The driver let them off at the front entrance, and they went inside, showing their badges again to the security people in the main lobby.

After three more security checks, they reached Antipov's office on the eighth floor.

"I will keep you only a few minutes, Comrade," Antipov said when they were settled at opposite ends of a long conference table. It was at this table every afternoon that all the department heads under Antipov's command met and discussed objectives. Normally the room was crowded. This afternoon Kozhevnikov and Antipov were alone.

Antipov opened a file folder on the table in front of him, hesitated, then looked up. "Against my recommendations, the chief of the First Chief Directorate has issued the following orders." He looked back down at the paper in front of him. Effective 1 November 1977, Kozhevnikov, Viktor Vasilievich, is elevated in position to chief of First Directorate Department A, Disinformation. Pay, housing, and peripheral privileges to commence upon date of rank."

If he were under suspicion it did not go as high as the directorate chief. Of that, at least, Kozhevnikov was certain. That meant Bolotin's report about his behavior in Paris and Munich was clean. In an effort to save his own skin, Bolotin had apparently lied to his chief here at KGB headquarters. Officially Kozhevnikov had been good during his vacation.

But Antipov had said the promotion was against his recommendation. Which meant Antipov was suspicious. Or was he?

"Congratulations, Comrade Kozhevnikov," Antipov said dryly.

Kozhevnikov nodded, but said nothing.

Again Antipov hesitated before he spoke, an odd expression on his face. "There is one other piece of information I want to give to you as well," he said.

Kozhevnikov sat forward slightly, his apprehension growing.

"I have here orders for Andrei Andreevich Bolotin, who was chief of your bodyguard detail during your European holiday. I will not bother to read you the details, however. Suffice it to say he no longer enjoys the luxury of a Moscow apartment or international assignments. In fact it may be a long time, a very long time indeed, before Comrade Bolotin ever sees a summer in which the temperatures climb above zero. Is my meaning clear, comrade?"

Kozhevnikov held his silence. Everything suddenly fell into place, and the new knowledge made him sick to his stomach. Antipov was Nadya's current lover. Nadya, not Bolotin, had spoken to Antipov about Kozhevnikov's behavior in Europe. Nadya, not Bolotin, had done this to him. And now it was going to be almost impossible for him to do any work for the Americans.

The revelation amazed him. Bolotin had been loyal, while his own wife had been . . . The thought stopped him. Nadya had been what—a traitor? The term was almost humorous considering the situation, but it made him even more physically ill.

CHAPTER 5

At eight o'clock, just after dinner, Laurie Andrews went to her room in the Park Motor Inn because she was tired. For two days she had searched Madison—university records, city directories, and the newspaper's clipping files—for any reference to Dr. Meitner. The picture she had been able to build so far was superficial. She had retrieved information anyone could get.

The *Who's Who in Science* had the most complete information. Meitner was born in Garmisch-Partenkirchen, a resort town in Southern Germany. He received his medical degree from the University of Heidelberg, worked until the war at a hospital in Berlin, then became a general practitioner in Hannover. In 1950 he emigrated to the United States, where he began work at the University of Wisconsin. Since that time he published more than two hundred scientific and medical papers in a number of journals and most recently made the discovery that would lead to his selection by the Nobel Prize Committee.

And that was it. She almost wished he would turn out to be a faggot. Without that bit of spice, the story she would turn in would be very dull indeed.

Yesterday she had tried to talk with two of his lab technicians. Both were very closemouthed and did not want to say anything about him. After exchanging only a few words with Laurie, they apologized to her for being late to a class and fled.

Only one alternative was left. And that was Meitner himself.

She sat down at the desk and asked the hotel operator to dial a Madison number. On the third ring the telephone was answered.

"Hello?" a man asked.

"May I speak with Dr. Robert Stewart, please?"

"Speaking," he said.

"Dr. Stewart, forgive me for bothering you so late, but I wanted to make sure I spoke to you before tomorrow."

"Who is this, please?" Stewart asked.

"Laurie Andrews. I'm a reporter with the *National Weekly* in New Orleans."

"I know the paper," Stewart said.

"I'm doing a story on Dr. Hans Meitner and the work that earned him the Nobel Prize."

"A wonderful man," Stewart said.

"I understand he works for you. That is, his department is part of your college."

"That's correct," Stewart said proudly. "What can I do for you, Miss Andrews?"

"I'd like an interview with Dr. Meitner—tomorrow if possible."

Stewart hesitated a moment. "Dr. Meitner is a very busy man."

"This would only take a short time. I'd like to ask him a few questions."

"I don't know, Miss Andrews. He is a very private person. He doesn't like publicity."

"I know," Laurie said, thinking of the thin file at the newspaper's morgue. "Of course, you would be present during the interview," she quickly added. "I mean it would only be right to have your views since Dr. Meitner's work would have been impossible without the backing and support of your college."

"Quite right," Stewart said, and Laurie smiled.

"Perhaps sometime in the morning?" she asked.

"He usually comes into the lab around nine," Stewart said, and she could almost hear his mind working.

"How about nine-fifteen then," she said. "I could talk with him before he gets started with his work. It would only take an hour or so."

Stewart hesitated again, and someone knocked at Laurie's door. She looked at the door as Stewart came back on the line.

"All right, Miss Andrews, I'll arrange it," he said.

"Fine," Laurie said, as the person knocked again. "Shall we meet at your office then? Say at nine?"

"That'll be fine," Stewart said.

"Good. I'll see you then," Laurie said and hung up. She went to the door and opened it just as the young woman standing there was raising her hand to knock.

"Yes?"

"Laurie Andrews?" the girl asked. She was very thin, with short hair, and was dressed in worn blue jeans, sneakers, a bulky sweater, and a blue jacket.

"That's right, Miss—?" Laurie said.

"Kathy Munson, Ms. Andrews. May I come in?"

"What do you want?" Laurie asked, making no move to invite the girl into her room.

"You were talking to Carl and Sanderson yesterday about Dr. Meitner. They told me about it. I work for him, too, and I think I might be able to tell you some interesting things about him."

"Sure," Laurie smiled, and she stepped away from the door. "Come on in."

The girl entered the room and hesitated. Then she walked over to the desk and sat down on the chair. She crossed her legs like a man and looked directly at Laurie. "You're very pretty," she said.

"Thank you," Laurie said smiling, but she groaned inwardly as she perched on the edge of the bed. The girl was a midwestern hick who was probably going to tell her how Meitner masturbated in the men's room, or liked to talk to little girls in the park.

"I suppose you've already checked university records, *Who's Who,* and the technical library?" the girl asked.

Laurie nodded, but said nothing.

"And you didn't find a thing, did you?"

"Not much," Laurie said guardedly.

"Your next step will be to interview Dr. Meitner himself, or at least try, although I doubt if you'll have much success."

"Look, Ms. Munson, I'm rather tired. I've had a busy day, and I'm going to be busy tomorrow. Why don't you get to the point. I'll need some sample information before we can discuss your fee."

The girl smiled. "Fair enough," she said. "Dr. Meitner is not married and never has been."

Laurie stared at her but said nothing.

"He came to the university directly from Germany right after World War Two."

"In 1950," Laurie said dryly.

"And no one knows what he really did during the war."

Laurie started to rise. "Look, Ms. Munson, if you don't mind, I'm tired."

The girl waved her down. "In the twenty-seven years Meitner has lived in Madison, no one has ever been to his home. Not Dr. Stewart, not any of us lab technicians, not even the dean of the university."

"He's a private man. So what?" Laurie said, impatient now. The girl was worse than she thought she would be.

"Perhaps you don't think that's unusual, but I do. Or did," the girl said. Her use of the past tense stopped Laurie from ordering her out.

The girl read the interest on Laurie's face. "Shall we discuss a price now?"

"Not yet," Laurie snapped. "But you're getting warmer. Go on."

"Dr. Meitner takes little naps in the afternoon in his office," Kathy said. "A couple months ago I wanted to talk to him about something and I went into his office. He was asleep, but he was having a dream. He was mumbling about something."

"Yes?" Laurie prompted.

"It was about the war."

"Go ahead."

"No," the girl said flatly. "First my fee."

Laurie reached over, and got her purse from the nightstand, opened it, and pulled out a hundred-dollar bill. "A hundred dollars," she said, holding the money out to the girl. "Standard fee."

The girl shook her head. "I don't want money."

Laurie's eyes narrowed. "What then?"

The girl stared at her for a long moment. "I've read your articles in the paper."

Laurie replaced the money in her purse. "So?"

"Most of it stinks, but I liked the one about you a couple of years ago. It was about your investigative work on the beauty contests in Arizona. They ran your picture. You were wearing a swimsuit."

"What are you getting at?" Laurie snapped. She suddenly felt uncomfortable under the girl's stare.

"You've been fascinating to me ever since that article," the girl said. She was smiling now.

"What the hell are you talking about?" Laurie said. But she had a sinking feeling in the pit of her stomach that she knew exactly what the girl wanted.

"In trade for what information I have on Dr. Meitner, information which you will be able to use for one hell of a story, I want to make love to you. I'm gay."

"Fuck you," Laurie snapped and jumped up. But Kathy also jumped up and shoved Laurie back down on the bed.

"This part's free. Another teaser," Kathy said quickly. "Meitner was mumbling something about the SS and machine guns."

Laurie was about to struggle out of the girl's surprisingly strong grasp, but suddenly what she said sunk in. The SS? Machine guns? What would a doctor know about those things?

Kathy stepped back. "Interested?"

Laurie sat up, the memory of last weekend on the Gulf flooding back into her mind. The man she had been with was like most men—interested only in his own pleasure, not hers.

In college she had a lesbian experience, and although she worried about it for months afterwards, afraid that somehow she would become tainted by it, it hadn't been all that bad. Oh, well, she told herself. Sex was sex in whatever package it came. The name of the game was pleasure, not marriage and children.

She looked up at the girl, who was waiting for her answer. Perhaps she would get some information out of her.

"Maybe," she said, and the girl smiled.

"Meitner also said something about killing the Jews but leaving the animals alone," Kathy said, as she took her jacket off and pulled her sweater over her head. She was not wearing a bra, and the sight of her small breasts, the nipples and dark areolae sharply defined against the white skin, fascinated Laurie.

"He didn't say much more that I could make out," Kathy continued as she kicked off her sneakers. "But I think we might find something at his house. I can keep him busy at the lab while you search his place."

"When?" Laurie asked huskily, as Kathy peeled off her blue jeans. She wore no panties either, and the sight of her pubic hair excited Laurie.

"Tomorrow morning," Kathy said, and she moved closer to the bed. "It won't be so bad, you'll see," she said.

CHAPTER 6

Rafn came around the corner, crossed the street against the light, and passed the telephone booth where Sigmund Schiller stood talking into the phone. The younger man was dressed in khaki trousers, with a dark green windbreaker zippered tightly up to his throat.

"Muskrat," Rafn said half under his breath as he passed. Schiller did not give any outward indication he had heard him.

Rafn continued walking, watching the distorted reflection of the sidewalk behind him in the store windows. A few minutes later he could see Schiller a few meters behind him.

Friday they had left the house on the Starnberger by six o'clock. Gleason flew to Frankfurt and caught the overnight flight to the States. Rafn spent the night in a hotel in Munich. Saturday morning Rafn flew into Tempelhof. By noon he had checked into a small hotel a few doors down from the Alsterhof where Schiller was staying under the name of Walter Goldmann.

That afternoon and evening Rafn watched the Alsterhof but saw no sign of the Israeli. Then early Sunday he called him from a house phone in the lobby.

"Gleason tells me it's a nice morning for a walk," Rafn said softly. Then he hung up and strolled out of the hotel and down the block where he stopped at a kiosk, purchased a copy of *Stern,* and idly flipped through its pages, waiting.

A few minutes later Schiller emerged from the hotel, lit a cigarette, then crossed the street and headed downtown. Rafn was across the street and a half block behind him.

They walked like that for nearly an hour, and when Rafn was finally sure that Schiller was not being followed, he passed him at a telephone booth.

A double-decker bus stopped at the corner, and a few people got off. Rafn climbed aboard, and Schiller had to run to catch up. By the time Schiller paid his fare, Rafn was already seated near the middle of the nearly deserted bus. Schiller came forward and sat one seat ahead.

The bus lumbered around the corner and headed down the Kurfürstendamm. Only a few people were out and around, although by the afternoon, Rafn knew, the streets would be more crowded. In Germany on Sunday, rain or shine, the entire nation came out for a walk. It was a national tradition.

"How is Herr Gleason these days?" Schiller asked quietly from the seat ahead.

"Concerned," Rafn said. "He's been having some trouble locating the doctor."

"Which doctor is that?"

"Predel. Perhaps we can help locate him."

"East," Schiller said.

"So I understand," Rafn answered. "I will rent a Mercedes and pick you up in front of the Lufthansa terminal at Tempelhof in an hour."

The bus stopped at a corner, and Rafn got up, hurried to the front door, and got off. As the bus moved away he could see Schiller in the window looking straight ahead. The Israeli was a professional and would do exactly as he was told. It was too bad he would have to be dumped sooner or later.

Rafn pulled up his coat collar to ward off the mist and hurried two blocks to a taxi stand where he directed a driver to take him to Tempelhof.

In twenty minutes they arrived. Rafn paid the driver and entered the huge building. Passing through one of the connecting corridors, he entered the airport's main mezzanine, which was busy with several overseas arrivals and departures. He went directly across the large room and entered one of the men's rooms near the main shopping area.

A man was washing his hands. When he finished and left, Rafn quickly opened the lid of one of the large trash containers and poked through the wads of paper until he found a Lufthansa boarding pass with a ticket stub still stapled to it. He stuffed it into his coat pocket and closed the container just as two men walked in. Nodding to them, he went back out into the mezzanine and entered one of the restaurants.

He stayed in the restaurant for fifteen minutes. When he finished his coffee and three cigarettes, he paid his bill and hurried out.

He went into a gift shop where he purchased a plastic Lufthansa flight bag and a stuffed animal, which he had the clerk wrap and put in the flight bag.

Back in the mezzanine, he put the bag over his shoulder, and clutching the boarding pass, hurried to the Lufthansa flight terminal where he stopped at the Schuldt Rental Car counter. In fifteen minutes he had filled out the necessary forms, paid the fee, and had the keys to a Mercedes sedan.

"Have an enjoyable vacation, Herr Van der Haarg," the clerk, a pretty young girl, said to him.

He nodded his thanks and hurried out of the terminal.

With five minutes to spare, Rafn slowly circled the large parking lot, and at exactly eleven-thirty, pulled up at the curb as Schiller was emerging. The Israeli crossed the wide sidewalk, opened the passenger door, and got in, throwing his single suitcase in the back seat as Rafn pulled smoothly away.

Schiller adjusted the rearview mirror so he could see out of it, and for twenty minutes they rode in silence.

Rafn finally broke the silence. "How does it look?"

"We're clean," Schiller said, and he readjusted the mirror.

"Tell me about Gustav Predel," Rafn said.

"Didn't Gleason brief you?" Schiller asked sharply.

"Yes, but I want your side of it."

"Predel murdered a few thousand Jews during the war. We want him."

"Medical experiments?"

"Yes."

"Why come to the Americans for help?"

"You are the only ones operating effectively in the East Zone."

"What happens when we find him?"

Schiller was silent for a moment. "If he's still in the East Zone, I want to bring him back here."

"So the attorney general's office can prosecute?" Rafn asked.

"Yes," Schiller said.

Rafn glanced at him. "You were doing fine, but if you're going to start playing games with me now, I'll drop you off at your hotel and make my report to Gleason."

"He'll send someone else," Schiller said.

"No, he won't. I wonder what a check with your boss in Tel Aviv would produce. Sigmund Schiller. Is he on vacation?"

Schiller's eyes narrowed. "What are you getting at?"

"The Americans are a trusting people. It may take them a week or more to check up on you. That gives you a week to do what you have come here to do."

Schiller held his breath for a moment, then let it out slowly. "What do you want?"

"Hard information."

"All right."

"Predel experimented with Jews. Were they exclusively women?"

"Yes, as far as I know," Schiller said, staring straight ahead.

"Are any of those women still alive in Israel?"

Schiller hesitated.

"If I'm going to help you, Schiller, you're going to have to tell me everything," Rafn said sharply.

"What's all this to you?" Schiller asked defensively.

"Nothing," Rafn snapped. "It's just an assignment. One I don't give a damn about one way or the other. But if I am going to put my neck on the line for you, I'll damned well not do it unless I know exactly what I'm getting myself into."

After another long pause, Schiller nodded. "A few of them are still alive."

"You've been sent here to take Predel back to stand trial. . . ." Rafn began, but then he stopped in mid-sentence. This was not going to be another Eichmann. With the Americans in on it, with Schiller obviously working alone, and with no official sanction, it could mean only one thing. "No, you're here to find Predel and assassinate him."

Schiller said nothing.

They stopped for a traffic light, and Rafn turned to the Israeli. "How did you come up with the town Tiefensee? How old is that information?"

Schiller looked at him, no expression in his eyes. For a moment Rafn was slightly unnerved. There were very few people whose eyes did not give them away. At first Schiller had been very obvious, but now that his guard was up, Rafn's estimation of him had risen considerably.

"Predel was stationed here in Berlin until 1940, when he was transferred to Tiefensee. It was a top-secret project under the direct authority of Goebbels."

The light changed. Rafn turned the corner and headed in the general direction of the Brandenburg Gate. "More medical experiments, I presume?"

"We don't know," Schiller admitted. "The only survivors are those upon whom he experimented here, in Berlin."

"And you expect to find something in Tiefensee?"

Schiller shrugged. "I don't know. It's a starting point."

"The man more than likely is dead. He probably was killed during the war, or died of old age," Rafn said.

"Someone in Tiefensee might remember," Schiller said insistently. "Such projects are always remembered by someone."

They came around another corner and the street opened into Brandenburg Square. Across the way from them was the Brandenburg Gate itself, below which were the East-West checkpoint buildings. On either side of the gate was the Berlin wall, nearly five meters high in most places, cutting the city in half.

Rafn pulled the Mercedes into the parking lot of the Tourist Center, maneuvered into an empty stall, and shut off the engine. The parking lot was nearly full. One interzone bus and several West Berlin tour buses were parked in the lot taking on passengers.

"Take the car and park it. There is an underground garage one block from your hotel. I will meet you in your room this evening after dinner."

Schiller looked from Rafn to the tour buses and back again. "Is this how you contact your East German network?"

Rafn smiled. "I don't trust you, Schiller. I am working with you merely because it interests me. If I lose interest I'll leave. If I find out you are playing a game with me, or you have lied to me about anything, I will kill you."

"The women——" Schiller started to say.

"The Nazis were here a long time ago and are of no consequence to me now. What they did to your people does not interest me, either. You Jews are stupid. You were like sheep during the war, and now you are like little children as you throw stones at the Arabs. One day the Russians will tire of your silly little games, they will arm the Arabs with tactical nuclear weapons, and your little kingdom will be at an end."

"Don't be so sure," Schiller said, his back stiffening.

Rafn smiled. "That's neither here nor there. Fuck with me, Schiller, and I'll cut your heart out. Literally."

"All I want is Predel," Schiller said evenly.

"If he's alive, you'll get him," Rafn said. Then he pulled a folded ten-mark bill from his wallet. Last night he had used a simple vinegar solution and a fine-tipped pen to write a message that would become visible when the bill was held over an open flame.

"Can your East German contacts be trusted?" Schiller asked.

"Don't be naive, Schiller," Rafn said impatiently. "Predel is of no interest to anyone but you and a few people in Israel. But even if he was, my contacts can be trusted."

"How can you be so sure?"

Rafn smiled. "Every one of them is a drug addict. Heroin is very difficult to come by in the East Zone."

Schiller's face contorted.

"Don't give me that tough-fighting Israeli soldier look," Rafn snapped. "Every one of my people is loyal. Not to each other. Not to their country. Not to any ideal. They are loyal only to their god, heroin. And I am god's messenger."

Rafn opened the car door and got out. He held the door open as Schiller slid behind the wheel. He looked down at the Israeli. "Contact no one, go nowhere, and do nothing after you have parked the car and returned to your hotel. I'll be there by eight o'clock."

"Good luck," Schiller said, and Rafn turned and headed for the interzone bus, which made tours several times a day, seven days a week into East Berlin.

The tour bus driver, Wilhelm Bermann, had been

working for Rafn for five years now, accepting messages written on folded ten-mark bills. When a message was returned from the East, the western contact would pay for the tour with a torn twenty-mark bill. Bermann would make change with the ten-marks.

Although Rafn knew Bermann by sight, the tour bus driver had never seen Rafn, nor did he even know his name. All Bermann and the others knew was that someone would take a tour of East Berlin on Bermann's bus from time to time, paying with a folded ten-mark bill. When an assignment was completed, payment in heroin was made at a prearranged spot along the wall. Someone from the West would throw a small package over the wall, late at night. For five years the system had worked, and it would work again, Rafn thought. Only this time he was handicapped by two things: First, he had to mix his real work with Schiller's, and second, time. Once it became known that inquiries were being made about Kummersdorf, the KGB would sit up and take notice, and Kozhevnikov would be in trouble.

Rafn took his place in the line of passengers slowly boarding the interzone tour bus. The service, offered by the East German Propaganda Ministry, allowed Western tourists to catch a glimpse of conditions in East Berlin. The tour, which never strayed off the streets that had been completely rebuilt after the war, also served as the only contact West Germans had with friends and relatives in the East Zone.

East Germans could board the bus in the East Zone but were required to get off before it returned its western passengers to the Brandenburg Gate.

In this way, friends and relatives separated by the wall could visit one another, although no gifts could be exchanged.

It was Rafn's turn now, and he stepped up to Bermann, who drove four tours a day, Tuesday through Sunday, and handed him a folded ten-mark bill. Rafn noticed that Bermann's hand shook slightly as he handed over the ticket, and then Rafn climbed aboard the bus.

If there was anything to find out about either Predel or Kozhevnikov's Kummersdorf Papers, the wheels for its discovery and disclosure were being set in motion. It would be only a matter of time now before he received a response.

STEINER. ONE KILO HEROIN FOR COMPLETE IN-FORMATION ON PRESENT WHEREABOUTS OF DR. GUSTAV PREDEL, NAZI MEDICAL EXPERIMENTER STATIONED 1940 TIEFENSEE. FULLEST REPORT ON NAZI RESEARCH PROJECT KUMMERSDORF AFTER 1940. FAT MAN

CHAPTER 7

Kozhevnikov entered the computer terminal control room carrying a glass of tea and three rolls of computer program tapes. Although it was after six, a half-dozen people were still at work in the large room filled with memory tape decks and printout machines. Ten rows of keypunch and data card readers radiated outward like spokes on a wheel from the main control console in the center.

He walked down one of the aisles to the main console where Alexander Dmitrievich Yurin, the chief computer technician, was poring over a batch of printouts.

Yurin looked up as Kozhevnikov approached and then glanced at the digital clock set in the console panel. "We're running a little late, Comrade Kozhevnikov, please forgive me."

"No matter, unless you are going to be all night. Perhaps I can schedule time for tomorrow?"

"It won't be possible," Yurin said, shaking his head. "Starting at twelve-hundred hours tomorrow we'll be doing a personnel analysis of the entire company. It'll probably take the rest of the week and most of the weekend." He glanced at the tapes Kozhevnikov held. "We'll be finished in a few minutes and the computer will be yours. Would you like some help with those?"

Kozhevnikov shook his head. "It's not necessary, Alexander Dmitrievich," he said, and he held up his glass of tea. "I've brought my tea with me and will be content to work alone."

Yurin, a young man with longish hair, smiled. "As you wish, Comrade." He casually waved toward a chair and went back to work.

Kozhevnikov sat down, placed the computer programs on the desk in front of him, and slowly sipped his tea. It had been a busy day, and he was tired.

As chief of the Disinformation Department, his first task was to familiarize himself with the organization and work of his department—from the top man here in Moscow to the lowest clerk in the smallest satellite station abroad.

What he had found this morning and this afternoon was appalling. From the beginning, the Cheka, the GPU and later the NKVD—all forerunners of the present Komitet organization—had maintained a disinformation desk, usually manned by only a few men. It wasn't until 1959, during the reorganization of the KGB, that the Disinformation Service became a full-fledged department. Then it was called Department D, and was headed by General Ivan Ivanovich Blok, the solemn Armenian.

It had been Blok's personal strength and ambition that finally pulled the disinformation service up from a haphazard organization to a full-fledged service of fifty officers in Moscow and an additional fifteen men at the Komitet's Karlshorst Residency in East Berlin.

Blok died in the mid-sixties, and in 1968, when the Komitet was again reorganized, the Disinformation Service became Department A, one of a few special departments directly under the First Chief Directorate.

It was time once again, Kozhevnikov thought, to reorganize the department, which had grown in stature and complexity so that now it directly employed more than seven hundred people and used the services of nearly every department and division in the KGB.

Blok was able to run roughshod over his people. He knew every one of them personally. But that was no longer possible. It was time for reorganization. The computer would help him with that tonight.

Kozhevnikov looked up as Yurin began stuffing his papers into a thick leather briefcase, and he could feel a stab of guilt in his gut.

In order to operate more effectively the Disinformation Department needed reorganization, and Kozhevnikov was just the man for it. But he was a traitor, and with luck he would be leaving his country very soon. For where? he asked himself. Or more accurately, for what?

He looked around the room. All but two of the keypunch operators had left, and they were deep in discussion with Yurin. Kozhevnikov watched them for a few moments and wondered what he was going to discover this evening.

Besides the reorganizational chart which he wanted the computer to analyze, there was a series of memory search and correlation questions he wanted to run.

There was no way he could directly obtain information on the Kummersdorf Project in Siberia, so he was going to have to do it indirectly.

If a hundred thousand Jews had been moved to Siberia, and if in fact there were no farming operations there, then what had become of those people? Even if they had all been murdered, it would take organization. It would require people, and lots of them.

Hopefully the computer would be able to supply him with a list of names of people transferred to Siberia within the past few years. From this list, he hoped to find the names of people he knew. People he could become sufficiently curious about enough to legitimately ask after their health and whereabouts.

It was a dangerous thing to do, he knew. Sooner or later Antipov would put two and two together. In addition to his mysterious disappearances in Europe, these inquiries would constitute a red flag waving directly in front of the bull.

He only hoped that the timing would not be so critical that he would be caught here, unable to make his escape.

Yurin turned and came to where Kozhevnikov was sitting. He was smiling. "We're finished, Comrade Kozhevnikov. The computer is yours."

Kozhevnikov rose. "Thank you. I'll take good care of it," he said lightly.

Again Yurin glanced at the programs Kozhevnikov had brought in. "Are you sure I can't stay and help with those?" he asked.

"No," Kozhevnikov said with finality. "I'm in the middle of reorganizing my department. I don't want any interference."

Yurin became suddenly apologetic. "I didn't mean to interfere, Comrade," he said.

Kozhevnikov reached out and touched his arm. "And I didn't mean to become angry with you, Alexander Dmitrievich. It's been a long, trying day, that's all."

Yurin nodded. "I understand," he said. "But if you should run into any problems, don't hesitate to call me. My number is listed on the console."

"Thank you," Kozhevnikov said. With one last glance at the programs, Yurin turned, picked up his overstuffed briefcase, and left the computer terminal room with the other two men.

Kozhevnikov watched as the door closed silently. He waited, holding his breath, and tried to listen for the sounds of the computer now running at idle. All he could hear was the ventilating fan that was keeping the room cool. Below him, in the subbasement, were the main racks of the computer—the heart— where the real work was done and where the information he needed was stored.

Kozhevnikov loosened his tie, took off his coat,

hung it over the back of his chair, and picked up the tapes.

He was leaving the Komitet, his wife, his home, and his country. But he would leave a legacy by making the reorganization. That much he would accomplish. After he was gone, his department would operate with a degree of efficiency that had never existed before.

But to what end was he doing this, he asked himself as he threaded the tapes onto the tape readers at one side of the main console. He was leaving. He was becoming a traitor to his country. He wanted to stop the Komitet from doing what it was doing to the Jews. So why not fix his department so that it would take years to straighten it out? Why not sabotage what he could?

He put the last tape in the machine and closed the glass front of the reader.

Because he was still a Soviet citizen. If there was a way to bring to a halt the project he was convinced would ultimately lead to the murders of a hundred thousand human beings, he would find it.

For the rest of his life he would regret his decision to defect. He knew it. But he also knew he had no other choice.

Back at the main console, he pushed the start buttons, then sat down to wait for the computer to do his bidding. Once the computer had read the tapes, it would begin its search and correlation by combining everything that had ever been fed into it—from every project and level in the KGB. All he had to do was wait.

It was after midnight when the first real information began spewing out. Besides the personnel lists, classifications, and present assignments he had wanted on his department, the tapes had also asked the computer to search for the term *Kummersdorf Papers*, as well as a list of personnel transferred to Siberia in the last four years.

The Kummersdorf query came up a blank, the computer merely printing out the response "Insufficient Data." But for the second part of the question, the computer began printing out a list of names, specialties, and dates of transfer to an unnamed Department T operation in Siberia.

Department T was where he had first seen the term Kummersdorf.

Kozhevnikov stood by the readout printer and watched the list of teachers, scientists, technicians, medical doctors, and researchers come out of the machine. There were hundreds of them. All being transferred to an unnamed project in Siberia.

Why? Were the Jews for some reason being trained by all these specialists and technicians? Somehow he knew this could not be the case. If they were training a hundred thousand people from all walks of life, he could understand it. But he was concerned with Jews—one hundred thousand Jews. Mostly women.

CHAPTER 8

At least a dozen cars and vans were parked in front of the Genetic Research building when Laurie Andrews showed up in a cab a few minutes before nine. She paid the driver, crossed the sidewalk, and mounted the steps.

Three of the vans were television mobile units and several of the cars were press cars, and Laurie was mad. Although Dr. Stewart had not promised her an exclusive interview in so many words, she was·led to believe that only she and Dr. Stewart would be talking with Meitner. This looked like a full-scale press conference.

Inside the building a university police officer directed her upstairs to the fourth floor. The press conference, he told her, was scheduled to begin in five minutes in the main lecture hall.

At the elevator a few steps away from the door, Laurie turned back to the guard. "Is Dr. Meitner still in his lab on the second floor?" she asked.

The guard turned to her. "Third floor," he automatically corrected. "But the press conference is on the fourth floor."

"Thanks," Laurie said as the elevator doors slid open. She stepped inside, punched the button for the third floor, and turned and smiled sweetly at the guard as the doors slid closed.

If Meitner was still in his laboratory she was going

to get a few answers out of him before the press conference started. Nothing very interesting, especially nothing personal, ever came from a press conference where more than one reporter was present. People just did not like to talk about themselves in front of a crowd. People, especially men, would tell Laurie some of the most intimate things about their lives during private interviews. And it was just this kind of information she wanted. That and the answers to a couple of questions Kathy raised last night.

The elevator bumped to a halt on the third floor, and the doors opened. She stepped out into a long, narrow corridor lined on either side with frosted glass doors.

Two doors down from the elevator she found a door marked with Meitner's name. No one else was in the corridor and she listened a moment at the door. She could hear someone talking on a telephone somewhere down the hall.

She took a deep breath, then opened the door and peeked inside. The small, book-lined office was deserted, and Laurie quickly slipped inside, closing the door behind her.

Across the room, she stopped to listen at another door and she could hear two men talking, one of them using the name Hans. She listened for a moment, but then the voices faded. A moment later she could hear them in the corridor. One of the men was Stewart, she guessed, and the other was probably Meitner. They were on their way upstairs to the press conference.

Although she had hoped to speak privately with Meitner, she had not really thought it would be possible. Not with all the other news people here this morning. She was sure Stewart or someone else would be keeping a close watch over the scientist. But now, finding herself alone in Meitner's office, was a better piece of luck.

She went to the desk, sat down in the chair, laid her purse down, and began going through the drawers. At first she found nothing of interest among the pencils, paper clips, rubber bands, and dozens of scientific articles evidently clipped from journals. But in the bottom drawer she discovered a bundle of canceled checks. Dr. Meitner's personal checking account.

She laid the checks on the top of the desk, removed the thick rubber band that held them together and began looking through them. Many of the canceled checks were for groceries, rent and utilities, but scattered through the thick pile were checks made out to a number of scientific supply houses. At the bottom of each check was a notation of what the money had been spent for.

Covering the last January-June period, Meitner had purchased nearly eight thousand dollars' worth of chemicals, test tubes and other glassware, and electronic equipment, and he had made six payments on a microscope. His neat handwriting not only revealed what the money was being spent for, but in the case of the microscope payments, the balance due. As of June the balance due on the one piece of equipment was more than five thousand dollars. An expensive toy.

Laurie bundled the checks up, stuffed them back into the desk drawer, and sat back in the chair.

Why would a scientist who had his pick of all the equipment a large university could supply him spend more than eight thousand dollars in six months on scientific equipment of his own? Two reasons formed in her mind. One was that he was a dedicated scientist who worked at home as well as here. And rather than bring university equipment home to his lab, he bought his own. The second reason seemed somehow more consistent with what Kathy had told her last night.

"He was a Nazi during the war," Kathy said after they had made love and were lying next to each other on the bed.

"How do you know that?" Laurie asked, coming out of a half sleep.

"I don't know for sure," Kathy admitted. "I'm just guessing. But he's so damned secretive, and that story of his about being a doctor in Hannover during and after the war is a bunch of bullshit."

Laurie propped herself up on one elbow and looked down at the girl. "What do you mean?"

"I know enough about medicine to realize that Meitner doesn't talk or think like any doctor. Once a researcher, always a researcher. He's just got that kind of mentality, that's all. He's cold. Dispassionate."

"No bedside manner," Laurie said.

"Exactly," Kathy exclaimed. "It's my guess he worked for the Nazis during the war. I'll bet he experimented on the Jews."

"That's a pretty serious charge," Laurie said sharply.

"After you talk to him in the morning, I'll make sure he stays at the lab and you can take a look around his house. Maybe you'll find something there."

Now Laurie got up from the desk and went to the door. If Meitner had indeed been experimenting during the war, might he not also be experimenting on his own now? Experimenting with something so delicate that he could not do it here at the lab?

It was probably a far-fetched idea, she told herself. But she had seen even more unlikely notions blossom into full-blown exclusives. Maybe this was one of them.

She slipped into the corridor, hurried to the elevator, and made it upstairs to the crowded auditorium, where she sat in a seat near the back. The news conference had already begun and Dr. Stewart was sitting with the man who must be Meitner at the front of the room.

Meitner was obviously nervous, and as the news conference progressed, Laurie kept silent, watching instead his reactions to the questions being thrown at him.

He seemed to enjoy answering those questions involving his work. But when the reporters began to ask questions about his background, he became tense, and his voice dropped to an inaudible level.

He was hiding something, Laurie was convinced of it. Just as she was convinced that the only place she would find out anything else would be at his home, and then possibly Germany itself.

If Kathy's guess that Meitner had never been a doctor was correct—and Laurie was beginning to believe the girl could be onto something—then what *had* he done during the war? Why was he so secretive that no one had ever been to his home? What was he hiding?

The press conference ended at nine-forty-five, and Laurie hurried out of the auditorium and downstairs past the guard.

She had to walk two blocks before she could find a pay phone to call a cab. Fifteen minutes later it pulled up in front of University Bookstore, and she directed the driver to Meitner's address.

Sooner or later she was going to have to face him, but she wanted to arm herself with as much information as possible so that when she confronted him, she would be on solid ground.

Meitner's house turned out to be a large, two-story colonial on a tree-lined street near the Nakoma Country Club.

Laurie asked the driver to wait, and she went up to the front door and unlocked it with the key Kathy had given her.

The girl and two other lab technicians had sneaked into Meitner's office several months before, made a wax impression of the house key lying on his desk, and planned to come out here one day to look around.

"We chickened out," Kathy explained to Laurie last night. "But I held onto the key." She handed it to Laurie.

"I'm just supposed to walk up to his front door, let myself in, and look around?"

Kathy nodded. "Just don't take anything, okay?"

Laurie now let herself in with a backward glance toward the driver, who was now reading a paperback.

Inside, the house was quiet and cool. A hallway led straight back to the kitchen. To the right was the living room, and to the left were double doors that opened onto a formal dining room. Stairs led up to four bedrooms on the second floor.

Everything was neat, almost sterile, in the upstairs rooms, and after a quick examination of some of the closets and the bureau drawers in what obviously was Meitner's bedroom, Laurie went back downstairs.

The first floor revealed nothing of interest, either. It was as if someone had once lived here, but had moved out, leaving nothing personal behind. There was the usual furniture, a few nondescript paintings on the walls, food in the refrigerator, but nothing else. Nothing in the wastepaper baskets. Nothing on the shelves or in the closets. No opened mail. No newspapers or magazines. No dirty ashtrays. Nothing.

In the hall, Laurie opened a door which led to the basement. Flipping on the light, she went down the stairs and found herself in a small room that contained the furnace, water heater, and a washer and dryer. The rest of the basement had been partitioned off, an oak door equipped with a combination lock and heavy hasp apparently the only access.

She fingered the lock a moment. There was no way she would be able to get in. At least not now. But she was convinced that Meitner's laboratory was behind the door. She could smell alcohol and some other undefinable odor, but knew that even if she were able to gain entrance, she would not know what to look for. That would have to be left to the others.

Hesitating, she went upstairs, careful to shut off the basement light and lock the front door. Then she went out to the cab and ordered the driver to take her back to the Park Motor Inn.

She was convinced now that Meitner definitely had something to hide. He had never invited people to his home, and it looked like he didn't really live there.

She had no doubt that his basement laboratory was equipped with not only the latest scientific equipment but also served as his real living quarters. In fact, she was certain that his entire world was confined to his lab and office at school and to the lab in his house.

But what else was in the lab? There had been another smell besides alcohol in the basement—an unpleasant odor that she had smelled before.

Back in her room, she called the airport and reserved a flight for Chicago in two hours and one for Munich. By tomorrow morning she would be in Germany.

Then she called Phil Shapiro.

"What?" Shapiro's guttural voice came over the line.

"Laurie—I'm in Madison."

"Hello, doll, what have you dug up so far?" he asked brightly. He had been trying to get Laurie into bed for as long as she had worked for the paper. And although he never let it interfere with his work or his treatment of her when she was on the job, when he was in a good mood he always managed to inject into his tone of voice a note of suggestiveness. It was something he probably did not realize he was doing, but it was something any woman worth a damn could read a mile away.

"Plenty," she said. "But I'm going to need a little backup here."

Shapiro suddenly became businesslike. "Can you talk?"

"Yes," she said, and she explained to him what had happened so far, leaving out only the events of last night. She also described Meitner's office and what she had found, and not found, in his home.

"Send me the key and I'll get a team up there immediately," Shapiro said without hesitation.

"I'm leaving for Munich tonight," Laurie said, holding her breath. If Shapiro was leveling with her about her expense account being unlimited, she would find out now.

"Have you got your passport?" he asked.

She smiled. "Yes, and enough clothes to last me a few days at least."

"Do you think you'll find anything?"

"I don't know," she admitted. "But I think it's worth a try. It's my guess Meitner was never anywhere near Hannover during the war, and probably never was a medical doctor. At least, not a civilian doctor."

"If Meitner is his real name," Shapiro added.

The comment stopped Laurie for a moment. "I'll check his birth and school records first. There's got to be something on him there somewhere."

"How about the other prizewinners?" Shapiro asked.

"Get someone else to dig up the routine stuff. I'd like to stick with this one until I come up with something."

"I thought as much. But we'll leave the real digging to you. Don't forget, you've got less than six weeks before you have to be in Stockholm. And I want something on every one of these people."

"You'll get it, don't worry," Laurie said. "I should be able to dig up something on Meitner within a few days. I'll check in with you by Friday to see what you've come up with at his home."

"All right, sweetheart, be careful," Shapiro said.

"Right," she answered and hung up.

CHAPTER 9

Nadya stood in front of the mirror in Antipov's bathroom and studied her reflection in the glass. She had
just stepped out of the shower and had not dried herself
yet, her wet skin glistening in the dim light over the
sink.

She was quite attractive for a woman of fifty-two,
she told herself frankly. And although her waist and
hips had become somewhat thicker in the last few
years, her muscle tone was still good, her complexion
excellent. Her breasts had begun to sag, contrary to
what Viktor believed, and if she had not begun using
the American cosmetics Antipov allowed her to buy at
the exchange store, the crow's feet and the lines around
her mouth and chin would be noticeable.

The fact was she was still a desirable woman. She
was still able to excite men with her body and with her
eyes. And she loved it.

She turned away from the mirror, dried herself carefully with a large Turkish towel, then applied powder
to her skin and Ultra-Ban to her underarms.

Since Monday, when Viktor's promotion became
official, he had worked like a demon, fifteen and eighteen hours a day. When he came home at night he went
directly to bed.

"There's so much to do, Nadya," he told her last
night. "The entire department needs reorganization. It's

181

why I was given the promotion—they know I am an organizer."

"How long will it take?" Nadya asked anxiously.

"I don't know," he shrugged. "A week or two."

"I want to be in our new apartment by New Year's Day," she insisted.

He smiled distantly. "I'll be finished by then," he said, and Nadya was left with the distinct impression that they were talking about two completely different things.

"Are you getting along better now with Sergei Antipov?" she asked.

He looked sharply at her. "Sergei Antipov is a fool. I will never get along with him."

Nadya winced at the harshness of his comment, but she did not want to start another argument. Ever since she had left him in Munich, she had been frightened; not so much of him, but frightened for their marriage. If he made her affairs public, it would be the end of both their careers.

Since he had returned he seemed subdued. Somehow he was different. Preoccupied. Worried. And except for his brief outburst at the mention of Antipov's name, he had been completely neutral about everything, even his medal.

Nadya left the bathroom and padded back into Antipov's huge bedroom. The key to comfort in any country, be it communist or capitalist, was money and power, she told herself, surveying the plush opulence of the room.

Thick shag carpeting, heavy brocaded draperies, and paintings—all of them originals—created the perfect setting for the huge Louis XIV four-poster bed with silk sheets in the center of the room.

Russians were like everyone else. They, too, loved luxury. The only difference here was that the haves did not flaunt their lives in front of the have-nots. It was a secret pleasure, and she loved it, too.

She came to the foot of the bed and stared down at Antipov, who was stretched out on his back, one arm over his hairy chest, the sheet barely covering his stomach. He was overweight, and unlike Viktor, had probably never satisfied a woman in his life—at least not sexually. But he had one thing that Viktor had never had until now, and that was power.

Nadya smiled wanly. Now that Viktor had power she no longer needed Antipov. Perhaps she no longer needed anyone but her husband. But was it too late? Had the damage to their marriage been done? And if it were too late, whose fault was that?

She turned away from the bed, suddenly cold, the gooseflesh rising on her arms and back. Vitya, she cried to herself. What have I done?

The sun had been shining when she arrived in Moscow, and after the dismal weather in Europe, she was buoyant and happy, certain that she would be able to mend their problems.

Antipov telephoned her that evening and sent a car for her. When she arrived he was waiting with an open bottle of champagne, wearing only a thin silk robe.

After she changed into the French negligee he kept for her and they were nestled in each other's arms on the sofa, she told him about her husband's odd behavior.

"I think he is seeing other women," Nadya said. She could feel Antipov suddenly stiffening in her arms.

She parted from him slightly and looked at his face. He was frowning.

"Did you discuss this with Andrei Bolotin?" he asked.

Nadya nodded. "Yes. He was upset. He said he could not keep up with Viktor."

"And this began in Paris?"

"Yes," Nadya said, realizing suddenly her mistake. "But I'm sure it is just women he is seeing."

"Why are you telling me this, my dear?" Antipov asked hesitantly.

Nadya's mind worked furiously. "Because I want my husband back. Because I think you can marshal the proper authority to promote him."

"Never," Antipov said, shaking his head. "Your husband is a traitor. And now I have him."

Nadya pulled away. "Then you will lose me," she said simply, gambling that Antipov was as weak a man as she had figured he was.

"Why do you need him?" Antipov said in amazement.

"Why do you need me?" Nadya countered.

"I love you."

"No. You never offered me marriage."

"Impossible. My career would be over. The mind must rule a man in my position, not love."

"Then it is your decision, Sergei Borisovich. It is in your hands. I want my husband with me as chief of Department A."

Nadya got dressed and went home without allowing Antipov to make love to her. Two days later when Viktor returned, he was promoted.

The next evening, while he worked late, Nadya went to Antipov's apartment where they made love for two hours. When he fell asleep she left, filled with hope that Viktor would come home and make love to her.

But it had not happened that way. When she arrived, Viktor was already asleep. The next morning he said nothing to her before he went to work, and for the last few days had been leaving for work before she got up, coming home very late, and going directly to bed.

She now crossed the room, gathered up her clothing, and began to dress, her back to the bed. This was the last time she would have a liaison with Antipov. In fact, she resolved, this was the last liaison she would ever have with anyone. Now that Viktor was in the position she wanted from the beginning, she would try to save their marriage, to bring her husband back—if it were not too late.

When she was dressed, she turned for a last glimpse

at Antipov. He would make trouble, or at least try to, but she would be able to handle him. She would make it crystal clear that if he dragged her husband down, she would drag him, too. If Antipov wanted to continue his career, he would have to make sure Viktor's position was secure, too. She had paid into the account for a long time; now it was time to collect interest.

She left the apartment and took the elevator to the underground garage where Antipov's driver was waiting to take her home—home for the last time.

CHAPTER 10

By the time Horst Steiner arrived at Maria Grindl's apartment he was worn out. The slightest amount of physical exertion seemed to tire him, but he knew that it would be over soon, and in a way he was glad.

The weather was still cold, and the sharp wind blew the rain in gusts that penetrated his body. But the rain would not matter if Maria came up with anything they could send to the West.

He stopped just inside the door of the decaying four-story brick building. Maria lived on the top floor, but right now he did not have the strength to climb the stairs.

He leaned against the mailboxes and tried to catch his breath. His eyes were sunken, his cheeks hollow, and his skin pale, almost translucent. Thin blue veins were visible in his face and neck. His nose was running, but he ignored it as he breathed deeply, trying to clear his spinning head.

One kilo of heroin, the message said. Translated, it meant a hundred grams for Maria, a hundred for Bermann, and two hundred divided among the others, leaving more than a half kilo for himself. Enough for a year of high living, or for a week of sweet agony that would lead to death. Release.

It had been five years since Steiner had made his first contact with the West. In that time he had progressed from money to hash to speed, and for a time, LSD. Then a year ago, to horse itself. The doses he received were carefully controlled by whoever supplied them—enough to hook him, but not enough to kill him. But one kilo, now that was something else.

He pushed himself away from the wall and began to trudge up the dark, narrow stairs. His thick rubber-soled shoes didn't make a sound on the wooden steps.

In the past, the quantity of drugs always matched the job required. If it were a big operation demanding the participation of many friends, the payment was so large that he could spread it around and have plenty left over for himself.

Two weeks ago they had returned from the Polish border where they took pictures of what the Russians were building in the forest. Payment for that job amounted to a hundred grams of heroin. And now, directly on the heels of that enormous payoff, was this.

Why? he wondered. What did Gustav Predel and Kummersdorf mean to the West? Something of vast importance, he was sure; otherwise the offer would never have been made.

On the deserted second-floor landing he had to stop for a few moments to catch his breath, the ragged gasps causing a deep, sharp pain in his chest.

The West Germans had never been that ruthless, at least not since the war; so the supplier had to be American. Steiner was sure of it. But he both loved and hated the man at the other end of the folded bills —loved him for the stuff he supplied, yet hated him for what was happening to him.

"Heroin will kill us all," Maria said one night ten months ago. It was the last time they had made love together.

"It will be better than this," he said, sweeping his hand around her shabby apartment. "What life do we have here?"

"None," she admitted flatly.

He tried to force a smile past his cracked, dry lips but it hurt too much, and he continued up the stairs.

They had planned to be married. They applied to the State Ministry of Records for the proper certificates, and when they received permission, they would move into Maria's apartment.

But all that had changed with the heroin. Now when they were with each other their intimacies were reduced to helping each other shoot horse into any clear spot on their bodies—in the anus, between the toes, in her vagina, behind his ear. Any place where the veins had not already collapsed to bring the sweet relief.

Maria stood in the doorway waiting for him. She was wearing a filthy housedress over which she had thrown a tattered sweater. Her lips were blue, and like him her eyes were sunken. Saliva was encrusted on the corners of her lips, but she was smiling and seemed excited.

She came out into the hall and helped him into her apartment. "I have found out what they wanted," she said breathlessly before they got inside.

"Do you have the information?" he asked, his heart skipping a beat.

She nodded. "Yes, Horst," she said, guiding him into the small apartment and closing the door behind them.

They stood by the door and stared at each other. Her eyes were bright and her face was more animated than he had ever seen it. For an instant he wanted to cry out that he did not want to hear what she had to say. He wanted to run away. But he heard himself talking as if someone else were controlling his vocal cords and his mouth.

"Then I will send a message this afternoon," he said softly. "Bermann says someone has been waiting every day."

"Yesterday you said Kummersdorf West had been moved before 1940," she said.

Steiner nodded. "Unless they made a mistake, there was no Kummersdorf West after that date."

"But it didn't say Kummersdorf *West*, it merely said Kummersdorf," Maria said, excitement in her voice.

"I don't understand, Maria," Steiner said, exhaustion washing through his body. It would be easier to lie down and sleep.

"They meant Kummersdorf *East*," she said.

"Another camp?"

"Yes. A sister camp. Gustav Predel was in Tiefensee. That gave me the clue. I learned that a research camp was at Tiefensee—Kummersdorf East."

"Then we have it?" Steiner asked. He too could feel the excitement rising within him.

"I don't know for sure," Maria said. "A half kilo of heroin means they might want more information."

A pang of guilt stabbed him. He had told them the payoff would be a half kilo, not the full kilo that it really was. He alone had seen the message; this way he would be able to have more for himself.

"Tell me what you know, and I will pass it on. If they need more information, we will have to go to Tiefensee."

"There is not much more. An old woman who lives here in East Berlin told me last night she remembered the Nazi camp near Tiefensee. She also remembered Gustav Predel."

"What became of him?"

"She doesn't know. She's too frightened to talk. She remembers the camp and Predel and some others. Nothing more."

"Why is she still frightened? It's been thirty years."

"I offered her cigarettes and more food, but she would only say that the Russians took the camp away after the trouble."

"What trouble?" Steiner said, trying to force his mind to work. It was difficult.

Maria shook her head. "I don't know, Horst. Will they give us our stuff?"

He took her by the shoulders and held her at arm's length. "What trouble, Maria? What was the old woman talking about?"

"I don't know," she said, tears coming to her eyes. "It was something terrible. She didn't want to talk about it."

"The war? Was it the war and the Russians?"

Maria shook her head again. "I don't know. I don't think so. She said she remembers Predel. He was the commandant of the camp and used to come to the town. She remembers the camp, but was never there. No one could go there. And she also remembers the Russians coming and taking the camp away. The buildings, the fences. Everything."

"And was that the trouble?"

"I don't know. No, I don't think so. There was something else. Something the woman remembered but could not talk about."

Steiner released his grip and turned toward the door. There was so little information for a full kilo of heroin. So little. And he knew that they would have to get more. They would have to go to Tiefensee.

He turned back to Maria. "Pack your things. I'll give Bermann the message and then we'll take the train to Tiefensee."

Marie stiffened. A look of terror crossed her face. "No . . . Horst, we can't. The woman was too frightened. Let's stay here with our . . . stuff."

Steiner shook his head. "It will be dangerous, perhaps, but it has been thirty years. An old woman's fright can mean nothing after all that time."

"Please . . ." Marie pleaded.

"We must," Steiner said, his head clearing somewhat. "It's the only way."

He turned and went out the door and started down the stairs. He could feel her eyes boring into him. This was the only way. He would send the message and advise them that they were going to Tiefensee. In a few days they would return with the rest of the information. They had found Kummersdorf. All that remained was to confirm that Predel had either been killed or captured by the Russians. Either way, their part in this would be finished and the payoff would be made.

Steiner stopped halfway down the stairs, another thought coming to mind. With a full kilo of heroin, they would never need any more. If they got their payoff and escaped to the West, they wouldn't have to share it with the others, and they wouldn't have to do this work anymore. They would be free at last.

He continued down the stairs. They would go to Tiefensee. And in two days they would return to Berlin and send a message that said Predel had been killed by the Russians. That would be the end of it. The payoff would be made, and the Americans would never know the difference.

It was a dangerous thing to do, to lie to them, but it didn't matter anymore. This was the last operation. Once they had the heroin they would be free.

CHAPTER 11

A husky young man with steel-blue eyes and short-cropped hair sat in a nearly bare apartment just off Karl-Marx-Allee in East Berlin reading dispatches from Tiefensee and other places. Most of the messages were routine, but one was different from the others.

He held it up and read the short, clipped sentences once again. "SUBJECT EB 7717 (MARIA GRINDL) OBSERVED. CONTACT WITH T 438 MADE THIS DATE 1924 HRS. ASSUME CONNECTION MADE. 4469A."

It elicited no surprise or concern in him, merely a response.

He destroyed the other messages, and stuffing this one in his pocket, left the apartment and walked to the Soviet embassy.

Downstairs, in the embassy's communications room he sent a message to Moscow. "AUNTY IS SICK STOP SHE IS BEING ATTENDED BY A DOCTOR STOP."

He signed the message "NEPHEW" and while the cipher clerk was busy sending it, he sat and waited for a reply.

One hour later it came. "FIRE THE DOCTOR." It was signed, "GRANDFATHER."

Maria came back into the apartment after Steiner had disappeared down the stairs. She closed the door and leaned against it, trying to catch her breath.

Last night after she had left the old woman's apartment she was sure that she had been followed. She had taken a circuitous route but the man kept up with her. She watched from the window as he walked away, and she almost collapsed with fright.

Who was he? Why had he followed her? There was only one answer. Somehow the East Germans or the Russians had discovered what she and Horst had been doing and were now investigating.

She took the last of the heroin last night and did not awaken until an hour ago, just before Horst showed up. Her head was splitting and a dull rushing sound filled her ears.

He sensed something was wrong, but she was unable to bring herself to tell him what had happened. She could not. If she did, he would call the entire thing off. Then they wouldn't get their payoff. If they didn't get it, she would die.

She moved away from the door and shuffled to the window. As she pushed back the curtains, Horst emerged from the front door and hurried down the street toward his apartment six blocks away. For a moment she debated whether to hurry after him and tell him, but then her heart nearly jumped out of her chest.

He was a half block away when a young man emerged from the doorway of a building across the way and headed down the street. It was the same man who had followed her last night, she was sure of it. He was young and husky and had short-cropped hair. And now he was following Horst.

She turned away from the window, her breath coming in short, ragged gasps. The room seemed to be spinning, and she had to hold onto the end of the bed to keep from falling.

The message would have to be sent. It would have to be. Except for one time, more than three years ago when Horst was sick, he had always sent the messages through Bermann. But he had showed her how the system worked, and she had prepared the ten-mark bill with the vinegar solution and given it to Bermann. It had worked then and there was no reason why it shouldn't work again.

She hurried into the kitchen and stopped in front of the cupboards, her mind working furiously. Vinegar. She didn't have any. Nor did she have the special pen used to write the message on the bill. The equipment she had used the last time was Horst's, and it was in his apartment. He was headed there now, but he was being followed.

She debated a moment whether to try to beat them there, but she knew it would be impossible. She was stuck.

Back in the other room she looked out the window again. No one was there now, and the rain was coming down harder than before. She leaned her head against the cool glass and began to cry. All she could think about was the stuff. She had to have it or die. The message must get to the West. There was no other way.

She pushed away from the window suddenly and hurried to the *Schrank* near her bed. She pulled out her coat and threw it on and then got her purse.

Withdrawing a ten-mark bill, the last of her money, and a pencil, she sat on the edge of the bed and wrote a short message in small print along the decorative edge. The guards on the tour bus wouldn't look at it closely; they would have no reason to, and unless Bermann gave it away they would be okay.

When she was finished, she signed her initials and then hurried out of the apartment to the rear of the building. There she opened a window and climbed out onto the fire escape.

They were probably waiting for her to go out the front again. Only this time she would be smarter.

She hurried down the fire escape and out through

the alley away from the building. The rain was already soaking through her thin cloth coat.

With this message their contact would not only have the information he needed, but he would also know that no more work would be possible here. Knowing that the couple had done their best, the man would have to send them the heroin. And when it arrived she would escape to another part of the city. There were lots of places where a woman alone with a half kilo could hide for a long time.

CHAPTER 12

The weather in Moscow had cleared, although it was very cold. Kozhevnikov sat in a straight-backed chair looking out the window as the sun came up. In the distance, beyond the children's park across the street, the trees and fields to the east were tinged with a golden red. For a moment he almost believed he was at peace with himself. It was a comforting feeling.

Today he would have to make his final decision to stay or leave. To remain loyal or become a traitor. To trade his life in for a very uncertain future. To give up an organized existence for a chaotic horizon.

For the last two days Nadya had become an attentive, loving wife. The sort of person she had been before Sasha had drowned.

He tried to bring his daughter's face into his mind, but he couldn't. It was too long ago. Now the memory of her was nothing more than a dull ache somewhere deep within his soul.

If it had not been for the death of their daughter, their lives would have been different, he had told himself innumerable times. But was that true? Or was there such a thing as predestination? Was each human life decided at birth? Was a man already on the road to what he was to become—toward his certain future—the moment he was born? Didn't the human spirit have any choice?

Last night Nadya and he had made love for the first time in a long while. And it was like coming home after being in a strange and terrible place. She had cried his name in the middle of it, and when they were finished she had drifted off to sleep nestled in his arms.

He laid his head in his hands and began to cry softly. Was there any way to back out? Could he turn away now and leave the Jews in Siberia to whatever fate they had been predestined for? Could he? Could he? The question hammered at his mind over and over like a malevolent pendulum.

More than one thousand teachers, technicians, linguists, and specialists had been sent to Siberia in the last few years. None of them had ever returned. What did it mean? Had he been wrong about the Jews? Were they being trained for some reason?

His mind boggled with the sheer logistics of such an operation. It was impossible to believe that nothing, not one shred of information had leaked out to raise questions. Not even he, as a high-ranking Komitet officer, knew anything about the program even though he had instituted an illegal search for data.

Such an operation was a gamble, he knew. His government wanted something done. But apparently it was so vastly important that the Central Committee or the Politburo had ordered the total disappearance of a hundred thousand human beings despite the risk that their absences would be noted and a hue and cry would go up worldwide.

But why? What was happening out there?

He had lain awake after they made love, listening to Nadya's breathing. Hours after she had gone to sleep he had slipped out of bed and come out into the living room to sit here by the window.

He had three choices. He could stay. He could defect. Or he could approach the head of the First Chief Directorate, tell him he had heard of the Siberian operation, was excited about it and wanted a transfer there.

The first choice was the most comforting. By selecting that one he would have a secure future.

The second decision hurt, not only because he would have to leave his wife, but also because he would have to leave a job undone. One thing he knew for certain was that he really cared about these people, even if they were Jews.

But the third choice, the one he knew Rafn would advise, was the most impossible. If he approached the First Directorate chief or even the chairman of the Komitet himself, he would be brought before a tribunal immediately. Antipov would make sure of that. The files, the computer analysis, all of it had been done illegally. Even if he had not contacted the Americans, he was now a criminal. And then, what would happen to Nadya? What would become of her if he were sent to Siberia? Would she go with him? Presumably she would—and no one would ever hear of them again.

Something touched his shoulder and he jerked around to look up into Nadya's eyes. She had a look of deep concern on her face.

"What is happening to you, Vitya?" she asked softly and knelt on the floor beside him.

He wanted to say that nothing was happening, but he could not even do that.

She took one of his hands in hers, kissed the palm, and then held it against her cheek. "Since Saigon," she began haltingly, "you haven't been yourself. You have changed. What is it, Vitya? Please."

He could not leave with the job undone, nor could he stay here in his present condition. Both options were closed to him. He knew it.

"In Paris and in Munich you were seeing the Americans, weren't you?"

It was like a fist clamping down over his heart. For a moment he remembered Auschwitz thirty years before. They were horrified as they looked through the fence at the piles of human corpses.

"When you returned to Moscow you called out some names in your sleep. One of them was Johnson, another was Gleason. They are Americans."

They had scoured the camp looking for people who were still alive. The ones they found were better off dead.

"Last night you talked about Kummersdorf, Jews, and death."

The stench of the place was still sharp in his mind. It was something he would never forget.

"Vitya, my darling, listen to me, please . . . listen to me. We . . . I can help."

Kozhevnikov looked down at his wife. She was crying, and the look of fright was deep in her eyes.

"You're right," he said without emotion. "I've contacted the Americans."

A low animal moan escaped from her lips and she closed her eyes tightly as if it would block out what she was hearing.

"The Jews," he said. "One hundred thousand of them are being murdered. Slaughtered."

"No, Vitya, darling . . . no. We can help you. The state, the Komitet will help you. It will protect you."

"Listen to me, Nadyenka. A hundred thousand Jews are being murdered. Our country is doing it. Right now. Do you understand that?"

She opened her eyes and looked at him, the fear slowly giving way to something else. "You mean you would become a traitor to your country? You would defect?"

Kozhevnikov nodded. "It's the only way."

She jumped to her feet. "No!" she shrieked. "I won't allow it! We have worked too hard for this! You can't throw it all away!"

She wheeled around and headed across the room

to the telephone. Kozhevnikov jumped up and went after her.

She reached the telephone, but before she could pick it up, he grabbed her arm and spun her around. Her face was a mixture of hate and fear.

"You can be helped, Viktor Vasilievich," she said coldly. "Let me do it for you."

"Who would you call?" Kozhevnikov asked, holding her tightly as she tried to pull free. "Antipov?"

Her eyes narrowed. "Yes!" she shouted.

"No," Kozhevnikov said evenly. "Not your lover."

"Then I'll call someone else. The chairman."

"You would have the blood of a hundred thousand people on your hands? Is that what you want, Nadya?" he said, not believing this was happening. His heart was pounding out of his chest, and his breath was coming rapidly, causing him to hyperventilate and become light-headed.

"They're nothing but Jews," Nadya said harshly.

There was a rushing sound in Kozhevnikov's ears. Everything was slipping down a long narrow tube. He let go of her arm. She turned and reached for the phone. His right hand came around, smashing her in the side of the head. She went down, spinning around as she fell, and her head cracked against the sharp corner of the table.

The apartment was still. The only sound he could hear was his own labored breathing. He bent down, picked her up, and carried her into the bedroom. Even before he laid her down, she was dead.

CHAPTER 13

Rafn got off the tour bus and took a cab back to the Alsterhof. It was still raining when he paid the driver, hurried into the lobby and took the elevator to Schiller's room, but he did not notice it.

Bermann had been extremely nervous. When he handed Rafn his change, he almost dropped the folded ten-mark bill, his hand was shaking so badly. Rafn casually stuffed the money into his pocket, took the tour, and came back here to the Alsterhof without looking at the message.

If Bermann was that nervous, he probably knew what the message said, and whatever it was, was important.

Rafn knocked three times and a moment later the door opened slowly. He went inside, and the door closed behind him. He could smell the sweetness of gun oil close behind him. Schiller sighed and Rafn turned around carefully.

Schiller was holstering his automatic. In the last few days he seemed to be coming apart at the seams. Something was eating at him, but Rafn knew enough not to ask questions. Everytime Rafn went down to the bus terminal, Schiller went to the Israeli embassy. Rafn had followed him on one occasion. Evidently he had learned something very upsetting. It must be something personal. Something he did not want to talk about.

"Did you get anything today?" Schiller asked, running his fingers nervously through his hair.

Rafn nodded, and Schiller almost collapsed with relief.

"Thank God," he breathed. "What did they find out about Predel?"

"I don't know yet," Rafn said, moving across the room and sitting down at the desk where his briefcase was. Schiller followed him across the room and stood behind him as he took a candle out of the large case, set it up in a holder on the desk, and lit it.

Rafn took the bill out of his pocket, unfolded it and was about to hold it over the flame.

Suddenly his heartbeat accelerated. This was all wrong. The message had been written in pencil on the border. Something must have happened.

Rafn took his glasses from his coat pocket, put them on, and smoothed the bill out on the table.

"What's the matter?" Schiller demanded. "What's wrong?"

Rafn wasn't listening; instead he was reading the message for a second time, his heart nearly bursting out of his chest, his gut constricting. "nothing to the west. check kummersdorf east. tiefensee. predel was there. danger. network blown. mg"

Schiller leaned over Rafn's shoulder and read the message. He snatched the bill off the table.

"It was written right on the bill. What the hell is happening?"

Rafn turned slowly in his chair and looked up at Schiller, but said nothing, his mind racing to a dozen possibilities. "network blown," the message said. "danger.'" And it was signed "mg." Maria Grindl. Horst Steiner's girlfriend. But why in pencil? And what did she mean, "network blown?" Bermann had delivered the message. He had not been stopped. Did that mean he knew nothing about this? Or did it mean

Bermann had been allowed to transmit the message so the entire operation would be broken?

"Who the hell is mg?" Schiller was demanding.

"Maria Grindl. She's one of my people," Rafn mumbled. Bermann must have read the message. That would explain his nervousness.

"That's one," Schiller was saying. "Now what the hell is Kummersdorf East?"

Rafn did not answer. Kummersdorf *East,* she had written. He could feel the gooseflesh on his arms. There had been a sister camp. One where Predel had worked. One where Jews had been experimented on. Gleason had been correct—there was a connection. It also meant Kozhevnikov's fears were probably well-founded. And that probably meant that the Soviets were still watching from this end.

He looked up at Schiller, who was studying his face. They would need more answers before they could pull Kozhevnikov out of Moscow. And they needed them fast. But they would have to have Schiller's cooperation. Since Predel was involved, Schiller's information was now of supreme importance.

"Are you really Gleason's man?" Rafn asked softly.

Schiller started to stammer, but Rafn cut him off.

"I have to know."

"I'm with the Israeli Secret Service," Schiller snapped.

"On assignment?"

Schiller didn't answer.

Rafn stood up slowly. "Listen to me, Schiller. This involves a hell of a lot more than just Predel. I have to know what your status is."

"I'm on assignment," Schiller said, subdued suddenly by Rafn's intensity. "But it is unofficial. I have no backing."

"Were you sent to assassinate Predel?"

"Yes."

"Because women—victims of Predel—are still alive in Israel?"

"Yes."

Rafn stared directly into the man's eyes. "Why have you been going to the Israeli embassy every day?"

Schiller shook his head. "I can't tell you," he said, a slight quaver in his voice. "It has nothing to do with this."

Rafn studied his face a moment longer. "Are you Gleason's man?"

"His department has helped me before."

Rafn turned away and sat down again at the desk. "Then I'm going to call him here to brief you. This time you're going to have to help us. Unofficially."

CHAPTER 14

It had been two days since Nadya's body had been cremated and her ashes destroyed. On both mornings Kozhevnikov had risen at the usual time, dressed in his black suit, white shirt and narrow tie, and hung the medal around his neck to wait for his summons.

He had been suspended from his duties in the seventy-two hours since Nadya had died. During that time he had done nothing and gone nowhere except to the cremation. He had not allowed himself to think of anything but the early years, when Sasha was a young girl.

Strangely he had not cried. There were no tears left in him, just a dull emptiness where emotion should have been.

When the knock came at his door this morning, he was ready.

"Comrade Kozhevnikov?" the husky man in the plain suit asked politely.

Kozhevnikov nodded. Two other men were standing in the corridor.

"We have a car for you, sir," the man said.

Kozhevnikov nodded again and went with them downstairs to where a fourth man was waiting with a black sedan. In a half hour they pulled up at KGB headquarters, where they were immediately ushered upstairs without being required to show their passes.

They left him alone in a large anteroom at the end

of the long corridor. He stood at attention facing a heavy metal door at the other side of the room and listened to the sounds of his escorts' footsteps echoing away. A moment later the door opened, and a young man emerged from the room within and beckoned for Kozhevnikov to enter.

The large room was carpeted. The far wall was a floor-to-ceiling window that looked out across the forests behind the building. A few meters in front of the window was a large desk behind which sat the chairman of the KGB. On either side sat Sergei Antipov, Alexander Yurin and Andrei Bolotin. A straight-backed wooden chair sat directly in front of the desk. The chairman, a large, barrel-chested man, motioned for Kozhevnikov to sit down.

"May I offer my condolences at your loss, Comrade Kozhevnikov," he said in a sonorous voice.

"Thank you, Comrade Chairman," Kozhevnikov said, cocking his head to one side.

"Did you murder your wife, Comrade?" the chairman said.

"Yes, sir," Kozhevnikov said. His insides felt weak.

Antipov sat forward and was about to speak, but the chairman silenced him with a glance. When he returned his gaze to Kozhevnikov, his expression was stern, his hands folded calmly in front of him on the desk.

"Why?" he asked.

The office was quiet. Out of the corner of his eye Kozhevnikov could see that although Yurin and Bolotin were looking straight ahead, Antipov was watching him. "My wife believed I was a traitor. She was going to make trouble for me. There was an accident," he said, and he could almost hear Antipov's shock at his admission.

"Are you a traitor, Viktor Vasilievich?" the chairman said calmly.

"No, I am not, Comrade Chairman," Kozhevnikov

said, and he held his breath. The chairman had always seemed to be on the same plane as the premier himself. They were men for whom lies were meaningless. They knew everything, even what was inside a man's soul. But they were also directly involved with the Kummersdorf Project, Kozhevnikov reminded himself.

The chairman said nothing, then turned to Bolotin. "Andrei Andreevich. You were assigned to watch over Comrade Kozhevnikov and his wife during their holiday?"

"Yes, Comrade Chairman," Bolotin said, his voice catching in his throat.

"You were privy to Comrade Kozhevnikov's private conversations with his wife?"

"Yes, Comrade Chairman," Bolotin said, his voice a little stronger. "At their hotel in Paris, on the train to Munich, and at the hotel room there."

"And the topic of their conversations. I mean the substantial meaning of their conversations was what, please?"

"Madame Kozhevnikov's lovers, and Comrade Kozhevnikov's desire for personal freedom, Comrade Chairman."

"Thank you, Bolotin," the chairman said. "That will be all."

Bolotin stood up and marched out of the room stiffly. When he was gone, the chairman turned to Antipov.

"Sergei Borisovich Antipov, were you Madame Kozhevnikov's lover?"

Antipov blanched, and he sat forward. "Comrade Chairman——"

"A simple yes or no, please."

Antipov slumped back in his chair. "Yes," he said softly.

"Do you believe Comrade Kozhevnikov is a traitor?"

"Yes," Antipov said with more feeling in his voice.

"Why?"

Antipov seemed to struggle for words for a moment,

but then he blurted, "His personal freedom, that is what Comrade Andreevich told me. His decided softening toward Western cultures. His frequent absences in Western Europe."

"Thank you, Sergei Borisovich, that will be all."

Antipov started to protest, but the chairman merely stared at him, and a moment later Antipov rose and went quietly out of the office. The chairman turned his attention now to Yurin, the chief computer technician who was visibly on the verge of collapse.

"Alexander Dmitrievich. You have finished tracing the tapes?"

"Yes, Comrade Chairman," Yurin barely squeaked. He handed across a thin file folder.

"Thank you, that will be all," the chairman said, taking the file but not looking at it for the moment.

Yurin jumped up and scurried out of the room like a rabbit. Kozhevnikov's gaze had not yet left the chairman's face.

When Yurin was gone, the chairman set the file aside and sat back in his chair. He studied Kozhevnikov for a long moment and then a sad smile came across his face and he shook his head.

"Viktor Vasilievich . . . what must we do with you?"

Kozhevnikov said nothing.

"Personal freedom is such an elusive thing, Viktor. Vasilievich. None of us are free. Certainly I am not free. I am answerable to my superiors, to the Politburo, the premier. You are answerable to Antipov and to me. Freedom from prying eyes is only a state of mind. Once it is accepted that men of our position and importance must be watched, it becomes like sunlight to us. Consider, Viktor Vasilievich: If we did not watch you, you would not be important. But you are watched and therefore you are important. And because you are important, you are therefore watched."

Kozhevnikov held his silence. The man was not a

simpleton, he was sure of it, but his logic was simplistic. It was as if the chairman were the father, and Kozhevnikov the infant son.

The chairman studied his expression for a few moments, and then he sighed. "I am truly sorry about Nadya. But you did not kill her, Viktor Vasilievich, she killed herself. It was unfortunate. And forgive Antipov, he is a dedicated man, although somewhat overzealous and lacking in tact." He looked down suddenly at the file folder, and then back up. "But this, Viktor Vasilievich, this is of a different nature. Tell me what you know about Operation Outlook."

The term was new to Kozhevnikov. "Comrade?" he said.

The chairman flipped open the file, read something, and then closed it again. "Perhaps you are not familiar with the code name. What do you know about the so-called Kummersdorf Papers?"

This was it then. He had been found out. He could not lie. "I ran across it a few years ago when I was in from Hanoi for a committee meeting."

"At that time you began your inquiries?"

"Yes, Comrade. I learned that a hundred thousand Jews had been sent to Siberia. I have also learned, from the computer, that a thousand technicians and instructors have been sent there also."

"You are a curious man."

"Yes, Comrade Chairman," Kozhevnikov said, every fiber in his body straining to hold himself in check. He knew that if the man asked him about his contact with the Americans he would tell everything.

"Now you believe we are murdering the Jews, is that correct?"

Kozhevnikov was surprised by the directness of the question, and it evidently showed on his face because the chairman smiled.

"That is simply not true, Viktor Vasilievich. We are not murdering a hundred thousand Jews. But you shall see."

"Sir?" Kozhevnikov said, sitting forward.

"Would you like to become involved in Operation Outlook, Viktor Vasilievich?"

"Yes, sir," Kozhevnikov said, his heart pounding.

"Then you shall be. I will arrange your reassignment. It is a reward for your excellent work in reorganizing your department. You shall leave tomorrow morning."

Kozhevnikov was speechless. The chairman knew nothing about the Americans. Or did he? Kozhevnikov turned that thought over in his mind for a moment. No one who had ever been sent to Siberia on this operation ever came back. Was his assignment now a reward or a punishment?

"Thank you, Viktor Vasilievich. That will be all," the chairman said.

PART THREE

CHAPTER 1

It was seven-thirty and finally light when Meitner got up and dressed in an old pair of slacks, a sweater, and his slippers. He had not been able to sleep, and now his back was sore from tossing and turning.

After he splashed some cold water on his face, he trudged down to the basement, unlocked the door to his laboratory, and turned on the light. Everything was the same as it had been yesterday. Nothing had changed. Nothing had been tampered with.

After the last of the reporters had finally departed, he left the lab and went home in a cab. Mounting the front steps, he was about to enter his house, when a woman came out of the house next door and hurried across the lawn to him.

"Dr. Meitner?" she asked, out of breath, stopping at the foot of the stairs and looking up at him.

He turned to her. "Yes?" he said, annoyed. He did not want to see any more people. He had had enough of them today to last a lifetime.

She apparently sensed his impatience, because she hurried. "I'm Mrs. Bernardi."

Meitner said nothing and waited for her to continue.

"I hate to bother you like this, but there was someone at your house today and I thought you would want to know about it. I mean, since you do value your privacy and all. And seeing as how you just won the Nobel Prize."

Meitner could feel a constriction in his chest. He thought immediately of his basement laboratory, but he forced himself to be calm. "When was that, Frau Bernardi?" he asked.

"This morning," she said, pleased that he would talk to her. "Just after ten-thirty. I was just——"

"Who was it, do you know?"

She shook her head. "It was a young woman. She was thin and had long blonde hair. Dressed to the nines. She came in a taxi and just walked up to your door and let herself in, pretty as you please."

He could feel the blood rushing from his face. The woman took a step forward as he turned, but he waved her off.

"Can I help . . ." she started to say, but he wasn't listening as he entered the house and slammed the door behind him.

Downstairs he studied the combination lock on the door to the lab. The dial was still set halfway between the numbers seventeen and eighteen, exactly where he had left it this morning. Whoever was here had not tampered with it, unless the lock had been reset to exactly the same spot.

With shaking hands he worked the combination, and when the lock clicked open he unlatched the door, went inside, and flipped on the light.

The low ceiling and walls in the large room were spotlessly white, and the perma-wax tiled floor gleamed under the overhead fluorescent lighting. The large work-table in the center of the room was neat and orderly, just as he had left it, and the chattering of the animals in the cages along the back wall was somehow comforting to him.

He closed the door behind him, locking it from the inside with a large deadbolt, and then crossed the room to the desk that was set in an alcove with a cot, a refrigerator, and a low bench with a hot plate and some dishes on it. Nothing in the room had been disturbed.

But now this morning, he was sure someone could have been there. Professionals who had known not to disturb anything. They could have come in, taken pictures, and left.

He sat down at the desk. The woman who had been here yesterday morning was probably a reporter. If that were the case he would be okay. She had probably just come in, looked around upstairs, and when she found nothing, left.

He picked up the telephone and dialed Dr. Stewart's office. After ten rings, he hung up and looked at his watch. It wasn't eight o'clock yet. Stewart would not be in his office until nine.

This time he dialed Stewart's home phone, and after a few rings it was answered by a woman.

"Stewarts' residence."

"This is Hans Meitner, let me talk with Dr. Stewart."

"Dr. Meitner," the woman said in surprise. "This is Charlene Stewart. I'd like to offer my congratulations."

"Thank you," Meitner mumbled. "But is Dr. Stewart there? It is of some importance."

"Of course," the woman said. "Just a moment."

One of the animals in the cages began to whimper, but as Meitner rose to go to it, Stewart came on the line.

"Hans, is something the matter?" he said. He sounded concerned.

But the guinea pig was silent now, and Meitner slumped down into his chair.

"Someone was here yesterday morning," he said.

"At the laboratory?" Stewart said, confused.

"No, here at my home," Meitner said impatiently. "My neighbor tells me a woman arrived in a taxi and let herself into my house."

"I don't know what to say, Hans," Stewart said.

"She was a young woman. She evidently had a key because she let herself in. What do you know about it?" Meitner could hear the bluntness in his own voice, and he tried to control it. If he made a big fuss out of this, Stewart might call the police. He could not have that.

"I don't know anything about it . . ." Stewart started to say, but then he paused a moment. "Wait a moment. You said a young woman?"

"Yes," Meitner said guardedly.

"Did your neighbor describe her?"

"Yes," Meitner said again.

"Long blonde hair. Dressed very nicely. Pretty."

"That is she," Meitner said, feeling his stomach churn. "Who is she? What does she want?"

"She spoke with me the night before last. Her name is Laurie Andrews. I was supposed to set her up for an interview with you yesterday morning. She was seated in the back of the auditorium during the news conference, but by the time it was over she was gone."

"How do you know it was the same woman?" Meitner asked.

"I'm just assuming that. Everyone else identified themselves at the news conference. Andrews wasn't among them, so I'm sure the woman in the back of the audience, the one who was at your house yesterday, was she."

"But who is she?" Meitner snapped. "And why was she here?"

"She's a reporter with the *National Weekly*. It's a newspaper in New Orleans. And like everyone else, she wants to do a story about you. Evidently she wanted to look around your house to see if she could find anything interesting. Do you want me to call the police? Is anything missing?"

"No . . . no, don't do that," Meitner quickly said. "Nothing was disturbed, so it is of no consequence."

"Are you sure?" Stewart said.

"Positive."

"All right, then, I'll see you at the lab."

Meitner was about to say yes, but then another thought stopped him. The other reporters had been content to interview him at the news conference, but she had not. She had come out here looking for something. What? What did she know?

"I won't be in this morning," he said after a moment. "I'm not feeling well."

There was instant concern in Stewart's voice. "Is something the matter, Hans?" he asked.

"No, I'm just a bit overtired. I'm going to stay home today, maybe all weekend."

"Is there anything I can do?" Stewart asked. "Can I call a doctor, or come out there?"

"No," Meitner said quickly. "Everything is fine. I'll be in on Monday. I just need to rest."

"All right, then," Stewart said after a slight hesitation. "But if you need anything, Hans, anything at all, don't hesitate to call me."

"Thank you," Meitner said and hung up. What did the woman want, and how much did she know? If she were still here in Madison he was sure she would have tried to contact him by now. Perhaps she had returned to New Orleans.

He knew he wasn't thinking straight, but he couldn't help himself as he picked up the phone and dialed the operator with a shaking hand. He would have to confront her and ask her directly what she knew and where she had gotten the key. He could see all of his work going down the drain.

The operator answered. "Operator."

"I want to place a call to the *National Weekly,* a newspaper in New Orleans. I don't know the number."

"Would you like me to dial it for you, sir?"

"Yes," Meitner said.

"One moment," the operator said.

Meitner closed his eyes and took a deep breath, letting it out slowly. He could feel the dull pain deep within his chest. Soon it would become more localized and more intense. When that happened he would have to begin taking pain killers and he would not be able to work. He was so close . . . so damned close.

The operator was back, and in the background he could hear the phone ringing. "What is your number, please?"

Meitner told the operator his telephone number, and on the third ring the phone was answered.

"National Weekly."

"Yes, hello," Meitner said. "I would like to speak with Laurie Andrews, please."

"One moment," the operator said, and she broke the connection. A few seconds later she was back. "Ms. Andrews is not here at the moment. Can anyone else help you?"

"Could you tell me where she is? I must speak with her," Meitner said. Perhaps she was still here in Madison.

The operator was gone for a much longer time, and when she came back she was apologetic. "Mr. Shapiro, the managing editor, has not come in yet. He would know specifically where Ms. Andrews is."

"Miss Andrews was in Madison, Wisconsin, yesterday. Perhaps she is still there?"

"No, sir," the operator said. "She is on assignment in Europe. Where specifically, I don't know. If you would care to call later——"

Meitner hung up the telephone, his breath catching in his throat. He could feel the rattle deep in his chest and it ached now. Europe. Germany. She did know something. And when she found out everything, she would expose him.

He rose slowly, left the laboratory without closing the door, and trudged upstairs to his bedroom where he began to pack a suitcase.

He would have to find her before it was too late. He

would have to find her and tell her the entire story if necessary. With a little bit of knowledge she would be dangerous, but if she knew everything, she would have to hold her story back. She would understand that what he had been doing for the past thirty-five years was so important it could not be stopped by some story in an inconsequential newspaper.

She would have to understand that. But if she didn't, he would have to stop her.

CHAPTER 2

Sylvan Bindrich had come alone to West Berlin and now he sat at a table on the Dobermann Terraces with Rafn and Schiller. Today was the first warm, sunny day in the past two weeks in Western Europe, and the open-air restaurant was moderately busy.

Bindrich looked up from the message at Rafn. "We're pulling you out of this. You can return to Copenhagen today."

"I sent for Gleason," Rafn said quietly. "Schiller is working for him."

Bindrich glanced at the Israeli. "Gleason has been pulled off this as well."

"Because of Schiller?"

Bindrich smiled. "That's company business. I'm running this operation now."

"What about Kozhevnikov?" Rafn said, keeping his voice even. He had half expected something like this. Gleason, like Kozhevnikov, was too mild-mannered and honest a man to be in this business. Only the bastards like Bindrich and himself survived.

Again Bindrich glanced toward the Israeli. "How much does he know?"

Rafn smiled. It was a wedge. "Enough to make him valuable."

Schiller, who had remained quiet through all of this, started to speak, but Bindrich cut him off.

"My president has been advised of your presence here, Schiller, and by now he has contacted your prime minister. I expect you will be receiving your recall orders today."

"Until then I'm on assignment," Schiller said.

Bindrich shook his head. "Tel Aviv knew nothing of your assignment. You're on vacation." Bindrich studied his face for a moment. "Perhaps the attorney general's office here in Berlin should be notified of your presence."

Schiller had turned white. "I would kill you first."

"I don't think so," Bindrich said after a moment. "You want this Predel, whoever he is. We're prepared to deliver him if and when we find him." He stood up. "Return to Tel Aviv, Schiller. We'll take care of this."

He was lying, Rafn knew it. Schiller, like Gleason, was a sacrificial lamb.

"I want to speak with you a moment, Rafn. Alone," Bindrich said.

Rafn rose and followed the man away from the table, and as they headed up the broad steps toward the parking lot, Bindrich glanced back at the table where Schiller remained seated.

"I don't like you very much, Rafn, but I'm not pulling you off this for that reason."

"For what, then?" Rafn asked.

"Kozhevnikov contacted our man in Moscow yesterday. His wife is dead and he is on his way to the Siberian operation. He's been reassigned."

"What if he can't get him out of there when he has the information we need?"

"Then we'll reopen the operation from this end."

"By then it will be too late. They will have backtracked and discovered everything."

Bindrich was frustrated. "It won't matter by then."

Rafn looked at him in amazement. He was stupid. "You still don't believe Kozhevnikov's story, do you?"

"It doesn't matter," Bindrich said after a moment.

"If he doesn't get out of there, we'll go further with this. There might be something to it, after all."

"But if he does, it's probably a disinformation plot and he'll be dumped," Rafn said.

"That's right, Rafn," Bindrich said drawing himself up. "I didn't make the rules for this game any more than you did, so let's not bullshit each other. You're in it for the money or for whatever perverse pleasure you get out of controlling a dozen people's lives with your heroin."

"And you're in it for God, country, and flag?" Rafn said sarcastically.

Bindrich said nothing at first. But when he spoke there was a cutting edge to his voice. "Gleason overstepped his authority on this one and he's out. Schiller is being pulled back by his own people. And you're next. You once told the director not to push you. I'm telling you now, Rafn, don't push us. You'll lose."

"You haven't got the man to do it," Rafn said softly.

"We'll cut you off."

"I'll go free lance."

Bindrich was about to say something else, but apparently thought better of it. He sighed tiredly. "I don't want to play this game with you, Rafn. You're a damned good operative—perhaps the best we have. They were pleased with your last assignment. Now leave this one alone. We'll handle it. Kozhevnikov came to us with a story. It's up to him to back it up with hard evidence. If he can do it we'll go along with him. If he can't, he'll be dumped. We'll make his contact with us known publicly."

Rafn started to speak, but Bindrich interrupted him.

"Your own people say the East Zone net is blown. That means either the East German authorities have stumbled onto their operation, or the Soviets are indeed watching from this end. Either way, if you go in there, they'll get you. That's the least that could happen. The worst is that Kozhevnikov's cover will be blown and we'll never find out what's happening."

Rafn remained silent. What Bindrich was saying was all true. But he was not being sincere. Rafn was certain of it. Kozhevnikov was going to be dumped. The decision had already been made. If Bindrich had been telling the truth, he would have stayed to find out exactly what Schiller knew and how Predel fit into all of this. But Bindrich did not care. He had pulled the necessary strings to have Schiller removed from the scene. Gleason was out and now Rafn, the last link in the chain, was being removed.

"Return to Copenhagen, Rafn," Bindrich was saying. "Take a vacation. Another assignment will be coming up soon."

Rafn nodded. "Have a good trip back," he said.

Bindrich studied his face for a moment, then shrugged. Without a word he turned and went up the steps, walked through the restaurant, and was gone.

Rafn watched until he was out of sight, and then turned and went back to Schiller. Bindrich had evidently convinced Washington that Kozhevnikov's story was nothing more than a disinformation plot. It was up to him now to convince them otherwise.

Before he sat down, the possibility that it was a disinformation plot crossed his mind. Maybe Bindrich was correct. He shrugged it off and sat down across from the Israeli.

"We're on our own," he said and Schiller sat forward.

"When I get my recall orders I'll have to return."

"*If* you get your orders," Rafn corrected. "Without them you're still on assignment. Correct?"

Schiller smiled. "Correct. Now who is Kozhevnikov, what is Kummersdorf, and what does all of this have to do with Predel?"

Rafn was silent while he lit a cigarette and ordered more cognac for them. When their drinks arrived he began.

"Kozhevnikov is a high-ranking KGB officer, Disinformation Service. Ten days ago he came to us with a story about a Jewish pogrom going on in the Soviet Union."

A strange look crossed Schiller's features and Rafn stopped. "What is it?"

"Continue," Schiller said, a choked sound to his voice.

"Have you heard of Kozhevnikov? The pogrom? What is it? What's the matter?"

"Finish your story first," Schiller said.

"There isn't much more," Rafn said slowly. "Kozhevnikov mentioned 'Kummersdorf' in connection with this pogrom. That has led us to Kummersdorf East at Tiefensee and coincidentally to Predel, who was the facility's director."

"Medical experimentation," Schiller said.

"That's my assumption," Rafn said. "Meanwhile, Kozhevnikov has been reassigned to the Kummersdorf operation somewhere in Siberia."

"Siberia?" Schiller said, nearly falling out of his chair.

Rafn nodded, and after a moment Schiller sank back, his face turning white.

"My God," he breathed.

"What is it, Schiller?" Rafn asked.

At first Schiller couldn't speak, but when he looked up he was almost on the verge of collapse. "My sister," he said. "That is why I have been going to my embassy every day. Before I left Tel Aviv I learned she had not made her regular contact in nearly nine months."

"What are you talking about?" Rafn demanded.

Schiller took a deep breath. "My sister is also in this business. She has been stationed in Moscow for the last two years. Jews have been quietly disappearing all over the Soviet Union for several years now, and we sent in some of our people to find out what was happening. About a year ago she learned that some of our people had been sent to a farming cooperative in Siberia. They were supposedly given land and equipment in exchange for developing the land."

"Go on," Rafn prompted after Schiller stopped.

"Nine months ago she sent out the message that she was trying to get assigned to that project so she could find out what was really happening."

"And since then no one has heard from her," Rafn completed it for him.

Schiller nodded. "Now you tell me this is somehow connected with Gustav Predel and the Kummersdorf facility. It sounds like the Nazis all over again."

CHAPTER 3

It was four o'clock in the afternoon when Laurie Andrews emerged from the domestic travel gate at Tempelhof. The short flight from Hannover aboard the aging twin-engine propeller-driven airplane had upset her stomach. Because of this and her weariness from constant running for the past few days, all she wanted to do was lie down and sleep. But she couldn't. Not yet. Meitner was a fraud, and she knew it. All she had to do now was prove it, and find out who he really was.

By five she had checked into the Berlin Hilton and was on the telephone to the Deutches Bundeskrankenhaus. The switchboard operator at the hospital had no trouble with English, but when she got the records section, the man she spoke with was barely understandable.

"Hans Meitner of the Nobel Prize?" the man asked again.

"Yes," Laurie repeated herself. "Did he work at the hospital?"

"No, Dr. Meitner does not work here. He is in the United States."

"I know that," Laurie said, frustrated. "I want to know if Dr. Meitner worked there during the war."

"The war?" the man said. "I don't understand."

"Did Dr. Meitner work at the hospital during the war?" Laurie said, enunciating each word carefully.

After a hesitation the man exclaimed, "I understand.

225

No, Dr. Meitner never worked here."

"Are you sure?" Laurie said excitedly.

"Sure? Yes, I am sure. Dr. Meitner not here. Never."

"Thank you. Thanks very much," Laurie said, and she hung up.

She opened her briefcase and pulled out the documents she had gathered so far.

Laurie held up the birth certificate she had purchased at the *Rathaus* in Garmisch-Partenkirchen.

"Meitner, Hans Dieter," had been born at 11:07 in the morning, August 5, 1911, which would have made him sixty-six. That fit.

She laid the birth certificate on the desk and pulled out the graduation record that she had obtained from the University of Heidelberg two days ago.

He had graduated from the Medical College in 1937 with honors. He had been immediately assigned to the Stanhof Krankenhaus, a large teaching hospital in Berlin.

A quick telephone call to the hospital had confirmed that as well. Meitner had indeed been assigned in 1937 and stayed until 1940, when he moved to Hannover to open his own practice.

Laurie laid the university record next to the birth certificate and extracted the next document from her briefcase. She stared at it for a long time and then smiled.

Yesterday she had flown up from Frankfurt to Hannover and taken a taxi directly to the ornate city hall building that had been rebuilt after the war. The clerk assured her that most of the city records had survived the war and that he would be able to help her.

"Do you have a record of medical doctors who were licensed to practice here before and during the war?" Laurie asked.

"Yes, of course," said the clerk, a mild-mannered young man with thick glasses. His English was good. "Who would you like to learn about?"

"A Dr. Hans Dieter Meitner. He transferred here from the Stanhof Hospital in Berlin in 1940. Ten years later he emigrated to the United States."

"If you would just take a seat, this will take a few minutes," the young man said, indicating a grouping of chairs to one side of the counter.

While she waited, she smoked a cigarette and looked through the magazines on the coffee table. In ten minutes the young man was back, a puzzled look on his face.

She got up and went to him at the counter. "Did you find anything?" she asked.

The clerk nodded. "Yes, I did. However, there seems to be some confusion."

"With what?" Laurie asked.

"Meitner received his license to practice here in 1940, but that ended in 1944, as you can see," he said and handed a document to her.

It was in German.

"This is a death certificate. Dr. Meitner was killed during the bombing of Hannover on May 17th, 1944." He looked up. "A mistake must have been made. He could not be the same man who emigrated to the United States in 1950."

Laurie stood perfectly still, barely breathing as she stared at the death certificate in her hand. When she finally looked up the clerk was watching her with a curious expression on his face.

"Is something the matter?" he asked politely.

"No," Laurie mumbled. "Can I have a copy of this?" she asked.

"That's a copy. I made it for you. I assumed you would want it."

Laurie laid it on the desk with the other documents and sat back and lit a cigarette. That had been the first crack in Meitner's armor, or rather the first crack in the story of the man who claimed he was Meitner.

Evidently he did something during the war that he wanted no one to know about, so he went to Hannover, found records on a doctor who had recently died, and then simply assumed his identity. Records were so confused that the Americans would believe almost anything. Obviously no one had checked through death records when Meitner applied for immigration status. He was a doctor, he had accepted a job at an American university, and he had been granted immigrant status.

She would have been completely lost, however, if Shapiro had not come up with the next step.

After she had paid for the copy of the death certificate, she went back to her hotel to think. She was at a dead end. There was no way she could trace the background of the man who claimed to be Meitner. She had nothing to go on.

In desperation she called Phil Shapiro. It was just after nine in the morning in New Orleans, and he seemed excited to hear from her.

She quickly told him what she had found out so far, which proved that the man who had just won the Nobel Prize was not named Hans Meitner. But she admitted she was now stumped.

"Maybe I can help," Shapiro said.

"Anything will help, Phil," she said. "If you haven't got anything for me, I might as well hang this one up, because I'm sure Meitner, or whoever the hell he really is, won't tell us anything."

"Oh, yes, he will," Shapiro said. "Maybe not directly, but he sure as hell is telling us something indirectly."

"What have you got?" she asked, picking up on his excitement.

"Number one," Shapiro began. "I sent our team up to Madison yesterday with the key you sent us. When they got there they found out Meitner had left town."

"Left town?" Laurie said. "Where did he go?"

"Are you ready for this, sweetheart?" Shapiro said. "He booked a flight to Munich. He's in Germany right now."

Laurie's mind was spinning. Meitner in Germany? "Why?" she asked out loud.

"From what I understand, Meitner's neighbor saw you entering the house. Someone at the university identified you, and Meitner put two and two together and figured you were hot on his trail. Whatever he did during the war, he's probably trying to cover up right now. It's my guess he's just a step behind you. So be careful, doll."

Laurie was silent for a moment. Meitner coming after her proved he had something to hide. But was he a dangerous man? She seriously doubted it.

"You said number one, Phil. Does that mean you've got something else?"

"Yes. The team got into his basement lab. There wasn't much there that made any sense except for his journal."

"His name was in it?"

"No," Shapiro said. "But there were several other names scattered throughout the book, one of them—Gustav Predel—was repeated at least three dozen times. That and the Deutches Bundeskrankenhaus, a hospital in Berlin.

"And listen to this. The DBK was one of the places where the Nazis did medical experimentation on Jews before the war. If Meitner was a part of it, and we can prove it, it'll make one hell of a story."

"OK, Phil, I'll check into it right away," Laurie said and hung up.

Now she was going to have to see those World War Two hospital records. Although she did not know Meitner's real name, she did know the name of someone he had been associated with at the hospital. Gustav Predel. Perhaps he would provide the next clue.

CHAPTER 4

Rafn and Schiller shared adjoining rooms in a run-down hotel on the far south side of the city. At night they could see the intense lights that shone on the Berlin wall two blocks away. During the day the view from their windows was of a European slum.

After Bindrich had left yesterday, they had moved to this hotel, Rafn had prepared another message and passed it to Bermann. This morning Schiller was to get the reply.

Rafn lay in bed, smoking a cigarette. The stubble of two days' whiskers was a dirty gray on his face. He had not put on a new change of clothes in three days.

He watched the smoke curl up toward the dirty, cracked ceiling of the small room and thought about how different he and Kozhevnikov were. Their only thing in common was the three months they had been together during the war. Other than that there were no similarities.

Externally they were different. Kozhevnikov was married, or at least had been. Rafn was not. Kozhevnikov was orderly in his appearance while Rafn was sloppy. Kozhevnikov was a Communist and Rafn was . . . what?

The major difference between them, he decided, was their idealism. Kozhevnikov was an idealistic man. He loved his wife, his job, and his country. He was motivated by devotion. It was what had convinced Rafn that something terrible was indeed going on in Siberia.

It had to be, otherwise Kozhevnikov would not have wanted to defect.

But Rafn was motivated for other reasons that did not include love of a person, a job, or a country, or even an ideal.

Ideals were for children, he firmly believed. Children and the infirm. The only reality was one's own existence, which in most cases was petty and miserable.

He turned over on his side, stubbed the cigarette out in the overflowing ashtray, and then got up and went to the window.

It was raining again after the one-day respite. And from the looks of the low-hanging clouds, it would rain for several more days.

He had no love for Denmark, and certainly none for the United States, or even for the loosely defined Western world. But he had no love for the Soviet Union or China or any of the Eastern bloc countries, either. Perhaps, he told himself, he was a man incapable of love.

He lit another cigarette, the last one, crumpled the pack, and let it drop to the floor at his feet.

The smoke burned his throat and lungs, but that did not matter, either. It was merely a part of living. Pain and pleasure were the same. They were signs of life. The Western world or the Eastern bloc meant nothing. They were terms merely indicating philosophies that were, in the last analysis, hardly different from one another.

In the Soviet Union there were dedicated people. Hardworking people. People who loved and hated. People who smoked and people who drank. People who went to the sports stadiums on Saturday and the churches on Sunday.

Was that any different from the United States? From Denmark or England or Albania or Germany?

The arguments were always the same. It always came back to the same point in Rafn's mind. He was a loner in a world of gregarious people. A single in a world of couples. Except for one time in his life, when he had become directly involved with and responsible for another human being, he had been a free man.

Patton's army was poised to the west of the city while the Russian artillery pounded from the east. For six days the shelling had been going on twenty-four hours a day, and yet no surrender message had come out of the city.

Hitler's bunker was the key, they had been told. Find it, capture or kill the Führer, and we can be done with this.

Kozhevnikov and Rafn had been sent as a team into the city to search for the bunker. They had been assigned a four-square-block area around the shell of the bombed-out Reichs Chancellory Bunker. Other Soviet-American teams were searching different sections of the city.

They had been working steadily at it for the past four days, and this evening both men were dead tired. On Rafn's suggestion they had been using telephone-tap equipment to cut into the underground lines beneath the streets. It was Rafn's idea that sooner or later they would tap into the phone lines that led out of the bunker and from there could direct a strike force to effect Hitler's capture and end the war.

Another fear also motivated the intelligence mission, however, and that was the so-called National Redoubt. It had been rumored that Hitler and an elite corps of his SS troops would move south into the mountains around Salzburg, and from there would wage guerrilla warfare, harrying the Allies, possibly for years.

It was possible, they had been told, that this had already happened. Hitler might already be out of Berlin and on his way to Salzburg. Find out.

It was late, two o'clock in the morning, when Rafn disconnected the equipment from the lines they were working on.

"Nothing," he said, looking up at Kozhevnikov.

They were in a narrow tunnel eight feet beneath the street. The cables attached to the walls disappeared into the distance through the darkness.

Kozhevnikov looked at his watch. "It's late," he said. "Shall we continue, or do you want to go back and get some sleep?"

Rafn had finished packing the equipment in the canvas bag. "Let's try once more, and then we can go back."

Kozhevnikov nodded and started up the ladder which led to the manhole cover in the middle of the street, his body momentarily blocking out the light from the burning buildings across from them. Once he was outside, Rafn scrambled up the ladder after him.

Kozhevnikov stood with his hands up, and as Rafn's head emerged from the manhole he could see two Germans in black *Waffen SS* uniforms holding machine guns on them.

"Komm raus!" one of them shouted at Rafn who stopped on the ladder.

Rafn carefully reached down for his knife in the leather scabbard strapped to his chest; using the canvas bag as a shield, he climbed awkwardly out of the manhole. The German who had ordered him up was about to say something else when Rafn shoved Kozhevnikov against him and in two steps was on the other, dropping the canvas bag and swinging the knife up, opening the man's gut. In the next instant the first guard had extricated himself from Kozhevnikov and was swinging a machine gun around directly at the Russian's head. Rafn flipped the knife underhanded, burying it to the handle in the man's throat.

For a few seconds it seemed as if the German would fire anyway, but then he pitched backwards without a sound, twitched on the ground a moment, and then died.

Kozhevnikov was shaking, and in the light from the burning buildings his face looked sickly white.

"You know your life belongs to me now," Rafn said.
Kozhevnikov's brows knitted. *"Bitte?"*

"It is an old custom. I've just saved your life, and now it belongs to me. For the rest of your life I will be responsible for you."

Kozheynikov smiled in understanding. "Treat me well, then, my friend," he said.

Someone was knocking at the door. Rafn moved quietly across the room.

"Yes?" he said.

"It's me," Schiller's voice came through the thin wooden door.

Rafn let him in, checked the corridor, and then closed the door and turned to the Israeli. "Was there a reply today?"

Schiller nodded and handed him the ten-mark bill.

Rafn took it and went across the room to a small table where he lit a candle and began heating the bill over the open flame. "Did you have any trouble?" he asked, as Schiller came up behind him.

"None, but Bermann looks about ready to crack."

Rafn watched carefully as faint brown lines appeared against the pale green ink around the border. In Rafn's message, directed at Bermann himself, he had merely asked if it were possible to get two men into the East Zone.

Despite Bindrich's warning, he and Schiller had agreed that more information would be needed—and fast—in case Kozhevnikov was not able to get out of Siberia. If they waited too long, whatever information was still available from this end would be covered up, Rafn was sure of it.

The reply from Bermann was simple and direct: "YES. IF OF UTMOST IMPORTANCE. STEINER IS MISSING AND MG IS AWAITING PAYMENT. GIVE PHYSICAL DESCRIPTIONS AND TIME-DATE YOU WISH TO ENTER. WB."

CHAPTER 5

Meitner was breathing hard, and the sharp pain throbbed in his chest as he paid the driver and stood on the sidewalk looking across the mall toward the hospital buildings that comprised the DBK. Nothing was the same. Everything had changed since the war.

The feelings he had expected to have upon returning did not come. He had never been at this place, at least not as it appeared now. Before the war the buildings had been old and substantial—brownstones with tall ceilings and high windows. The scene he looked upon now was almost exactly the opposite. The buildings were modern—steel, glass, and cement. Doctors and white-uniformed nurses hurried through the mall, but not one uniformed soldier could be seen.

So much had changed, he mused. Not only here, but everywhere he had been, change had been evident.

It was due mostly, he knew, to the war. This place had been completely destroyed by the Allied bombing, as had many of the other places he had visited in the last two days. But the change ran deeper than that. Deeper than just reconstruction. The entire feeling of the country, of the people, of attitudes, was different. Americanized. He no longer felt comfortable here in his own country.

Meitner felt like an old man, tired and used up, as he began to shuffle across the parklike mall and up the

235

wide steps into the main building. He was frightened, too, of what he might find here, for the reporter from the *National Weekly,* Laurie Andrews, had already been making inquiries. She knew now that Meitner was not his real name.

Twice this morning he had gotten into a cab and ordered the driver to bring him here to the DBK. Both times he had changed his mind and had the driver take him back to his hotel.

Even though the young woman knew his real name was not Meitner, she still did not know his real identity, or what he had done during the war. Unless . . .

He turned the thought over in his mind. Unless she had learned something here at the hospital. This was the only place where there was any possibility of a record, and he was frightened to ask if a young woman had been here inquiring about him.

He stopped a few meters away from the information desk in the center of the huge lobby.

There was no way the woman could connect him with this hospital. Meitner had worked at the Stanhof before the war. He had never practiced here.

Once she had come up with his death certificate in Hannover, she would be at a dead end. There was no reason for her to come here. None.

He would return to his hotel, pack his bags and go home. He was only being foolish. She had found out nothing, really, except that his name was not Meitner. Not really Hans *Dieter* Meitner, at any rate. Perhaps he could convince her that his name was Hans Wilhelm Meitner. Or Hans Peter Meitner. That would explain the mix-up.

He shook his head. She would never believe it. She would check his new story, in all likelihood. And sooner or later she would want to know his real name and what he did during the war. But before he faced her, he would have to make certain that there was no record here at the DBK she could eventually uncover.

The woman at the information desk directed him to the elevators which would take him down to the hospital's records section.

Two other people got off the elevator with him and directed him to the right.

Standing before the door to the records section, he realized with a shock that he recognized the place. This was part of the old hospital. Very little had changed, and he could remember being down here more than thirty-five years ago.

He could feel his heart pounding against his ribs. Each time he breathed, the pain in his chest throbbed and grew worse, making him almost faint.

The young woman could not have been here. There was no reason for her to suspect he had ever worked here. None.

He pushed through the large swinging doors finally and found himself in a small room divided by a short narrow counter. Beyond it a large steel door stood partially open. A man with a pinched expression on his face emerged from the back room, and when he noticed Meitner standing there he approached the counter.

"*Mein Herr?*" he asked politely.

Meitner came to the counter and in German introduced himself. The man's eyes grew a little larger.

"Dr. Hans Meitner, the Nobel Prize winner?"

Meitner's stomach fluttered. "Yes."

"It is an honor to meet you, sir," the man said, and he stuck out his hand. "I am Gunther Braunschweig. Curator of Records."

Meitner shook the man's hand. His throat felt dry and he was acutely conscious of his beating heart. What could he say to this man? How was he going to put it?

"You have been quite popular around here," Braunschweig said.

Again Meitner's stomach turned over. "Please?" he asked.

"A young woman telephoned two days ago about

you, and then yesterday she came here asking to see our war period records."

A wave of nausea and dizziness washed over Meitner, and he reached out to grip the counter to stop himself from falling. "Her name. Was it Laurie Andrews?" he squeaked, his throat constricting. "From the United States?"

Braunschweig looked instantly concerned. "Dr. Meitner, is something the matter? Are you ill?"

Meitner shook his head. "It passes," he said. "The young woman who came here, was her name Laurie Andrews?"

"Yes, as a matter of fact, it was," Braunschweig said. "Of course, I denied her request to see the records —at first. But she returned yesterday afternoon with authorization from the attorney general's office, so I had to let her look at what she wanted to see. And it was curious, too . . ." Braunschweig said, trailing off.

Through a haze which was filling Meitner's sight and hearing, the man's last statement had nearly knocked him down. "She saw the records?" he asked.

Braunschweig looked at him sharply. "Yes," he said. "The same records another man was looking at. He claimed to be from the attorney general's office, but he wasn't. I found that out later."

Meitner could feel his world coming down around him. It was going to be the end of his work. So long. So many years for nothing. He was close. And yet there would be no prize for the knowledge at the end. It was over.

"May I see those records?" he heard himself asking.

The pinched expression on Braunschweig's face tightened. "This is highly irregular," he said. "Without authorization either from the hospital administration or from the attorney general's office, my hands are tied."

"It is important to me, Herr Braunschweig," Meitner said, and he could hear the pleading tone in his voice. The woman and someone else, someone unknown, had been looking at war records. Why? Did they all know? Or suspect?

Braunschweig seemed to be debating with himself, and Meitner could feel the dizziness and nausea wash over him again in wave after wave. He could not remain on his feet much longer.

The clerk finally relented, his expression softening somewhat. "It can hurt nothing," he said. "I'll bring the book the other two looked at. A moment, please."

Braunschweig turned and went back through the steel door, leaving Meitner standing alone.

Why had the woman come here? How had she come up with the DBK? Suddenly it struck him, and his knees went weak. He reached out and grabbed the counter, this time with both hands, struggling to remain standing.

The laboratory. The woman had been at his house, she must have been in his laboratory and seen his journal. It was the only answer. She knew everything. Everything.

Braunschweig was back, and he laid a large, leather-bound book on the counter in front of Meitner who tried as best he could to compose himself. The records clerk studied his face for a moment.

"*Herr Doktor*, are you sure you are feeling all right? May I call a doctor for you? After all, this is a hospital. I'm sure someone could help you."

Meitner shook his head and took his hands away from the counter to show he was feeling better. "No, it is not necessary. It is merely a little dizziness that is passing. It is nothing. Thank you."

Braunschweig studied his face a moment longer, then sighed. "As you wish, *Herr Doktor*." He pushed the book forward. "I cannot allow you to take this out of here, or take too long with it."

"I understand," Meitner said, and he reached for the book and opened it to the first page as Braunschweig moved back to his desk.

The woman and the other man knew, he was certain of it now. This was the 1940 record book. The year they had moved out of the hospital. He quickly flipped the pages until he came to the notations for July. Flipping through the book more slowly now, he finally came to the pages for July 16, the day they had moved.

Gustav Predel's name leaped off the page at him, and ten lines below that his own name appeared. He stared at it for a long time, a strange feeling passing through him. He had not seen his real name for more than twenty-five years, ever since Hannover. And now it brought back a flood of memories.

About to close the book, he noticed something else at the bottom of the list. A single word inked in the margin. He adjusted his glasses and bent down so that he could read what it said. Suddenly the word made sense. Tiefensee.

He stared at it for a long time, barely conscious of the passage of time or his own breathing or heart beat. They knew. The woman and the man, whoever he was, they knew. They knew.

Braunschweig was bent over his desk writing something when Meitner straightened up, looked briefly his way, and then turned and shuffled out the door.

CHAPTER 6

It was already dark although it was only early afternoon when the four-engine military jet transport touched down on the snow-covered runway. From the air Kozhevnikov had caught brief glimpses of the facility, which was spread out over several square kilometers. Beyond the bright lights of the runway, and beyond the camp itself, he could see nothing but featureless tundra that stretched in every direction as far as the eye could see.

They had come over a mountain range only a few minutes earlier, and although Kozhevnikov did not know their exact position, he suspected they were close to the Bering Sea. He thought he had caught sight of a town toward the east, but the aircraft had banked sharply and begun its descent, cutting off his view.

The engines whined in reverse as the plane braked and began to slow down, and Kozhevnikov stretched in the canvas-covered seat bolted to the hull of the aircraft. Besides the pilot and the navigator, he was the only person aboard.

During the long flight from Moscow he had tried to sleep, but the airplane was too cold, and he had managed to doze for only a few minutes at a time. Now, as the plane taxied toward the brightly lit hangar, he was tired and there was a foul metallic taste in his mouth.

He unfastened his seat belt and got up as the plane came to a halt and the engines began to whine down. A moment later the door to the cockpit opened and the pilot emerged.

"We are here, Comrade," the man said, grinning. "I trust you had a pleasant flight."

Kozhevnikov managed a weak smile. "Thank you for your concern, but I didn't."

"A glass of hot tea and a warm bed will fix what ails you," the pilot said pleasantly. He moved to the side of the aircraft, undogged the hatch lever, and pushed the door open.

A blast of Arctic air immediately swirled through the aircraft. Kozhevnikov zippered up his parka and stepped past the pilot to the boarding stairs that had been pushed up to the plane by two heavily clad flight attendants who were now hurrying back to the hangar.

He paused at the top a moment, but he could see nothing beyond the lights illuminating the huge hangar and he started down.

A man dressed in an unzippered parka, the hood down, got out of an enclosed military jeep and met him at the bottom of the stairs. He was about twenty-five, had short-cropped hair, square features, and steel-blue eyes. He was not smiling, nor did he offer his hand.

"Comrade Kozhevnikov, welcome to Operation Outlook," he said in a deep, rough voice.

"Thank you," Kozhevnikov said. "My bags——"

"Will be brought to your quarters," the young man smoothly interrupted. "If you will follow me." He turned and headed toward the jeep.

Kozhevnikov fell in behind him and climbed in the passenger side of the unheated jeep. Without a word the man got behind the wheel, and a moment later they were heading away from the hangar and down a narrow dirt road toward the camp a half kilometer away.

"What time is it here?" Kozhevnikov asked after a few moments.

"Sixteen-twenty hours, Comrade," the man said, not turning.

"Am I to be briefed immediately?"

"No. The colonel will see you in the morning. You are to rest in your quarters until then."

"How about dinner?"

"It is waiting for you in your quarters."

"I see," Kozhevnikov said, and he fell silent as they approached a large gate, an opening in the tall, wire fence. Every three hundred meters spotlighted guard towers rose around the camp. From here, Kozhevnikov could see that the camp consisted of row upon row of long, wide, but very low ramshackle-looking buildings.

The facility looked like a wartime concentration camp. Kozhevnikov again had the strong feeling that he had been sent here for punishment, not as a reward.

He shivered, more in apprehension than from the bone-chilling cold that had begun to penetrate his heavy military parka, as the driver hurried between the windowless low buildings toward the center of the compound.

They emerged into a large, well-lit open area, the center of which was dominated by a four-story cement-block building. Several two-story wings jutted out from it randomly. Beyond it, in the distance, Kozhevnikov could see some barnlike buildings ringed by strong lights.

He pointed as they headed directly for the big building in the center. "What is that?"

The driver did not look that way. "It will be explained to you in the morning, Comrade," he said.

Again Kozhevnikov fell silent as they pulled up and parked at the end of one of the wings. Several military vehicles, including two heavy trucks, were also parked nearby; except for the flight attendants and the guards in the tower at the gate, he had seen no one; there was no movement anywhere. His feelings of apprehension increased.

The driver got out of the jeep, and Kozhevnikov followed him into the building and up a flight of stairs to the second floor, where he found himself in a wide corridor.

Halfway down the corridor, the driver opened a door and motioned Kozhevnikov into a well-appointed suite of rooms that included a large living room, a small efficiency kitchen, and a compact bathroom with shower off a large bedroom.

His dinner was waiting for him on a low table in front of a sofa in the living room.

Everything seemed new and spotlessly clean. The draperies in the living room were closed, but soft ceiling lighting cast no shadows.

"This is nice," Kozhevnikov said, turning back to the driver.

"Yes," the man said, an almost distasteful expression on his face. "You will stay here this evening, Comrade. Do not attempt to leave your suite. If you should need anything, pick up the telephone and inform the controller. In the morning you will be summoned."

"You mentioned a colonel," Kozhevnikov said. "Is he the facility director?"

The driver stared at him a moment. "No further questions, Comrade. I am Fedor Udalov. I will be your assistant disinformation officer, and after your briefing in the morning I will be of assistance. Until then do not leave these quarters. Everything you may need is here. There is even liquor in the kitchen."

Again Kozhevnikov detected a sense of distaste in the man's expression. "Thank you, Comrade Udalov," he said. "I will do as you say."

Without further word, Udalov turned and went out of the apartment, closing the door firmly behind him.

Kozhevnikov took off his parka and laid it over a chair, and then picked up the telephone on the table next to the sofa. The smell of the food in the covered dishes made him hungry.

"Yes," a rough, low-pitched male voice answered.

"This is Kozhevnikov. Can someone awaken me at oh-six-hundred hours?"

"Yes," the man said and hung up.

Kozhevnikov stood with the telephone to his ear

for a moment before he hung up. The voice on the telephone sounded exactly like Udalov's.

The harsh jangling of the telephone woke Kozhevnikov out of a deep, dreamless sleep, and as he stumbled out of bed and went to answer it, he looked at his watch. It was exactly six o'clock.

He picked up the phone. "Yes?" he said.

"It is oh-six-hundred hours, Comrade," said the same voice as last night, and the phone went dead.

Kozhevnikov hung up and turned to go back to the bedroom when he spotted his bags on the floor next to the sofa. The dirty dishes were gone and the bottle of cognac and glass he had used also were missing. Someone had been here while he slept last night, and the disquieting feeling of apprehension that had begun to fade last night was back.

He took a deep breath and let it out slowly. The events with Rafn and the Americans seemed to have happened centuries ago. There was no way he was going to get out of this. He was certain of that now. When he had left Moscow he had managed to contact the man in the American embassy, but all he was able to tell him was the name, Operation Outlook, and that he was being assigned to it somewhere in Siberia. There was nothing they could do for him now. He was on his own, and for the first time since this entire thing had begun, Kozhevnikov suddenly felt very alone and lost.

In the bathroom, he took a long, hot shower and shaved. Then he dressed in a gray suit and soft black boots. The boots had been a present from Nadya two years ago, and the thought of her made him ache inside. He missed her, he would always miss her; the ache in his gut was something that would become very familiar.

He decided against wearing a tie and for a brief moment fingered the Order of Lenin medal, but decided against that, too.

Under his parka Udalov had worn plain gray fatigues with no visible markings of rank. Kozhevnikov supposed he would also be issued a similar uniform.

When he was finished he went into the living room, but stopped suddenly. Udalov was standing silently by the front door. He was not smiling.

"I didn't hear you come in, Comrade Udalov," Kozhevnikov said, regaining his composure.

"No," the man said. "The colonel is waiting to brief you."

"This early?" Kozhevnikov said, looking at his watch. It was just after six-thirty.

"Are you ready?" Udalov said.

Kozhevnikov nodded. He donned his parka and followed the man out into the corridor.

Instead of going back outside the way they had come in last night, Udalov led Kozhevnikov in the opposite direction. At the end of the corridor, they took the stairs leading up to the fourth floor.

They emerged into a large spartan auditorium with a podium on a raised dais at the front. Seating for at least a hundred persons fanned out like a theater.

Udalov, looking neither right nor left, continued across the auditorium and through a door at the opposite side, which led into a large, carpeted room. Along one wall was a plate-glass window overlooking the camp toward the airstrip in the distance. It was still dark, and the wind was whipping the snow around the corners of the buildings across the open space below. There was still no sign of any activity.

In the center of the room was a large desk equipped with a telephone console. Across from it was an open stairwell, and on the wall opposite the window was a single, unmarked door.

Udalov sat down at the desk, punched a button on the console, and leaned forward slightly. "He is here," he said, and a moment later he looked up and motioned toward the door. "I will wait here for you."

Kozhevnikov nodded, took a deep breath, crossed the room, knocked once on the door and entered.

Inside he found himself in a luxurious office, dominated by a massive oak desk. Three of the walls were lined with bookcases. No one was here, and confused, Kozhevnikov was about to turn and go back to Udalov when a door at the back of the office opened and a large man entered. Kozhevnikov guessed him to be in his early fifties, nearly two meters tall, and at least a hundred and ten kilograms. Bald, his eyes were deepset and dark, and he had slightly Mongoloid features. He broke into a grin when he saw Kozhevnikov.

In several long strides he was across the room and embraced Kozhevnikov in a crushing bear hug. When he parted and stepped back he was smiling.

"Welcome, Viktor Vasilievich, to Operation Outlook. I am very pleased to have you with us."

His voice was deep, rich, and cultured. Kozhevnikov nodded uncertainly and returned the man's broad smile.

"But permit me to introduce myself," the man said. "I am Colonel Safar Pavlovich Agayan, commandant of Operation Outlook. Have you had your breakfast yet?"

"No, sir," Kozhevnikov said.

"Please," Agayan said, taking Kozhevnikov by the arm and leading him past the desk. "We do not stand on formality here. You may call me Safar Pavlovich, or if that is uncomfortable to your Moscow manners, simply Comrade."

"Thank you, Comrade," Kozhevnikov said.

Agayan led him through the door at the back of his office into a large, luxurious apartment. Off the living room was a formal dining room. Breakfast was laid out and waiting for them. No one else was in the room.

Kozhevnikov took off his parka and draped it over a chair, and when they were seated at opposite ends of the table, Agayan proposed a toast, raising his steaming glass of tea.

"Now that you are here, Viktor Vasilievich, Operation Outlook is certain to succeed. May I toast your health, and give congratulations on your Order of Lenin."

Kozhevnikov raised his glass. "Thank you, Comrade," he said, and he sipped the hot, sweet tea that tasted slightly of lemon.

"So," Agayan said. "Please eat and we shall talk. I am sure there is much you will want to learn."

CHAPTER 7

Breakfast consisted of smoked salmon, caviar, small crackers, hard rolls with butter, and a selection of cheeses. When Kozhevnikov was finished he looked up. Agayan was studying his face.

"May I offer my condolences, Viktor Vasilievich, on the unfortunate death of your wife."

"Thank you," Kozhevnikov mumbled.

"I hope you are sufficiently recovered so that your work here can be effective."

So far everything indicated this assignment was exactly what the chairman said it was: a reward for the good work he had done in reorganizing his department. If that were truly the case, he needed more information. First the information and then a way to transmit it to the West. Or some plan to stop what was likely happening here. Kozhevnikov turned that thought over briefly.

What if he were wrong about the Jews? Nothing he had seen here indicated any operation such as Auschwitz. There were no tall smokestacks, no crematoriums evident.

"It would help if I knew exactly what Operation Outlook was. And where exactly we are?", Kozhevnikov finally said. "I was not briefed before I left Moscow."

Agayan laughed. "No, I don't suppose you were briefed. You must understand, Viktor Vasilievich, that this operation is a very closely guarded state secret."

Kozhevnikov said nothing, waiting for Agayan to continue.

"This project alone will guarantee that the Soviet Union takes its rightful place as supreme master of the world," Agayan said. "And that is not an idle boast. It will happen. And soon, very soon."

Kozhevnikov felt a chill. There was something in the man's eyes that was not exactly right. For a moment Kozhevnikov wondered if the man was mad. But Agayan was continuing.

"I am getting ahead of myself," he said, pouring himself another glass of tea from the samovar. He offered some to Kozhevnikov, who declined.

"Udalov will take you on a tour of the facility this morning, but first I must give you some background information."

Kozhevnikov sat back and lit a cigarette as Agayan watched him closely. When Kozhevnikov was settled, Agayan began his explanation, and as he talked, all the pieces of the puzzle dropped into place, one by one.

"In the late thirties the Nazis established a rocket research station south of Berlin. The code name for that facility was Station Kummersdorf West. You may have heard of it. It was the same group of men who later moved to Peenemünde on the north coast and developed the V-2 rockets.

"At any rate, another facility, this one very secret, was established northeast of Berlin near the town of Tiefensee. It began its operations in 1940 under the code name Station Kummersdorf East. Scientists from all over Germany working independently on this project were pulled together in one facility to get the job done a little more quickly."

"What job?" Kozhevnikov asked carefully.

"I'm getting to that," Agayan said impatiently. He took a sip of his tea and continued. "The name Kummersdorf was the only thing the two facilities had in common. The scientists at Kummersdorf West were developing wonder weapons, while the scientists at Kummersdorf East were trying to do something else. Something quite different.

"Near the end of the war, Hitler almost single-handedly developed something called the National Redoubt. The plan was made against the possibility that the Allies would win the war and invade Germany. If this happened Hitler and an elite corps of *Waffen SS,* Gestapo, and members of the high command, as well as the entire facility of Kummersdorf East, would establish themselves in the mountains south of Salzburg near Hitler's Eagles' Nest at Berchtesgaden. From there they would wage guerrilla warfare against the invaders, an action that would have prolonged the war to such an extent that the Allies would never have completely won, would sooner or later have given up, and Germany would be returned to the Germans.

"At that time Hitler and his elite corps would return from the mountains to start the rebuilding of the Thousand-Year Reich."

Kozhevnikov was having trouble accepting all of this, and it evidently showed on his face, because Agayan looked at him sharply.

"This fantastic plot was not lunacy on Hitler's part, my dear Kozhevnikov. Not at all. He had something that would have made it all possible. Namely the research efforts of Kummersdorf East."

"Which were?" Kozhevnikov asked very carefully.

Agayan smiled. "Genetic control," he said simply.

For a moment Kozhevnikov was stunned. This wasn't making any sense. Why the secrecy? Why the hundred thousand Jews? "I don't understand, Comrade," he finally said. "What exactly do you mean?"

"Listen carefully, then," Agayan said. "The scientists at Kummersdorf East had been working independently on genetic control since the early thirties. But of course even their best efforts at the time were crude compared with what is happening now.

"Nevertheless, they were making great strides. Without the electron microscope, of course, they were merely stabbing in the dark, but stabbing nonetheless.

"Despite the handicaps, the Germans had learned a great deal about the makeup of the human cell. And although they had no inkling of the existence of DNA, they knew there had to be some way of manipulating or controlling the structure of each individual human being."

"Wait a moment," Kozhevnikov said, holding up his hand. "You're losing me. First of all DNA. I think I've heard of it, but what exactly is it?"

Agayan smiled pleasantly again. "I'm not a scientist myself, Viktor Vasilievich, but in order to understand what is happening here, you must understand a little something about these matters.

"First of all, DNA is an abbreviation for a substance called deoxyribonucleic acid. It's found in every living cell. And it works like a computer. The scientists say it is shaped like a pair of very long ladders that are twisted around into a spiral. The rungs of the ladders contain certain chemical substances, four of them to be exact. Depending upon the sequence in which these chemicals are arranged as rungs on the ladders, the individual DNA molecules instruct other chemicals to make hair, or to make blood, or to make any of the thousands of substances that make up a living organism."

"The combinations must be vast," Kozhevnikov said, trying to make some sense of Agayan's explanation, and wondering what this had to do with the Jews.

"In the hundreds of thousands," Agayan said. "But let me continue. The Germans as early as the thirties suspected they could control the very structure of the human form through the control of the cell of the male sperm and the female egg. This, you have to remember, was before they even suspected the existence of DNA."

"Why? What were they trying to accomplish?"

"The idea the Germans had was to build millions, literally millions, of tailor-made human beings. They wanted to construct an entire race of supermen. Superwarriors to fight for the new Germany. Their factories would have been located in the mountains, and they could have sent their expendable, easily replaceable armies down into Germany to defeat the Allies."

"Unbelievable," Kozhevnikov said softly.

"They were successful to a point," Agayan said. "They were using radiation techniques to break down cell walls, and unknown to them, to tamper with genetic codes, and then they combined the male sperm cells with the doctored female eggs. A baby was conceived by fusing the two together and implanting the fertilized egg into the womb of a woman. In theory it would have been the perfectly engineered specimen."

Kozhevnikov was unable to speak, and Agayan continued.

"By duplicating each engineered sperm and egg combination a million times in the laboratory, using a process of biological duplication called cloning, and implanting the fertilized egg in a million women we would have turned out a million human beings all exactly alike. The ideal fighting force for Hitler's National Redoubt."

"But it didn't work," Kozhevnikov managed to say.

"No," Agayan said. "The end came too soon for Hitler. The Americans had heard rumors of the National Redoubt but, fortunately for us, nothing about Kummersdorf East.

"We knew about it, though, and before entering Berlin we picked up the station, its buildings, what was left of its personnel, and its equipment and records. Everything was scoured clean. Nothing that even hinted of the station remained.

"When General Patton was outside Berlin, he was held back from entering the city as a political gesture to us. The Americans stupidly did not realize we were calling the shots, that our technicians needed the extra time to strip Kummersdorf East. Not telling anyone what we had discovered put us ahead in this field. But more importantly it gave our Operation Outlook a complete cloak of secrecy. Since that time, the operation has been moving forward from here."

"I'm having difficulty accepting this, Comrade," Kozhevnikov said, recovering somewhat from his initial shock. "You can't mean to tell me that actual human beings are constructed to a pattern and artificially produced. It can't be true."

"Indeed it is, Viktor Vasilievich. We have succeeded where Hitler's scientists failed. The original Kummersdorf experiments were hideous failures. Fortunately most of the monsters were born dead, and the few that did survive birth were insane, misshapen creatures that had to be destroyed.

"But we have produced the perfect technique. Our job now is to implant the fertilized eggs into a hundred thousand host women at a time. Nine months later we'll have a crop of identical babies, and the implanting process will begin again."

"The Jews?" Kozhevnikov said.

Agayan nodded. "The process is actually quite simple. We have a sperm bank filled with cells whose DNA coding structure has been precisely altered. The sperm samples in the form of fertilized eggs are merely emplanted in the female womb, and because of the nature of the dominant traits in the changed sperm, the resulting babies are exactly what we want."

"Don't the women object?" Kozhevnikov asked, still struggling with the things he had been told.

Agayan waved that aside. "We tranquilize them. They're harmless."

"And the scientists and teachers, they are here to train the children?"

"The children are called clones," Agayan corrected. "And yes, the teachers are here to train them."

"But it will be years from now before the children are grown enough to become soldiers."

Agayan arose from where he was sitting and came around the table. Kozhevnikov got to his feet and followed him back into his office.

"There is material in your office which Udalov will show you. It will explain more fully what I have told you. You will understand that our scientists have completely altered the genetic structure of these clones. They grow to maturity in eight years, not twenty. They are fast, intelligent, strong, but emotionally neutral. For them, killing and warfare are of no more consequence than killing a fly."

"Why?" Kozhevnikov asked.

"Why are we doing this, do you mean?" Agayan asked, an amused expression on his face.

Kozhevnikov nodded dumbly.

"Raw technology will no longer win wars, not when so many thermonuclear devices are in existence. If such a war began it would mean the end of all life on the earth. But consider sending five million identically perfect soldiers against the Chinese. If they were led by normal men, and directed to kill without fear for their own safety, they would be invincible.

"Once China was overrun, Western Europe would be taken, or perhaps the Near East. The soldiers would be easily replaceable. They eat nothing but soy concentrate so they are easy to care for in the field, and they are programmed never to rebel."

"Automatons," Kozhevnikov said.

"Exactly," Agayan agreed. "Biological robots. With them we will conquer the world."

"And what is my job here? What am I to do?"

Agayan took Kozhevnikov's arm and led him toward the outer door. "Work up a series of disinformation programs. I understand you are very good at that. With an operation of this size, sooner or later the Western world will begin to become suspicious. It is up to you to give us the margin of time we need to complete our program. Convince the world that this is nothing more than an Agrarian Reform Project."

They were at the door. "I'd like to return to Moscow," Kozhevnikov said on impulse.

Agayan looked at him with curiosity. "Whatever for?"

"I think such a program could better be directed from there."

Agayan shook his head. "Impossible, my dear Viktor Vasilievich. No one who comes here to Markovo returns. You will stay here like us for the rest of your life."

PART FOUR

CHAPTER 1

The young man with short-cropped hair, square, regular features and steel-blue eyes entered the Soviet embassy in East Berlin and was ushered immediately into the *Referentura,* the meeting room for sensitive affairs.

The ambassador and his assistant were out of the city, so the only person present at the meeting this morning was the KGB resident, who was also the officer in charge of the Komitet's East Berlin Karlshorst Residency. His name was Vasili Vasilievich Baturin.

"Sit down, Comrade Udalov," Baturin said from where he was seated at the end of a long conference table.

The young man took a seat at the opposite end of the table, and waited for the KGB officer to begin. He neither smiled nor frowned, merely stared at the officer, who returned his steady gaze.

"There has been some trouble," Baturin said after a long silence.

"Yes, Comrade, there has been trouble," Udalov said.

"Was there an original dispatch?" Baturin asked.

"Yes, sir," Udalov said, and he pulled a slip of paper from his jacket as he got up and came around the table. He handed it to Baturin and then went back to his seat.

Baturin studied the dispatch for a few moments, and when he looked up he was frowning. "This T 438, who is it?"

"An old woman who was a former resident of Tiefensee. We have numbers for all of them. She lived here in Berlin."

"And Maria Grindl? There is a file number here for her as well?"

"It is a new number, sir."

"She has not previously been on your files?"

"No, sir, nor yours," Udalov said calmly.

"I see," Baturin said, and he leaned back slightly in his chair, the dispatch lying open on the table. "On the basis of this, you queried Moscow?"

"Yes, sir," Udalov said.

"I see," Baturin said again. "What did you do after you received the go-ahead from Moscow?"

For the first time the young man seemed slightly uncomfortable. "First the Tiefensee woman was picked up and disposed of."

"Next," Baturin said sharply.

"Maria Grindl was observed making contact with a man we later identified as Horst Steiner."

Baturin snapped forward. "There were two people in on this?"

"There may be more, Comrade. It is why I requested this meeting."

Baturin's eyes narrowed. "Continue."

"In an attempt to gain more information, Horst Steiner was followed from Maria Grindl's apartment. He went directly to his apartment."

"You picked him up there?"

"Not at first, Comrade," Udalov said, his discomfort becoming more obvious.

"Why?"

"We wanted to see if Steiner would make contact with anyone else."

"What caused you to change your mind and pick up this Steiner?" Baturin said impatiently.

"The unit watching Maria Grindl lost her. She left her apartment unobserved. The order was then given to pick up Steiner."

"I see. And what information did you get from Steiner? Where is he now?"

"Steiner died of heart failure when we arrested him. However, we found this," Udalov said. He got up again and came around the table, this time handing Baturin a crumpled ten-mark bill.

When Udalov was back in his seat he continued his explanation. "At the time of his arrest, Steiner was writing on the bill. The message was incomplete, but as you can observe, it included the words *Tiefensee* and *Kummersdorf*."

Baturin was studying the dull brown writing on the bill. He had turned pale. "Who was this meant for?" he said, looking up finally.

"We do not know, Comrade. Presumably someone in the West."

"And Maria Grindl, has she been picked up?"

"Yes, sir," Udalov said. "She is undergoing questioning at this moment."

Baturin fell silent for several minutes and thought. When he looked up again, Udalov had regained his earlier calm.

"You did right to dispatch Moscow with this," he said. "However, I do not want any mistakes made with Maria Grindl. She is to be treated delicately until she provides us with the information we need. If this was merely a random inquiry, which I seriously doubt, she will be disposed of routinely. However, if this was a directed inquiry into the operation, then we will have to lay a delicate trap to snare whoever is in the West. Do I make my meaning clear, Comrade Udalov?"

"Yes, sir," Udalov said and he rose.

"With delicacy," Baturin said.

CHAPTER 2

Traffic was light around the Brandenburg Square as Laurie Andrews got out of the cab, paid the driver, and headed toward the tour bus parked near the terminal, swinging her heavy leather purse over her shoulder. She had not combed her hair this morning, and had used no makeup. The clothes she wore now, she had slept in last night, and she knew she must look a sight. But it was an image she wanted to project.

There were a number of people waiting for the bus despite the fact that the weather had turned very cold, and the sky was heavily overcast. They stood in a ragged line that snaked away from the large Mercedes diesel bus idling in the chill morning air. Most of them were old women who wanted to visit their East German relatives aboard the bus. But there were several men among them, one of whom might be the one who was searching for the same information she was.

She stopped near the back of the line and searched the crowd for him. Gertrude Vogel had not given her a description, other than the fact he was Jewish.

The statue of the Four Horsemen of the Apocalypse atop the Brandenburg Gate was half lost in the mist, and as she moved to the end of the line she looked up at it in awe.

This was the big leagues now, and despite her assurances to herself that she could pull this off, she was

261

frightened. She had told herself over and over again that she was a journalist with a valid American passport. The worst they could do was arrest her and expel her from East Germany. If that happened, Shapiro wouldn't be able to fault her for trying.

Still, she was frightened. Anything could go wrong. A nervous guard, an upset policeman, the man who was searching for Predel. How did he fit into all of this? And would he threaten her if she got in his way?

Her eyes wandered to the guard emplacements at the gate and she shuddered involuntarily, pulling up her coat collar against the sudden chill.

The East German guards wore steel helmets and had deadly looking machine guns hanging from straps over their shoulders. Would they hesitate to shoot her because she was a woman? Would they wait long enough to find out she was an American journalist? Or would they shoot first and ask questions later, like they did in all the war movies she had seen?

The line began to move suddenly as the bus driver emerged and began to collect fares. For a moment Laurie tensed, unwilling to move forward. She had not called Shapiro and no one knew where she was going or what she was trying to do.

Gertrude Vogel had warned Laurie to be careful. But that had not deterred her, especially not after she had seen the record book at the DBK.

She had gone to the hospital after she called Shapiro about Meitner's laboratory journal, but the man in the records section had refused to help her.

"Authorization for any examination of war records must come from the attorney general's office," he had told her in his broken English. "There is nothing I can do for you unless you get the proper authorization, Fräulein Andrews."

Laurie had immediately gone to the attorney general's office in the Government Center. Inside, she told the receptionist that she was interested in looking at

World War Two records kept on file at the DBK, and the woman had given her a strange look but had shown her into Gertrude Vogel's office.

"May I see your press credentials, please, Miss Andrews?" the assistant attorney general had asked. The receptionist had remained standing by the open office door.

Laurie handed across her press pass, and after Gertrude Vogel quickly scrutinized it, she handed it to the receptionist. "Verify this, please, Hilde," she said, and the receptionist left.

"Please sit down, Miss Andrews," Gertrude Vogel said pleasantly, and when they were seated her voice took on a slightly conciliatory tone. "I'm sorry to have to check your credentials, but you must understand that we are somewhat sensitive about that period in our history."

"I understand," Laurie said, but she felt the woman had been surprised at her presence and she was holding something back.

"What exactly are you interested in finding out?" the woman asked.

Laurie had the urge to tell her the entire story. Instead she chose her words carefully. "I'm doing a story on Dr. Hans Meitner who has just won the Nobel Prize for physiology and medicine."

"Yes, I read it in the newspapers earlier this week," the woman said. "But what brings you specifically to the DBK?"

"It is my understanding that Dr. Meitner may have worked there during or before the war," Laurie said.

Gertrude Vogel hesitated a moment and seemed to make a decision before she spoke again. When she did her voice had a strange, almost demanding tone. It was almost as if she were in a courtroom and this was a trial. "Do you know a Walter Goldmann with the Israeli News Service?"

Laurie shook her head. "No, I don't think so. At least the name isn't familiar."

"I see," the woman said. "Does the name Gustav Predel mean anything to you?"

Laurie hesitated for a brief moment, hoping that the woman hadn't noticed. "No, I haven't heard that name, either."

Again Gertrude Vogel paused a moment. "In what capacity did Dr. Meitner work for the DBK, do you know?"

Laurie shook her head. "I presume he was a medical doctor. From what I understand, he may have done his internship there after he graduated."

"If you know that, why do you want to see the records?" Gertrude Vogel said, her eyes narrowing slightly.

It was the one question Laurie was afraid she would ask because she had no answer for it unless she admitted some of her suspicions.

"It's more than that, isn't it?" the woman said, not waiting for an answer. "You suspect Dr. Meitner may have been involved in the medical experimentation going on at the DBK. That's it, isn't it?"

"I——" Laurie started to say.

"Listen to me, Miss Andrews. I cannot stop you from pursuing a legitimate journalistic assignment. But I must warn you that someone else may be interested in the same thing. And that man may be dangerous if you get in his way. We are looking for him at this moment, but I do not expect to have much luck. He's a professional."

A professional *what*, Laurie wanted to ask, but she held her silence as the woman continued.

"Provided your press credentials check out, I will give you authorization to see the DBK records. But be careful. While in Germany you must obey German laws, and if you don't, you will be arrested and prosecuted."

"I don't understand," Laurie said.

"Then let me explain. If the information you want concerns war crimes committed here in Germany by German nationals, the law requires you to report the information immediately to this office. Failure to do so will result in your arrest."

Laurie nodded, but said nothing. She had been right from the beginning; there was something Meitner wanted to hide. But then there was the other thing—the man, Walter Goldmann, whoever he was. The woman said he was dangerous.

Laurie looked up as the line moved closer to the bus driver. After she had left the attorney general's office with her authorization to see the records, she had returned to the hospital.

She had not admitted to the Vogel woman the name Predel meant anything to her. Nor was she concerned about the Israeli newsman.

At the hospital it was a different story. Whatever Goldmann was seeking, so was she.

The clerk looked up from the authorization letter Laurie handed him. "This is a different matter, now," he said, smiling. "May I be of help, Fräulein?"

"Yes," she said, again enunciating her words carefully so that he would understand her. "Several days ago a man was here looking at World War Two records. I believe he was looking for information on a Gustav Predel."

The clerk's eyes narrowed. "Yes?"

"I would like to see those records," Laurie said with a straight face.

The clerk again glanced down at the letter, then sighed and shrugged. "It doesn't matter," he said. "You have the authorization. One moment."

He turned and went through a thick steel door on the other side of the counter and was gone for a few minutes. When he returned he was lugging a huge, leather-bound book, the year 1940 stamped on the spine above the figure of a swastika. Laurie's heart skipped a beat.

"This is the only record the man looked at," the clerk said, laying the book down on the counter. "You may not take it out of this room."

"Thank you," Laurie said, and she opened the book to the first page and began scanning its contents.

She was almost up to the bus now. Several more people had arrived since she had, and now they were in line as well.

Looking through the book, she had immediately come to Predel's name, but not being able to read German, the references beneath it meant nothing, and she continued, looking for anything that might give her a clue.

At one point she looked up at the clerk, who was seated at his desk on the opposite side of the counter. *"Tot,"* she asked. "What does that word mean in English?"

The clerk looked up. "Dead, or death," he said, and he studied her face for a long moment. She went back to the book, suddenly comprehending what she was reading.

Most of the names beneath Predel's were Jewish-sounding, and sooner or later most of them were listed under the *Tot* heading. Dead, or death. They were Jews; Predel had killed them. If Meitner had been associated with Predel, had he, too, killed Jews?

An hour and a half later, Laurie came to the section for July 16, 1940, and her eyes riveted on the page. Below Predel's name was a list of people, none of them Jews, and below that was the signature of Goebbels, the Nazi Propaganda Minister.

She called for the clerk, who got up and came over to the counter. She turned the book halfway around on the counter so he could see the page.

"What is this?" she said, pointing to the list.

The clerk studied the notation a moment, then looked up at Laurie. "It is a transfer list."

"What do you mean?"

The clerk again looked down at the notations. "Dr. Predel evidently headed a research unit here in the hospital that on July sixteenth of that year was transferred somewhere else."

"Where did they go?" Laurie asked, her heart hammering even harder.

The clerk shrugged and peered again at the page, but then he stiffened. "Here," he said, pointing his finger at an inked notation at the bottom of the list. He turned the book back so Laurie could see better. The single, blurred word was *Tiefensee*.

She looked up after a moment, a questioning expression on her face.

Again the clerk shrugged. "It is where Dr. Predel and his group were apparently moved. Tiefensee is a small town, unfortunately now in the Eastern Zone."

The next day she had learned the exact location of the town and learned that Westerners were not allowed into the Eastern Zone except on the tour bus.

She moved forward now, handed the driver her money, took her ticket, and boarded the bus. The aisle seat by the front door was vacant, and she sat down next to an old woman talking animatedly with a woman one seat back. They glanced in her direction, then went back to their discussion, and Laurie returned to her thoughts.

She did not know what she expected to find when she actually got to Tiefensee, nor did she know exactly how she was going to get there. She only knew she was going to have to try, because there was something more to this story than just Dr. Hans Meitner trying to cover up his war crimes. She had the feeling that she was onto something much larger, much more important, and she wanted to have the exclusive story.

CHAPTER 3

"What is your sister like?"

Sigmund Schiller turned away from the window of the cab as it neared the Brandenburg Gate and looked at Rafn through squinted eyes for a moment. He shrugged. "She's prettier than me."

Rafn chuckled. "How did she come to be a member of the service?" he asked. He was trying to be conversational. Schiller had not slept all night, and now this morning he seemed a bit nervous, on edge.

"Our father was in it," Schiller said. "We were at Gan Habe, a kibbutz near Beersheba. I joined the service and they stuck me in intelligence because of my father. When I came home on leave, Raya liked the intelligence service patch I wore so much that she decided to join when she grew up. That's all. It's a family thing." He turned away and stared out the window.

"How old is she?" Rafn asked softly.

"Twenty-nine," Schiller said, his voice choking.

Rafn looked over the driver's shoulder. They were two blocks from the bus terminal now; within a few hours they would be in a car headed for Tiefensee.

Bermann had agreed to supply two men of similar build and age who wanted to defect to the West. Yesterday he had given them passports to put in Schiller's and Rafn's coat pockets. Rafn was to wear a long green leather overcoat, and Schiller, a short, tan raincoat.

268

The plan was relatively simple but demanded good timing and, Rafn hated to admit, a certain amount of luck.

Rafn and Schiller were to sit as close to the back of the bus as possible, saving two seats next to them. The two defectors would get on at the East side of the gate, take the seats next to them, and switch coats sometime during the tour.

Bermann's last message said that travel permits and wine sellers' licenses would be in the defectors' coat pockets, as well as the keys to a Mercedes diesel sedan that would be parked near the East Berlin bus terminal.

The passports Bermann had given Rafn and Schiller guaranteed that once the defectors entered the West Zone they would be able to disappear without causing a fuss. Once the East Germans suspected someone had used the tour bus to defect, they would begin a nationwide search, something Rafn had cautioned Bermann must not happen.

Yesterday they had purchased coats from secondhand stores and hidden their papers in their hotel room.

With any luck they would only be gone a day or two at the most, although they would not be able to return on the bus. They would have to figure out some other way of returning to the West.

It was a risky business, Rafn thought to himself, but he had taken risks all of his life. Only now too many people were involved. He did not like to depend upon others for anything, especially his own life.

The cab rounded a corner, drove across the Brandenburg Square through the thin traffic, and stopped at the curb near the terminal. A number of people were boarding the bus, which was nearly full.

They got out of the cab, Rafn paid the driver, and they took their places in the slowly moving line. Rafn could sense Schiller's increasing nervousness, and it surprised him. Even though he seemed professional, he was now on the verge of falling apart. Rafn only hoped the Israeli would hold together long enough for them to get the car and head out of the city. He didn't want to start anything he knew they wouldn't be able to finish if Schiller bolted.

Bermann's head was bent down as he made change and punched tickets, and when Rafn handed him a folded ten-mark bill, the man looked up with a start. For a moment his eyes locked with Rafn's and then he smiled nervously, accepted the money, and gave Rafn a ticket.

Rafn nodded pleasantly and climbed aboard the bus. Schiller was right behind. He had to stop while a young woman sat down in the front seat, and then he headed toward the back of the bus, where the last two rows of seats were empty.

He turned and stepped aside to allow Schiller to take the window seat, and when the Israeli was seated, Rafn took his coat off and sat down heavily in the aisle seat.

The last few passengers finally boarded the bus and a few moments later Bermann climbed on and quickly counted the passengers. His eyes locked with Rafn's for a moment, but then he turned and sat down in the driver's seat. A minute later the door closed, the bus lumbered out of the parking lot and headed across the plaza toward the West Zone checkpoint.

"Achtung, meine Herren und Damen," Bermann's voice came over the bus's public address system. "We will be stopping at the American checkpoint for pass-port verification and again on the East Zone side where we will take on additional passengers. Please have your passports ready, and please do not attempt to leave your seats. Thank you."

As they approached the heavily reinforced concrete wall beneath the Brandenburg Gate, Rafn could feel Schiller stiffening beside him. He turned to the man. "What's the matter, Schiller?" he asked softly.

Schiller turned to him, and there was almost a wild expression in his eyes. He shook his head slightly. "I don't know," he said barely audibly. "It's something. A feeling. I don't know."

"Are you going to be all right?"

"Yes . . . yes."

Rafn gazed at him for a moment, and then shrugged. It was too late now. He only hoped the man would hold together.

The bus stopped at the West checkpoint, the doors opened, and two American guards boarded, one of them remaining by the door, his hand resting lightly on the strap of a rifle that was slung over his shoulder, and the other soldier working his way down the aisle looking at passports.

The guards were young and obviously bored. At each seat the one coming down the aisle only stopped long enough to open the passport, check its date, glance at the photograph, and then look down at the passenger it was supposed to match. The photos in Rafn's and Schiller's passports, although blurred and faded, looked very little like them, and Rafn felt himself tensing. He was picking up Schiller's mood.

In a few minutes the guard came by and Rafn handed over his passport. He took it, flipped it open, looked down at Rafn, then closed it and handed it back. He did the same with Schiller's and then turned and went back to the front. He said something to Bermann, and then he and the other guard got off the bus.

Bermann closed the door and the bus eased forward around the first in the series of concrete barriers that had been set up so that any vehicle coming through would have to drive slowly in order to negotiate the sharp turns.

When they made it through the gate, Bermann stopped the bus and opened the door. An East German guard, a machine gun over his shoulder and an automatic strapped to his hip, boarded the bus, said something to Bermann and laughed, and then looked up and made a quick head count. Then he climbed down and waved the bus on.

Rafn could feel Schiller relaxing now, and he turned toward him as the bus lumbered across the wide avenue and pulled up to the East Zone terminal where a dozen people were waiting.

"What kind of feeling do you have?" Rafn asked.

Schiller was looking out the window at the two East German guards who were checking travel permits. "It's nothing," he mumbled.

Rafn was about to pursue the subject, but the bus door was open and the first of the East Zone passengers were boarding.

There were several cries of recognition as East Berliners suddenly saw relatives, and for a minute there was some commotion near the front of the bus. But then the aisle was cleared, and two men were heading their way. One of them was an older man, short with white hair. The other was much larger and younger. They both wore long gray overcoats.

Rafn flipped his coat across his knee to straighten it out, and Schiller began to take his off. The two men noticed the action and slid into the seats across from them, first taking off their coats. Neither of them looked directly at Rafn or Schiller, and a few moments later they were deep in conversation, their heads turned away.

Rafn smiled.

The two guards got on the bus, looked at the passengers, and then said something to Bermann, who closed the door, put the bus in gear, and eased the bus out of the parking lot.

Rafn kept his eyes on the guards standing at the front of the bus as Bermann announced, "Ladies and gentlemen, the Democratic Republic of Germany's Ministry of Tourism welcomes you to this guided tour of East Berlin and its environs. May I remind you to remain in your seats at all times. The guards at the front of the bus are here for your protection; however, may I also remind you not to speak to them during the tour." Bermann paused as he shifted smoothly. "We will be traveling along the Karl-Marx-Allee, which has become the pride of East Berlin. Later in the tour . . ."

Rafn could feel a constriction building in his gut as he continued to stare at the guards. Unless they looked the other way it would be impossible to switch coats. He could see out of the corner of his eye that the men seated across the aisle were also aware of the problem, and they looked nervous.

"Bermann is going to have to distract them," Schiller said softly. Rafn looked at him and smiled for the benefit of anyone watching them. "We have two hours. We will be patient."

Bermann's voice droned on as the bus lumbered around a corner and they came into an area which was obviously a shopping district. Although there were very few cars or trucks on the wide road, the sidewalks were filled with shoppers.

Rafn leaned forward to get a better look when a woman screamed at the front of the bus. Rafn jumped around to see the young woman in the front seat stand up and then double over, clutching her stomach as if she were about to vomit.

Bermann slammed on the brakes and the bus came to an abrupt stop, throwing the guards off balance.

"I'm sick, help me!" the woman cried.

Bermann opened the door, and before the guards could recover, the young woman shoved them hard against the windshield and then bolted from the bus.

"Halt! Halt!" one of the guards shouted as he regained his balance and jumped off the bus.

Rafn quickly grabbed the coats and keeping his eyes on the guard who had remained on the bus, but whose back was to them, shoved them across the aisle. The two men grabbed them and shoved theirs across.

It was over in a second and Rafn craned his neck to look out the window, just catching a glimpse of the young woman dashing into a department store.

The first guard was now in the middle of the street and had raised his machine gun, but then the woman was gone. A moment later he lowered the gun, unclipped the walkie-talkie from his belt, and spoke into it. Then he turned and came back to the bus.

Whoever the woman was, Rafn thought, she had provided the necessary diversion for them. Without her they might never have made the switch.

But he wondered who she was and why she had wanted to enter East Berlin.

CHAPTER 4

Maria Grindl awoke screaming, every muscle in her body straining against the leather straps that held her down on the padded table. She could see, but she was not really conscious of the featureless white confines of the narrow room she was in as the pains wracked her stomach, searing her insides as if someone had opened a hole in her stomach and poured hot metal into it.

"Maria." It was a soft, male voice near her ear, but she tried to blot out the sound that intruded on her misery.

"It will be all right, Maria. Everything will be better soon," he said.

She turned her head and a face above her swam slowly and unsteadily into focus. He smiled.

The pains came at her again and she wanted to double over, but she could not. A roaring was in her ears and she started to scream, but the man placed a gentle hand on her shoulder.

"Can you hear me, Maria? Do you understand what I am saying?"

She looked curiously at the man and then beyond him, but her eyes had trouble focusing on the whiteness over his shoulder, so she looked back at his face.

His hand was around her wrist. She could feel his probing fingers, and for a moment she could not understand what he was doing; then it dawned on her that he was taking her pulse. She was in a hospital. Had she been hurt?

She struggled now to remember who she was and how she had gotten here.

His fingers were gone, but now he was rubbing the inside of her forearm with something cold. She looked down as he pulled the cotton ball away. It smelled strong. Alcohol.

A minute later he tied a rubber tube around her upper arm. She almost laughed now that the pain had subsided. He wouldn't find a vein that way. They had all collapsed.

Horst. The word flashed through her mind almost as painfully as her cramps. Suddenly she knew where she was and why, and she began to tremble.

Horst had been followed. She had seen the man from her window. After she had written the message on the ten-mark bill, she had left her apartment the back way and walked across town to the bus terminal.

Inside, Bermann had taken the money and left to pick up the passengers in the Western Zone while the East German police checked travel permits. She didn't have one.

She recalled now how she had suddenly remembered the travel permits. Horst had mentioned it once, but she had forgotten to get one.

The rubber tube was gone from her arm now, but the man was cutting her gown away. Suddenly she was ashamed. She did not want him to see her nude. She struggled, but it was no use against the restraints at her wrists and ankles. Soon she could feel the coolness of the air on her body. It frightened her even more, so she closed her eyes.

When they turned her away at the bus terminal, she had returned to her apartment. Two days later they came after her.

Her left arm was free and she could feel the man's

gentle hands lifting it up, over her head. A moment later there was a coolness in her armpit.

She opened her eyes and turned her head to the left. The man's hand was large, his fingernails trimmed neatly, the smell of alcohol strong as he disinfected her skin and hair.

She looked up at his smiling face as he threw the cotton away and unhooked the needle attached to the rubber tube that snaked upwards somewhere behind her field of vision.

The meaning of the cotton, the alcohol, and the rubber tube around her arm now clicked into place. Stuff. He was going to give her some stuff. It *would* be all right. Everything would be all right.

She closed her eyes again and let her body relax. A moment later she felt the brief prick of the needle in her armpit, and then a warm flow that felt strange at first, then faded to nothing.

She waited for the high to come; for the floating and weightlessness to begin; for the colors and beautiful roaring to fill her ears—but none of it happened.

Maria opened her eyes. She was completely lucid for the first time in four days. She knew exactly what had happened to her and why. And she knew where she was —the basement of the Karlshorst Residency Hall. The man smiling down at her now was a doctor. And whatever he had injected into her armpit was definitely not heroin. They had lost.

"Did you kill Horst?" she heard herself asking, and she immediately tried to bite her lip, but she could not stop herself. "Horst Steiner—did you kill him?"

The doctor sat down next to the table she was lying on and pulled a metal cart closer to him. He adjusted the controls on what looked like a tape recorder, then he turned back to her, the pleasant smile still on his face.

"Horst died of a heart attack four days ago, Maria,"

he said. "During his arrest. We did everything we could to save him, but by the time he was brought here it was too late. We are sorry."

Maria felt sorrow, but she could not cry. "Are you going to kill me?"

"Yes," the doctor said. "But first I would like to talk with you."

"All right," Maria could hear herself saying. One part of her mind was screaming, trying to make her free arm flail out and dislodge the needle. But it would not work. Some other part of her had taken control. She felt sleepy, but completely rested and relaxed, not tired at all.

"Were you and Horst friends?" the doctor was asking.

"Yes," Maria said.

"Were you lovers?"

"Once. But not since we started with the horse."

"I see," the doctor said, again adjusting the tape recorder. "And where did you get the heroin? Who supplied it to you and Horst?"

"I don't know."

"Where did you get it?"

"It was thrown over the wall at the end of Strasse B whenever we finished a job."

"Who did you work for, Maria?" the doctor asked.

"I don't know."

"Was it an East German?"

"No."

"Did you ever see this person you and Horst worked for?"

"No."

The doctor paused for a moment, and Maria marveled at herself and the things she was saying. She only hoped he would not ask her about Bermann.

"What was that you said?" the doctor asked pleasantly.

For an instant Maria stiffened. She had evidently

been thinking aloud. "I hope you do not ask me about Bermann."

"Who is Bermann?"

"The tour bus driver."

"What is his first name?"

"Wilhelm."

"Does he deliver the heroin?"

Maria giggled. "No."

"Does he deliver messages?"

"Yes," Maria said, and inside she screamed, trying to hold back about the money.

"You said money, Maria. Is that how the messages are sent?" the doctor asked.

Once again Maria realized she had been thinking aloud. "Yes," she said.

"How does the system work? Will you explain it to me?"

"The message was written on a folded ten-mark bill. The money was paid to Bermann, who gave it to a man in the West in change for a torn twenty-mark bill."

"How long have you been doing this, Maria?"

"Almost five years," Maria heard herself saying.

"What information did you gather, Maria?" the doctor was saying, and she knew she could not answer. Suddenly she knew what she was doing, and she screamed inside.

"I don't know," she whimpered.

"Surely you remember, Maria. Please tell me," the doctor said.

"I don't remember," Maria whimpered again.

The doctor stood up and reached behind her, then sat down again. He watched her for a moment, then smiled again.

"Maria," he asked, "what information did you and Horst gather for Bermann this time?"

"Kummersdorf East and Gustav Predel," she heard herself saying. There was an unpleasant hot feeling in her armpit, and she could feel her heart racing. It felt strange, like her heart was fluttering, skipping a beat. Sometimes it felt like that when she was coming down from a big high. It made her uneasy.

"And what did you and Horst find out about them?" the doctor asked.

"Gustav Predel was the director of the research station Kummersdorf East near Tiefensee."

"Did Horst send that message to the West?"

"No."

"The message was not sent?"

"Yes. It was sent."

"Who sent it, Maria?"

"I did," Maria said, and her heart speeded up even more, making her short of breath.

The doctor suddenly jumped up, the smile gone from his face. "Are you sure you sent the message, Maria?" he asked, almost shouting.

"Yes," she managed to gasp between breaths. She could not get enough air, and her heart was racing so fast that her chest was beginning to ache.

"What other projects, Maria?" the doctor was shouting next to her ear. But it seemed far away.

"Missiles," she managed to say, and then a tremendous weight crushed down on her chest. For a brief moment before she died, she was conscious of the fact that her heart had suddenly and completely stopped.

CHAPTER 5

Hans Meitner was seated alone at a small table in the dining room of the Europäischer Hof's eating his breakfast. The dull pain had throbbed in his chest all night and he had gotten very little sleep so that this morning he was tired, more weary than he had ever been in his life. It was as if the thing in his chest were draining away his vitality, his life force. And there was nothing he could do about it.

He had been in Germany for nearly a week now, and had successfully tracked Laurie Andrews's progress all the way to the DBK. Then he had lost her yesterday. She had completely disappeared.

Meitner had considered going to the Berlin police and reporting her as a missing person, but he immediately dismissed it as foolish. They would ask too many questions; questions for which he had no answers.

Yesterday afternoon, after he returned to his hotel, he had finally telephoned Dr. Stewart. The man had been beside himself with worry.

"My God, Hans," Stewart's voice had come over the transatlantic line. "We didn't know what to think. We feared you had been kidnapped or something."

"Nothing so dramatic as that, Dr. Stewart," Meitner said, his voice wavering.

Stewart picked up the uncertainty in his voice. "What's the matter, Hans? Are you sick?"

"No," Meitner said. "I just had to get away. They were hounding me."

"The·reporters are all over the place now. You've been reported as missing. There's nothing much I can do."

"I'm sorry, I couldn't help it."

"Are you in some kind of trouble?" Dr. Stewart asked, his voice lower and more guarded.

Meitner managed to chuckle. "No, Dr. Stewart, it's nothing like that, either. As I said, I merely wanted to get away from the clamor. I needed time to think. Come home for a while."

Stewart hesitated a moment before he spoke again. "Are you coming back soon, Hans?" he asked.

"Yes," Meitner said. "In a day or two. I want to see some friends first."

"What should I tell the reporters?"

"Tell them I'm resting. I'll be back soon to give them all their interviews."

Stewart seemed somewhat relieved, but there was still a note of concern in his voice. "Hans . . ." he began and then paused. "Is there anything I can do for you? You sound . . . tired."

"No, I am all right, I assure you, Dr. Stewart. I will return in a day or two. Everything will be all right."

"If you need anything at all . . ." Stewart said, trailing off.

"Nothing," Meitner said. "I will see you in a few days. Good-bye."

"Good-bye, Hans."

Stewart's concern had touched Meitner, and he had the urge now to return to the States. But he could not leave Germany yet, not knowing that the Andrews woman had learned about Tiefensee.

Meitner's reveries were interrupted by a young man dressed in a rumpled suit and crooked tie.

"Aren't you Dr. Hans Meitner from the United States?" the young man asked in German.

Meitner looked up into his smiling face and nodded uncertainly.

"May I join you?" he asked enthusiastically and pulled up a chair.

Meitner noticed that the young man was carrying a leather bag over his shoulder.

"Permit me to introduce myself, *Herr Doktor*. I am Hermann Müller, a photographer with the *West Berliner Zeitung*. Your photograph came over the wire this morning. You have been reported missing."

Meitner managed a slight smile, although his heart was racing. "As you can see, Herr Müller, I am not missing."

"Yes," the photographer said, grinning. "But may I ask you what brings you to Berlin unannounced? Is there a scientific congress in progress?"

"I am on a short holiday," Meitner said, at a loss for any other explanation.

"Unannounced, sir?" the man said, his eyes narrowing. "That is a bit unusual."

"Do you announce your holidays, Herr Müller?" Meitner said angrily.

The man laughed. "No, sir, but then I have not won the Nobel Prize."

Meitner sighed. He wished this brash young man would go away and leave him alone. He was like Laurie Andrews and all the others. They were pecking at him, and everything was coming apart at the seams. It was all being ruined. An entire lifetime of effort going for nothing.

A look of concern came across the photographer's face and he leaned forward in his chair.

"Are you quite all right, *Herr Doktor*?" the man was saying.

"Yes," Meitner mumbled and nodded his head, but the photographer persisted.

"You do not look well, sir. May I call a doctor for you?"

Meitner shook his head. "What you can do for me, young man, is go away and stop bothering me. I came here to be alone, away from your kind." He got to his feet unsteadily and headed away from the table.

He suddenly felt he had to lie down. He felt so tired. If they would stop pestering him, if they would leave him alone, he could get back to his work. There was so much to be done and so little time in which to do it. It had been the same, years ago, in Tiefensee. Time had always been against them. There was always the rush to accomplish the impossible. And they had nearly done it.

He heard his name being called, and he turned around. A bright flash of light momentarily blinded him, and a second later he saw the photographer lowering his camera.

"Thank you, *Herr Doktor*. I hope you have a pleasant stay in Germany," the man said, and he turned on his heel and hurried for the outside door.

Meitner stood near a table and he put his hand on the chair to steady himself as several diners in the room looked his way. His photograph would undoubtedly appear in the afternoon edition of the newspaper. The story would be out that Dr. Hans Meitner, the recent Nobel Prize laureate, had been seen in West Berlin. Then the others would descend upon him. The hordes of reporters would besiege him with questions for which he had no answers.

The dizziness subsided after a moment, and Meitner turned and shuffled toward the lobby.

By this evening everyone in West Berlin would know he was here. Everyone.

The thought stopped him in his tracks. Everyone would know he was here. That included Laurie Andrews if she were still in the city.

The photo caption would undoubtedly give the name of his hotel, and Laurie Andrews would see it and seek him. Her search would have ended at the Berlin wall— there was no way she would be able to get to Tiefensee.

And even if she had she would have found nothing. She would learn nothing unless she talked with him.

And he would tell her everything. Make her understand a life's worth of work. Make her understand the importance of his research for all of mankind. Make her understand so that she would not print the story.

She would have to see that, of course. Anyone with any modicum of intelligence would have to see that.

With a somewhat lighter step, Meitner crossed the lobby to the elevators. He would simply wait until she came to him, probably no later than this evening.

By tomorrow he would be on his way back to the States. By Christmas this foolishness with the Nobel Prize would be completed, and with the new year he would begin the last leg of his research unhampered, at long last, by his fears of discovery and exposure.

CHAPTER 6

The first thought that crossed Schiller's mind as the bus pulled into the East Berlin terminal and parked was to get rid of the overcoat and stay on the bus until it returned to the West Zone. But he immediately rejected the idea. He was committed now to this course of action. With only East German papers to identify him, he would never make it out. In all probability he would be arrested and returned to the East Zone where his life would be forfeit, and he would not be able to help his sister.

That was it exactly, he told himself, as the doors opened and the East German passengers filed out past the guards. Since he had learned about the possible connection between Gustav Predel and his sister's disappearance, he had been running scared.

David Sherman's description of what Predel had done to the women, especially his wife, kept running through his mind. The thought of his sister being an experimental animal made him break out in a cold sweat.

"Let's go," Rafn said, nudging him, and they both stood up and moved to the front of the bus.

He and his sister had always been close. When they were children the other boys in the kibbutz would pick on her, but he would always come to her defense, sometimes suffering a bloody nose for his trouble. And she had always looked up to him as her natural protector.

Their father had been away in the intelligence service most of the time, but the few leaves he spent at home had been times of happiness for them. Schiller and his sister had idolized the man. They both wanted to grow up to be like him.

Schiller had joined the service when he was sixteen, and two years later, when he returned home for the first time, he was surprised and saddened to see how much his sister had grown. No longer was she just a little girl dependent upon him for her protection. She had, in those two years without a father or an older brother, become fiercely independent. A scrapper. All of the boys who had taunted and teased her were now maintaining a respectable distance.

Schiller looked up as the East German guard spoke to him. *"Bitte?"* he said, confused.

"Your travel permit," the guard snapped harshly.

Schiller could feel his muscles tense, and from the corner of his eye he could see Rafn hesitating a moment on the steps. Schiller relaxed slightly and withdrew the permit from his coat pocket and handed it to the guard. "Sorry," he said contritely.

The guard took the permit, looked at it a moment, and then looked at Schiller's face as if he were memorizing it for future reference.

"Geh!" he finally said, and Schiller got off the bus and fell in step with Rafn and headed for the parking lot behind the building.

When they were out of earshot, Rafn asked angrily, "What the hell was all that about?"

"I was preoccupied," Schiller said absently. "It went all right."

"Like hell," Rafn hissed. "That guard knows your face, and right now he's trying to figure out why he doesn't remember giving you the travel permit before the tour began. That was stupid, Schiller."

"I said it's all right," Schiller repeated, turning to look at him.

They came to the battered Mercedes diesel sedan and Rafn fished the keys from his pocket, unlocked the doors, and they got in, Rafn slipping behind the wheel. The back seat had been removed and a large board had been wedged into place on the floor to make a flat space for several wooden crates filled with wine bottles.

Rafn started the engine with some difficulty, but before he put the car in gear he turned to Schiller. "If you fall apart on me now, I'll dump you."

Schiller had the same gut reaction now that he had on the bus. "I'm sorry," he said.

None of this had any personal effect on Rafn, who was in it, Schiller suspected, for some kind of perverse pleasure. Although the Dane was good, this was nothing more than a game to him. A game that Schiller decided he would play only as long as Rafn didn't get in his way. Nothing was going to stop his primary mission: that of finding and killing Gustav Predel, even if it meant eliminating Rafn himself.

Schiller seriously doubted if they would find anything of Predel in Tiefensee. When this operation was completed he was going to have to go into the Soviet Union. Somehow he would find his sister.

Rafn was talking to him, and he looked up.

"What did you say?"

Rafn stared at him. "What the hell is happening to you. . . ? he started to ask, but he stopped in mid-sentence, stiffened, and nudged Schiller's leg. "Trouble," he said under his breath.

Schiller turned as the guard from the bus who had taken their travel permits came across the parking lot to Rafn's side of the car.

Rafn rolled down the window as the second guard from the bus came around the corner of the building about twenty meters away and stopped to watch them.

"Your identification and car registration papers," the first guard snapped.

"Of course," Rafn said pleasantly, and he took a thick leather wallet from his coat pocket, withdrew the papers, and handed them to the unsmiling guard.

The guard, one hand on the strap of the machine gun over his shoulder, reached out and took the papers, then leaned down so he could see into the car.

"Your papers, as well," he said to Schiller.

Schiller handed his papers out to the guard and tensed. There was no way they were going to be stopped here. They had been told there would be weapons under the front seat. If need be, he would take the guard out and they would make a run for it. Somehow they would make it over the wall. But at all costs he could not be stopped. He was going to have to get out so that he could find out about his sister. He could not leave that undone.

The guard looked at their papers for a long moment, then peered in the window at the crates of wine bottles.

When he glanced back at Rafn, he seemed about to say something, but the other guard shouted at him and he looked away.

The guard by the building held up his walkie-talkie, and the first guard turned and threw the papers back into Rafn's lap, stared at them for a long moment, and then briskly walked back across the parking lot.

Schiller sighed deeply as he pulled a .38 revolver from under the seat.

Rafn put the car in gear and eased out of the parking lot, but said nothing to Schiller until they had gone several blocks.

"He knew something was wrong because of the way you acted on the bus."

"It's all right now," Schiller said, his mind already back on his sister. If there were some kind of an operation in Siberia, and if Gustav Predel were still alive, it probably meant she was there now. The only thing they could possibly learn in Tiefensee, he decided, was whether the Russians had captured the research facility and its personnel. If that were true, it was very likely that his sister was in deep trouble.

But once they learned what there was to learn in Tiefensee about Predel's present whereabouts, Schiller was going to return to the West Zone, with or without Rafn.

Nothing was going to stop him, he decided firmly. Nothing.

CHAPTER 7

"We'll wait here for a few minutes, Miss Andrews," the police officer said to her pleasantly. His English was perfect, and from the moment he had arrested her in the intercity bus depot, he had been polite. She felt more like a guest than a prisoner, and she relaxed now after the initial shock.

"What's going to happen to me?" she asked. They were standing outside of the depot on the sidewalk. After her arrest, the policeman had taken her out of the building, had spoken to someone by walkie-talkie, and now they stood chatting almost like friends, it seemed, although Laurie was cold.

"You will be asked a few questions, and then I imagine they will send you back to the Brandenburg Gate. That's where you entered, isn't it?"

"Yes," Laurie said, nodding, and she smiled slightly, remembering the startled, almost frightened look on the guards' faces when she pushed them aside and took off running.

The policeman returned her smile. "Whatever possessed you to jump off the bus and come here?"

"I want to get to Tiefensee," Laurie said.

The policeman looked startled. "All the way to Tiefensee?" he said. "Do you have relatives there?"

Laurie shook her head. "I'm on an assignment for my newspaper," she said.

"Is this normal procedure for American journalists?" he asked.

"We do whatever we have to do in order to complete an assignment," she said. "I don't suppose there is any chance I would be allowed to go to Tiefensee? It wouldn't take very long."

The officer smiled and shook his head. "I'm afraid such things are not allowed. It is different here than in the United States."

"Yes," Laurie said dryly. At least, she thought to herself, Shapiro wouldn't fault her for trying. And her arrest would make an interesting sidebar to her story on Meitner. If there were going to be a story at all, now.

She was going to have to find Meitner and talk with him. If she were to confront him with the fact that she knew his real name wasn't Meitner, he would tell her what he had done during the war. She doubted it, but anything was possible.

The policeman had been studying her face with interest, and she looked up at him, a questioning expression in her eyes.

"I was wondering about you, Miss Andrews," the officer said almost apologetically. "In Europe most journalists are somewhat older—shall we say—distinguished men."

"As you say," Laurie said, smiling, "things are different here."

The officer nodded. "Whatever could you be looking for in Tiefensee?"

"I'm doing a story on a Nazi war project that was located there," Laurie said. There was no reason for her to lie to him.

His expression darkened. "None of that is left in Germany," he said. His manner had suddenly turned brusque, and for the first time since she had been arrested she realized that she was an American in a communist country. An enemy country. In more trouble than she realized.

When she had jumped off the bus, she had run across the street and into the nearest building, which turned out to be a department store. Not looking over her shoulder, she had rushed past startled clerks and customers, through the back door of the establishment and into an alleyway, and had not stopped running until she was two blocks away.

For the next ten minutes she had wandered aimlessly, not knowing what her next step would be, and certain that her arrest would come at any moment.

She was out of place. Her clothes and even her bearing were different from everyone she passed, and as she walked, everyone stared.

She happened on the bus depot, entered, handed the clerk some money, and spoke the only word of German she knew that would mean anything: "Tiefensee."

It came as no surprise to her when the police officer came in the front door a few moments later and in English told her she was under arrest.

"How did you know I was here?" Laurie asked now, breaking the silence.

The police officer looked at her but said nothing. A minute later a large black sedan came around the corner a half block away and glided to a halt at the curb in front of them. Two men in drab gray suits jumped out and came up to them.

One of them said something in German to the officer. He smiled, pointed back to the depot, and then handed Laurie's heavy purse over to the man, who turned to her.

"Miss Andrews?" he said politely, his German accent heavy.

She nodded uncertainly.

"If you will come with us, please, we will have this straightened out in a very short time."

The man took her arm while the other hurried to the car and opened the back door for her. She got in the back seat, the one who opened the door sliding in beside her, while the other man went around the car and got in behind the wheel.

She turned to wave to the police officer, but he had already turned and was heading away from them; a moment later they pulled away from the curb.

"Where are you taking me?" Laurie asked the man who sat beside her.

"To police headquarters," he said.

"Will I be returned to West Berlin?"

The driver said something brief, and the man in the back seat stopped talking and turned to stare straight ahead.

Laurie could feel her apprehension; for once she wished she had not been so flippant with Shapiro. She wished she had told him where she was going. He would have tried to stop her, which would have made no difference, but at least he would have known where she was.

She did not want to end up like the American woman who was still in a Turkish prison, or the hundreds of POWs she was sure were still captives in North Vietnamese jails.

For the first time she realized what being an American in the United States meant in terms of personal freedom. And she was frightened now. More frightened than she had ever been in her life.

CHAPTER 8

Despite the fact that Rafn could feel there was something wrong with this town, he was looking forward to talking with the priest in the Catholic church as he walked along the main street past the post office. He turned the corner and continued down the block toward the stucco-and-wood structure that faced the cemetery marking the outer limits of the village.

He was not only concerned about Schiller, whom he had left at the Hülsterhof Gasthaus, but also about the feeling of impending doom that hung in the air of this town. At first he felt paranoid but later dismissed it. There was something else.

Crossing the cobblestone street, he passed under the wrought-iron gate, went up the stone walk, and mounted the steps to the church. The priest had summoned him earlier this afternoon while he was having lunch in the Hülsterhof's dining room. The word had gotten around that two wine salesmen from Leipzig were in Tiefensee to demonstrate their wares and the priest wanted to talk to them.

Rafn accepted and sent a message back with the altar boy that he would meet with the priest at the church at three o'clock.

It was a few minutes before three now, and as Rafn pulled the heavy wooden door open by its thick metal ring, he thought about Schiller.

Schiller had held his silence during the drive out of the city, but once they hit the open road, he turned to Rafn. There was a wild look in his eyes.

"Let's go back," he said quietly.

Rafn glanced at him and then returned his attention to the road. "What the hell's the matter with you, Schiller?"

"I want to go back."

Rafn had seen other operatives lose their nerve and it was not a pretty thing to witness. And now the same thing seemed to be happening with Schiller. If it went too far, Rafn promised himself, he would have to take him out. Too much now depended on speed and keeping a low profile to risk a scene with Schiller.

But first he wanted to find out what was eating away at the Israeli. He took a stab in the dark. "You won't be able to help your sister very well without some hard information." It had to be her or fear for his own safety that he was concerned about.

He could see the muscles cording on Schiller's neck, and he tensed, one hand sliding off the wheel toward the buttons on the front of his coat. His knife was in the scabbard beneath his left arm.

A moment passed and Schiller relaxed slightly. "We're tracking a dead end, Rafn. We'll find nothing in Tiefensee."

"It's our only remaining clue," Rafn said. "If Kozhevnikov doesn't get out we'll be stuck without any information. And if they figure out his operation, they'll backtrack here and cover anything that's in the open. This is our one and only chance."

"The trail is too old," Schiller said, shaking his head.

"What about Predel?" Rafn snapped, keeping his eyes on the road.

"I don't care about him," Schiller said softly.

"Or the women in Israel—the ones who were Predel's guinea pigs?"

"I don't care!" Schiller said, raising his voice. "That happened in the past. My sister is right now."

Rafn turned to him. "You won't be doing a fucking thing for her if you lose your nerve!"

The harsh truth stopped Schiller. He turned and looked out the window and sighed deeply. "I don't think I can handle it anymore."

With a sinking feeling, Rafn realized that he was witnessing an operative lose his nerve, and he wondered if it would be the same with him one day.

"You won't have to do anything," he said finally to the man's back.

They had not said anything to each other for the rest of the trip, and when they had pulled into Tiefensee and had checked into the *Gasthaus,* Schiller had gone immediately to their room. Rafn started spreading the story that they were wine salesmen from a new vineyard and would be happy to conduct a wine-tasting demonstration at the *Gasthaus* tomorrow evening.

It was cold inside the church. Rafn stood facing the altar just inside the doorway at the end of a narrow aisle between the pews. A very old wooden crucifix hung from a heavy rope attached to the vaulted ceiling, and Rafn stared at it.

He had never been a very religious man. His parents in Jutland had been Protestant, and when he was a young boy he went to church regularly. But he had never liked it. For him church was nothing more than a place for the well-to-do to show how well-to-do they were, and for the poor to come and gawk at them under the pretense of worshiping.

As a young man, his conviction that organized religion was a sham deepened and he all but put it out of his mind. He had to admit to himself that lately he had begun to give the matter some thought. People were the hypocrites, not the philosophy.

"Gutten Nachmittag," a pleasant voice said from

the shadows to Rafn's left. He turned as an aged, frail man got up from one of the pews, shuffled into the aisle, and painfully approached.

"It is a beautiful crucifix," the priest said simply.

"Yes, it is," Rafn agreed, studying him. He wore a black cassock that dragged on the floor as he walked, and he carried a cane which he used to relieve the weight on his right leg. The man's face was deeply lined and there was the same haunted look in his eyes that Rafn felt everywhere in this town.

"When I came here fifty-two years ago, there was only a small figure of Christ on the altar. After the war we received permission to salvage this one from the ruins of St. Theresa's in Magdeburg."

"Many places were ruined during the war," Rafn said carefully.

"Yes," the priest said, a slight catch in his voice. "Even our little Tiefensee, although we were not destroyed by bombs, became a *kümmerliches Dorf,* a sorrowful village."

Sorrowful village. Rafn began to tense. "Sorrow comes in many forms, Father. Does it still plague your village?"

The priest studied Rafn's eyes, and then he sighed, a look of weariness and sadness crossing his features. "In the work of the Antichrist, himself," he said.

Rafn felt slightly uncomfortable. He motioned toward one of the pews. "May we sit and talk awhile, Father?"

The old priest shook his head. "No. Leave Tiefensee this afternoon, Herr . . ."

"Shultenbrunner," Rafn said. "But my wine-tasting demonstration is tomorrow night at the Hülsterhof."

The priest did not smile. "I have the luxury of a telephone here, and I have friends in Leipzig who purchase wine for the sacraments. Leave Tiefensee, Herr Shultenbrunner, you cannot help us."

Rafn wanted a cigarette, but he restrained himself. "I will leave Tiefensee, Father, but first I must get some information on someone who was here during the war."

The priest shook his head. "Go away. I can't help you."

"A hundred thousand lives may depend upon it," Rafn said softly.

The old man's eyes seemed out of focus, but now he looked directly at Rafn, his eyes sad and moist.

For several minutes they stood and stared at each other in silence. Rafn could hear the light wind coming through a partially open window somewhere. A truck rumbled past. When it was gone, the priest spoke.

"Is it still happening?"

"Yes it is. I want to stop it."

The priest seemed to debate with himself, and for a moment Rafn was certain the man was on the verge of collapse. But then he took a deep breath, as if he had drawn strength from an inner reserve, and his eyes cleared. "Then I must help you. What would you know?"

Rafn shuddered involuntarily. Once the connection was made, and he was certain it would be sooner or later, the Soviets would come for the priest and others in the village who knew what had happened. But too much depended upon this for Rafn to give up.

"There was a Nazi experimental station here during the war," he finally said.

"Yes. It was called Station Kummersdorf."

"Headed by Gustav Predel?"

"Yes. The man without a soul. He was a monster."

"Did you know him?"

"Not personally," the priest said. "He came to town from time to time, but for the most part he remained at the station."

"Where was it located?"

The priest looked at him. "A few kilometers east of town at the foot of the hills; there is nothing left. Everything is gone."

"Gone where?" Rafn asked.

"The Russians took everything. The people, the buildings, even the fences. There was nothing left but the foundations of the buildings. Even those are gone now."

"What became of Predel?" Rafn asked.

"He was murdered by the SS. All of the Germans were murdered by the SS the night before the Russians came. The Jews were murdered, too."

"Why?"

The priest thought a moment, and when he looked at Rafn again there was fear in his eyes. "Leave this place while you can."

"Why was everyone murdered that night?" Rafn insisted.

The priest held his silence for a moment, then shook his head. "I don't know. Perhaps there was a shred of decency left among those who were still in Berlin. Perhaps it was guilt. Or fear of discovery."

"What were the scientists doing at Station Kummersdorf, Father?"

Again the old priest's eyes seemed to go out of focus, but he straightened up. "Leave," he said, his voice rising. "Go away and leave us alone."

"I cannot, Father. One hundred thousand Soviet Jews have been taken to Siberia. The phrase *Kummersdorf Papers* was mentioned in connection with the project. I think that whatever the Nazis did here to the Jews, the Russians are doing to them in Siberia."

The priest turned white; his entire body was quivering. He made the sign of the cross as tears began to slip down his cheeks. "Forgive me," he mumbled and shuffled away from Rafn toward the front of the church.

"Father, help me," Rafn called after him, but the old priest didn't seem to hear him as he moved slowly to the altar where he kneeled down. laid his cane by his side, and clasped his hands together and began to pray.

Rafn watched him for a while, and then he turned and went to the door. When he opened it, he turned to look at the priest again.

"There are watchers here," the old man said without turning around; his voice sounded hollow.

Rafn strained to hear him, but the priest fell silent, and a moment later Rafn was headed toward the *Gasthaus*.

If there were watchers, they had to be Russian. They would be the only ones expecting anyone to come here. Between them and the fact that Schiller had become a useless piece of baggage, Rafn was going to have to hurry.

CHAPTER 9

Bermann was dead tired when he braked his empty bus to a halt at the West Zone checkpoint, put it in neutral, and opened the door to admit the two American guards. This was his last run of the day, and now all he wanted to do was return to his apartment on the outskirts of East Berlin, sink into a hot tub, and have a light dinner before going to bed.

The two Americans climbed aboard without a word and quickly began to search the bus.

Today had been doubly tiring because of the operatives he had gotten in and out of the East Zone. The young woman who wanted to remain in East Berlin had created more excitement than he wanted, too.

When she had jumped up out of her seat, he was sure she was going to vomit. If that had happened, he would have had to clean up the filthy mess.

The last time it happened he had vowed to hustle the passenger off the bus before it was too late.

He had done exactly that today. Only he never dreamed she wanted to escape.

For a moment he was sure the guard would fire at her, and was relieved when she made it across the sidewalk and into the department store. For the life of him he could not figure why the woman, obviously a well-to-do American, would want to come into East Berlin.

He sighed as the guards finished their task and got off the bus.

He closed the door, put the bus in gear, and eased forward through the gate back into the Eastern sector.

On the other side the East German guard waved him across the avenue, and he drove around behind the terminal and eased into the parking lot next to four other buses.

As he shut off the engine and switched off the lights, he wondered about the four men.

He could understand the two men who had escaped. He thought about doing it himself, only every time he thought about it a mental picture of his wife and three children stopped him.

He could probably manage to make it across the wall alone, but with his wife and children it would be impossible. And he was certain that many of the people who lived in East Berlin stayed there for similar reasons.

But the two men who had entered East Berlin and taken the car were another matter. What could possibly be so important that they were willing to risk their lives?

The papers he had provided them would not withstand close scrutiny. A quick telephone call would disclose that the travel permits had been used more than a month ago; the wine sellers' permits had been stolen more than a year ago from a small wine shop here in East Berlin; and the automobile registration belonged to an East German *Apotheke* owner whom Bermann had bribed with ten grams of heroin.

Bermann got wearily to his feet and stepped off the bus, closing the door behind him. He had turned in his money before the last run, and now he would walk to the corner and wait for the city bus to take him home.

It was cold. He zippered his jacket all the way up and shivered.

At least the rain had stopped, he mused, looking

up at the darkening sky, but the weather would not hold. It looked as if it would begin to rain at any moment.

He supposed the two men were looking for more information on the project that Horst and Maria had been busy with before they disappeared.

The thought stopped him. First Horst disappeared, and then Maria was reported missing by the others. They had melted into the city somewhere, and now there was no telling if any of them would be able to receive payment for this job. Horst had promised to split the half kilo evenly, and Bermann needed the payoff.

Although he was not a drug addict himself, he still accepted payment in the heroin because it was easily marketable through a man he knew. Another fifty grams of heroin would pay for a small car, and he could take his family on picnics in the country when the weather turned warm.

If Horst or Maria didn't show up, they wouldn't be able to receive payment, and his plans for a car would be ruined. Unless . . .

A second thought stopped him, and he pondered it as he stood in the shadows near the maintenance garage a half block away.

. . . unless they paid only him for bringing the two operatives into the East Zone. He had taken all the risks. There was no reason anyone else had to share.

Tomorrow was his day off. Perhaps he could take a bus to Tiefensee and talk with these two men. Perhaps he could arrange for an immediate payment—enough for a car, or maybe a motorcycle. Yes, a motorcycle. He would settle for that.

Bermann's step was lighter now as he again headed for the bus stop two blocks away.

Even if Horst and Maria had been arrested, no one had connected him with the network. If they had, they would have come for him by now.

Yes, he told himself, everything was going to be all

right. There was even a possibility that he might receive payment of the entire half kilo himself. Keeping Horst's and Maria's large shares for himself would leave him more money than he would earn in ten years as a bus driver.

His peace of mind was suddenly shattered, however, when a voice called his name from the shadows. He stopped and swiveled around as two men came into view about ten meters behind him. They were walking fast and had apparently followed him from the bus terminal.

"Herr Bermann," one of them called again. "Wait a moment, please. We would like to talk with you."

They were Russian. He could hear it in the man's voice.

Bermann moaned, turned, and headed away in a dead run.

"Halt!" one of them shouted, and Bermann could feel his bowels loosening. He suddenly soiled his trousers but kept running. Horst and Maria had disappeared. They had been arrested. And they had talked. Everything was finished. Everything.

He had no specific last thought as something hard slammed into the back of his head, except that whatever it was seemed terribly hot.

He was dead before he hit the pavement.

CHAPTER 10

"Good evening, Miss Andrews. I'm Fedor Udalov."

Laurie Andrews looked up tiredly as the young man who had just entered the office where she had been sequestered for the past ten hours came across the room to her. He sat down in an easy chair across from the sofa where she was lying. She sat up.

"When am I going to be allowed to return to West Berlin?" she asked.

Udalov smiled. "That depends upon you, Miss Andrews," he said.

Laurie ran her fingers through her hair. She was a mess, and she wished they had at least allowed her to keep her cosmetics.

"What do you want from me?" she said. "It's late and I'm tired."

"I understand," Udalov said sympathetically. "But I must know why you did such a foolish thing this morning. What could you possibly hope to find by wandering around East Berlin?"

"I told the policeman who arrested me. I wanted to go to Tiefensee."

"Whatever for?" Udalov said, smiling slightly.

"I'm a journalist. I was assigned to do a story on Dr. Hans Meitner. He's just won the Nobel Prize. I learned that during the war he worked on some project in Tiefensee. I wanted to go there to see if anyone remembered him."

Udalov gave her a long stare, and Laurie felt uncomfortable. There was something about his eyes, his bearing, that did not seem quite right.

The two men who had picked her up at the bus depot and driven her here to police headquarters had said nothing. When they arrived she had been led through a back entrance, taken upstairs to the second floor and, in a small room adjacent to this one, been searched by a stout, closemouthed woman.

Afterward, the woman had brought her to this room and left, locking the door behind her.

The only furniture in the room besides the couch and easy chair was an empty desk, a chair, and an empty bookcase against one wall. A small bathroom with a sink and toilet adjoined the room, and there were no windows anywhere. The only light came from the recessed fluorescent tubes in the ceiling.

She had lost track of time and had slept for a while, but she was certain that it was late.

"Look," she said, breaking the silence. "I'm an American citizen and I demand to see the ambassador or consulate or someone."

"There are no such people representing the United States in this country, Miss Andrews," Udalov said matter-of-factly. "As to your American citizenship, there is some doubt, but we are checking it now."

"What!" she screamed, snapping forward. "Listen, you sonofabitch, I demand to be released at once. When my paper finds out that I'm being held for no reason here, they'll . . ." She let it trail off.

Udalov stared impassively at her. "Tell me about Dr. Meitner," he said softly.

Again Laurie ran her fingers through her hair. This was all wrong, and somehow Meitner was at the center of it. She remembered Gertrude Vogel's warning. The other man seeking information on Predel, and therefore on Meitner, was a professional, and probably dangerous. This man, too, seemed professional—

deadly. Laurie felt as if she were caught in the middle of something very big.

"I told you everything I know," she said finally, and for the first time there was a change in Udalov's expression. He seemed impatient.

"I don't believe you understand the seriousness of what has happened to you, Miss Andrews," he said. "You have been arrested in a country that does not have friendly relations with the United States. No one can help you. If it is determined that you are a spy, you could very well be shot. Do you understand?"

The gravity of the situation suddenly hit her, and she marveled at her naiveté and stupidity. She had been playing a child's game in the world of adults. She began to tremble.

"If you cooperate with me," Udalov continued, "your belongings will be returned to you, and you will be driven back to the Brandenburg checkpoint."

Laurie looked up at him. She was finished with this Meitner business now. Whoever he was and whatever he had done during the war would probably make one hell of a story, but it simply was not worth her life. Two years ago she had been jailed for contempt of court when she refused to answer questions about an unidentified source for a story she had written. A murder trial had taken place, and she had been subpoenaed, but refused to testify about her source. The charges were dropped when the defendant was acquitted.

But the two weeks in jail had not been terribly bad. Although she had chafed at the confinement, there had never been any doubt about the ultimate outcome. Her stand was correct. Her newspaper was behind her. She had the best attorneys money could hire. And even her jailers knew she was not a criminal, so they treated her accordingly.

This now was a totally different story. If she were not shot, she would in all likelihood be jailed. But jailed as a foreigner, a criminal against the state.

Although she was naive, she had no illusions about what that would be like. Meitner's story was simply not worth it.

"All right," she said. "What do you want to know?"

Udalov's pleasant manner returned. "Tell me about Dr. Meitner and the story you are pursuing that made you attempt to go to Tiefensee."

Laurie took a deep breath and sighed. "Hans Meitner is a geneticist at the University of Wisconsin. Last week he was named this year's winner of the Nobel Prize in physiology and medicine. My paper assigned me to do a story about him and the other winners." She paused.

Udalov said nothing, waiting for her to continue.

Resigned now, she told Udalov everything she had done and learned since she left New Orleans, including her sexual liaison with Meitner's laboratory assistant.

Udalov remained quiet, sitting in the chair staring at her, the slight smile still on his lips. His expression changed, however, when she came to the part about Gertrude Vogel's warning that someone else was interested in Meitner.

"Who is this other person?" Udalov interrupted, sitting forward.

Laurie shrugged her shoulders. "Walter Goldmann. He's supposedly an Israeli News Service correspondent, but I got the impression from Vogel that he was something else. She called him a professional and said he was dangerous."

Udalov thought a moment before he asked his next question. "That still does not explain how you came to find out that Meitner, or whatever his name is, worked in Tiefensee."

"When I went back to the hospital with the attorney general's authorization, I was looking for some record of Gustav Predel and his associates. Since his name had been mentioned in Meitner's laboratory journal, he was the only lead I had. In a record book for 1940, beneath Predel's name and the names of about fifteen other people, was the notation *Tiefensee*. They had been transferred there to some kind of a project."

"I see," Udalov said. "And what about the Jew, Walter Goldmann, have you had contact with him?"

Laurie shook her head. "No, but the hospital records clerk said the man had looked at the same book I had."

"What?" Udalov asked. He looked surprised.

"I said the man, Walter Goldmann, had been to the hospital a day or so before I was, and had looked at the same book. He, too, was looking for Gustav Predel."

Udalov seemed to be struggling with himself and looked annoyed. For several moments he seemed almost angry, but then the look of amusement came across his features again.

"That is when you decided to take the tour bus and escape to Tiefensee?" he asked.

"Yes," Laurie said. "But it was stupid of me." She stared at Udalov for a long moment, certain that the fear showed on her face. "But I am no spy, Mr. Udalov. I only wanted to do a story on Meitner."

Udalov smiled, stood up, and helped Laurie to her feet. "I believe you, Miss Andrews," he said, and he led her to the door.

"Are you going to let me go?" she said, her heart racing.

He knocked once on the door and glanced at her. "We will drive you back to the Brandenburg Gate," he said, and the matron opened the door.

They left the room and started down the long corridor toward the back of the building.

Laurie wanted to sing out. She had made it, and once she got back to the States she would confront Meitner with what she had learned and still come up with one hell of a story. Her arrest would make the best reading of all.

They went downstairs and out the back door. It

was dark and cold now. The slight breeze felt damp, and Laurie shivered.

The lights on a black sedan parked in the lot across a narrow alleyway came on and the car headed their way. Udalov turned to her.

"Where is Dr. Meitner now?" he asked. "Is he still in Wisconsin?"

"No. He followed me here to Germany. He suspected I was on his trail."

Udalov seemed startled with this news, but he said nothing more as the sedan pulled up in front of them and he stepped off the curb, opened the door, and motioned for her to get in.

"My purse," Laurie said, hesitating a moment.

"It's in the car," Udalov said. "Let's go."

Something was drastically wrong here. Laurie could suddenly feel it. She turned and was about to protest, but Udalov shoved her in the back seat and slipped in beside her, pulling the door shut as the car moved away.

"Der Flughafen," Udalov said to the driver.

It was the German word for airport, Laurie knew that much from the road signs in West Berlin. She was about to protest again when the driver turned to acknowledge the command. Suddenly alarm bells jangled along her nerves, and she felt almost dizzy. Everything was wrong. She was not being returned home. She would never get home. She was in the middle of something now that was even bigger than she had ever suspected.

"Jawohl," said the driver, an exact twin of Udalov.

CHAPTER 11

Rafn sat alone in the Mercedes, the nearly shot engine idling roughly in the still night air, the headlights illuminating what had obviously been a wide road at one time. The road led away from the dirt track he had followed down the steep hills east of Tiefensee, toward an area of farm fields that was flatter than anything else around it.

He had not really expected to find anything more than this, and yet he was slightly disappointed. He turned in his seat and looked back the way he had come, but the dirt road was lost in the darkness as it wound its way back through the trees.

Forty years ago there had been a fence and buildings here, but now there was nothing but a farm field.

Given sufficient time, enough manpower and tools, Rafn was certain that clues could be dug up. A foundation, some wire, even a piece of metal would prove that the research facility had been located on this exact spot.

But even that would not provide them with any more information than they already had.

Rafn turned that thought over in his mind. Why had he come here in the first place? Was it merely to strike back at Bindrich for taking him off the operation? Or had he come here because he still had some doubts about Kozhevnikov?

Bindrich could be correct in his assessment. Perhaps Kozhevnikov was involved in a disinformation plot.

There was no doubt in Rafn's mind that Kozhevnikov believed what he had told them, but it still did not make the existence of the Russian research station a fact. Kozhevnikov simply believed it existed.

Two points supported it, however. Schiller's sister had disappeared. But that was no sure indication that anything unusual was going on in Russia. She was an Israeli operative. Perhaps the Russians had merely stumbled onto her operation and she had been arrested.

But then there was the priest, obviously frightened not only by what had happened forty years ago but by what was still happening today. If there were watchers here, it would mean the Russians were up to something connected with the Nazis, something important enough that they had to station someone here to watch for inquiries.

He smiled. Arguing with himself like this had become a habit and was a result of living alone, of depending upon no one for his day-to-day existence.

He opened the door and got out. Lighting a cigarette he perched on the edge of the hood, one headlight shining on the back of his pants leg. It was cold, and the sky was still overcast. Beyond the swath of light from the car he could not tell where the land ended and the sky began.

For the first time in his life he felt his aloneness as something real, something so tangible that he could almost reach out and touch it.

He was old, and he felt his age. There had been more than one chance to commit his life to someone else. But every time he walked away from a relationship, he congratulated himself afterward. He was in the wrong kind of business for such entanglements. Men like Gleason and Kozhevnikov, who were both committed to their wives, were only effective as long as they could keep their personal lives from becoming entangled with their professional worlds. It always became impossible sooner or later.

Gleason had suffered because of it. He was not an intelligence officer. Never had been. He was a husband and a father, and the two worlds were mutually exclusive.

Kozhevnikov was the same, only he was in worse straits than Gleason, now that his wife was dead.

And Schiller—Schiller had gone to pieces over his sister's welfare.

Rafn envied them in a way. They all had someone else to think about. To worry about. To be concerned with. But was that enviable? he wondered. Or was it a rock around their necks? Gleason had been pulled off the case. Kozhevnikov had lost his wife and was now somewhere in Siberia. And Schiller had fallen apart.

He took one last drag on his cigarette and flipped it away from him, the glowing end arching in the darkness.

This operation was sour. It had been from the beginning. Nothing further could be done here in East Germany. It all depended upon Kozhevnikov getting out of Siberia and bringing them the proof they needed.

It was a foregone conclusion that Kozhevnikov would try to get out. The man was dedicated, but his chances for success were slight. What was left?

The watcher. Rafn hoped that by coming here this evening he would flush him out of the woodwork. So far it had not happened. If there were a watcher it would prove that the Russians were up to something important indeed, or at least provide enough proof to satisfy him, if not Bindrich. But even that had not happened.

He turned and was about to get back in the car when he noticed a flash on the hill above him. He stopped and stared, not certain he had seen anything. A few seconds later he saw the flash of light through the trees again, and he could make out the twin beams of headlights moving very fast down the dirt road. He smiled.

Rafn quickly doused the Mercedes' headlights and

hurried to the back of the car where he took out his knife and broke out the taillights with the handle.

He jumped in the car, put it in gear, and backed onto the dirt road and took off as fast as he dared in the darkness.

Whoever was coming down the hill had not followed him from the *Gasthaus*. Evidently it had taken them all day to discover strangers were in town, and when they discovered Rafn was missing, they had come directly out here.

If there were only one watcher, they would be all right. Rafn would be able to make it back to town, where he could pick up Schiller and they could make their escape.

But if there were more than one, they would have gotten to the Israeli already.

Rafn glanced in the rearview mirror, and for a moment he could see nothing but blackness. Then he saw the headlights in the flat part of the valley where he had parked a few moments ago.

The dirt road curved to the right and climbed up the hill toward the paved highway on the other side.

When he left the hotel this evening, Schiller had been completely distraught and had practically begged for them to leave while they still had the chance.

Rafn didn't tell him about the priest, but assured him they would leave as soon as he returned.

Schiller didn't ask Rafn where he was going, but merely nodded his head in relief and laid down on the bed, one arm over his eyes.

Earlier in the evening Schiller had told him about the briefing he had received in Tel Aviv. And he had told Rafn that he was certain his sister was now one of Predel's victims.

"You've got to finish this for me," Schiller said.

Rafn said nothing at first, forcing himself to look away.

Schiller came across the room and grabbed Rafn's

arm, pulling him around. "You've got to promise me that if something happens to me, you'll finish this. I've got to know that."

Rafn pushed his hand away and faced him. "I'll finish it, Schiller," he said softly.

Schiller stared at him for a long time, then went across the room and sat on the bed. "I'll wait for you," he said.

If they had gotten to Schiller, he wouldn't have been able to defend himself. Rafn was sure of it. And for a moment he wondered if Schiller had experienced a premonition of his own death when they had entered the East Zone on the tour bus.

He had heard of such things, but always dismissed them as fantasy, as he did now. Schiller had lost his nerve and was blaming it on his concern for his sister. Whatever the cause, he was finished as an operative, and until Rafn was able to get him back into West Germany the man would be a stone around his neck.

It was a few minutes after two when Rafn finally stopped a hundred meters from the Hülsterhof, shut off the engine, and sat for a moment. There was no movement in the town, and he had seen no sign of his pursuer since he left him in the valley.

His thoughts turned to Kozhevnikov. The connection between him and these inquiries had probably been made now, and very shortly Kozhevnikov would either escape or be captured.

One way or the other, Rafn thought as he got out of the car and started toward the *Gasthaus,* this operation would be over very soon.

The Hülsterhof was a large, three-story Bavarian-style building that was set well back off the street. Across the street was a row of shops, the night shutters down over the front windows and doors. To the left were more shuttered shops, and to the right, across a single set of railroad tracks, was the small depot.

Beyond that was the center of town. Behind the *Gasthaus* a large field sloped upwards toward the wooded hills outside town.

Rafn slipped around the side of the building and entered a rear door which led through a short corridor to a flight of stairs. No one was awake, and a single light bulb on the wall illuminated the stairs. Rafn stopped long enough to unscrew the light bulb, and then he continued up in the darkness, withdrawing his knife. He had never liked firearms because, even with silencers, they were noisy.

Their room was on the second floor, along with four others that all opened into a large common room at the center of the building. Rafn stopped on the second-floor landing and listened. The building was quiet.

There was something wrong. As he started across the common room, he noticed that there was no light shining from under the door to their room. Schiller would be waiting for him. He would have a light on. Rafn was certain of it.

He had never liked violence, but it was part of his job, and he could handle it despite his age.

At the door to their room, he stopped and listened, his ear against the wood. At first there was no sound. He was about to open the door when he heard someone walking toward him. The doorknob turned and the door swung open. He quickly stepped to the side, his knife up and ready.

At first Rafn thought it was Schiller. The man was tall and broad-shouldered. But as he came all the way out he sensed his presence and turned quickly.

Rafn caught a glimpse of the man's surprised face in the dim light. His arm swung around and automatically pulled the knife across the man's exposed neck. Blood spurted out of the severed jugular and the man's breath gurgled out of his throat. Rafn pushed him back into the room with his left arm and drove the knife into the man's chest with his right.

CHAPTER 12

Everything that could be done here was done. This part of the operation was over with. There were watchers. More than one of them. This was as serious as Kozhevnikov had predicted it would be, and all of them were in deep trouble.

Whoever had followed Rafn into the woods would come back here to discover the body. Shortly after that, a message would be sent from here to East Berlin and from there to Moscow. It might take a day or two, then a message would be sent to Siberia: *Arrest Kozhevnikov.* Then the real war would begin.

Rafn sighed deeply as he caught his breath and leaned against the door. After he killed the man, he had listened to learn if the noise had awakened anyone in the *Gasthaus.* There was no sound, so he entered the room, closing the door behind him.

Schiller was dead. His body was sprawled on the bed, his head bent at an impossible angle.

He never had a chance, Rafn decided. A week ago, he would have come out of this all right. But not now. Taking him out must have been child's play.

The man Rafn had killed lay flat on his back in a pool of blood. A wide stain spread across the front of his light gray suit coat where the Belgian hunting knife had penetrated his heart.

The room had been searched. Schiller's papers lay scattered around his body on the bed.

Rafn pushed away from the door, went to the bed,

gathered up the papers and stuffed them into his coat pocket. He would have to leave Schiller's body here. Without papers it would take a long time to identify him, but by that time this operation would be finished.

Quickly now, Rafn pulled the knife out, wiped it on the man's trouser leg and replaced it in the scabbard.

The man was large, almost two meters, and at least a hundred kilos, Rafn decided. His hair was cropped short, and his open eyes, already beginning to film over in death, were a harsh, steel blue. He looked Eastern European, almost Jewish, but the cut of his hair and his clothes definitely stamped him as Russian.

Rafn searched the man's pockets but came up with nothing. No papers, no weapons, not even money. He sat back on his haunches for a moment. The man had come here to kill Schiller and was expecting trouble. Whoever sent him did not want to leave any clues if he were taken out. He was expendable.

Rafn shuddered. This was a dirty operation in a filthy business. And it was far from being over.

Checking the room a last time, Rafn left and locked the door behind him. Then he quickly walked down the stairs and on the first floor stopped long enough to screw the light bulb back in. Then he slipped outside.

There was no one in sight as Rafn made his way around the front and down the street to where he had parked the Mercedes. In a few minutes he was heading out of town toward the northeast.

Before they had entered the East Zone, Rafn had planned their route back to West Germany. From Tiefensee they would skirt East Berlin and drive northwest to an area above Wittenberge near the village of Lenzen, directly on the wall. There was a swampy area along the Elbe River where the wall itself was nothing more than a high wire-mesh fence topped with rolls of barbed wire. It would be an area difficult to patrol, and therefore easy to penetrate.

He had made two mistakes with Schiller, he told

himself as he drove through the damp, chill night. The first was agreeing to work with him at all and the second was in leaving him alone in their room.

Mistakes like that ended up being very costly sooner or later. This one had cost Schiller his life, and unless Kozhevnikov was working on his own escape at this moment, his life was probably forfeit as well.

There was virtually no traffic on the narrow highways. But as he crossed under the E74 *Autobahn* near Lanke, a large convoy of military vehicles was headed north. Most of the trucks were troop transports, and Rafn idly wondered where they were going. Probably to maneuvers somewhere near the Polish border, or perhaps even to the missile site his East German network had photographed for him ten days ago. It seemed like ten years ago.

It was nearing six o'clock in the morning when Rafn pulled off the paved highway south of Lenzen and onto a dirt road that led west. He was exhausted and his back hurt him. A fine rain had begun to fall that at times was turning into snow.

The Elbe River was less than five kilometers away now, in the West Zone, but once he crossed over the fence he could make his way along this side of the river to the highway bridge that led south toward Gartow.

He would be arrested by the American border guards, and it would take most of the morning before he was properly identified and could return to West Berlin. From there . . .

He let that thought trail off as he shut off the car lights and slowed down.

This road, like hundreds of others along the border, served as an access to the guard towers that rose above the wall at five-hundred-meter intervals. Each tower was manned by two guards, one who stayed in the tower and the other who patrolled the fence between the towers.

Because the area was swampy, the road was built up above the water. About a kilometer off the main highway, Rafn stopped the car so that it blocked the road, got out, and threw the keys into the swamp. If anyone were following him they would have to walk, unless they were able to push his car off the road.

He reached under the seat, took the revolvers out and threw them deep into the swamp, and then stood perfectly still, listening for sounds. But he could hear nothing, the fine rain blanketing any possible noises.

A moment later he headed down the road toward the fence which he figured could not be much more than half a kilometer away. As he walked he thought again about Kozhevnikov. Even if he did escape, he would have a hard time convincing the Americans that this was anything more than a disinformation plot.

What did they have at this point? The testimony of a high-ranking KGB officer, himself a disinformation expert. The search of an Israeli operative for a Nazi war criminal. The oblique remarks of an aging priest, remarks that only Rafn had been privy to. The murder of Schiller would be blamed on Rafn. And Schiller's sister would no doubt be totally untraceable.

Bindrich's position would be clear, and Rafn could almost hear the man speaking now. "Kozhevnikov is being used by his own people."

That was the first step in writing Kozhevnikov off.

"Schiller was killed, and you would have been, because they discovered that a pair of enemy agents were poking around the countryside."

In other words, "I told you so."

And the old priest? Rafn had to smile at that himself, because Bindrich would laugh out loud.

Schiller's sister was not worth mentioning, either. She was simply too unknown a quantity in this for any consideration, especially by Bindrich.

Rafn was about to carry that thought forward when he realized that the road had opened into a clearing, and through the mist he was suddenly able to see the lights atop the guard tower directly across from where he stood.

He turned, intending to get off the road and make his way through the swamp between the guard towers, but he stopped short, his heart skipping a beat.

The same man who had murdered Schiller came out of the mist toward him like an apparition. He was smiling slightly, the simple gesture completely unnerving Rafn. For the first time in his life, he was truly frightened. Deeply frightened. Not only for his life, but for his sanity.

When the man was about two meters away, he stopped and held out his hand.

"It is over, Herr Shultenbrunner. Your knife, please," he said.

Rafn slowly reached for his knife, but his hand stopped as he touched the handle, and his mind began to clear from the sudden shock. It wasn't the same man. It could not be. There were no marks on his throat or chest. And yet he was the same. Same enough to be the dead man's identical twin. Then it came to him what was happening—what had been happening since the war and the Kummersdorf experiments. Everything suddenly fit. Everything Kozhevnikov had said, all of Schiller's testimony, and the fear that had been in the old priest's eyes.

He was afraid for his own life now because he was the only one, other than Kozhevnikov, who knew what was happening. Kozhevnikov was in Siberia and would possibly be dead soon. Rafn was the only one who knew.

He withdrew his knife, but held it low, by his side. The man reached in his coat pocket and pulled out an automatic.

"By the time you throw that and hit me, I will kill you," the man said, casually pointing the gun at Rafn.

"Then you would never find out how much information I have already sent out to my people."

"Maria Grindl, Horst Steiner, Wilhelm Bermann, and the rest of your East German network are dead. Your friend back in Tiefensee is dead, and so is the priest you spoke with yesterday afternoon, Herr Shultenbrunner."

Rafn tensed, and he ached for a cigarette. He knew that sooner or later they would all be found out and killed. But hearing it all at once now was a shock. For a moment he was amazed with himself. Rafn, the man who never needed or cared about anyone in his life, was shocked and saddened by the deaths of these people. What was motivating him was now preventing him from taking decisive action.

He shrugged it off. Shultenbrunner. The man had called him by that name, which meant that Bermann's contacts had been followed up, the travel documents had been discovered, and the name Shultenbrunner exposed. Shultenbrunner, not Rafn. There still was a chance.

"You forgot one thing," Rafn said, forcing himself to smile. "You didn't search my car. You didn't look in the trunk."

The man frowned and half turned to look at where the car was parked. In the next instant Rafn flipped the knife forward and buried it deep in the left side of the man's chest.

The man staggered back a step, regained his balance and turned toward Rafn, raising the automatic to fire. There was a surprised look on his face.

Rafn leaped down off the road, and as the first shot slammed into a tree next to him, crashed away through the thick undergrowth parallel to the fence.

A siren sounded from the guard tower, spotlights came on, and Rafn could hear dogs barking behind and ahead of him.

He turned and headed directly for the fence. The water was now above his knees and his legs were numb.

A machine gun fired to his right, and he could hear

several men shouting, their voices muffled by the rain that was falling much harder now.

The fence suddenly appeared ahead of him. Rafn stopped for a moment while he tore off his coat, and then he cautiously crawled to the path next to the fence and looked both ways. No one was in sight, but the sounds of the pursuit were directly behind him now.

He threw the coat over his shoulder, leaped up as high on the fence as he could, and began scrambling. By now his hands were completely numb and his legs and feet had no feeling in them.

He was certain he would not make it to the top, which seemed to be hundreds of meters above. He was too old and too tired for this sort of thing. But while he hung on with one hand, he flipped the rain-sodden coat over the barbed wire, and climbed all the way over. It seemed to take an eternity.

He lost his grip at the top and fell the five meters to the other side. The only thing that saved him from serious injury was the soft muck and water of the swamp.

The wind knocked out of him, he lay on his side for a few seconds before crawling into the heavy undergrowth in the rain that was now pouring. Within a few seconds he was away, and safe, the picture of the twins indelibly etched in his mind.

CHAPTER 13

Rafn sat on a stool in the American checkpoint shack located on the approach to the Elbe River bridge seven kilometers north of Gartow, sipping a cup of coffee. One of the young American guards had brought out an olive-drab wool blanket and had thrown it over his shoulders. Neither of the guards had said much to him from the time he stumbled out of the woods, but they were expecting him.

Dawn had broken, the rain had let up, and the overcast sky had lifted considerably by the time Rafn finally made it to the bridge. He had walked less than ten meters on it when a jeep with two guards in it came across from the Western side.

Rafn stopped and watched them as they pulled up alongside him.

"Mr. Svend Rafn?" the driver asked. He was wearing a raincoat, and a plastic cover was over his hat.

"Yes," Rafn said tiredly.

"Colonel Bindrich is expecting you, sir."

Rafn climbed wearily onto the back seat of the jeep. "Where is he now?"

The driver put the jeep in gear, made a U-turn on the bridge, and headed back to the checkpoint shack. The other man turned in his seat toward Rafn.

"He's on his way here, sir. We heard the commotion earlier and expected it was you, so we called him."

Rafn closed his eyes against the wind and shivered. He was cold, tired, and hungry, but before he was going to get any rest he was going to have to endure an attack of self-righteousness from Bindrich. It wouldn't be pleasant, but it was a fact of life. At least life in this business.

They had pulled up at the checkpoint shack, and the guards had led Rafn inside where they gave him coffee and a pack of cigarettes and threw the blanket over his shoulders.

That was three hours ago. During that time the only other thing he had learned from the young men was that Colonel Bindrich had taken a military jet from Berlin to Hannover and would be coming here by helicopter.

He was due any minute.

It was all up to Kozhevnikov now, Rafn thought as he put his coffee cup on the counter in front of him and looked out the large plate-glass window and down at the bridge. He lit a cigarette and inhaled deeply. The smoke burned his lungs, but it felt good.

If they wanted to convince the Americans to take action, Kozhevnikov would have to escape with hard information. Bindrich would never buy Rafn's scanty details. Schiller's death, the old priest's story, and the two identical men amounted to very little.

Rafn could not really blame Bindrich. The man was simply doing the best job he could. If this were a disinformation plot, or worse yet, if it were real and they had no proof, and the Americans took action anyway, it would create an international scandal. And that, as Bindrich explained, could not be allowed to happen.

Kozhevnikov. It all hinged on his getting out. And there would be very little they could do for him.

The heavy chop of helicopter rotors intruded on Rafn's thoughts, and he looked up as one of the guards went outside. A moment later the man came back in.

"The helicopter is here, sir," he said.

Rafn got up, took the blanket and handed it to the young man, who was watching him with a mixture of awe and suspicion. "Thanks for the blanket and the coffee," he said and went out to meet the helicopter that was touching down in a parking lot beside the bridge.

He got there just as it touched down and the big Sikorsky engine slowly unwound. The door opened and Bindrich got out, ducked low beneath the still whirling blades, and hurried up to meet him.

"You've created quite a stir, Rafn," Bindrich said, puffing.

Rafn was cold again, but Bindrich made no move to return to the helicopter or go up to the shack.

"How did you know I had gone in?" Rafn asked.

Bindrich ignored the question for the moment, looking past Rafn toward the bridge. "Where's Schiller?" he asked, looking back.

"Dead," Rafn said.

"I see," Bindrich nodded. "They found you out?"

"Yes."

"I stuck around after we talked, and when you dropped out of sight, I figured you must be up to something."

"Why didn't you try to stop us?"

Bindrich smiled. "At first I didn't figure you'd be going in, but when you didn't show up in Copenhagen, and when Schiller turned up missing as well, I distributed your photograph to every checkpoint on the border. I missed you at Brandenburg by a couple of hours."

"Would you have stopped us?" Rafn asked out of idle curiosity. Bindrich was a bureaucrat, but at one time he had been a field man. He was hard to figure.

"That's a moot point now," Bindrich snapped. "All hell started breaking loose along the border last night, so I figured you had gotten into something and were on the way out. Every position reported increased activity from the other side. You've stirred up a hornet's nest."

"And Schiller is dead," Rafn said.

"Yes," Bindrich said dryly. "Did you find anything?"

"Only that Kozhevnikov is probably telling the truth."

Rafn quickly sketched for Bindrich the happenings of the past few days, including his conversations with Schiller and the information his network had come up with that pointed toward Tiefensee as the site of a Nazi experimental medical station. The only thing he omitted was the description of the man in Tiefensee and the one at the border fence. Bindrich would not accept it, Rafn was sure. At least not until they had more information.

"Kozhevnikov is as good as dead," Bindrich said when Rafn was finished.

"Unless he's already got the information he needs and is on the way out," Rafn said.

"From Siberia?" Bindrich snapped. "Don't be a fool, Rafn. This is finished."

"No, it's not," Rafn said. He was so tired now that he was almost asleep on his feet.

"You're not going back in," Bindrich said. "I'll see to that even if I have to arrest you myself."

Rafn shook his head. "I'm coming back to Langley with you."

"What?"

"I said I'm coming back to the States with you."

"Why?" Bindrich said, his eyes narrowing.

"A couple of loose ends need tying up."

"I'm not going to play your silly games any longer, Rafn."

Rafn shook his head again. "If I come up with what I think I'm going to come up with, this won't be any game, as you put it. I'll be able to tell you where Kozhevnikov is and exactly what's happening."

PART FIVE

CHAPTER 1

Kozhevnikov zippered his heavy Arctic parka, stepped from the rear door of the administration building, and climbed into the enclosed jeep he had been assigned ten days ago. With shaking hands he turned on the ignition and the engine came to life.

Proof, Bindrich had told him in Seeshaupt a century ago. They needed proof.

He sat for several long minutes in the idling jeep and tried to calm down. Udalov had not even looked up from his desk when Kozhevnikov walked out the door. But he was certain the man suspected something. All of them did, including Agayan, whose attitude had changed from the moment Kozhevnikov began interviewing the Jewish women.

For an instant a picture of Nadya flashed into his mind. If there were some way to go back, to turn time around, he knew he would do it without a moment's hesitation.

But Nadya had known, or had at least suspected, that it was already too late for him. He had gone too far to turn back.

And now he was going to have to get proof for Bindrich and escape with it somehow.

He shivered. Far from being the pleasant, well-mannered, cultured man he appeared to be, Agayan was a monster. And it was possibly one of the reasons the man had been so adamantly against Kozhevnikov talking with the women.

"What the hell are you talking about?" Agayan had screamed at him last week.

Kozhevnikov had gone to the man's office for permission to begin interviewing a selected number of the Jewish women.

"If I'm going to do my job I'm going to have to have a free hand," Kozhevnikov said with more calmness than he felt.

"Impossible," Agayan said, dismissing the subject. But Kozhevnikov persisted.

"There are one hundred thousand Jews here at this moment. Correct?"

"I don't see what . . . what that has to do with——"

"Hear me out, Comrade," Kozhevnikov said, and Agayan fell silent. "One hundred thousand Jews. All of them from somewhere within the Soviet borders. Their disappearances over the past few years have attracted the attention of someone, somewhere. The Israeli Secret Service, perhaps. Maybe some of our own dissident writers. But someone, somewhere knows something is going on."

Agayan held his silence, waiting for Kozhevnikov to continue.

"What I am trying to do, Comrade, is to come up with a disinformation plan that will satisfy everyone. This is just too big an operation to go unnoticed for much longer. Frankly, I'm surprised that it hasn't blown wide open already."

"We have our methods, as well, Comrade," Agayan said dryly.

"Yes," Kozhevnikov said. His persistence was becoming dangerous. But it could not be helped. If he were going to come up with the proof the Americans needed, he would need specific names.

It was not enough that here a hundred thousand Jews were imprisoned. He would have to prove that they were being used to create a monstrous army—a story that he did not completely believe himself.

"And I have my methods as well, Comrade, which is why I was sent here."

Agayan sat back in his chair, carefully placed a cigarette in a long, black holder, and peered at Kozhevnikov once he lit it.

"What exactly do you have in mind—assuming, that is, I give you the permission to talk with the Jewish bitches?"

"Simply this," Kozhevnikov said, sitting forward. "I need to find a number of women who will be able to pose as farmers—the workers in this supposedly 'Agrarian Reform' Project."

"Go on," Agayan prompted.

Kozhevnikov smiled. "When they are found, they will be programmed with the proper responses. A model farm situation will be arranged in one section of the base, and we will invite a carefully selected group of Western journalists here to inspect our handiwork."

For a moment it looked like Agayan was going to have a heart attack, and at that moment Kozhevnikov was certain the man was insane and was going to have him shot. But he could not back down now.

"Never!" Agayan managed to shout, rising from his chair.

Kozhevnikov jumped to his feet. "Then replace me, Commandant. Get rid of me. Ship me back home. One way or the other don't tie my hands, goddamn it! I was sent here to do a job. Let me do it!"

Udalov, who had come upstairs with Kozhevnikov, burst into the office, and Agayan looked at him.

"Get out of here, you fucking machine!" he screamed.

Udalov swiveled on his heel smoothly and went out, closing the door softly. Kozhevnikov's heart nearly stopped. He knew! Suddenly it all came together: Udalov's odd, almost inhuman behavior; the rows upon rows of babies in the barracks, every one hundred of them being attended by a Jewish nurse, none of the infants crying, all of them staring quietly up at the ceiling. He knew, and he was more frightened now than ever before.

"You'll never get out of here. None of us will," Agayan shouted, turning back to him.

"Then I demand a tribunal with the director himself. I will not have my hands tied."

Agayan was about to shout again, but suddenly his jaw went rigid, and obviously under great strain, he sat down, took a deep breath, and motioned toward the chair behind Kozhevnikov. "Sit down, Comrade, and we will discuss this as gentlemen, not fishwives."

Kozhevnikov sat and managed a slight smile. His insides were churning. But he had to be careful. Agayan was no fool, and the control he was exhibiting now proved he was highly intelligent, albeit insane. A dangerous combination.

"All I am saying to you, Commandant, is that this is such a huge operation, it will soon attract attention. We must be ready for it."

Agayan nodded. "I see the wisdom of your concern, Comrade," he said. "But it's impossible."

"Perhaps another installation can be constructed and staffed with the Jews I select."

"That's possible," Agayan said thoughtfully, but Kozhevnikov was sure the man was not sincere. He was holding something back.

"Then I can talk with the women?"

Again a look of rage crossed Agayan's features, but it was instantly replaced with the artificial smile. "When would you begin?"

"Immediately."

"And what would you ask them?"

Kozhevnikov paused. "I don't know yet. I merely want to find two dozen who could pass as happy Soviet citizen-farmers."

Agayan stared at him, and Kozhevnikov was certain

the man could see through his lie. But a moment later the commandant sighed.

"I'll give your program one week. At the end of that time I'll review what you have accomplished. If it looks to me as though there is merit to what you are trying to do, I'll authorize what you are proposing," Agayan said. He got to his feet, came around to where Kozhevnikov was sitting and perched on the edge of his desk. "I'll want you to tape all the interviews. I'll want to listen to them at the end of the week."

Kozhevnikov put the jeep in gear, pulled away from the parking lot, and headed across the base. That had been one week ago today. Seven days. Agayan had been too busy for their promised meeting, but he was sure he would call him tomorrow. And he would have to bring the tapes to that meeting.

Operation Outlook, located twenty kilometers to the west of the small Siberian town of Markovo, was laid out in a fenced-in square at least four kilometers on a side. At the center of the huge square was the administration complex, the only modern-looking building on the base.

The other buildings were of exactly the same construction, at least from the outside. Row after row of the long, barnlike structures were distinguishable from each other only by identification numbers and letter.

A buildings housed the scientific personnel and laboratories. Inside they were modern and spotlessly clean.

B buildings housed the Jewish population and were scattered throughout the base. No guards were needed for these buildings because all Jews were given heavy doses of tranquilizers in their food each day. Inside, the buildings looked like military barracks, with row after row of low cots. At one end was the dining hall, and at the opposite was a small exercise area that they used in shifts each day. A few of the *B* buildings housed the Jewish men, of whom there were less than a thousand. Their barracks were exactly the same as the women's, and their purpose was to produce live sperm.

The few C buildings housed the maintenance personnel and shops that kept the base operating.

And the D buildings, one for every twenty Jewish barracks, housed a clinic and medical staff that examined the women daily. The women were artificially inseminated in these buildings, Kozhevnikov had been told. And it was here that the women delivered their babies, which were immediately transferred to the E buildings, which were the nurseries where he had seen the endless rows of infants, each lying in its own basket, and none of them crying.

All of that, however, comprised only half the base. The other half, the area he was heading toward now, was the F section—off limits to everyone. Last week Udalov had dismissed his questions about this area with a shrug.

"Those are more nurseries," he said.

"Why the F designation, then?" Kozhevnikov had persisted.

They were in his office, and Udalov looked down at him. "They are special children, you know that."

Kozhevnikov nodded.

"They all mature quite rapidly. You also know that."

Again Kozhevnikov nodded.

"That is their growing-up section."

"How old is it?"

"It is new," Udalov said, and for the first time Kozhevnikov wondered if the man were lying.

Then, the next day, when he argued with Agayan, he knew the man was lying. Now he was going to find out just what was contained in the huge F section. If it contained what he thought it did, he would have all the proof he needed. Somehow he would have to force Agayan into sending him back to Moscow.

It was just after two o'clock in the afternoon, but

already dark and the lights atop the buildings gave a ghastly air to the place.

As he drove down the narrow snow-covered road, bits and pieces of the interviews he had conducted ran through his mind. The tapes of them were in his briefcase in his apartment.

Although the women were dull and lifeless, all of them were pregnant and in good health and they had been here for more years than they could count. All had been pregnant over and over again.

They all knew what was happening to them, but because of the tranquilizers, none of them seemed to care. And after each interview, Kozhevnikov found himself physically sick to his stomach.

They were not human beings. They were animals—nothing more than cows in barns. They were fed and watered each day, exercised and examined for diseases, and then impregnated. Every ten months—without letup—the process began again.

Although Kozhevnikov's questions about what happened to the women who got sick or lost their babies were met with frightened silences, he was certain they were destroyed like any nonproductive cow would be destroyed.

The program had been going on since World War Two. The women had been pregnant more times than they could remember. He had seen a huge number of infants in the nurseries. And yet he could not completely accept Agayan's prediction that in eight years these children would become mature men. An army. He had to see it himself before he could leave. Without it he would never be able to convince the Americans of what was going on here.

F section was separated from the rest of the base by a strip of land about the width of a soccer field that ran the entire length of the facility. Several dirt roads crossed the no-man's-land, each with the same large warning sign:

ENTRY FORBIDDEN
TO ALL BUT AUTHORIZED PERSONNEL

Kozhevnikov had gone this far before in his wanderings around the base, but each time he had turned back at the sign.

"During the first few months of the infants' lives," Udalov had explained, "they are for some reason very susceptible to infection. That is why no one is allowed over there."

Kozhevnikov had accepted the explanation until now. He continued past the warning sign, across the empty field toward the row of identical barracks. Alongside the road, near the first building, was a guard shack, and as Kozhevnikov's jeep approached, two men with machine guns on their shoulders barricaded the road and motioned for him to stop.

He pulled up beside them and pushed the plastic side curtain back. "Kozhevnikov: Administration," he snapped.

The guard smiled pleasantly. "I'm sorry, Major, but you will have to leave. Entry is forbidden."

Kozhevnikov was about to protest, until he saw Fedor Udalov emerge from the front door of the barracks.

He stuck his head out the window and was about to shout at him when another man came out of the building. The sound died in his throat. The second man was Udalov's identical twin. Tall. Husky. Square-featured. Short hair.

"If you will leave, Major," the guard was saying. But Kozhevnikov wasn't listening as a third and a fourth man came out of the building, all of them identical in appearance.

It was true. The only thing Agayan had lied about was the degree to which the program had progressed. Agayan had led him to believe they had just begun. In reality, the Soviet government's new army already existed. Perhaps it was already too late for anyone, even the Americans, to do anything about it.

CHAPTER 2

Dr. Hans Meitner looked over his shoulder and out the rear window of the car as it entered Vorobyevskoye Road and sped away from Moscow State University, where he had been quartered for the past week. He was sad in a way, to be leaving the university, yet he was looking forward to the next year or so of his life.

He turned around and sat back in his seat, folding his hands on his lap. The past week had been a kaleidoscopic jumble, but one thing was clear: He was glad it had happened. Now, at long last, he could get on with his life's work. And from what he had been told, the progress that had been made here in the last thirty years was unbelievable.

"This could never have been possible in the United States," he mumbled aloud to himself.

Dr. Ivan Damarovich Zagreb, his host at the university who was seated next to him, turned. "Pardon me, Doctor?" he said in German.

Meitner looked up and smiled, switching to German. "Just thinking aloud, my dear Ivan Damarovich."

Dr. Zagreb returned the smile and patted Meitner on the arm. "The trip out will be tiring, but I think you will agree it is worth it."

"Yes," Meitner said, nodding. "I only wish you were coming with me. There is so much more to discuss."

"I will join you in two weeks, and then we will be able to work together."

Meitner settled deeper into the seat and closed his eyes. He could feel the cancer heavy in his chest now, but even that no longer mattered. The doctors at the state medical center had told him what he had expected to hear after they had examined him; but they had assured him that with chemotherapy once a week, he could expect to live at least two more years, of which eighteen months could be productive.

It was such a terribly short time in one respect. But it would be unfettered by distractions or restrictions.

"No avenue of research will be closed to you," Zagreb and the Komitět men who first talked with him had said. "Absolutely any experimental situation will be open to you."

Those had been the key words that had unlocked his reticence after his kidnapping in West Berlin.

Two men had come to his hotel room at two in the morning, and at gunpoint had taken him outside to a waiting car. They drove half the night, it seemed, passing through several checkpoints.

Finally he had been put on a flight to Leipzig. From there he was spirited aboard a military jet transport and arrived in Moscow that afternoon.

They knew everything about his work in Tiefensee, except how he had escaped from the *Waffen SS* that night.

When he had finally told them the entire story, including his real name, they had reacted sympathetically and told him that he didn't need to run anymore.

"You need never be fearful of discovery again, Doctor," the Komitět man said. "The work that began at Kummersdorf continues here in the Soviet Union. And we would be honored if you would join our research efforts."

At first Meitner had been incredulous. But later he had finally come to realize that the Soviet Union would be the only place in the world where his research could be completed.

And now he was on his way to Markovo. No longer would he have to worry about the woman newspaper reporter, the stupid, inane Dr. Stewart, or being discovered.

Any avenue of research, they had told him. Any avenue. It was an exciting prospect.

CHAPTER 3

Rafn looked up from the light table as Nathaniel Gleason entered the Reconnaissance Photo Laboratory. It was five o'clock in the morning in Langley, West Virginia, and Rafn was dead tired. He had not showered in three days, and the three packs of Camels he had been smoking each day had given him a bad case of heartburn. But he was satisfied that he had finally found what he was looking for.

Gleason came across the large room, dimly lit with blue light, to where Rafn was seated at the photo examination table. He didn't look happy.

"This had better be good, Rafn," he said angrily.

Rafn nodded as he stubbed out his cigarette in the overflowing ashtray. "I know where Kozhevnikov is."

Gleason looked startled. "So what?" he said. "I have nothing to do with that any longer. Bindrich pulled me off this, remember?"

Rafn took off his thick glasses and carefully cleaned the lenses with a tissue. When he put them back on he looked up at Gleason and smiled. The man was like Kozhevnikov in many respects—sensitive, yet naive. It was a curious quality in the Russian, but very typical of Americans.

"I need your help," Rafn said simply.

Gleason sighed after a moment, then pulled a tall stool over to Rafn and sat down. "What have you got?"

For five days Rafn had worked here in the photo lab, as well as in the computer record terminal. But it was not until early this morning that he had come up with anything concrete. What he found made him suddenly aware of just how limited even his own abilities were. This was simply too large for one man alone to handle.

It had been an interesting revelation to him. Very seldom had he admitted to himself that he needed help. Even his East German network had always been more of a luxury to him than a necessity. He had known that if his network failed to produce what he wanted, he could go in and get the information himself. He had done just that with this business.

But now he was going to need Gleason's help. Bindrich, he knew, would block him. But Gleason could be convinced. That was the first step.

"Have you been following this at all?" Rafn asked. Gleason shook his head. "Bindrich has cut me off."

"Are you on your way out?"

"I suppose so, if Bindrich gets his way. But even for him it's a slow process."

"One you're not fighting."

"That's right," Gleason said, the anger back in his voice. "Bindrich is the same kind of a sonofabitch that you are. I'm just tired of the whole business."

"Then why did you come this morning when I called?"

Gleason didn't answer at first, and for a moment Rafn felt almost sorry for him. "I don't know."

"Are you going to help me?" Rafn asked softly.

Gleason nodded. "If I can," he said, and then paused for a moment. "You were right in Germany. Kozhevnikov is a lot like me. I could feel it when we were talking with him."

Rafn wondered briefly how anyone ever became involved in this business, which was, after all, nothing more than the fine art of using people. The more people you could use, the more effectively you could use them, the better an operative you were.

The best operatives were the pimps, the whores, the drug addicts, and the men like himself who used them. It was a filthy business. He found himself wishing now that Bindrich would have his way and force Gleason out.

There was little hope for Kozhevnikov, even if they managed to get him out. But Gleason was still relatively untainted. There was hope for him.

"I need to see the president this morning," Rafn said.

Gleason's eyes widened. "Do you have proof this is a pogrom?"

"Worse than that," Rafn replied. "But we're going to have to move fast if Kozhevnikov is going to get out."

Gleason shook his head. "I don't know if I can get you in to see the president. We'd have to go through the director."

"No," Rafn said sharply, the memory of his conversation with the man clear in his mind.

When he had arrived five days ago; he had been ushered immediately into the director's office, where he was told in no uncertain terms that relations with the Soviet Union at this time were already shaky enough without adding something else to upset the balance.

"You may work here to your heart's content, Mr. Rafn," the director, a stern man, said. "But there will be no more Western European operations on this."

"And Kozhevnikov?" Rafn asked softly.

"We are writing him off."

Bindrich was in the room, and he nodded. "My feelings exactly, sir. It's nothing more than a disinformation plot. A finely tuned one, perhaps, but it had enough rough edges, so we thankfully did not fall for it."

Rafn turned and peered at Bindrich through his thick

glasses. The man was a fool. But a high-placed fool, which made him dangerous.

He turned back to the director. It was ironic, he told himself. The Americans had been the fierce liberators of World War Two. They had been the ones who had screamed the loudest about the atrocities the Germans had committed on the Jews. In the Arab-Israeli wars, it was the Americans who had supplied the Jews with arms. And yet even in this liberal country there was still the same holdover distrust of the Jew.

If the people being experimented on in Siberia had been Catholics, or farmers—anything but Jews—the entire CIA would have been at his instant disposal.

But they were Jews.

Gleason looked up at Rafn. "If we're going to do this, it'll have to be done in the next two and a half hours. When Bindrich comes in he'll go over the nightly logs. When he sees that I signed in early he'll be down here loaded for bear."

"Can you get me in to see the president?"

"I think so," Gleason said carefully. "If you can convince me that you've actually got something."

It was fifteen minutes to eight in the morning when Rafn and Gleason left Langley and drove into Washington. The weather was clear and cool, but at this moment Rafn knew that in Markovo it would be dark and very cold. Winter in the Arctic came early. And if Kozhevnikov was going to attempt to escape, he was going to have a tough time of it.

"He was mad," Gleason said as they entered the city. It was the first thing he had said since he had hung up from his telephone call to the White House.

"What kind of a man is he?" Rafn asked. He knew very little about the American president.

Gleason glanced nervously at him. "If you mean will he buy what we're going to tell him, I don't know, I just hope so."

"But he agreed to see us."

"Yes," Gleason said, gripping the steering wheel. "He couldn't understand why I hadn't gone through the director." He turned again to Rafn. "What the hell was I supposed to tell him?"

Rafn shrugged. "It doesn't matter now, as long as he will listen to us."

The guards at the gate were expecting them, and they were ushered into the president's office in the West Wing.

Rafn had seen photographs of him in the newspapers and on television, but he was mildly surprised at how short and husky the man was in person.

"Good morning, gentlemen," the president said with a soft southern drawl when they came in. He got up from his desk and came around to them. But he did not offer his hand.

"I'm sorry to have to bother you this way, Mr. President," Gleason began, but Rafn cut him off.

"Mr. President, we are in possession of some very grave information that could be of the utmost importance to the United States. I believe you should listen with an open mind to what we have to say."

The president turned to Rafn. "Mr. Svend Rafn, our Danish operative?"

Rafn nodded.

"I've heard about you."

"If we can begin, Mr. President," Rafn said without acknowledging the comment.

"Make it brief."

The president was a young man and at this moment Rafn felt old and tired. But he was going to have to be careful with how he presented this. Rafn suspected that the president would not react favorably if he became patronizing. And if he blew it, Kozhevnikov would be lost.

He took the briefcase that Gleason had carried in and withdrew from it two sets of photographs which he spread on the president's desk. "These are reconnaissance photographs of an area in far eastern Siberia."

The president moved next to Rafn and looked down at the photographs, but said nothing.

"Are you aware of the defection of the KGB officer recently in Paris?"

The president looked up. "Kozhevnikov. A Disinformation Department officer. It was in my daily summaries. It's been dismissed, as I understand it."

"Which is why we came directly to you."

The president studied Rafn's face for a long moment, then nodded. "Get on with it."

"Kozhevnikov suspected that one hundred thousand Jews are being used as medical guinea pigs somewhere in Siberia. He was sent back to get more information for us," Rafn began.

He quickly related for the president everything that had happened to date, including Kozhevnikov's contact with Douville in Paris, the Munich meeting, the death of his wife and his transfer to the Kummersdorf Papers base somewhere in Siberia. He also went into detail about his connection with Schiller and their search in Tiefensee which led to Schiller's death. But he held back about the identical men.

When he was finished, the president seemed more impatient than before. "I've seen everything that you've told me so far in the daily intelligence summaries. You've told me nothing new."

"There is more, Mr. President," Rafn said.

"I hope so."

Gleason seemed very uncomfortable, but Rafn ignored him for the moment. "First the photographs. I know where Kozhevnikov is stationed."

The president looked with interest at the two sets of photos as Rafn continued.

"These two groups of photos were taken ten years apart. I compared the two sets for any differences."

"And?" the president said tersely.

Rafn took a magnifying glass from the briefcase and handed it to the president. He pointed to one of the photos. "In the upper right-hand corner you will see a series of buildings. It is an installation of some kind."

The president bent over the desk and studied the photograph for a long minute. When he stood up his expression was still one of impatience.

"What is it?" he said.

"It has been listed as a Siberian farming station. A place where they grow crops indoors, year-round. But this one is new. The beginnings of it show up in the fifties photographs, but in the last ten years the size of the place has increased ten times. At this moment it is at least four or five kilometers on a side."

"And you don't think it's a farming operation?"

Rafn shook his head. "No, sir. I've seen photographs of those operations. There isn't one of them with a five-thousand-foot airstrip like this one."

The president looked again at the photograph, and then straightened up. "So you believe Kozhevnikov is there."

"Yes I do. And I also believe that he will be trying to escape at any moment."

"Why?"

Rafn quickly explained Kozhevnikov's warning to them in Seeshaupt not to make inquiries in Western Europe.

"Since Schiller and I were compromised, I'm sure they've put it together by now and will have Kozhevnikov arrested."

"What makes you think he will be able to escape?"

"Wishful thinking, Mr. President," Rafn said honestly. And it was exactly that, he told himself. Because if Kozhevnikov did not escape they would all be in trouble.

The telephone on the president's desk burred softly

and he picked it up. "Yes?" he said into the mouthpiece. He listened. "Have him wait just a few moments please, Mrs. Williams," he said, and he hung up the phone and turned back to Gleason. "Your boss is here for the morning intelligence briefing."

Gleason blanched at this news, but Rafn said nothing. The next move was the president's.

"Mr. Rafn," he said, going back around his desk and sitting down. "You believe Kozhevnikov is telling us the truth and there are a hundred thousand Jews incarcerated at this place near Markovo. Is that right?"

"Yes," Rafn said, not moving.

"And it is also your opinion that Kozhevnikov has either been compromised or will soon be compromised."

"Yes."

"And now he will be attempting his escape."

Rafn nodded.

"How?"

Rafn moved forward, withdrew a map of eastern Siberia from the briefcase and spread it out on top of the photographs. Also shown on the map was the Bering Sea and the far western coastline of Alaska.

"Markovo is about three hundred kilometers inland from the seaport of Anadyr," Rafn said, pointing them out.

The president bent forward to get a better look.

"At first I thought he might try to talk his way back to Moscow and from there your embassy people could have helped him out of the country. But I don't believe that is possible now. Once he is compromised, he'll be arrested."

"So you're depending on him to make a break for it."

"Yes," Rafn said, looking directly into his eyes. "He is a resourceful man. He knows that once he is arrested he can't escape."

The president looked down at the map. "You are expecting him to steal an airplane, perhaps, and make his way across the Gulf of Anadyr to St. Lawrence Island?"

Rafn nodded. "Either that or a land vehicle. Much of the ocean in that area is frozen over this time of year. He might be able to make it far enough out for us to pick him up."

The president again looked up at Rafn. This time a slight smile played across his features. "I was told you were a devious sort; now I understand why."

Rafn returned the smile. "I would like to borrow one of your nuclear submarines for a few days."

"To patrol the waters off St. Lawrence Island."

"Yes," Rafn said. "It would have to be a ship with Soviet radio-monitoring equipment. I'm sure if Kozhevnikov breaks out there will be heavy radio traffic. It'll let us know he's coming."

The president sat back and with his elbows on the arms of his chair, he put his fingers together in front of him. "Let's assume Kozhevnikov is successful and does break out of Markovo, and does make it to a point where we can pick him up without compromising ourselves. And let me stress that point, Mr. Rafn—without compromising ourselves. Then what?"

"Kozhevnikov was to get proof of what he told us. I would presume he will be bringing some of it with him."

"Let's assume that he does. Then what?" the president asked, his gaze steady and his expression completely neutral.

Rafn relaxed and lit a cigarette. The action seemed to upset the president. It didn't matter, Rafn told himself. The man was hooked.

"At that point it becomes your ball game, Mr. President. I will have done my job."

"I see," the president said, and he sat forward. He started to reach for his telephone, but hesitated for a moment. "What are you holding back, Rafn?"

Rafn was startled. "Mr. President?"

"Every good operative always holds back an ace card. What's yours, Rafn?"

"No good poker player uses his ace card until it's absolutely necessary. Are you calling me, Mr. President?"

The president shook his head after a moment. "No, I don't believe so. But the submarine will not leave international waters under any circumstances, nor will it take any aggressive action against Soviet vessels or aircraft. Under no circumstances. Do I make myself clear?"

"Perfectly, Mr. President," Rafn said.

CHAPTER 4

At fifty-three Kozhevnikov was no longer a young man, and although he was in outstanding physical condition for a man of his age, he felt tired, washed out, and used up right now.

He lay on his back in his bed listening to the wind outside moan around the corner of the building. The lights in his quarters were turned off, and from time to time he could hear a truck or a jeep outside, but the building itself was quiet.

It was after eight o'clock and most of the staff were either in their quarters or in the officers' dining hall in the opposite wing of the administration building. Agayan had not called for him today, and Udalov was not there when he had returned from his attempt to see *F* section.

The faces, the erect posture, and the military bearing of the men he had seen coming out of the barracks there, however, were firmly etched in his mind. In one chilling respect it made him proud of his country.

They had done it. Soviet scientists, standing on the shoulders of the earlier German efforts, had successfully learned the secret of the human gene. Not only learned the secret, but developed the technology to alter it at will.

In his mind's eye Kozhevnikov could see universities staffed with entire armies of brilliant scientists; manufactured geniuses who would work for peaceful domination of the world by the Soviet Union. No longer would war, or famine, or disease be necessary. The greatest assemblage of minds the world had ever seen could be set to work on the tens of thousands of problems that plagued mankind.

It was all within his country's grasp. All here for the asking.

But it was not happening that way, he reflected sadly.

The telephone in the other room rang, and he sat up with a start. In the ten days he had been here he had gotten to know no one except for Udalov and Agayan himself. It had to be one or the other of them on the phone now.

It rang again and Kozhevnikov got out of bed and went into the sitting room and picked it up. "Yes?" he said.

"Viktor Vasilievich, this is your commandant. I would like the pleasure of your company this evening in my quarters."

"Yes, sir," Kozhevnikov said, his heart sinking. Of course Agayan had been told about his abortive attempt to get into the F section of the base.

Agayan hung up without another word and Kozhevnikov slowly replaced the receiver and turned toward his bedroom. His briefcase stuffed with the interview tapes sat open next to his bed. Would they be enough proof for Bindrich and the Americans?

He had asked himself that question every day for the past week, each time telling himself no. Talk to one more Jew. Gather one more piece of evidence. And then today when he had seen the men coming out of the barracks, he had wanted to stay and gather more details.

If Agayan had told him the truth and the cloned men had very simple needs and wants, then F section, which was easily as large as the rest of the base combined, could house upwards of a quarter million men.

And was this installation at Markovo the only one? Or were there others across Siberia? Depots of cloned soldiers. Ready to move out and attack China, or Western Europe.

Would the Americans believe all this?

The situation was beginning to close in on him. He could feel it thick in the air. Udalov had changed, and all week Agayan had been too busy to see him. Suddenly tonight he was being called to the commandant's quarters.

Kozhevnikov left his apartment, hurried down the empty corridor, up the stairs and through the auditorium into the reception room outside of Agayan's office.

Tonight, one way or the other, he was going to have to make his escape, or at least set the wheels in motion. There were two possibilities.

The first was Moscow—across the entire Russian continent. But his only chance to escape that way was through Agayan. If he could somehow convince the man to send him home he would be able to contact the people in the American embassy. From there it would be relatively simple to get out of the Soviet Union and into Western Europe.

The second possibility, the one he had not wanted to think about, was the American-owned St. Lawrence Island off the Alaskan coast in the Bering Sea. Nine hundred kilometers of featureless tundra and windswept frozen Arctic waters. An impossible distance.

Agayan was waiting in his outer office when Kozhevnikov knocked and entered. The man stood looking out his window across the base toward F section, and when Kozhevnikov entered the room he turned and smiled.

Kozhevnikov's gut tightened. During the several meetings he had had with Agayan, the man had always been good-natured and friendly, but with reserve. Tonight he was not the same person. His eyes were bright, his manner almost artificially energetic, and a thin sheen of perspiration glistened on his forehead.

"How is your little project coming along, Viktor Vasilievich?" Agayan asked.

Kozhevnikov stood just inside the doorway and managed a slight smile. "It goes well, Commandant," he said. "I didn't bring the tapes tonight because I didn't think you wanted to work on them."

"No need to apologize, Viktor Vasilievich," Agayan said. "You are right. Tonight is no night for work. It is a night to celebrate."

"Sir?" Kozhevnikov said, a sick feeling growing in the pit of his stomach.

Agayan moved toward the door to his personal quarters, gesturing for Kozhevnikov to follow. "Come with me, Viktor Vasilievich, there is something I want to show you, and much I would like to tell you."

Agayan's use of his first and paternal names was beginning to grate on Kozhevnikov's nerves, but he followed the commandant into the luxurious apartment that took up half of the third floor.

The living room, plushly carpeted and tastefully furnished, was located in the back corner of the building. Along one wall were several large windows which overlooked the western half of the base. The curtains were open, and Kozhevnikov could see the lights glinting harshly on the newly fallen snow. A brisk wind had come up, and long plumes of snow whipped around the corners of the buildings.

But Kozhevnikov's eyes had gone to the adjacent wall, which faced the inside of the building. A long set of drapes, drawn closed, covered most of it, and Agayan chuckled at Kozhevnikov's questioning stare.

"Behind those curtains is a hobby I find necessary to pass the time here," the commandant said brightly. "But first we must sit and talk. There is much I must tell you."

Agayan indicated a sofa positioned directly in front

of the drapes. Kozhevnikov sat down at one end while Agayan poured champagne and sat down.

He handed Kozhevnikov a glass and lifted his in a salute.

"A toast," Agayan said, and Kozhevnikov raised his glass. "To the success of Operation Outlook."

Kozhevnikov nodded and sipped the champagne. He put it down on a low table in front of him and turned directly to the commandant. There was definitely something wrong with him and Kozhevnikov did not want to be toyed with. One way or the other he was going to have to force the issue. Either Agayan would let him return to Moscow or he would arrest him. If that happened, Kozhevnikov would have to overpower the commandant somehow and escape.

He glanced toward the window and shivered. There would probably be a storm tonight, which would make the nine hundred kilometers even more impossible than it already was.

Agayan noticed Kozhevnikov's glance, and he, too, put his glass down. "It is freezing tonight—too cold to be out in."

"Commandant," Kozhevnikov said, taking a deep breath. "I am glad that you called me up here this evening. There is something we must discuss."

Agayan seemed startled by Kozhevnikov's directness but nodded for him to continue.

"It is about my work here. The project. Actually it is going entirely unsatisfactorily."

"Yes?" Agayan said, his smile back.

"I must be allowed to return to Moscow in order to complete my work. If I am to manage any kind of a disinformation scheme to cover this facility, I'll need my staff."

Agayan laughed. "You may get your wish, Viktor Vasilievich," he said. "But first let me tell you the entire truth about our operation here and why you were sent to us."

Kozhevnikov's eyes narrowed reflexively, and Agayan laughed again.

"Do not look so surprised, Viktor Vasilievich. One of my few hobbies is psychology. You know I have not told you the entire story."

Kozhevnikov suddenly felt cold. He said nothing and did not move. He knew now that he would never get out of here alive.

"When I placed the listening devices in your office and heard the questions you were asking the Jewish bitches I knew I was right. You do not trust us, Viktor. You perhaps are a traitor as Sergei Antipov suspected."

Kozhevnikov could not respond. Agayan was right, of course. How could he have been so blind, so stupid? He had acted more like a schoolboy than a high-ranking Komitĕt officer. Maybe Nadya had been right after all. Maybe his career had been totally dependent upon her machinations.

"Then this afternoon when you had the audacity to drive across base to *F* section, I knew I had you. But now you also know our little secret."

Kozhevnikov's mouth was dry, but he couldn't reach for his champagne. In his mind he could see the piles of emaciated corpses at Auschwitz. And he could smell the putrefying flesh.

"We have half a million cloned soldiers billeted here at this facility. And soon a new base, even larger than this one, will be constructed. After that, there will be others, all Agrarian Reform Farms. Ingenious, don't you agree?"

Kozhevnikov's assignment was to search the bodies and find identifications. The Americans had arrived and between them they had gone through the camp, had uncovered the mass graves, and worked side by side in growing horror as they picked through bins of false teeth, bales of hair, and mounds of clothing.

"But enough of that for now," Agayan said jovially.

He got up from the sofa, went to the draperies and reached for the draw cord. Before he pulled it, he turned back to Kozhevnikov.

"I have been here a long time, Viktor Vasilievich. I do not know why I was taken from the military and given this assignment, but suffice it to say I have enjoyed the challenge it has provided me."

He turned away for a moment, apparently deep in thought, and when he returned his gaze to Kozhevnikov there was an odd, almost maniacal expression in his eyes. Kozhevnikov was certain the man was insane.

"It is very lonely at this place. The scientists and teachers working here are dedicated. And the Jewish bitches who can have children are untouchable." He smiled. "However, of the hundred thousand women, Viktor Vasilievich, there are enough who are sterile. Enough for my pleasure."

Kozhevnikov knew what Agayan was about to show him, but his imagination was no match for reality.

Agayan turned and pulled the drapes open across a plate-glass window which looked down into what appeared to be a small handball court.

For what seemed an eternity, Kozhevnikov sat rooted to his spot and stared down at the scene below him. The bile rose from his stomach, bitter in his throat.

A dozen women, all nude, fought wildly against a number of horribly misshapen, monstrous creatures who bit their breasts, ripped at their legs, raped them and beat them into masses of blood and mucous. The women were screaming, but Kozhevnikov could not hear them. The room had evidently been soundproofed.

He tore his gaze away from the scene to look at Agayan, who seemed highly agitated now. Spittle drooled down his chin.

"Lovely, isn't it?" Agayan breathed.

Kozhevnikov started to rise, but a motion from below caught his eye and he turned again to look down into the room. One of the women had managed to extricate herself and ran for the door which was set in the opposite wall.

The creature who was on top of her scrambled to his feet and rushed across the narrow room. He towered over the tiny woman, and with one pawlike hand slammed her against the wall, splitting her head open. Blood gushed from the wound.

Before the woman could slump to the floor, the creature hauled her backwards toward the center of the room and threw her on top of another woman who seemed to be dead.

Kozhevnikov stood up and stepped to the window as the monster, his huge erection glistening red with blood, leaped on the woman, entered her, and pounded violently.

"The Jewish sluts are sterile," Agayan said in a high-pitched voice.

Kozhevnikov snapped around to face the commandant, who was now fondling himself.

"The monsters are defective clones. Recessive genes, I'm told." He giggled. "Base. Vile. Dangerous. Lovely."

Kozhevnikov was horror-stricken. This was worse than Auschwitz.

"You don't approve, I see," Agayan said gaily. He was enjoying this.

"Why?" Kozhevnikov managed to ask.

"Don't you mean how?" Agayan said laughing. "Amphetamines and a chemical which causes a urinary tract irritation in the defective clones makes them wild. They will fuck anything. The women, on the other hand, have been taken off their daily Thorazine so they can enjoy it. And I watch. It's lovely."

Kozhevnikov started for him, but Agayan pulled a 9mm automatic from his jacket and pointed it at him.

"You're going to stay for the fun, Viktor Vasilievich," he said calmly now.

Kozhevnikov stopped short as Agayan reached be-. hind him and drew the drapes.

"Sit down, please, there is someone I would like you to meet. Your partner for the evening."

Kozhevnikov's mind was racing now as his stomach continued to churn.

"Why are you doing this to me, Commandant?" Kozhevnikov asked, trying to keep his voice calm. The man was insane, and he did not want to provoke him.

Agayan pulled a crumpled sheet of paper from his pocket with his left hand and threw it across the room. Kozhevnikov bent down, picked it up, and unfolded it. It was a copy of a telex to Agayan from KGB headquarters in Moscow. The message was simple and very direct.

HOLD V. V. KOZHEVNIKOV, MAJ., KGB, FOR QUESTIONING. SUSPECT HIM TO BE COUNTER AGENT WORKING FOR AMERICANS. INTERROGATION TEAM ARRIVING OUTLOOK WITHIN 24 HOURS.

The message was signed ANTIPOV.

"That is tomorrow morning, my dear Viktor Vasilievich," Agayan said happily. "Which means we have the whole evening to ourselves. And what will happen to you will not leave a mark, at least not a physical mark."

CHAPTER 5

It was late afternoon when Laurie Andrews was taken from her jail cell and driven to Frunze Central Airfield on the far northwestern side of Moscow. The guards who had driven her crosstown handed her over to a pair of airport security men without a word, and she was hustled immediately aboard a four-engine military jet transport that was warming up on the parking apron.

Just inside the doorway of the aircraft a short ferret-like man she had never seen before smiled up at her and pointed down the aisle. "If you will just take a seat, Miss Andrews, we can depart."

Laurie was tired, hungry, and dirty. Since her capture they had fed her only twice a day and had not allowed her out of her cell. And even though she had been allowed to keep her purse, she was not allowed to bathe. She had never felt so uncomfortable in her life. But she managed to keep her voice steady. "Where are you taking me?" she demanded.

"To your new home," the man grinned.

He made her feel doubly uncomfortable. Her light fall coat, the only one she had brought with her to Germany, was unbuttoned in the front, and she was acutely conscious of her thin blouse and uplifting bra which accentuated her breasts. He was staring directly at them.

She pulled her coat tightly around her. "I demand to see the American ambassador," she snapped.

The man's patience and forced good humor seemed to depart. "Miss Andrews," he said, raising his voice. "You will either take your seat voluntarily, or you will be drugged."

There was a clutch of fear at her stomach, and she started down the aisle. When they had taken her from East Berlin, she had been given a tranquilizer. When she had regained consciousness it had felt like her head would explode.

Later, in her cell, she had been given the same thing again, and through a thick haze she could vaguely remember talking with someone about her life, telling her questioner everything he asked.

The next morning when she awoke, she had the same feeling that someone had been beating on her head with a sledgehammer. She did not want to repeat that experience.

Halfway down the aisle an old man got up from his seat and smiled at her. He looked vaguely familiar.

"Miss Andrews?" he said in a soft voice. "Miss Laurie Andrews, the newspaper reporter?"

Although the short little man was directly behind her, Laurie stopped and nodded. There was something about him. He was someone she should know.

The old man glanced behind her. "Comrade Antipov," he said, "would it be all right if Miss Andrews sat with me for part of the trip?"

Laurie did not turn; instead, she continued to stare at him. Surely her tiredness and disorientation were causing this memory block. But she was certain she should know this man.

"I suppose it won't hurt, Dr. Meitner," the man behind Laurie said, still in English. The old man moved to the window seat and motioned for her to sit down.

She stared at him. The sudden revelation hit her like a ton of bricks. Meitner! Of course. But here?

Meitner managed a slight smile. "Please, Miss Andrews, we are about to take off. Won't you join me? We have a lot to talk about. I, for one, have several questions I would like to ask you."

Nothing made sense to her any longer, and for some reason she suddenly remembered the identical twins outside the police station in East Berlin. There was a colossal story here, her reporter's instinct told her. But her instinct for survival told her that she wasn't going to get out of this one. There would be no Phil Shapiro to bail her out. No company lawyers, no public opinion to vindicate her. She was completely alone in a foreign land—a hostile foreign land. And she knew that she would never see New Orleans again.

She sat down and methodically buckled her seat belt, not bothering to take off her coat. She stared at Meitner, her mouth half open, but she could not help herself. What did it all mean?

He was about to speak when the door at the front of the aircraft was closed with a heavy thump and the jet began to taxi down the runway. He turned and looked out the window, and for a moment Laurie was once again alone with her chaotic thoughts.

She had spent three months in the Canary Islands investigating the crash of the 747 jet airliners. And a few days before she was due to leave, she began to have nightmares. Each time she was on an airplane that was crashing and she would awake as the flames began to consume her body. When she returned to the States, the dreams stopped, but she still remembered them.

They were at the end of the runway now, and the aircraft was turning ponderously. A moment later the jet engines revved up to a deafening noise, and they began to move; slowly at first, and then faster and faster. A few seconds later they were airborne, heading . . . where? she asked herself, coming back to the present.

Meitner turned to her as the noise began to decrease. "I am quite surprised to see you."

"What are you doing here?" she managed to ask.

"I might well ask you the same question," Meitner said. There was a self-assurance about the man now that was not present when she had watched him answer questions at the news conference in Madison. But there was also an unnatural pallor to his skin, like that of a sick man, a very sick man.

"I found out that your name really isn't Meitner. He died in Hannover. And I found out about Tiefensee," Laurie said. It didn't really matter now, but she found that she could not stop herself from getting the rest of the story. She had never left puzzles unfinished.

"How did you find out about Tiefensee?" Meitner asked.

"After you left Madison, some people from my newspaper got into your basement laboratory."

"My journal," Meitner said softly, his brows knitting. And then he brightened. "You saw Dr. Predel's name, and mention of the DBK. That's what led you to look for the World War Two records."

Laurie nodded.

"But what brings you here?" he asked.

"I tried to go to Tiefensee," she said simply.

"And you were arrested. In East Berlin?"

She nodded tiredly.

He sat back in his seat, a thoughtful expression on his face. "So now you will learn everything. Unfortunately for you," he said under his breath.

Through the haze that began to cloud her mind, she heard Meitner's remarks; but his pronouncement of doom had no effect on her. From the moment she saw the identical men in the car in East Berlin she knew she would not come out of this one. At the time the thought had frightened her. But now somehow it didn't mean much to her. But she was a fighter. She had always been a fighter.

She turned finally to Meitner, her mind clearing somewhat. There was still hope, she told herself. At least that was what heroines told themselves in hopeless situations.

"What is your real name?" she asked.

Meitner looked up, surprised at her question.

He smiled and shook his head. "After all these years it is Meitner. But I was born Abel Brenner in Ludwigshafen, on the Rhine."

"And you were Abel Brenner in Tiefensee?"

"Station Kummersdorf East. Yes. *Leutnant* Brenner. Young. Idealistic. And a good scientist even then."

"And why are you here?" she heard herself asking. Did any of this really matter?

Genuine surprise showed on his face. "To work, of course," he said matter-of-factly.

"Work?" she managed to say.

Meitner nodded and was about to answer when the man who had directed Laurie aboard the aircraft came up to them.

"How is everything, Dr. Meitner?" he said, smiling.

Meitner looked up past Laurie. "It will be better when we arrive at Markovo, Comrade Antipov," he said.

Laurie looked up at the man who was leering down at her now.

"Is Miss Andrews bothering you, Doctor?"

"Not at all," Meitner said. "Her company is welcome."

"I see," Antipov said, staring directly into her eyes. "If there is anything you need, please ask me. I'm seated three rows back."

"Thank you," Meitner said.

Antipov took one last lingering look at Laurie, then turned and went back to his seat. For the first time she noticed that there were others on the aircraft. Two men seated across the aisle from her looked familiar, and when one of them turned toward her she almost fainted. He was a husky man, with short-cropped hair, square features, and steel-blue eyes. He was identical to the two men in East Berlin.

The man glanced at her, his expression completely devoid of interest, and then he turned to stare straight ahead.

Laurie turned to Meitner, who had been watching her. There was an amused expression on his face.

"Unbelievable, isn't it?" he asked.

She stared at him without comprehension, and a look of impatience crossed his face. "You know nothing about our work at Tiefensee?" he asked.

"Only that you and Predel and the others murdered Jews," she said. She could feel anger mounting, directed at Meitner's smugness.

Meitner dismissed her comment with a shrug. "That is the difference between us and you," he said in a lecturing tone. "We are fighting a battle against ignorance. And as in all battles there are casualties. At least they are only Jews."

"Are the Russians doing the same thing the Nazis did?" she asked incredulously.

"Of course," Meitner said, surprised. "All this time in the United States I've been hampered in my experiments. Nothing beyond a certain point can be accomplished with guinea pigs and rabbits. If I had only known that the Soviet scientists were working on the Kummersdorf Project, I would have come here years ago."

"Why?" Laurie stammered. "What are you doing that you have to kill people?"

Meitner smiled condescendingly. "If I took the day to explain it to you, Miss Andrews, I am sure you would not follow half of it. Suffice it to say we are building an army of perfect men." He nodded toward the two men sitting across the aisle from them. "And we have been successful."

Laurie looked across the aisle. None of this made

any sense. What was he trying to tell her? She looked back as he continued to talk.

"In the thirties, we were stabbing in the dark. But we had the Jewish women to experiment with. An unending supply to do research on—a luxury I have not had in the United States."

As he continued, a growing horror began to fill Laurie's body. She began to shake uncontrollably. Human guinea pigs. Hideous medical experiments. Irreversible operations to test the limits of human endurance. Meitner was telling all of it now, completely lost in his own world.

This man had won the Nobel Prize. The Nobel Prize. And men such as Jonas Salk and other giants of humanitarian medicine had received nothing.

She was going to end up as one of those test victims, she knew it. Wherever Markovo was, it apparently had a Soviet research station there modeled after the one the Nazis had maintained in Tiefensee. She was going there now. She was going to be one of them.

She glanced again at the men seated across the aisle, but she could not make the connection. Such things were science fiction. Unacceptable. Unthinkable.

They had let her keep her purse and her cosmetics. She carefully opened her bag and reached inside, cautious not to move fast and attract attention. Whatever Meitner had been during the war, he had done good work in the United States. Work that had earned him the Nobel Prize.

Her fingers curled around the ten-inch-long metal fingernail file, but she hesitated for a moment. She turned to look at Meitner, who was staring straight ahead as he talked. He was wearing a worn-out black suit and white shirt that was open at the collar. His neck was gray and wrinkled. He was a sick man, she was sure of it. But he was also sick in the mind. He could not be allowed to do this.

In one smooth motion, Laurie withdrew the fingernail file from her purse and plunged it deep into Meitner's neck. Instantly blood spurted out, staining her coat sleeve and splashing on her face.

Meitner jerked around, almost like a marionette, and looked at her with a shocked expression on his face, his mouth open, blood bubbling up from his throat as he tried to breathe.

Strong hands suddenly grabbed her head and sharply twisted it around; but before her neck broke she was satisfied to see Meitner slump forward and the arterial blood stop pumping from his neck.

CHAPTER 6

Rafn could not sleep, so he sat up, swung his feet around to the floor, and flipped on the light over his bunk. He lit a cigarette as he listened to the sounds of the nuclear submarine *Tyrannosaurus*. There was a thrumming noise that seemed to vibrate everywhere, and the whir of electrical machinery was close. An air-conditioning fan, he thought.

He looked at his watch. It was after two in the morning. Yesterday afternoon the captain, Elias Rothman, had told him they would be in position off St. Lawrence Island by early this morning. The captain had not been told specifically what the mission was, but he had been warned that under no circumstances should contact with the Soviets be made. Under no circumstances.

At first that didn't bother Rafn. He had gone along, pleased that he had managed to convince the president to go this far. But now other contingencies began to weigh on his mind.

What if Kozhevnikov did make it, what if he needed help at the last minute? Were they going to stand by and watch him fall without lifting a finger to help him?

There were a lot of big ifs in this, but there had been from the beginning. Only they had gone too far now to abandon the mission. If they could grab Kozhevnikov and if he could convince the Americans, they would be out of the fire.

There are too many ifs, Rafn thought glumly as he inhaled. Too many chances for a foul-up. Too few places that were controllable.

Eliminate all uncontrollables, the old line went, and success is assured. Black and white. Nothing was really that way, though. Everything was grays and grays.

Somehow then, he was going to have to minimize the uncontrollable factors.

He started to get up from the bunk but then sat back. The president had called for his ace card. But this was more like a wild card in a poker game in which the rules had been suspended.

He had refrained from telling Bindrich about it, nor had he told Gleason or the president himself. But why? Why had he held back? Why hadn't he shared his suspicions with them?

The two men in East Germany were only the tip of the iceberg.

The clues had come from Kozhevnikov and then from Schiller in East Germany. Kozhevnikov had said that most of the Jews were women. Schiller had said that the experiments at Tiefensee had been with women. Women. Why only women? What were they doing?

And then the identical twins gave him a clue.

In Langley he had used what the company called its Idento-Print computer to come up with a composite drawing of a face, the same face of the identical twins in Germany. Combined with a physical description of the men, he had run the information through the company's incident report files. It spun out sixty-nine separate incidents over the past five years involving men of the same description—ranging over a wide area of Western Europe.

Each incident had been minor and had attracted very little attention—enough to qualify for the files, but not enough to make any analyst sit up and take notice. At least not until Rafn.

Sixty-nine separate incidents. Plus the one in Tiefensee. And the one at the border. Seventy-one separate incidents. The same face. The same description.

Bindrich would never have believed it, nor would Gleason. And the president?

He got up, pulled a threadbare sweater from his suitcase and pulled it over his head. When he had boarded the submarine in San Francisco two days ago, he had changed from his suit to a pair of workman's trousers, soft-soled shoes, and an old dress shirt. Now he was cold despite the warmth of the submarine. It was purely a psychological reaction, he knew, to being submerged, but it didn't matter. The sweater was like an old friend. Warm and comfortable. Qualities he had never found in people.

He left his cabin, shuffled down the narrow corridor, and ducked into the officers' wardroom. The lights were on, and there was coffee in the machine on the sideboard, but no one was here at this hour. Just as well, he thought as he poured himself a mug of the strong coffee and sank wearily down in one of the chairs at the long mahogany table.

He did not like the confinement of the submarine. A few days at a time would be all he could handle. Having to accept his own limitations made his sour mood even worse.

Age was a strange thing, he thought. As a young man this would not have bothered him. In fact he would have enjoyed it. But now thoughts about his own vulnerability, his own frailty, had begun to creep into his lexicon of justifying the things he was doing.

He smiled. Perhaps he was getting too old for the games. Perhaps when this mess was straightened out, he would go to Spain and never return.

Something prevented him from picking up the pack of cigarettes he had laid on the table. He cocked his head slightly and listened. At first he could hear nothing unusual, but then he knew what was happening.

The steady thrumming of the submarine's motors had

lowered in pitch. And as he listened now, the sound slid lower, then stopped.

He grabbed his cigarettes, jumped up and hurried out into the corrdor; just then the ship's PA system clicked on.

"Attention all hands. Attention all hands. This is the captain speaking. We have stopped at the hundred-meter level to get a better look at an ice floe directly in front of us."

As Captain Rothman spoke to the crew over the PA system, Rafn hurried down the corridor and up the ladder into the control room.

Keith Saunders, the executive officer, who was standing next to Rothman behind the sonar operator, turned as Rafn came up through the hatch in the deck. He said something to the captain, who glanced toward Rafn but then turned back to the sonar set. Saunders came across the room as Rafn stepped up onto the deck.

"You'll have to return to your quarters, Mr. Rafn," the young officer said.

Rafn tried to push past him, but the man held him back. "Please, sir," he said.

Rafn stepped back, suddenly realizing what he had done. "Sorry," he said. "I thought we were stopping." It was his one failing. When he was no longer in control of a situation, he wanted one of two things. To regain control or turn away completely. This time he could do neither, and he had become tense, something he could not allow. He would have to remain clear-headed and dispassionate in order to handle this situation properly.

Rothman turned again toward them, hung up the microphone and then walked over to where they were standing. "I want you back in your quarters, Mr. Rafn," he said.

Rafn studied his face for a moment. They were about the same age, but where Rafn looked ten years older than he really was, the captain looked ten years younger.

"I thought we were stopping," he said.

"We are," the captain barked. "I'm scrubbing this mission. We're turning back."

"No," Rafn said loud enough so that the others in the room looked toward them.

The captain looked thunderstruck, and he turned to his exec. "Mr. Saunders, would you escort this man back to his quarters and see that he remains there until we berth in San Francisco?"

"Yes, sir," Saunders snapped.

Too many mistakes were being made, Rafn told himself. But it had been like this from the beginning. Maybe he was getting too old. Losing control.

"We're going to talk first," Rafn said, taking a deep breath. "Either here or in your quarters."

"By God, Mr. . . ." the captain began, but something in Rafn's expression, combined with the import of the mission, made him stop.

"Either here or in your quarters," Rafn repeated more softly.

The captain's resolve seemed to waver, and he turned to his exec. "Hold her steady, Mr. Saunders. I'll be right back."

"Aye, aye, sir," Saunders said, and Rothman motioned for Rafn to leave the control room.

The major difference between Rothman's tiny quarters and Rafn's was the communications console built into the bulkhead above the desk. The captain sat next to it now while Rafn sat opposite him. The captain did not seem happy.

"I think you'd better explain your actions and damned quickly, mister," Rothman began, and Rafn smiled. He was regaining his control.

"I am not an engineer, and this is not a routine mission to show me your ship, Captain," Rafn said. He pulled out a letter the president had written for him, and handed it across to the captain. In a few short, simple sentences, the president merely introduced Rafn as a CIA operative who was on an undefined mission in the Bering Strait. Rafn was to be cooperated with up to, but not including, the point they confronted Soviet forces.

The captain read the letter once, looked up at Rafn with a new respect in his eyes, and then reread it. When he was done, he folded it and handed it back.

"I was told that you were a NATO engineer, and that this was to be a routine cruise beneath the ice in the Bering Strait."

"Yes," Rafn said dryly.

Rothman seemed somewhat uncomfortable. "Of course, I will cooperate with you in any way possible. What is the mission?"

Rafn ignored the question for the moment. "Where are we right now? Exactly."

The captain studied Rafn's eyes a moment, then reached behind him and pulled a chart from a narrow cabinet next to his bunk. He unfolded it on his desk, and Rafn got up and came around so that he could see it.

"We're a hundred and fifty nautical miles south-southwest of St. Lawrence. We passed the western tip of Hall Island late last night."

With his finger Rafn indicated a course that would take them almost due west from their present position to the dividing line between international waters and the Soviet border waters.

"What are the chances of surfacing there?" he said.

Rothman studied the map a moment, and then looked up. "It'd raise a lot of questions once we were detected."

"Would it precipitate any action?" Rafn asked carefully.

"Hard to tell. I don't think I'd care to risk it unless I knew beforehand what the stakes were."

Rafn was on familiar territory now, and he felt more comfortable than he had since the beginning of this in San Francisco. Manipulating people was his stock-in-trade.

The map indicated the Soviet coastal town of Anadyr across the Gulf from St. Lawrence Island, and Rafn pointed his finger at it. "A high-ranking Soviet officer may be defecting. If he does, it will be across from there."

The captain looked at the map and then up at Rafn again. "You're crazy," he said after a moment.

"Yes," Rafn said, smiling. "Nevertheless, I want us to surface as closely as possible and have a look. We can monitor Soviet military radio channels. If he is coming, there'll be chatter about him."

"He's important?"

"Very," Rafn said.

"Then they'll be coming after him."

"Most likely."

Rothman smiled now. "That letter of yours says to cooperate short of confrontation."

"That's right," Rafn said. "And that is exactly what I expect from you until a confrontation occurs."

"It will, once we surface. There is a MIG base at Anadyr."

"I know," Rafn said. "There also is a long-range submarine-detection station. We're probably being monitored right now."

"You do get around, don't you," the captain said. The Soviet's submarine-detection capabilities were top secret. Rafn had ony learned about it during the short briefing the president had arranged for him.

The president had agreed to cooperate with Rafn, over the CIA director's protestations, just this once. Though Gleason was behind him one hundred percent, he was probably completely out by now.

"I don't want an incident any more than you do, Captain," Rafn said levelly. "If we can surface directly off Anadyr just enough so that your radar and radio antennas can work, we shouldn't be immediately detected as having surfaced."

"For how long?" Rothman asked.

"Until our man comes out to meet us."

"Is he expecting us?"

Rafn shook his head. "He may expect some kind of help, but there is no way for him to know in what form it might come."

"You're not even sure if he's going to attempt the escape then, are you?" the captain said sharply. "Or when he'll try to escape. Or how."

"That's correct. But we're going to be there watching for him nevertheless."

Rothman grunted and got to his feet. "Watching for him out of one eye, and the opposition out of the other. Whoever makes it to us first will determine the outcome, for which I will call the shots."

CHAPTER 7

Fedor Udalov came into Agayan's living room dragging a baby-faced young woman by the arm. She was wearing the same light gray fatigues that everyone else wore, except the Star of David was stamped on the front and back of the jacket. When Udalov saw the automatic in Agayan's hand, he stopped. The girl's struggles were ineffectual against his bulk.

"Commandant?" he said.

"That will be all for this evening. Leave the girl now and return to your quarters," Agayan said, the expression on his face even more animated than before.

Udalov nodded, pushed the girl forward and then turned and left. As Kozhevnikov stared at the obviously frightened young woman who cowered in a half crouch across the room from them, the outer door of Agayan's apartment closed, and then the room became quiet.

The girl was about twenty-five years old, obviously Jewish, and pretty in an athletic way.

Her face, however, held a determined expression. Kozhevnikov could not help but admire her spirit.

"Allow me to introduce you to Miss Raya Kisselstein," Agayan said, his gun still trained on Kozhevnikov. "Or should I say Raya Schiller."

At the mention of the second name the young woman winced. For that instant Kozhevnikov had the distinct impression that she was getting ready to do something drastic.

Agayan also noticed her reaction. "I've taken her off Thorazine and given her a light dose of Valium so she would be a more able, active partner," he said, glancing at her. "Miss Schiller has spent nearly a year with us, mostly in isolation. Before that she spent a couple of years in Moscow, and before that in Tel Aviv. Israeli Secret Service."

A startled expression crossed Kozhevnikov's face, and Agayan laughed.

"Yes, my dear Viktor Vasilievich, you were correct. Our little project has been attracting some attention."

"Then others will be coming," Kozhevnikov said. His mouth and throat were dry. For a moment he thought about the Jewish girl who had stayed with them while his wife was sick. But he could not remember her name or face, only Nadya's accusing stare.

"Yes, they may," Agayan said jovially, a strange tone in his voice. "But that is no longer your concern. This evening you shall be part of my little hobby."

Agayan reached behind him and drew open the curtains. The room beyond the plate-glass window was now empty. "You two will give me a pleasant diversion this evening."

Kozhevnikov's insides felt queasy. "Then you'll have to kill me," he heard himself saying. "Because I won't play your little games."

Agayan turned back and laughed out loud. "No . . . no, my dear Viktor Vasilievich, it won't be so easy as that. You are a Jew-lover. Would you like to watch while Miss Schiller is tortured to death? Or would you rather cooperate?"

It had finally come to the end, and it was as if he were on a roller coaster. He had climbed aboard at Auschwitz in 1945 and ever since then he had been riding toward the crest of the tallest trestle. Although he had gone down short hills and around curves, he was always headed toward the tallest point on the tracks. And when he saw the Kummersdorf files in Moscow, the ride speeded up. Once he contacted Douville in Paris, he got his first clear view of what lay ahead. The heights were impossible.

But there was still a chance, he told himself, his heart hammering nearly out of his chest. There was still a chance.

He had the Order of Lenin. The premier had called him a hero. The director of the Komitët had believed in him. Only Antipov wanted to push him over the edge.

He could stay here and fight this. Antipov would come in the morning, but the man could have no real proof. He was certain that Rafn had not allowed the Americans to push the inquiries in Germany. He would not have allowed that. So there were only suspicions. He could stay and fight it. His record was clean, except for his contact in Paris and Munich. He had done outstanding work for his country, especially in Vietnam.

He could remain here, fight it out, and once his name was cleared, work to abolish this place. Work as he had always worked, to make his country great. The Union of Soviet Socialist Republics. The greatest, largest, finest nation this earth has ever seen.

Wasn't it? Wasn't that what he had been told in school as a young man? Wasn't that what he had worked for all of his life? Wasn't that what he had devoted every gram of his strength, every particle of his being toward?

Many peoples, many tongues, many lands. From the shores of the Caspian to the top of Communist Peak. From the Sea of Okhotsk to the borders of Western Europe. All of it was his country.

One nation, one land, one people all bound by a common destiny.

There were tears in his eyes when he focused again

on Agayan, who was watching him. Traitor. The word kept pounding on his mind.

He was a traitor to his country, but not to the ideal. Because it all came back to this. To the hundred thousand Jews here on the Siberian tundra.

He bent down and picked up his half-empty champagne glass and turned toward Agayan. "A little more champagne first, Commandant?"

Agayan smiled broadly. "Of course, Viktor Vasilievich. And for Miss Schiller as well," beckoning the woman to come forward. He moved away from the window, shifted the automatic to his left hand, and bent down to reach for the champagne bottle.

At that moment Agayan was less than a meter and a half away. Kozhevnikov threw his champagne into the man's face and leaped forward over the coffee table.

Agayan bellowed like a wounded bull and crashed sideways against the end table, upsetting the champagne bottle and losing his balance.

In the next instant Kozhevnikov was on him, and they both crashed to the floor, the gun flying out of Agayan's hand.

The commandant was huge, and he shook Kozhevnikov like a rag doll, tossing him half across the room.

When Kozhevnikov untangled himself and sat up, Agayan was slowly getting up and the young woman was holding the gun on him.

"You get up," she snapped at Agayan.

Kozhevnikov's heart was hammering. They had made it. At least this far.

Agayan got to his feet and started across the room, but the young woman waved the gun menacingly at him. "No further."

He laughed. "Where will you go, little girl?" he said, and she seemed to waver.

She was determined, but still she was on Valium, Kozhevnikov could see it in her sluggish actions and slurred speech. She would not be able to hold on much longer.

Once again Kozhevnikov found himself at the crest of the hill. If he helped Agayan now, it would be a power case in his favor. But he could not.

"Miss Schiller, I am on your side," he said, taking a step forward.

"No," she cried uncertainly, and took a step backwards.

Agayan leaped forward and was on her before she could react. As they struggled for the gun, Kozhevnikov leaped forward and scooped the champagne bottle up off the floor. He swung it over his head and in one smooth motion brought it crashing down on the back of Agayan's head. The man went down on top of the young woman, and in the next instant Kozhevnikov grabbed the pistol and backed off behind the sofa.

He was committed now, he told himself, trying to steady his shaking hands. He was now over the crest and was starting the downhill run.

The girl extricated herself and got shakily to her feet. She backed away from Agayan, eyeing Kozhevnikov and the automatic.

"Is it true?" Kozhevnikov said. "Are you with the Israeli Secret Service?"

The girl said nothing.

"We don't have time to play games," Kozhevnikov said tersely. "You are either with me, or you're not. I'm getting out of here. I will take you along if you want."

"How?"

"There's a light airplane on the runway. I can fly it."

"Where?" the girl said. Agayan started to regain consciousness and he sat up, holding his head in his hands.

"St. Lawrence Island, across the Gulf. It's American-owned."

"It's impossible."

"Do you want to stay here?" Kozhevnikov shouted.

Agayan got slowly to his feet, and the young woman backed farther away from him.

"Kill him," she said.

Kozhevnikov shook his head. "He's our passport to the airstrip," he said. He turned to the commandant. "Let's go."

Agayan smiled. "You're an amateur, Viktor Vasilievich. You'll never get out of here alive."

"Perhaps," Kozhevnikov said more calmly than he felt. His insides were churning. "But if I don't make it, you won't either." He raised the heavy automatic and pointed it directly at Agayan's head. "So move."

Color drained from Agayan's face. "If you kill me you'll have no chance whatsoever."

"It won't matter to you then, will it?" Kozhevnikov asked. "Move."

The commandant edged away from the sofa. "Where are we going?"

"To my quarters," Kozhevnikov said. He glanced at Raya. "Check his office and the reception room. Udalov might still be there."

"Which Udalov?" she asked. "Thirty-three fifty-seven was assigned to me."

Her voice was still slurred; none of this seemed very important to her.

"You're either with me or you're not," Kozhevnikov shouted, and Agayan laughed.

"You won't even get out of this office, let alone the base," Agayan said, his jovial attitude coming back.

"Then I'll kill you now and get it over with," Kozhevnikov said. "It doesn't really matter, anyway. The Americans already know about this place."

Agayan dropped his hands and started toward Kozhevnikov. "You traitor!" he screamed.

Kozhevnikov reached up, snapped the slide back on the gun and then held it stiff-armed with both hands. "Another step and you are a dead man, so help me God!"

Agayan stopped abruptly. "So help me God, Kozhevnikov. *You* are the dead man."

"Then so are you," Kozhevnikov said. He started to squeeze the trigger when Raya shouted.

"Stop!"

Kozhevnikov released the pressure on the trigger and relaxed his grip on the gun.

"I'll go with you," she said. "I'll help." She turned and went out of the living room.

Agayan, for the first time, looked frightened. "Why, Viktor Vasilievich? Why are you doing this?"

Kozhevnikov ignored him, and a moment later the woman was back.

"It's all clear."

"My room is twenty-three A. It's on the second floor in the west wing," Kozhevnikov said, and then he motioned toward Agayan with the gun. "You first, Commandant. If we run into any resistance, I will kill you instantly."

Without a word Agayan got his heavy parka and the three of them left his apartment.

CHAPTER 8

They met no one in the briefing auditorium, on the stairs which led down to the west wing of the administration building, or in the second-floor corridor. The three of them now stood facing each other in the living room of Kozhevnikov's apartment.

On the way out of Agayan's office, they had stopped long enough for Raya to put on the heavy Arctic boots and parka. Now she looked like a rabbit in its burrow, beneath the heavy clothing.

Agayan looked like a bear.

If the situation were not so serious, Kozhevnikov thought, it would be ludicrous. He could envision Nadya's reaction to all of this. She would have laughed at him. But she had always been the strong one, the conservative element of their marriage. She had been the one who supported him when he doubted his work. And after a while he had come to lean on her. Whenever a decision was to be made, he found himself looking across at Nadya to get her reaction first. But she wasn't here. There was only a girl, a dangerously insane man, and. . . . The thought stopped him. And a traitor. The word made him ache inside.

Agayan was watching him with an amused expression on his face. "You'll not make it off this base alive, Viktor Vasilievich," he said contemptuously.

Kozhevnikov ignored the commandant and turned toward Raya. "In my bedroom, by my bed, is my briefcase. Get it, please. We have to take it with us."

A look of uncertainty passed over Agayan's face as Raya turned and went into the bedroom. A moment later she came out lugging the open briefcase.

"What are these tapes?" she asked, setting the heavy leather satchel down next to Kozhevnikov.

Kozhevnikov kept his eyes on Agayan. "Interviews with two dozen Jewish women. Proof for the Americans."

Agayan took a step forward, a pained expression on his face. "Viktor Vasilievich, reconsider what you are doing," he said through clenched teeth.

"I have thought about it, Commandant. I have thought about it long and hard," Kozhevnikov said and turned toward Raya. "My parka and boots are in the closet. Get them for me."

"You are determined to go through with this, then?" Agayan said almost sadly as Raya went across the room to the closet near the corridor door and pulled out Kozhevnikov's Arctic clothing.

Kozhevnikov nodded. "Yes. But that does not mean I love my country less——"

"Save me the philosophical discussions, traitor."

The word cut deeply, but Kozhevnikov said nothing.

Raya came back with his boots and parka and put them on the floor near the briefcase. He handed the pistol to her.

"Cover him while I dress."

She nodded and trained the automatic on Agayan, who stood about two meters away, as Kozhevnikov quickly pulled on his Arctic boots, laced them tightly, and then pulled on his down-filled parka.

When he was dressed he took the gun from Raya and motioned toward the door. "My jeep is out back. We'll take that to the airstrip," he said.

Agayan did not move. "Are you really going to take that material to the Americans?" he asked, nodding toward the briefcase.

"Yes," Kozhevnikov said. "This insanity must stop."

Agayan started to move but in an instant swiveled around, howled like an animal, and charged across the room.

Kozhevnikov was taken completely off guard and had no time to fire before Agayan's large hand swung around and slapped the gun out of his hand. In the next moment Agayan was on him, and they both went crashing to the floor.

Kozhevnikov's mind was racing now. Everything seemed to be happening in slow motion. But he could not get his body to function fast enough as Agayan grabbed the hood of his parka and began to bang his head on the floor.

The smell of stale wine and perspiration was strong enough to make Kozhevnikov gag.

He felt like a small child being beaten by his father; there was nothing he could do to stop him. The man was too large, and too strong. Sounds were coming to him from down a long tunnel and the lights in the room were dimming. There was a sudden, sharp pain in his left arm that shot up to his shoulder and down his spine so that his hip began to ache.

Agayan was rolling off him now, and he could feel the man kicking him in the legs. From a distance he could dimly see Raya bringing the heavy briefcase down on the back of Agayan's head, the brown leather case was making a perfect arc in the air over and over again.

And then Agayan's kicking ceased, and Raya was bending over Kozhevnikov and helping him up as the room came back into focus.

He got to his feet. The pain in his arm was so sharp it brought tears to his eyes.

"Is your arm broken?" Raya asked, deep concern in her eyes.

Kozhevnikov nodded. "I think so."

"Oh, God," she breathed.

Escape had seemed almost impossible from the beginning, and now their chances seemed even more remote. Kozhevnikov wanted to cry out in anger and frustration, but he hurt too badly for that. They were committed now. They would have to continue.

He turned stiffly and bent down over Agayan's nearly inert form. His head was a mass of blood, but he was breathing, and when Kozhevnikov touched him, he moved.

"I thought I had killed him," Raya said.

Kozhevnikov looked up. "We won't be able to get out of here without him."

Agayan rolled over and started to sit up, and Kozhevnikov backed away from him. "Get a wet rag from the bathroom," he said to Raya. "We're going to have to clean him up before we take him out of here."

Raya quickly went into the bathroom. Kozhevnikov looked around until he found the commandant's gun lying near the bedroom door. He picked it up and turned around, startled.

Agayan had gotten to his feet and was weaving drunkenly across the room toward him. Kozhevnikov raised the gun tiredly and pointed it at the man.

"I've got nothing to lose now, Agayan. I'll kill you if you come any closer."

Agayan stopped where he was and weaved. His eyes were narrowed nearly to slits, his hate radiating from him almost visibly. "When this is over, Viktor Vasilievich, I will see to your execution personally. And it will not be pleasant. So help me. You will live a long time before I am through with you."

Raya came into the room carrying a wet towel. When she saw that Agayan had recovered, she gasped.

Agayan turned toward her. "And the little Jewish slut. She, too, will become a toy before she is allowed to die."

"Never mind the towel," Kozhevnikov said to Raya. He motioned with the gun toward the door. "Let's go, Commandant."

Agayan stood perfectly still, and Kozhevnikov raised the gun again.

"Don't make me kill you."

"You won't get out of here," Agayan said.

Kozhevnikov said nothing. His arm hurt and the back of his head throbbed. He felt tired and sluggish.

Agayan turned slowly and walked out into the corridor.

"Pull up your hood," Kozhevnikov said from behind him.

Agayan did not look around, but he pulled the hood over his head as he continued down the still-deserted hall toward the back door where Kozhevnikov's jeep was parked.

Raya had grabbed the bloodied briefcase, and she followed behind Kozhevnikov.

Agayan went out the back door without stopping and marched directly to Kozhevnikov's jeep. He turned back to them. "Front seat or back?" he asked simply.

"Front seat, passenger's side," Kozhevnikov said and turned to Raya. "You drive. I'll cover him from the back seat."

Without a word, Agayan climbed in and stared rigidly ahead. He did not move as Kozhevnikov painfully climbed in from the driver's side and Raya got in behind the wheel and started the engine.

Alarm bells were jangling along Kozhevnikov's nerves. The commandant had become too subdued. He was offering no resistance. Something was wrong, but there was nothing he could do. His arm was throbbing all the way up to his shoulder, and he was colder than he had ever been in his life. The wind had begun to blow, and by the looks of the weather they would be in for an Arctic storm before long.

Everything that could go wrong had gone wrong. And yet the toughest part of the escape was still ahead of them. If they were not stopped at the main gate, they probably would be at the airstrip. If not that, the airplane might be gone or not ready to fly. Then they would be lost.

Raya put the jeep in gear and they headed away from the administration building along the snow-covered road that led to the main gates. Like the afternoon he arrived, it looked cold and dark and seemed completely deserted except for the lights on top of the barracks.

Agayan was silent, and Raya concentrated on her driving. In a few minutes they were approaching the main gate.

Looking between Raya and Agayan, Kozhevnikov could see that no one was manning the guardhouse on the ground but he could see soldiers in the towers that rose above the fence.

No one had come out to challenge them and Raya turned back to Kozhevnikov. "What should I do?"

"Why aren't there any guards at the gate?" Kozhevnikov asked Agayan.

The commandant did not turn around. "There are guards at the lower gate only when a shipment of Jews comes in. They are not drugged, so they have to be watched."

Something was drastically wrong. Kozhevnikov could feel it. "Go on through," he said to Raya.

They passed through the gate and headed toward the airstrip, which was dark except for a single light on top of the main hangar. Like the base, it looked deserted.

There were two planes parked outside the hangar. One was a large twin-engine cargo plane that was used for supply runs to Anadyr. The other was a small two-seat single-engine plane that, Udalov had explained to Kozhevnikov last week, was used to spot the occasional Jew who wandered off the base.

"It happens from time to time," Udalov had said nonchalantly. "They never get very far, but the plane helps track them down."

It was then that Kozhevnikov decided to use it for his escape if he was not able to talk Agayan into sending him back to Moscow. It was a dim possibility at best, one that he had never really envisioned himself using. After the war he had learned to fly the small spotter planes the KGB used to patrol rural prison areas, but that was a long time ago. And he had had the use of both arms.

Raya pulled off the road and onto the snow-swept concrete surface of the parking apron leading toward the runway and slowed down.

"Which airplane?" she asked.

"The little one," Kozhevnikov said.

Agayan began to laugh as Raya pulled across the apron and stopped a few meters from the little black airplane.

Raya got out of the jeep, and Kozhevnikov painfully climbed out after her, keeping the gun trained on the commandant as best he could.

"Get out of the jeep," Kozhevnikov said. He was already cold and shivering, and as the commandant climbed out the opposite side, he directed Raya to remove the tiedowns holding the airplane in place.

She silently went to work as Agayan came to where Kozhevnikov stood. "It is all over now, Viktor Vasilievich. You have had your little fun. We have seen how far you would go. It is my turn now." He turned and looked in the jeep.

Kozhevnikov followed his gaze and suddenly he went cold. The microphone from the communications radio was dangling by its cord. Agayan had turned it on. Someone on the base had monitored their every word.

Raya was back at his side. "The ropes are off and the door is open."

"Take the briefcase and strap yourself in the back seat," Kozhevnikov snapped. "Hurry!"

She grabbed the heavy briefcase, came around Kozhevnikov, and was about to get in the airplane when lights all around the airstrip came on, a spotlight swept toward them from atop the hangar and sirens began to scream.

Kozhevnikov and Raya, both distracted by the sudden light and noise, looked toward the base. At that instant Agayan lunged forward, pushing Kozhevnikov back against Raya. He grabbed the briefcase, turned, and started running toward the hangar as a long line of jeeps came streaming through the main gate.

"Stop!" Kozhevnikov screamed at Agayan, who was moving away at a dead run.

He raised the pistol, aimed it the best he could, and squeezed off a shot, the heavy gun bucking in his hand. Agayan stumbled, then regained his balance and continued running, more slowly now. Kozhevnikov squeezed off another shot and then a third and a fourth. Each time Agayan's body seemed to be propelled forward in a little jerk, and then he fell.

"The airplane," Kozhevnikov shouted at Raya, and he started toward Agayan.

"There's no time for the briefcase," Raya screamed and pulled him back.

For a moment he stood rooted to his spot, his eyes darting from the briefcase lying fifty meters away to the line of jeeps screaming their way from the camp.

Raya was right. He might make it to the briefcase, but he would not make it back to the plane in time.

He turned and rushed back to the plane, as Raya scrambled into the back seat. He climbed into the pilot's seat and with his right hand reached over and flipped on the ignition switch.

If the plane was out of gas, they were dead. If it had been sitting for too long in this cold, it would not start, and they would be dead. If the oil had been removed because of the cold, they would be dead. If the battery was too low, they would be dead. If. If. If.

Raya slammed the door shut as Kozhevnikov pumped the primer knob a half-dozen times, then punched the starter button. In the distance he could hear the sounds of gunfire over the wailing of the siren.

For an eternity nothing happened, but then the propeller slowly started to turn. The battery was almost dead.

The gunfire was closer now as the propeller came down and around, the engine grinding, barely able to move the stiff metal parts. Suddenly, as a bullet crashed through the side window and pierced a corner of the windshield, the engine popped to life.

Immediately Kozhevnikov released the starter button and with his right hand slammed the throttle and carburetor heat controls on his left side all the way forward, and then he quickly grabbed the wheel as the plane lurched ahead.

The little plane was building speed fast, and as he began the wide turn around the transport airplane on the apron, a bullet smashed through the rear of their plane, grazing the side of his head before going through the windshield. He was thrown violently forward, his vision suddenly going black. The plane lurched sharply to the left, but he managed to pull himself upright and push hard on the right rudder pedal. The plane straightened out and they were heading down the taxiway.

The oil pressure was coming up painfully slowly, and with this kind of treatment Kozhevnikov was sure the plane would fall apart before they even reached the runway, even if he could hold himself together.

His head was throbbing and his vision was fading in and out as the plane bumped once when they came off the taxiway. Instead of trying to make the turn down the runway, he continued across it, and at the edge, near the landing lights, he hauled back on the stick. The plane jumped sickeningly into the air, bouncing once on the snow alongside the runway and then becoming airborne again.

Kozhevnikov held the plane flat, only a few meters off the ground, until the speed built up to 110 kilometers per hour. Then he hauled back on the control again, and the little plane began to climb into the black Arctic sky, heading due east toward the Gulf of Anadyr.

CHAPTER 9

"Mobile seven, Anadyr Ops. State your position."

How long had he been flying?

"Anadyr Ops, Mobile seven. Grid seven-seven."

The question suddenly flashed across Kozhevnikov's mind, and he sat forward in his seat, conscious of the pressure of the headphones against his ears.

"Red Star leader three, Anadyr Ops. Negative radar scan. Repeat, negative radar scan, grid Delta three-five."

It seemed that for the first time he was aware that his arm hurt and his head throbbed. For the first time. How long had he been in a state of semitorpor?

"Anadyr Ops, Mobile three for a radio check."

He scanned the instrument panel, and everything seemed normal. He was flying almost exactly due east, his airspeed indicator was steady on 180 kilometers per hour, and the fuel gauge read. . . .

"Mobile three, Anadyr Ops, you are breaking up. Repeat, you are breaking up. Red Star leader three, can you relay?"

Kozhevnikov stared at the tiny instrument on the right side of the panel. It had been three-quarters full. He was certain of it. But now the needle hovered a hairline above the empty mark.

"Anadyr Ops, Red Star leader three, negative relay. Am not reading Mobile three. Repeat negative contact."

He let go of the stick, reached out with his good hand, and tapped the dial. The needle jumped but settled back to the empty mark.

"Anadyr Ops, Red Star leader one. Passing over grid five-five. Mobile three in sight."

It was cold. The airplane's small heater, never designed for this kind of climate, was barely able to keep the windshield clear and did little to warm the cabin. Kozhevnikov shivered.

"Red star leader one, Anadyr Ops. Can you relay Mobile three?"

"Negative Andyr Ops. Mobile three does not respond." There was a pause in the radio traffic. "Anadyr Ops, positive radar contact."

Below them the featureless tundra rolled in all directions, faintly gray under the overcast sky. It looked almost like an ocean. Somewhere to the east was Anadyr. But how far away? How long had they been flying? And something else was bothersome. The radio. He must pay attention to it.

"Red Star leader one, Anadyr Ops. Take no action. Repeat, take no action. Report positive visual ident."

The pain in Kozhevnikov's arm was receding with the cold. He felt warm and soft. Nadya was smiling at him. They were making love.

"Anadyr Ops, Red Star leader one. Am showing a slow-moving target. One-eight-oh klicks, on an oh-nine-three heading. It's right on the deck."

Someone was screaming in his ear. It was like a siren going on and on.

"Red Star Leader one, Anadyr Ops. Say again his altitude?"

The irritating engine sounds were gone, but the screaming seemed to go on.

"Target radar shows less than five-oh meters. He's right on the deck!"

There was a tremendous bumping, as if someone were shaking him, and a sharp pain stabbed up from his arm.

"Red Star leader one, Anadyr Ops, have you got a visual yet?"

The floating came again.

"Negative Anadyr Ops. I've lost him."

The bumping came again, and then the floating. The screaming was continuous.

"Switch to infrared!" someone was shouting in his ear.

"Mobile three, Mobile three, do you read?"

The grinding and bumping came again, and it seemed to Kozhevnikov that Agayan had pulled him out of bed and was shaking him, harder and harder. The screaming was going on and on. And then something smashed into his forehead, and there was nothing.

The wind was blowing through the broken windshield of the airplane, and for a moment Kozhevnikov was not sure where he was. But then his mind cleared, and he opened his eyes.

Raya Schiller was stooping over him, tying a bandage around his head.

"I thought you were dead," she said, her voice curiously far away and hollow.

"What happened?" he heard himself asking, his voice like hers seeming to come from a canyon below him.

"We must have run out of fuel. We crashed. You hit your head on the instrument panel."

She finished with the bandage, stood up and stepped back. Kozhevnikov sat up, still seated in the pilot's position, and Raya helped him out of the wreckage.

Leaning on her shoulder, he looked at the airplane. The landing gear was collapsed, the fuselage was broken in two near the tail section, and one wing was completely missing. The plane had bounced several times on the ground, and then stopped against a low snowbank.

"Where are we?" he said, his voice coming to him a little more clearly now.

"I don't know," Raya said. "But there was a jet

plane overhead. It left just before you woke up."

He looked at her and shook his head. "I'm afraid I've messed this up."

She managed a slight smile. "They haven't gotten us yet."

"We'll never make it," he said, and he looked up and then stood away from her. His arm hung uselessly at his side, swollen now. Every movement shot excruciating pains past his elbow to his shoulder. His head throbbed, and there was a faint ringing in his ears.

Raya went back to the airplane, and supporting herself with both hands on the top of the fuselage, she kicked at something inside the plane. A moment later she reached inside, pulled at something, then turned and came back to him, carrying the aircraft's compass, which had been mounted atop the panel.

"Before we went down I saw a road a few kilometers to the south of us. It ran directly east. If we can make it that far, we should be able to get at least into Anadvr."

Kozhevnikov started to shake his head. "What are——"

"I'm not going back, Comrade," she shouted. "I'll die here first."

He looked at her. Nothing was quite right yet. If he concentrated hard, he could feel his broken arm and it hurt him. But then if he thought about the ringing in his ears or the throbbing in his head, he could not focus on the cold and the wind. His office in Hanoi seemed closer to him than anything else, even Operation Outlook.

He turned and looked at the wreckage. He would have to get the briefcase before they left. He took a step toward the airplane, then stopped. Agavan had taken the briefcase. Kozhevnikov had killed him.

He stuck his right hand into his coat pocket, and his mittened fingers felt the automatic. He had shot Agayan. There was someone coming and there was no time to retrieve the briefcase. No time.

He turned back toward Raya, who was staring at him. There was fear on her face. It was almost the same expression on Nadya's face the morning in their apartment. . . .

"My country 'tis of thee. . . ." The first few words of a song came into his mind, but for a moment he could not identify the tune.

Then it struck him. The American embassy in Saigon. When they had moved in after the Americans had retreated, he had found a child's windup record player in one of the family quarters. He had wound up the toy and played the record that was still on the spindle. It was that song.

"My country 'tis of thee . . . Sweet land of liberty. . . ." The first words of the song stuck with him. He could not remember any more of it, only that he liked it. It was a song American schoolchildren sang often. The record was well worn.

"My country 'tis of thee. . . ." The United States to the owner of the record player. The Union of Soviet Socialist Republics to Kozhevnikov.

"My country 'tis of thee . . ." Moscow and Nadya and Sasha. The park across from their apartment.

". . . Sweet land of liberty. . . ." Antipov, Agayan. Operation Outlook. Udalov. Udalov. Udalov.

They walked along a narrow, snow-covered road that was drifted over in places. Nadya led him by his right arm, and he could feel one foot move ahead, step down, then his other foot. Step by step they moved along the road.

They had been marching behind the tanks for two days when they came to the fenced-in concentration camp. The first men stopped and stared through the wire mesh at something mounded up in a field beyond a series of low brick buildings, each with a tall smokestack jutting into the air.

The odor they had smelled on the wind for the last twelve hours was so strong now it made Kozhevnikov sick to his stomach.

He pushed his way through the row of men at the fence and looked across the field at the pile. Bodies. Hundreds and hundreds of human corpses. Piled high like a scene directly out of hell.

"The Jews of Auschwitz," Kozhevnikov said out loud.

They stopped suddenly. "Shut up," Raya said sharply.

He started to turn toward her, but suddenly she was dragging him off the road, and they were scrambling over a high snowbank. On the other side, she pushed him down in the snow, the movement shooting an unbelievably sharp pain up his arm, clearing his mind. And then he could hear it.

"It's a tank," he mumbled. The woman ignored him as she peered over the top of the snowbank.

Kozhevnikov lay on his good side, reality coming into focus again. He was tired, thirsty, hungry, and cold. The pain from his broken arm and the wounds on his head were sharp and clear now, and he knew that he was only semiconscious even before the plane crashed.

He looked up at Raya, who lay on her stomach on the snowbank above him. Without her he would be dead.

The heavy rumble of a diesel engine was very close now, and Kozhevnikov carefully edged his way alongside Raya and peeked over the edge of the snowbank as a twelve-metric-ton half-track vehicle with a radar antenna on its roof rumbled by them. It stopped about fifty meters down the road.

Bits and pieces of the radio traffic he had monitored while they were in the air came back to him. This was one of the mobile radar units that had been dispatched from the MIG base at Anadyr. The radio traffic had begun within minutes after they had taken off, and he had listened while not only the MIG squadrons had been scrambled to look for them, but the mobile ground radar units as well.

They had been flying too low for the main radar antennas at Anadyr to pick them up, so the mobile units were sent out to pinpoint their position as they came toward the coast.

They must be very close.

The half-track was still halted. Its engines were idling and the radar antenna was sweeping back and forth.

"Can you drive one of those things?" Kozhevnikov said. He knew exactly what they would have to do if they were going to survive.

She turned to look at him and smiled. "You're back."

He ignored the comment. "Can you drive one of those things?"

She nodded. "We captured six of these units from the Syrians in the Golan Heights. Yes, I can drive it."

"Fine," he said, and he pulled himself to his feet and scrambled over the top of the snowbank and down to the road.

Raya shouted at him to stop but he continued running, as he crouched low. The back of the unit was its blind side. The driver would be operating the radio, and the radar man would be watching the screen.

As he hurried toward the rear of the half-track he pulled the mitten on his right hand off with his teeth and took the automatic from his pocket. The metal was so cold it hurt his hand, almost numbing his fingers.

The half-track was ten meters away when he stumbled and dropped the gun. He started to bend down but Raya got to his side, scooped it up, then helped him back to his feet.

"You're in no shape to do this," she said gently.

For a moment he stared at her and she looked like Nadya. He shook his head and her face became that of a little girl.

"St. Lawrence Island," he said.

"I saw the map in the airplane. We'll never make it, but I'm willing to try."

"The Americans know about Operation Outlook. I told them. But they need proof."

She smiled. "We'll try," she said. "But we won't make it to St. Lawrence Island in this."

Kozhevnikov stared at her, but said nothing.

She turned suddenly and hurried to the back door of the half-track. She looked back at Kozhevnikov, motioned for him to get down, then banged on the door with the gun.

She took one step backward and raised the pistol as Kozhevnikov dropped to his knees.

The door opened, and Kozhevnikov could hear someone shouting. Then Raya was firing into the van, and someone was screaming.

CHAPTER 10

"Anadyr is about three hundred and fifty kilometers almost due west, but the northern coast of the bay is less than two hundred kilometers northeast of us," the captain said.

Rafn was not listening. The two of them, plus Saunders, stood on the conning tower bridge, staring across the open water. Icebergs were dimly visible in all directions through the swirling wind-driven spray, and Rafn's hopes were fading fast.

The Soviet radio traffic from the MIG base at Anadyr they had monitored three hours ago had proved Rafn correct. A massive search was on. Jets had been deployed in a routine search pattern, and mobile radar units had been sent out to ring the coastal area and watch for the low-flying plane.

"The sum and substance of what we've intercepted," Rothman told him before they came out on the deck ten minutes ago, "is that your friend broke out with a light plane that has crashed about twenty-five kilometers west of Anadyr."

"Then he'll come on foot if he can't commandeer a land vehicle or another airplane," Rafn said stubbornly.

The captain smiled. "Rather naive, don't you think?"

Rafn glared at him, but said nothing. The man was right.

"Have you any idea what it's like out there? Your man has picked what is probably the most bleak and uninhabitable piece of real estate in the world for his little jaunt. Except for Anadyr and to the north Uel'-Kal, there is nothing there. No people, no vehicles."

"Anadyr is there, and so is the MIG base," Rafn said.

"Jesus Christ! Rafn," Rothman exploded and slammed his fist down on the navigation table. "What the hell do you expect him to do? Is he a superman? Is he supposed to hike twenty-five kilometers across the tundra, waltz up to the base, and say: 'Pardon me, old chaps, I've sort of wrecked the aircraft I borrowed. Could you possibly lend me an AATV?'"

Rafn could feel a gigantic fist closing inside his chest. He leaned over the chart table to look directly into Rothman's eyes. The others in the control room studiously worked at their duties, avoiding even a glance their way.

"What is an AATV?" he asked calmly.

The captain looked at him blankly for a moment, but then realization dawned on him, and he straightened up. "You haven't been watching the latest sonar reports, have you?"

Rafn said nothing.

The captain turned to the planesman. "Bring her up ten meters. I want the upper con hatch cleared."

"Aye, aye, sir," the young seaman said.

Rafn could feel the ballast tanks being blown. A few moments later a green light winked on an overhead panel.

"Get your parka. I want to show you something," the captain said to him.

A few minutes later they were standing on the upper conning tower bridge. The main deck of the submarine was still submerged, and Rafn had the impression that he was on a narrow tower that was sinking into the choppy water.

"An AATV," the captain shouted over the wind, "is

an Amphibious All-Terrain Vehicle. He'd need it to get to us."

"I thought there was pack ice in these waters," Rafn shouted back.

"Later in the winter, toward spring, the pack ice will get this far. But not now."

"How about the Gulf itself?"

The captain thought a moment. "It's iffy, but I'd say the chances are good that he'd have pack ice for the first hundred and fifty kilometers, maybe as far out as two hundred kilometers. Beyond that it would be risky. And out here in the Bering Sea itself, it is open water, as you can see."

Rafn stared morosely toward the west. The weather was closed in, and the wind was unbelievably cold. He had been standing out in it for only ten minutes, and already he was colder than he had ever been in his life.

He conjured up a mental image of Kozhevnikov, but he could not picture him out in this. His airplane had crashed. That meant he had been compromised, had broken out of Markovo, stolen the airplane, and made it almost to the coast. And now?

The man would not give up. Rafn was certain of that. Or was he? The thought stopped him momentarily. Had he been honest when he told the president it was merely wishful thinking on his part? Did he really know Kozhevnikov that well? Perhaps Bindrich was correct.

"If the man gets out of there, we'll know damned well it's a disinformation plot," Bindrich had said at the briefing before Rafn left for San Francisco to catch the submarine. "No one could get out of there without help. If he makes it, I'd bet my last dollar it was arranged."

Arranged or not, Rafn told himself now, Kozhevnikov had managed to make it to within twenty-five kilometers of the coast. What would he do now?

"Have you seen enough?" the captain was asking.

Rafn looked up and nodded. He turned and started back through the hatch, when another thought intruded in his dejection.

Kozhevnikov was not going to give up. That was the key. Stick with that.

He hurried down the steel rungs into the comforting warmth of the control room, the captain and exec right behind him, and went across to the radio operator's position. The young man who had been monitoring and translating the Anadyr MIG base transmissions was sitting back, the earphones draped around his neck. He looked up in surprise as Rafn spun him around in his swivel chair.

"Have they found him?" Rafn asked. "Have the transmissions stopped?"

"I don't know, sir," the young Russian translator said, confused.

"What do you mean?" Rafn shouted. He could feel himself losing his control. It was not good. But it was something that had been happening almost from the beginning of this operation.

The captain came up behind him, and the young man looked up at him, a blank expression on his face.

"ECM?" Rothman asked quietly, and the young man nodded.

Rafn looked up.

"They're jamming us," the captain said, a slightly pinched expression on his face. "That means they know we're here."

"Which means Kozhevnikov is still at large. They haven't gotten him yet," Rafn said. He turned back to the young man. "What about the last transmissions you received. Did they say anything about the wreckage of the airplane?"

The young man shook his head. "No, sir. The last I received was about their Mobile three."

"What is a Mobile three?" Rafn said, guarding his impatience.

"From what I could gather, it is a mobile ground radar unit. A half dozen or so were dispatched from Anadyr."

"Go on," Rafn prompted.

"It's missing," the boy said, shrugging. "At least it wasn't answering its radio queries."

Rafn held himself carefully in check. "It's a mobile radar unit. Mounted on a truck?"

The young man shook his head. "No, sir. I imagine it's mounted on a half-track."

Rafn snapped around to the captain. "Kozhevnikov got it. I'm sure of it."

The captain stared openmouthed at him.

"He'll probably be skirting north of Anadyr, away from the base, and then he'll be coming across the pack ice."

"You're insane," Rothman said, barely breathing the words.

"Nevertheless, we're going to wait for him," Rafn said more calmly now. "I want you to bring this ship right up to the edge of the ice pack. From there we'll watch with the infrared detectors. We should be able to pick up his engine."

The captain began to stammer, but Rafn led him away by the arm. "Before you say anything, we're going to talk again," Rafn said.

Rothman, recovering, pulled away from Rafn's grasp. Everyone in the control room was staring at them.

"There is nothing you can say to me to make me compromise my ship and crew. We've already been detected. They know we're out here. If we go barging in it will precipitate an incident."

"Incident or no incident, we are going in," Rafn said softly. "And if you'll step out of this room for a moment, I'll tell you why."

CHAPTER 11

He and Nadya had taken the train down to Gur'yev on the Caspian Sea that summer. The Ural River, placid and soft blue, had set the mood of peaceful relaxation for their holiday.

Native dancers in costume performed on the front lawn of the resort hotel every evening. Afterward, the couples would walk along the seashore, hand in hand, humming the gay love songs they had heard.

.They had argued only once during the four days, and he had to laugh about it later. Their fight had not been about her lovers, or about his job, or even about living in Moscow. It had been about what they were going to name their first child. Nadya had selected the name Aleksandra, while Kozhevnikov, certain it would be a boy, wanted to name him Vasily, after his father.

. Six weeks after they had returned from their vacation. Nadya had announced she was pregnant. They had gone out that night and danced until dawn. And both drunk, they had stumbled home singing.

Above him two dim red lights on the metal ceiling were protected by wire mesh. Kozhevnikov stared at them as he listened to the idling diesel engine, which had drowned out the sweet native dance melodies running through his mind.

Jan DeHeus had been very good. Almost too good

for Kozhevnikov, so that when he uncovered him he knew immediately he was perfect.

Disconnected thoughts continued to drift through his mind.

At the last minute in Munich he had almost turned back from driving out to Dachau. Not because he was having second thoughts about what he was doing, but because he did not think he could face the sight of another concentration camp, even if it were now only a museum.

Slowly other aspects of his surroundings began to intrude in his dreams. His broken arm felt as if it had been dipped to the shoulder in a vat of boiling oil while being squeezed tightly in a vise.

His head felt battered and bruised where the bullet had grazed him and where he had struck the instrument panel in the crash.

Then he could feel that he was lying flat on his back on something cold and unyielding.

Finally, he heard someone sobbing. But in the distance. Softly. Quietly. Barely audible.

He strained to hear, but the sounds were nearly blanked out by the sound of an idling engine. Idling. They were no longer moving.

Kozhevnikov sat up, the sudden action sending a wave of nausea and dizziness sweeping through him. Agavan. The airstrip. The crash. The half-track. Raya Schiller.

He got to his feet shakily, and with his hand atop the still-warm electronic equipment cabinets that lined both sides of the van, he went painfully forward to the driver's compartment where Raya Schiller sat slumped over the huge steering wheel. She was crying, her shoulders moving in pitiful jerks.

Kozhevnikov touched her shoulder with his good hand. She jumped, then swiveled around to look up at him. There was defeat in her eyes and fear.

At first he could not speak. His throat was parched,

his head throbbed, and the pain from his broken arm was so intense it was hard for him to concentrate.

"We're going to die," she said in a weak voice.

Kozhevnikov shook his head slowly. "No," he managed to say, but he immediately felt stupid.

She looked deeply into his eyes, and then slowly turned in her seat so that she was staring out the huge windshield. Kozhevnikov looked up. The shock of what he saw was almost physical, making his knees weak and bringing the bitter taste of vomit up his throat.

They were parked on a rock-strewn beach that stretched as far as he could see to either side of them. Directly ahead, less than twenty meters away, a gigantic twisted wall of wind-blown ice and snow directly barred their way. The ice was twisted into fantastic shapes and blocks that jutted at all angles, rising up from the beach at least fifteen meters in some places.

He stared openmouthed at it.

"The Gulf of Andyr," Raya said softly.

"My God, what is it?" Kozhevnikov croaked.

Raya shook her head. "I don't know. Maybe as the water freezes the waves push the ice up like this."

He stared at the sight for several minutes before he could shake himself out of his stupor. And when he looked down Raya was staring up at him.

"We cannot go any further," she said simply.

Despite the pain, Kozhevnikov felt somewhat rested now, and his mind was clearer.

"Where are we?" he asked.

"North of the base at Anadyr," she said. She pulled a map from a case attached to the floor and spread it on the steering wheel.

Kozhevnikov bent down to look more closely at it in the dim red light. She pointed at a spot on the coast.

"We're here. I'd guess about thirty kilometers north of the base."

"How about the radio?" he asked. "Are they looking for us?"

Raya shrugged. "I don't know. The radio has been dead. I think it went bad."

"There have been no aircraft overhead?"

"None that I have seen," she said.

He looked again at the fantastic, impassable jumble of ice ahead of them, and then looked down at the map.

"We're north of the Anadyr River?" he asked.

"We crossed it about five kilometers back."

"What did the shoreline look like there?" he asked.

She shrugged again. "I wasn't close enough to see."

Kozhevnikov took a deep breath. "That's where we will get out," he said.

"Are you crazy?" she suddenly screamed. "You fucking crazy sonofabitch!"

Kozhevnikov was stunned by the outburst.

"Look!" she screamed again, staring out the windshield. "How the hell do you think we're going to get across that?"

"It won't be like this at the mouth of the river," he said.

"How do you know?"

"I don't," he said quietly.

She slumped in her seat. "We're dead," she sobbed.

He grabbed her shoulder with his right hand and pulled her around to face him. "Then we stay here or we turn ourselves in—and they'll ship us back to Markovo. Is that what you want?"

"No," she cried, shaking her head. "God, no!"

"Then we'll try at the river," he said.

The buzzing was back in his head, and he could feel his heart hammering. His father had died of a heart attack when he was fifty. His uncle had dropped dead in his store when he was forty-five. Maybe this was his moment, now.

Raya turned and spun the steering wheel all the way around to the right, jammed down on the right track brake, and gunned the engine.

They spun around, the acceleration nearly throwing Kozhevnikov against the equipment bays, and they headed down the beach, the huge machine bucking and slamming over the rocks.

The ifs began piling up in his mind again as he managed to slip into the passenger's seat and hung on with his right hand the best he could.

If the river path was clear to the open ice in the Gulf. If the half-track did not break down. If they were not spotted and attacked by the searching MIGs. If they did not hit a crevasse or a thin spot in the ice and crash into the water.

If . . . if . . . if.

But even then, Kozhevnikov told himself through the haze building in his mind, what would he tell the Americans? How would he convince them?

CHAPTER 12

The submarine was almost completely submerged. The only elements of the ship that protruded from the surface were the fully extended periscope, one wide-band radio whip antenna, and an infrared heat detector.

All hands were at Alert stations. Rothman was peering through the periscope, the executive officer was standing behind the radio-monitoring position, and Rafn stood staring at the infrared head, which looked much like a radar screen ony it was square and the blotches it showed were red.

"The heat patterns stop about fifty meters out," the young operator was telling Rafn.

"From us?"

"Yes, sir," the boy said. "We're warming up the water and the ice around us."

The captain turned away from the periscope across the control room. "Your hour is nearly up, Mr. Rafn."

Rafn did not turn toward him. "We have five minutes," he said.

The captain said nothing, and Rafn continued to stare at the small television screen in front of him, as if he could will Kozhevnikov to show up.

Rothman, who had been born in Duluth, Minnesota, and had not gone farther than St. Paul until he joined the navy when he was twenty-two and directly out of college, was cowed by Rafn's explanation of what had happened to date.

Rafn had not gone into detail, but he had managed to convey more information to the man than he had to anyone else, including the president, Bindrich, and Gleason.

But although he had been impressed and deeply affected by what Rafn had told him, Rothman nevertheless set an absolute time limit on the operation.

"I'll not only get you to the ice pack, but we'll duck under it," the captain had said in his cabin. "We'll find an open spot and then surface. That way, if your man has been able to make it out of the Gulf, we'll be able to get to him."

Rafn got to his feet and was about to go out the door when the captain stopped him.

"But hear me well, Rafn," he said.

Rafn turned and peered at the captain through his thick glasses, but said nothing.

"From the moment we poke through the ice pack and begin watching for him, I'm giving you one hour. No more, no less. If he's not out to us by then, we're leaving."

Rafn continued to stare at the man without saying anything.

"Beyond that point I don't care what happens. If need be, I'll put you in the brig. But we're leaving. Do you understand, Mr. Rafn?"

Rafn had turned on his heel without a word and stalked into the control room. A few moments later the captain joined him and ordered the submarine beneath the ice pack.

For fifty-five minutes now they had been watching for Kozhevnikov without results. And as the time ran out, Rafn's mind worked harder and harder.

Most likely Kozhevnikov was lying at this moment in the plane wreckage somewhere west of Anadyr. The crash had killed him. The missing mobile radar unit was merely a coincidence.

And yet. . . .

Rafn casually reached under his bulky sweater, as if to scratch himself. His fingers curled around the grip of the military .45 automatic he had stolen from the captain's cabin earlier this evening.

If Kozhevnikov did not show up in the next five minutes, they would not leave. In fact, they would not leave until the armaments this ship had at its command were finally dispersed in her defense, if it came to that.

CHAPTER 13

From the Urals to the Volga, from the Caspian to the Barents—the Union of Soviet Socialist Republics spread over more than eight and a half million square miles.

From the shining lights of Moscow to the windswept hills of the Taymyr Peninsula, Mother Russia was populated by nearly a quarter of a billion people, speaking twenty-one major languages.

Yes, there were men like Antipov and Agayan. But they were the exception. Kozhevnikov had to believe it. Had to.

But Nadya. She was a traitor to him. He was a traitor to his country. Could he live with that? Traitor! Traitor!

Louder and louder. Echoes. Hollow. Distant.

Kozhevnikov was thrown violently from his seat as the half-track pitched over on its side two hundred kilometers due east of Anadyr.

Nadya was below him for an instant as he tumbled over the driver's seat, his broken arm smashing against the side of the equipment bay.

He flipped completely upside down, landing on his back atop Raya Schiller. A million bright lights flashed, sirens screamed and the grating of metal went on and on and on.

It was quiet and Kozhevnikov was certain he was dead. But then he realized that if he had the ability to think he was dead, he must be alive.

414

"I think therefore I am. . . ."

He sat up. Raya Schiller lay next to him, her face against the passenger's window of the driver's compartment. For the first few moments he felt good; lightheaded, as if he were floating a few centimeters off the floor. But then the pain slowly intruded on his peacefulness and he began to scream.

He was warm. Too warm. He opened his eyes. Raya lay by his side, a thin trickle of blood seeping from her forehead.

He pushed himself up to his knees and looked around. Everything seemed out of place. The passenger seat was directly above him, and he reached up with his good arm to touch it. The metal frame of the seat was warm. That was odd.

Something else intruded into his consciousness as well. Something he should know about. Something that should frighten him.

Smoke. It was hard to think, but the single word sunk into his fuzzed mind. Smoke. Heat. Fire.

He suddenly straightened up, everything coming clear again to him. They had made it down the river through an opening in the pressure ridges to the open ice in the bay. That was hours ago. Raya was worried about running out of fuel. He dozed off, and then they hit something and overturned. And now they were on fire.

He pulled himself painfully to his feet and stood looking out of the windshield, which now rose from the floor to the ceiling. The entire front and side of the half-track was in flames, and he could feel the heat and the stifling smoke. He could see nothing beyond the flames.

The end.

Like a bright fluorescent sign, the letters flashed through his mind.

He grabbed Raya by one arm, pulled her body around, and then dragged her toward the rear of the van, stepping and sliding over the faces of the instruments and radar screens which were now the floor.

Her head bumped against the dials and gauges. If her neck or back was broken, or if she had suffered internal injuries, he was killing her. He knew it. But he could not leave her here. She had brought him this far. He could not leave her.

The door slammed open downward on its hinges and Kozhevnikov stumbled into the wind and the incredible cold, onto the snow-crusted surface of the ice.

Raya's body slumped from the van into the snow and she moaned, but Kozhevnikov did not stop. He continued to drag her, step by step, away from the half-track that now was burning furiously, lighting up the night sky.

One foot in front of the other, the pain was no longer localized anywhere on his body. The heat finally went away and was replaced by the biting cold against his bare cheeks.

He managed to drag her nearly seventy-five meters away from the burning van when the flames finally reached the diesel fuel tank, and his world erupted in a tremendous thunderclap.

He was drifting then. Floating. Sailing. Someone was calling his name.

"Kozhevnikov . . . Kozhevnikov . . ."

He tried to struggle to his feet, but then there were strong hands around his shoulders and legs, and he was certain someone was lifting him, and then carrying him. Running.

"Be careful," he said, looking up into Rafn's face. "My arm is broken."

PART SIX
Spring 1978

CHAPTER 1

The husky young man with short-cropped hair and steel-blue eyes entered the KGB's Karlshorst Residency in East Berlin shortly before noon, where he was directed to the interrogation rooms in the basement.

Orders had come directly from Moscow that all field units were to report to the residency for disposition.

What began as a ripple in a large pond in Markovo—with the detection of the American submarine and the probable escape of Kozhevnikov and the girl— had developed over the past two months into huge waves that threatened to overturn the ship. Fear dominated all the upper-echelon officers.

Those were words and terms foreign to Field Operative Fedor Udalov-7797, but they were things he had been hearing for several weeks now. The talk elicited no fear in this Udalov, however. His brain did not have that capacity. But he was curious.

Two men he had never met were waiting for him in a vestibule at the foot of the stairs, and without a word they guided him through a heavy metal door into a long, narrow room. Coffinlike crates were stacked along one wall near a ramp that led up to a large service door.

In the center of the room Udalov was directed to stop. One of the men went across the room and turned on a garden hose, and Udalov watched as the water flowed toward the floor drain a few meters away.

He was curious about the water, about the crates, and about the talk he had been hearing, but even when the other man stepped away from him and pulled a Soviet officer's automatic from his shoulder holster, he was not frightened.

Expendable was the operative word in school. He dimly remembered his military tactics instructor telling them that they were like armed rockets, set to go off at any moment. Usable in the field but too dangerous to transport home. Expendable.

Udalov had never given much thought to life, no more than a tank or a mortar or a rocket thinks about its own existence. But he was curious about expendability, and exactly what it meant.

The KGB *mokrie dela* operative raised the heavy automatic and fired point-blank into Udalov's head. And then there was nothing.

Nathaniel Gleason was in the kitchen of his house in Chevy Chase finishing his coffee when the doorbell rang and Pat jumped up to answer it. Their camper was loaded and they would be leaving soon on their long-awaited vacation.

His son, Kevin, was out of school and Pat had never been happier or more relaxed. His job with the CIA was all but finished and when he returned in two weeks he would be giving notice. Already he had been given a tentative job offer at Harvard as lecturer in foreign policy.

Which was fine with him, except for the unfinished business with Kozhevnikov. Because of Kozhevnikov's condition he had not been invited to any of the debriefing sessions, which were being held at Bethesda Naval Hospital.

In fact, the only word he had heard from his assistant, who would be taking over the department when he left, was that Kozhevnikov was in serious condition. It had something to do with a weak heart. But he had heard nothing further.

Nor did he want to hear any more. He was through with the agency. He wanted nothing more to do with any of them.

And yet. . . . He did not like to leave things undone.

Pat came into the kitchen, a look of worry on her face. He got up from his chair.

"There's someone here to see you, Nate," she said quietly.

Gleason looked past her toward the living room, but he could see no one waiting. He glanced at his wife.

"He didn't want to come in. He's waiting outside for you."

Gleason put down his coffee cup and headed for the kitchen door, but as he passed her, she stopped him.

"Whatever it is, don't get involved," she said, with intensity in her voice. "Please. For our sake."

Gleason said nothing, but a feeling of apprehension grew into a hard knot as he left the kitchen, walked through the living room and out the front door.

Rafn was leaning against a plain gray Chevrolet sedan parked in the driveway behind the camper. It was a motor pool vehicle from the agency. Gleason was suddenly angry. He was being drawn back into the mess. He could feel it.

He stopped three feet away from Rafn and shook his head. "I'm through with this business. I don't want to get involved," he said.

Rafn smiled tiredly and pushed away from the car. When he spoke his voice was low. "I need your help again."

Gleason continued to shake his head. "I don't want to hear it."

"They don't believe his story," Rafn said.

"I don't care," Gleason shouted and immediately lowered his voice. "I'm leaving on vacation. And when I return I'm resigning."

"We're meeting with the president this afternoon. We have until then to come up with the proof we need."

"No," Gleason said flatly.

"They've locked me out of the incident files."

"Go home, Rafn. Leave me alone."

"Kozhevnikov was right, you know," Rafn continued, as if Gleason had said nothing. "He did get to the Siberian operation. It's near the town of Markovo. There are a hundred thousand Jews there. It's worse than a pogrom. Much worse."

Gleason could feel himself weakening and cursed himself for it. "There's nothing I can do for you. I'm on my way out."

"The president won't listen to me alone. Bindrich will make sure of that. And Kozhevnikov brought nothing with him."

"He brought a woman. An Israeli operative," Rafn said, coming a step closer.

Pat called for Gleason from the doorway of the house, and he turned around. She was staring at him, a frightened expression on her face.

"In a minute," he called, and he turned again to Rafn.

"They didn't believe her, either," Rafn said. "And they'll probably try to keep her here. Tel Aviv has not been notified of her presence."

Gleason said nothing, but he was seeing Kozhevnikov talking to them on the beach at Seeshaupt.

"I need you to get into the incident files and pull sixty-nine jackets. I've got them all indexed and addressed. You can be in and out of there in ten minutes. You could combine it with a routine request. I'm sure Bindrich won't be watching that close. Not now."

"And you want me to go with you to see the president with those files?"

Rafn nodded.

"What's it all about? What is happening at Markovo?"

"I won't tell you that now. If I did, you'd back out. You wouldn't believe me."

"But if I see the files, I will?"

"Yes. I think so. And combined with Kozhevnikov's testimony and that of Raya Schiller, we might be able to convince them."

"What happens if they bounce it right back?" Gleason said, feeling hemmed in. "What happens if this is finally dismissed as a disinformation plot?"

"Then we've got to get Raya Schiller out of the country," Rafn said simply. Gleason could feel his heart skip a beat.

"I won't do it, goddamn it, Rafn!" he shouted.

"I'm not asking you for that," Rafn said, still calm. "All I am asking is that you dig out those files and come with me when we meet with the president. Nothing more. If it doesn't work, you can go on your vacation. I'll take care of it from that point."

Pat came out on the porch and called again. Gleason felt torn between his wife and Rafn. Or more accurately, between his peace of mind and a bizarre plot against the Jews in a remote corner of Russia.

It wasn't fair, he told himself. But then nothing was ever fair.

Pat called again, but he ignored her, sighed deeply, and then nodded. "What time is the meeting?"

"Three this afternoon," Rafn said.

"Stay away from me for the rest of the day," Gleason said. "If Bindrich gets the idea you and I are working together again, he'll stop me."

"I'll meet you at your office at two-thirty."

Gleason shook his head. "Just go to the meeting alone. If I can get the files I'll show up. If not . . ." he let it trail off.

CHAPTER 2

It was nearly eleven o'clock by the time Rafn got back to Bethesda Naval Hospital where Kozhevnikov was being kept in isolation under the name Harold Miller. The man seated in an alcove down the hall from Kozhevnikov's room looked up and nodded when Rafn came around the corner and paused by the Russian's door.

For two months Kozhevnikov had lain here, mostly alone. The first two weeks he had been only semiconscious, and after that the doctors would only allow the interrogation teams to be with him one hour in the morning and one hour in the afternoon. As a result, the debriefing had gone slowly. Yesterday it was finished.

Kozhevnikov told them everything. The entire fantastic story of Operation Outlook. The cloned men. Agayan. His escape. And through the sessions Bindrich remained silent.

Two weeks ago a company psychologist was included on the debriefing, and he, like Bindrich, had very little to say. Rafn knew that none of them believed the man.

He entered the darkened room, closed the door behind him and went to the bed where Kozhevnikov lay half propped up. An IV tube was connected to his right arm, and a wire trailed from his left arm to a machine mounted on the wall over his bed. On a dim green screen Kozhevnikov's heartbeat traced an erratic path, accompanied by a thin high-pitched beep each time it peaked.

Kozhevnikov was asleep when Rafn pulled the heavy chair next to the bed and sank wearily into it.

For two months he had gotten too little sleep, had eaten too infrequently, had smoked too many cigarettes and drunk too much beer. He felt old and tired now. Used up.

He had been issued only a Class C pass for the CIA building, and his movements had been restricted to a temporary office in Operations on the fifth floor. He had been barred from the computer rooms and the Recon Photo Lab, and his "need-to-know" status had been sharply curtailed.

He was working in the dark now, and for the past few weeks the only real contact he had with this business was the daily sessions with Kozhevnikov.

He looked up at his friend, and shook his head. There was no longer any doubt in his mind that Kozhevnikov was telling the truth—had been telling the truth all along. The Soviets were building an army, as fantastic as it seemed, in Markovo. And it would only be a short time before that army was used. Probably against the Chinese. And when that happened, the next world war would not be far away.

But it was too enormous a concept, too vast an idea for Bindrich and the others to swallow. They would have to have been there, like Kozhevnikov and like Raya Schiller, who had confirmed his story, to fully believe it.

And now that Kozhevnikov's debriefing was completed, and he assumed that Rava Schiller's was also done, only he and Gleason remained.

He was certain that the CIA director would go along with Bindrich's assessment when they met with the president this afternoon, and they were two powerful voices. From the beginning, Bindrich especially had set the tone of skepticism for the debriefings.

"He got out, goddamn it, Rafn," Bindrich shouted after one session. "Over impossible odds he made it. What the hell does that tell you?"

"That he is a dedicated man," Rafn replied.

"Bullshit," Bindrich exploded. "It was set up from the beginning, and you know it."

"What if it wasn't?" Rafn said carefully. "What if he is telling the truth——"

Bindrich interrupted him. "The man is telling the truth, don't get me wrong. At least the truth as he sees it. But he was set up, too. From the beginning. This has been nothing but a huge stage show. They knew he was coming over to us, they knew he would be interrogated, they knew we would use drugs—the entire gambit. It was the only way they could pull it off. And it very nearly worked."

"And Raya Schiller? What has she told you?" Rafn asked.

Bindrich laughed. "She confirmed everything he told us, right down to the last detail, which in itself struck me as odd. But there were so many traces of Thorazine and Valium in her system, the medicos estimated she had been on one tranquilizer or another continuously for at least a year. It's a wonder she even knew her own name."

"But what if they are telling the truth?" Rafn said and could feel his self-control slipping again.

"We don't operate that way," Bindrich snapped.

"You mean your existence is too comfortable for you to believe such a thing could be possible," Rafn retorted angrily.

Bindrich stood up abruptly and came around from behind his desk, indicating the meeting was at an end. Rafn stood, too, and followed him to the door.

"The only reason you're still in on this, Rafn, is because I am a fair man. I want to give you a shot at proving that what Kozhevnikov and the Schiller woman say is true. As soon as the debriefings are completed, we'll meet with the president. I want all sides of the story presented. I'll want as many opinions as possible."

"Admirable," Rafn said, "considering the deck is stacked in your favor."

Bindrich straightened to his full height and obviously worked to hold himself in check. "When this is finished, you will be, too. We won't be needing your services any longer."

Rafn smiled tiredly. "My services will not be for sale. To you."

A stir in the bed brought him back to the present and he looked up. Kozhevnikov had regained consciousness and turned his head. His eyes were open.

"Good morning," Rafn said. "How are you feeling?"

Kozhevnikov shook his head and started to speak, but nothing came out. Rafn took a glass of water with a straw from the bedside stand and held it to Kozhevnikov's lips. The man drank and it seemed to help.

"How is Raya Schiller?" he asked.

"She's fine," Rafn said.

"Where is she now?"

"At Fort Belvoir. It's a military base southwest of here."

Kozhevnikov seemed to digest that for a moment, and then his moist eyes narrowed. "There was no session today. What are they doing?"

"We're meeting with the president this afternoon."

Kozhevnikov stared at Rafn, then sighed deeply as if he were in great pain. "Bindrich does not believe me."

Rafn shook his head. "He is a fool."

"But he is in charge."

"Yes."

Kozhevnikov reached out slowly and touched Rafn's shoulder. "Make them believe me, Svend. Make them see that I am telling the truth before it is too late."

Rafn could feel a constriction in his chest. For almost all his life he had been called by his last name, or referred to as a line number in the nonbudgeted fund. An operative. Kozhevnikov's use of his first name now came as a surprise.

Kozhevnikov shuddered, turned his head back and closed his eyes. Rafn's eyes darted from Kozhevnikov's face up to the machine above the bed, but the green line still indicated a heartbeat. How long that line would continue to pulse, no one knew. But Rafn knew that when it did stop, he would have lost the only real friend he had ever known in his life.

CHAPTER 3

At 3:20 Rafn was seated at the long table in the president's cabinet room. In addition to the president, who sat on one side of the table, were the director of the CIA, his assistant, Sylvan Bindrich, the head of the Joint Chiefs of Staff, the secretary of defense, the secretary of state, the CIA Soviet affairs résearch chief Marty Romberg, and the White House doctor, who was acting as a scientific advisor for this particular meeting.

Gleason had not shown up yet, and Rafn glumly suspected that he had decided against helping, or, worse yet, that Bindrich had found out what he was doing and had stopped him.

For the first twenty minutes Bindrich brought the president and the others up to date on everything that had happened so far, including the sum and substance of Kozhevnikov's and Raya Schiller's debriefings. And at this point it was clear to Rafn that no one believed the story.

The president was speaking. "Dr. Barnes, what is your opinion?"

The White House physician, Dr. Alphonse Barnes, was a tall, distinguished-looking man with gray hair and a white moustache. Rafn estimated him to be in his mid or late fifties, and when he spoke his voice held a soft southeastern drawl.

"As far as I know there are only two similar projects

in this country. The army has got one going with guinea pigs at M.I.T. And Dr. Meitner has made some significant breakthroughs at the University of Wisconsin."

"I know about the M.I.T. project," the president said, "but what about Meitner? Isn't he the one who won the Nobel Prize and then disappeared?"

"Yes," Dr. Barnes said, and Rafn sat forward. He had not read a newspaper in months, and this came as a surprise to him.

"Dr. Barnes?" he said, and everyone turned his way. "What was Dr. Meitner working on? Specifically."

"Genetic control," the doctor said.

"And you say he disappeared."

The doctor nodded. "It's been at least three months," he said.

"When you say disappeared, what do you mean?"

"I don't see . . ." the doctor began to say.

"Please, Doctor, this could be significant."

The doctor turned to look at the president, who nodded for him to continue. Bindrich looked disgusted.

"His name was announced by the Nobel Prize Committee, and a few days later he went to Germany . . . West Berlin, I believe . . . and disappeared. There was a big hullabaloo in the newspapers about it, and then someone from the university where he worked told everyone that Meitner had telephoned him. A reporter in Berlin saw Meitner one afternoon, and by the next day the man had simply disappeared."

"No trace of him has been found?" Rafn persisted.

The doctor started to answer, but Bindrich sat forward. "We were assigned to look into his disappearance because it happened on foreign soil."

Rafn waited for the man to continue.

"We found nothing."

"Are you still looking?"

Bindrich nodded and turned to the president. "He wasn't of interest to national security, Mr. President, but we are continuing the search."

Rafn sat back. "The Soviets have him. He's probably at Markovo now."

Bindrich started to protest, but the president waved him silent. He was looking at Rafn with interest in his eyes. "I think before we draw any conclusions from this, I would like to hear from Mr. Rafn. He was correct, after all, in his prediction that Kozhevnikov would be coming out of Markovo."

Without Gleason and the incident files he did not think he would be able to convince the president that Kozhevnikov was telling the truth. But he was going to have to try, because if that didn't work there was only one other option open to him.

"Mr. President," he began. All eyes were on him, and except for Bindrich's cold stare, everyone seemed genuinely interested and curious. But Bindrich swung the weight.

"This is like a gigantic puzzle, but before you make any decision, I think we should look at all the pieces and try to see how they fit together."

Bindrich's features relaxed, and he sat back in his chair, a slight smile playing across his face. Rafn paused to look at the man, and the thought briefly crossed his mind that Bindrich was not interested in the truth. He had never been interested in the truth, just the game itself.

"But instead of lecturing or even summarizing everything we've found so far—you've heard most of it— I'll make an assumption and look at it from that angle.

"Let's assume for the moment that Mr. Bindrich is correct in his assessment. Kozhevnikov's contact with us in Paris and then in Seeshaupt, his subsequent transfer to Markovo, and his escape are all part of a large disinformation plot. The Soviets would hope that you would be convinced there is something terrible going on in Markovo, would exert pressure on them to stop, and when it was proved that nothing was going on, the United States would be embarrassed."

"Exactly," Bindrich said.

"Hear me out, please," Rafn said, and Bindrich sat back.

Everyone in the room seemed pleased. They were being told exactly what they wanted to hear. A nefarious plot uncovered. But a plot they could handle with relative ease.

"Everything seems to fit this picture," Rafn began again. "The arms limitation talks, I understand, have been postponed, presumably until the United States makes a fool of itself over this issue.

"Kozhevnikov did manage to escape despite impossible odds, although he probably will not survive. And as an added bonus, Raya Schiller, an Israeli operative, was allowed to escape with him.

"And there is still another point in favor of this idea. Dr. Barnes supplied it for us. The genetic research you are doing in this country is in its infancy. And even if the Soviets were far ahead in the field, could they be so far ahead they have the ability to manufacture the army that Kozhevnikov and Miss Schiller have described?"

Rafn paused for effect, slowly stood up, and lit a cigarette. This was his last shot. He would have to make it count.

"And one last point," he said. "The next war, if there is one, I presume would be fought with missiles and nuclear weapons. What good would a few million soldiers do?"

At that the head of the Joint Chiefs of Staff seemed somewhat uncomfortable. Rafn continued.

"A wonderful disinformation plot the Soviets almost foisted on you. Or was it?"

Rafn had been smiling, but now a grim expression crossed his face.

"Number one. My East German network did uncover references to a Nazi research camp called Station Kummersdorf East near Tiefensee. It was something we uncovered—not something Kozhevnikov planted on us.

"Number two. Kozhevnikov's wife was killed. Your observers in Moscow confirmed that. That's a fairly high price for even a dedicated KGB officer to pay to make a plot work.

"Number three. Kozhevnikov was sent to Markovo, the site of a huge installation that supposedly is an Agrarian Reform Project. However, it is an installation that is equipped with a five-thousand-foot runway; an installation to which an Israeli Secret Service operative was also sent."

Bindrich had sat forward again. "May I comment?" he said, sarcastically polite.

Rafn nodded.

"Kozhevnikov did tell us about the Kummersdorf camp, at least indirectly. He mentioned the term *Kummersdorf Papers*, which at first we took to mean the Nazi Kummersdorf installation that was a rocket research station. So Tiefensee could have been part of the plot."

"And Kozhevnikov's wife?" Rafn asked, already knowing what Bindrich's answer would be.

"That's simple," Bindrich said. "You know I've never disagreed with you that Kozhevnikov is a good man. He himself is the victim of this plot. From the beginning, even in Vietnam when he uncovered our deep-cover man DeHeus, he believed what he was doing. Because of that his wife's death was maneuvered."

Bindrich looked around him, and then back at Rafn. "As for Raya Schiller, she was working as a deep-cover agent in Moscow. They knew about her. What better topping for the pudding than to allow her to escape with Kozhevnikov?"

Bindrich fell silent and for several moments Rafn said nothing, either. He had maneuvered the discussion to exactly the point he wanted. And it was now or never.

"You're right, Bindrich," he said softly. "Everything

I've mentioned could have been part of the disinformation plot. A grand plot, on a larger scale than anything the Soviets have ever attempted, for only a questionable gain. Think of it. This plot was set up as early as five years ago in Vietnam. Raya Schiller was captured. Kozhevnikov was maneuvered into meeting with us. The installation at Markovo was selected as the site for this plot. And how long has that installation been there? And Sigmund Schiller, somehow he was set up from Tel Aviv to help us at Tiefensee . . . no small coincidence that his sister would at the same time be involved in this."

Rafn paused again, and for the first time he was gratified to see that Bindrich and the others were somewhat uncomfortable.

He turned to the president. "Mr. President, when we met last, you gave me the use of a submarine to pick up Kozhevnikov, and you asked me what my ace card was."

The president nodded.

"I'll play it now."

Bindrich was squirming, but the others were interested.

"In Tiefensee, while I was searching for references to the Nazi Kummersdorf East installation, an old priest told me there were watchers in Tiefensee.

"When I returned that evening to the hotel, I had to kill a man who had just murdered Schiller." He stopped, remembering clearly the man's face. "He was dead, I'm sure of it, because I slit his throat."

The president had a distasteful look on his face. "Your point, Mr. Rafn?"

Rafn smiled sadly. "First. If this was a disinformation plot, why kill Schiller, and why attempt to kill me? Wouldn't our being alive have been of more use to support the plot?"

Bindrich was about to speak, but Rafn held him off. "The man whose throat I slit was tall, heavyset, wore his hair short, and had blue eyes."

A look of recognition crossed the president's face, and Rafn nodded. "Yes, Mr. President, the man I killed fit Kozhevnikov's and Schiller's description of the cloned men at Markovo. But let me continue.

"In my attempt to escape from East Germany, I was forced to kill another man. An exact twin of the man whose throat I had just slit a few hours earlier in Tiefensee."

There was a stunned silence in the room for a moment. The president was the first to recover. "Is that your ace card?"

"Not quite, Mr. President," Rafn said. "When I returned to Langley after that operation, I ran the description of those men through the CIA's incident files. And I came up with sixty-nine separate incidents over the past few years, all minor, but all involving men of the same description."

"I thought you would bring that up," Bindrich said, and he withdrew a thick bundle of files from his briefcase on the floor next to his chair. He was smiling indulgently, and Rafn knew suddenly that Kozhevnikov had lost.

"Gleason led me to these this morning, and I did a follow-up study on them," Bindrich said to Rafn. He turned to the president and handed him several composite drawings of husky men. All of them looked similar to the men Rafn had killed.

"These are composite portraits from our Idento-Print computer. We are able to feed into the computer a description and the machine will print out the picture.

"Rafn, when he returned from Germany, fed in the description of the two men he claims to have killed, and came up with sixty-nine incidents. All of them minor, as he says. But he should have gone a step further."

As the president studied the pictures and then handed them around, Bindrich turned to Rafn. "I did take it a step further this morning. By varying slightly the descriptions, I came up with several slightly different composite drawings. Sending those drawings through the incident files, I came up with several hundred incidents. Some of them Soviet. Some of them British, Italian, Spanish, and even a few Israeli."

Bindrich turned to the president. "In our experience, Mr. President, we have found that ten operatives, even highly trained and skilled observers, will describe the same person in ten slightly different ways. Mr. Rafn's description fit sixty-nine incidents. My variations fit hundreds. There simply is no substance to Mr. Rafn's contentions. This was from the beginning a cunningly conceived and brilliantly executed disinformation plot. One that almost worked. But one that, thank God, we were sharp enough to catch."

The president pondered Bindrich's words for a minute, and when he looked again at Rafn he seemed tired, but untroubled. "Mr. Rafn, anything to add?"

Rafn shook his head. "In all of this I only wanted the truth. I sincerely hope that Mr. Bindrich is correct in his assessment."

"But you still do not think he is," the president said.

"No, I do not."

The president looked at the others around the room. "Gentlemen? Any comments?"

There were none.

"Then I think this meeting is adjourned. I will ask Mr. Bindrich that he continue to keep a watchful eye on developments in and around Markovo."

Bindrich started to protest, but the president cut him off sharply. "Keep me posted, Mr. Bindrich. Although at this moment I tend to agree with your assessment of this operation, there still is a slight doubt in my mind. I want the situation monitored."

"Yes, sir," Bindrich replied.

The president turned to Rafn. "Is that satisfactory?"

"Yes," Rafn said. "Except for Kozhevnikov and Miss Schiller."

Dr. Barnes spoke up in a subdued voice. "I'm sorry to say that I believe Mr. Kozhevnikov will not live." He looked down at a report in front of him. "He has a congenital atrophy of the heart muscle tissue itself. It is not a cancer, but it acts similarly."

"A transplant?" Rafn asked.

The doctor shook his head. "It might have been possible three months ago. But in his present weakened condition, he would never survive the operation."

Rafn turned to the president. This was the last chance. "And Miss Schiller?"

The president glanced at Bindrich, who spoke up.

"She should remain here."

"Why?" Rafn snapped. He would have to control himself. But it was difficult.

"She knows too much that could be potentially embarrassing to us. We will be putting a military base in Israel soon. Negotiations are——"

The president cut in brusquely. "You forget yourself, Mr. Bindrich." He was angry. "Your purview is intelligence gathering, not politics."

"Sorry, Mr. President," Bindrich mumbled.

The president stared at him before he returned his gaze to Rafn. "What is your interest in Miss Schiller?" he asked directly.

"I worked with her brother, and she did help save my friend. I want her returned home."

The president shook his head. "I tend to go along with Mr. Bindrich, at least for the moment."

Rafn sat forward. "I will inform Tel Aviv," he said calmly.

The president looked thunderstruck, and Bindrich began to stammer.

"We'd stop you," the president said.

Rafn smiled. "Would you assassinate me?" He looked around at the others in the room. "After we discussed it in front of all these witnesses, with Gleason still out there?"

The president stared at Rafn for a long time, everyone else in the room frightened by his audacity.

"And if Miss Schiller is allowed to return home?" the president asked.

"Then it will be the Israeli's problem, not yours. There are a hundred thousand Jews at Markovo."

"Farmers," Bindrich snapped.

The president waved him off. "We will return Miss Schiller. To avoid any trouble. But we will also inform the Israelis of our conclusions."

Rafn smiled. "Thank you."

CHAPTER 4

It had been a dirty business from the beginning, and now it looked as if it would end that way.

The day was bright and very warm as he rode in the back seat of the plain gray staff car from Langley to Bethesda Naval Hospital. His own debriefing was done at long last, and the only thing holding him here now was Kozhevnikov, who was not expected to live much longer.

It had been one month since the operation had been officially shut down and Raya Schiller sent home. And during that time Rafn had waited for something to happen. But it hadn't.

He had hoped that once Raya Schiller returned to Tel Aviv and told her story the Israelis would do something about it. They seemed to be the only nation doing anything positive anymore. He had hoped it might end up like the raid on Entebbe. Only on a much larger and more difficult scale. But nothing had happened—yet.

It was the perfect season in Spain now. Most of Europe was still gripped by a lingering spring weather system that was alternately dumping snow and cold rain everywhere except along the Mediterranean. Spain was warm, friendly, and inexpensive. Maybe he would find a house and live out the rest of his life there. Away from any thoughts about this operation.

He had met Gleason for coffee three days ago and the man seemed happy. He was the only one who had come out of it unscathed.

"Pat and Kevin are happy about it, too," Gleason said across the table. They were in a restaurant in downtown Washington. Gleason had telephoned Rafn when he returned from his vacation and Rafn had agreed to meet him.

"What will you do, now that you are out of the business?" Rafn asked. Gleason was a lot like Kozhevnikov, he told himself. Only luckier.

"I'm going to write a book about the CIA."

Rafn laughed humorlessly. "Bindrich won't like that."

"I don't care," Gleason said, unperturbed. "All of this mess has to be told."

Rafn stirred sugar into his coffee, wishing for a beer. "Am I going to be in your book?"

"Yes," Gleason said evenly. "Are you going to fight it?"

Rafn slowly shook his head. "No. I'm getting out of the business, too. Maybe you'll let me help you."

"Maybe," Gleason said noncommittally.

And now, to see Kozhevnikov.

The staff car driver pulled up and parked at a back entrance to the huge hospital's main building, and he turned in his seat. "Shall I wait for you here, sir?"

Rafn shook his head. "It won't be necessary. I may be a while."

"I can wait, sir——" the man started to say, but Rafn cut him off.

"No. I might be here all night. Thank you."

"Suit yourself, sir," the man said, and Rafn got out of the car.

His bags were packed at his hotel, and tomorrow or the next day, or whenever, he would be returning home. To Copenhagen. And after that, Spain.

The nurse on the sixth floor wanted to stop Rafn from going in to see the man she knew as Harold

Miller, but something in his eyes made her back away and only halfheartedly warn him not to excite the patient.

Kozhevnikov had been transferred four days ago to an intensive-care ward; he lay on his back in the bed which was cranked up so he was half sitting. No one else was in the small room, and a television set had been placed on a stand at the foot of the bed. An inane children's program was in progress, the sound turned off. Kozhevnikov was staring at it. His hair had turned completely white, and the skin on his arms, his neck, and his face hung slack, as if he had not eaten in six months. But what irritated Rafn most of all was the fact that they had not shaved him for what appeared to be several days. A gray stubble of whiskers was on his chin and face, which made him look even older and more vulnerable than he was.

Rafn came into the room, pulled a chair to the bed, and sat down. At first Kozhevnikov did not move, but then, apparently sensing that someone was in the room with him, he turned and looked down at Rafn. He smiled tiredly.

"We've lost, old friend," Rafn said.

Kozhevnikov tried to struggle up. "No . . . no . . . we can't." His voice was thin and frail.

Rafn could feel tears coming to his eyes. It was an empty feeling in one respect but welcome in another. As far back as he could remember he had never cried.

"How about Raya Schiller? Has she been able to do anything in Tel Aviv? Did they believe her?" Kozhevnikov whispered.

Kozhevnikov had asked that same question over and over again during the past month, and each time Rafn had to tell him he did not know. There had been no word.

Rafn bent his head and cried silently. All of his life he wanted . . . what? A friend? A brother? A father?

Someone. Anyone whom he could talk with. Anyone he could feel responsible for.

"Dear God," Rafn heard himself saying.

He looked up after a long time. Kozhevnikov's head was back on the pillows and he was staring at the television, his mouth half open.

Rafn reached up and touched the man's arm, and he knew instantly without looking up at the heart monitor over the bed that Kozhevnikov was dead. Internal injuries, the doctor had said earlier. Exposure. Shock. Inhalation of oil and diesel fumes. And the weak heart. He should have died on the ice.

Rafn stood, but before he left the room he glanced up at the television set. The children's program had been replaced by a stern-faced announcer standing in front of a huge map. For a few moments it did not register on Rafn's mind what he was seeing, but then he realized what was happening.

He went back to the bed, and with shaking hands grabbed the television control from beside Kozhevnikov's body and turned up the volume.

The announcer was speaking, as a bright dot illuminated the area around the Siberian town of Markovo.

". . . repeating the bulletin. An explosion, possibly nuclear, near the Siberian village of Markovo early this morning was no test according to Tass, the Soviet News Service. . . ."

The Israelis, Rafn knew it. He turned and looked down at Kozhevnikov. What a terrible price to pay for victory, he told himself. Schiller, Kozhevnikov, and now how many people at Operation Outlook. A hundred thousand Jews. A thousand or more technicians and scientists. And several hundred thousand manufactured soldiers—human beings, nevertheless.

"We've won, my friend," he said softly, placing his hand on Kozhevnikov's shoulder, and then he turned and shuffled slowly out of the room.

SWAP

Walter Wager

The toughest way to pay a debt.

'I've only got six months, captain, which means you've got less. I'm asking you to go into the Soviet Union, a police state with some of the most heavily guarded frontiers in the world, and bring out the girl – illegally.'

Vietnam veteran David Garrison had a debt to pay – and the price was high. Bring a very special person out of Russia.

But a dying man's dream and an orphan girl's future had to be bought. With another human being.

Fast, tense and violent, the action sweeps from Washington to Tel Aviv, from Moscow to Paris in a Cold War confrontation of horrifying dimensions.

THE CAESAR CODE

Johannes Mario Simmel

Beneath the peaceful, prosperous surface of today's
Europe – a twisting trail of guilt and terror . . .

A young man searching for his father's mysterious
assassin . . . the woman who might be the dead man's
mistress or murderess or both . . . a harmless old
bookseller with a carefully concealed past . . . the
madame of a brothel that caters only to the most
bizarre erotic appetites . . .

These people form part of the spellbinding mosaic of
suspense and intrigue in this magnificent novel. THE
CAESAR CODE combines the explosive power of a
great thriller with a terrifying investigation into the
horrors of the violent past and present.

THE DEFECTOR

Donald Seaman

'EXPERTLY CONSTRUCTED THRILLER' *Daily Express*

From the author of THE BOMB THAT COULD
LIP-READ, a second brilliantly realistic thriller – THE
DEFECTOR.

A vital Russian scientist leaves the Soviet Union in
order to save his wife from torture and imprisonment.
In Britain their faces are changed by plastic surgery
and they learn to play the roles of Mr. and Mrs. John
Stevens. It is the perfect defection, until John Stevens
shoots and kills a housekeeper and becomes the pawn
in a deadly struggle between the English courts of law,
British Intelligence and the KGB.

'A slow-fuse thriller that GRIPS FIERCELY' *Birmingham
Post*